To Marianne,

Here's to our
meandering yet
potent connection.
Enjoy!
Mary Ann Cain

DOWN FROM MOONSHINE

A NOVEL

MARY ANN CAIN

A 13th Moon Press Book
Copyright © 2009 by Mary Ann Cain; All rights reserved under International and Pan-American Copyright Conventions.
Library of Congress Control Number: 2009900623
Mary Ann Cain, 2009
Down From Moonshine / May Ann Cain—1st American ed.
ISBN 978-0-9819559-0-2
First Edition: February 2009
Manufactured in the United States of America

13th Moon website=Http://www.albany.edu/jej84/~13thmoon
Mary Ann Cain's website= http://www.ipfw.edu/engl/fsmcain.htm
Cover design by Judith E. Johnson
Cover painting by Alvaro Cardona-Hine
Cardona Hine Gallery at http://www.cardonahine.com
Reproduced with permission of the artist

Also by Mary Ann Cain:
Revisioning Writers' Talk: Gender and Culture in Acts of Composing (SUNY Press, 1995)
Breathing Space: Composing Public Places for Writing and Teaching (with co-authors Michelle Comstock and Lil Brannon) (forthcoming: Heinemann/Boynton/Cook 2009)
This is a work of fiction. All characters in this novel are fictional, and refer to no real persons, living or dead.
Sections of this novel were published in *13th Moon: a Feminist Literary Magazine, Volume XIX, Hawai'i Pacific Review, Flying Island* and *Terra Incognita, # 3, 2002-2003.*

13th Moon Press
2 Horizon Road, G20
Fort Lee, NJ 07024

DOWN FROM MOONSHINE

A NOVEL

MARY ANN CAIN

Acknowledgments

I am grateful to the following individuals and institutions for their assistance in the research, writing, and revision of this novel.

For assistance on the history, culture, and society of the South Side/Bronzeville neighborhood of Chicago: Dr. Margaret Burroughs, co-founder of the DuSable Museum of African American history; Theresa Christopher, curator at the DuSable Museum; LeRoy Winbush, graphic artist extraordinaire; the staff of the Vivian Harsh Collection at the Carter G. Woodson library, Chicago; David Meyers, proprietor, Ace Hardware (formerly Louis Armstrong's Sunset café); the Chicago Defender; the Harold Washington Public Library, Chicago.

For insight into horse racing: Jeff Johnson, The Chicago Sun Times; Tim Carey, President, Hawthorne Race Course.

On horses and horse sense: John and Elta Moreland, retired ranchers, Big Timber, MT; Bobby and Kathleen Lindner, retired ranchers and thoroughbred racers, Big Timber, MT; Lisa Zimmerman, horsewoman and poet, Fort Collins, Colorado, Karen Walasek, master riding teacher; Candice Phillips, horsewoman and midwife, Chris Rensfield, trainer and Feldenkrais practitioner.

For financial and other support: The Mary Hambidge Center for the Arts, Rabun Gap, Georgia; Hill House Writer's Retreat, Nashville, Tennessee; Indiana Arts Commission; Linda Cain, journalist; Three Rivers Jenbe Ensemble, Fort Wayne, Indiana; Indiana University Purdue University Summer Research grant; Lil Brannon, teacher and mentor, Clark Waterfall, retired veterinarian and fly fisherman, Big Timber, Montana and Columbia City, Indiana.

For feedback on drafts: George Kalamaras; Toni Morrison; Lisa Tsetse; Judith Johnson; Ron MacLean; Michelle Comstock; Kathy Hayes; Peter Leach; Linda Cain; Sue Tungate; Kirin Narayan; Candice Phillips; Sarah Sandman; Ryan Shepherd; Cecilia Rodriguez Milanes; Peggy Woods; Tobey Ray.

For sharing Chicago stories and memories: Linda Cain; Ruth Cain; Tom Cain; Richard and Pat Seaman; Dorothy Gillespie; Gina and Jack Allen; Dan and Eleanor Avgerinos.

For learning, inspiration, and good company in the long processes of writing: My students at Indiana University Purdue University Fort Wayne.

To George Kalamaras, heart of my heart

In memory of Barney, beloved beagle

Table of Contents

Prologue..1

Part I..3
Chapter One: Tack Room...4
Chapter Two: Two Way..19
Chapter Three: Pasture..37
Chapter Four: Kitchen...58

Part II..73
Chapter Five: Rose Garden...74
Chapter Six: Laundry..97
Chapter Seven: Lobby...103
Chapter Eight: Coat Room...115
Chapter Nine: Derby Room...123

Part III..139
Chapter Ten: Attic...140
Chapter Eleven: Horse Barn...143
Chapter Twelve: Big Willow...161
Chapter Thirteen: Walk-in..171
Chapter Fourteen: Service Bar..181

Part IV...197
Chapter Fifteen: Powder Room...198
Chapter Sixteen: Safe Room...209
Chapter Seventeen: Business Office...................................222
Chapter Eighteen: Swamp..243
Chapter Nineteen: Broom Closet.......................................258

Author's Biographical Note...269

Prologue

She stands alone in the pasture while fire twists and groans through the horse barn. Night has already fallen. Against the shifting light, dozens of figures hunch in ghostly silhouette. The water they pour from buckets and hoses rises up from the flames in clouds of steam.

It is a sultry Midwestern summer night, and she is covered in sweat. Yet she shivers. Her arms hug her bare breasts; her thighs press together, as if to protect her exposed pubis. Fire has singed the hair on top of her head and burned off her eyebrows. Her eyes swell with tears.

She has no idea how long she has been standing there when someone comes up behind her and wraps a man's flannel overcoat around her shoulders.

"Sister," Mildred whispers. She hears the familiar female voice but cannot move, cannot shift her eyes from the horror before her.

The barn door had been locked. All seven had been inside.

"Darlin, it won't do you no good to keep looking." Arms hugging her around the waist. Sniffling from a tear-moistened nose. Smells of fried chicken and lye soap on her neck.

She had been ready to die. She had lain there, sprawled across the soiled hay, stinking of shit and piss. Bruised, her man's shirt ripped open, exposing her soft, never-seen-the-light belly. Dying would have been a comfort.

"Nigger," he'd called her. And for the first time, she understood what that word was: the kind of stain that would not come clean, no matter how hard a body scrubbed it.

The arms around her now tighter and tighter. Tear drops on her neck. Breath warm in her ear. Like Mama, who used to whisper her to sleep at night. And then the whole body shaking. Hers? Mama's? The voice behind her? All shaking, sweating, crying.

Like a well-loved, worn blanket, the thought of death had covered her. Her eyes had closed to the flames eating up the hay around her.

"Viney-girl, don't train your eyes on the Devil's work," Mildred moans.

Her eyes have closed, but with Mildred's sad drawl, she opens them. It isn't the Devil she is searching for. It is Baby.

"Babylon's a-falling, falling, falling. Babylon's a-falling to rise no more." The song rolls out from Mildred's throat, slow and deep.

Baby's eyes dark globes hovering over her, flames playing across their glassy surface. His long neck bent all the way to the barn floor. He had sniffed her, nudging her hand with his hairy lips, his nostrils wide with fear. He whinnied, then began to stomp his thin, elegant hooves.

Stomp on me, she had thought. *Then she'd smelled the smoke. The smoke had brought her back to the barn, the soiled hay, the overturned lantern, the tender, burning places on her cheeks, arms, and thighs. Suddenly she realized that she was alone. Only she could open the horse barn's door. Only she could free Baby and the others before it was too late.*

Now, Mildred's singing breath in her ears, up her nose, under her eyelids, between her lips. Breath like water. Buttermilk, honey, and hominy breath. All that milk-soaked breath that babies depend upon. Breath close to the cow. Milk-fed, soft, slightly sour breath.

No one else could have saved them. She loved them more than life.

As she stands in the dark, hugged by an old overcoat reeking of cigar smoke, stars flash greetings to each other, unaware of the infinitesimally tragic fire below. Or wise in ways she cannot grasp. She cannot even remember how she was saved but not the seven, who mattered so much. Not even Baby, who had warned her.

The barn door had been locked from the outside. That is all she remembers.

Behind her, Mildred keeps singing, "If you get there before I do, Babylon's a falling to rise no more." She feels arms under her arms press against the overcoat, holding her, holding up the coat. The coat remains. But she disappears into the solemn wind of the stars.

Part I

If you surrendered to the air, you could ride it.
---Toni Morrison
Song of Solomon

Chapter One: Tack Room

Most days the Tack Room greeted Viney with a sullen stillness, like a child holding its breath. But today, as she entered the Stables' oldest dining room, she sensed something had already stirred the air, unsettling the dust.

From the doorway, she inspected harnesses that hovered over curved red leather booths, dust burrowing in buckles and seams, and in the slouch of reins. In the decades since horses had raced for the Stables, the surviving tack had lost so much suppleness and strength that by 1978, it had shriveled into the shapes of the horses it once held.

However, at her touch, the tack would yield and soften to a tender gleam as she massaged the memory of those horses between her fingers, speaking to a brow band or cheek strap as if to the thoroughbreds themselves. Only after she'd rubbed a mile of elbow grease into every groove and bulge, only after she'd whispered until she was hoarse, *Viney's here. Never you mind no more,* would the harnesses and bridles, stirrups and saddle horns scattered across the Tack Room's mahogany walls raise up in hopes of riding once more.

Smoke snaked through the empty dining room as her ears followed the rise and fall of a distant siren. For Viney, fire was a way of life at the Stables. Yet the rest of the hired help panicked as if every fire was the first. They tore through the kitchen, clutching their heads and sucking their lips, blaming everyone around them for the disaster sure to claim them. But after 40-some years of cleaningbuffingshining, of bendingscrapingpatching the Stables, Viney stuck to her morning routine. She'd already been through the worst. No mere kitchen fire could change that.

She shoved an old A&P buggy full of rags, soaps, and brushes ahead of her into the Tack Room. Halfway in, the buggy stalled, straining against the carpet. The harder she pushed, the more the buggy bucked back. Whatever had managed to stir the air had unsettled the carpet, too. As she rested, catching her breath, a slight wind slid over her, sifting through the hair on her arms.

The buggy's groans muffled as she pushed across to the fireplace. Silver loving cups on the mantle pointed their elbows at her accusingly. Outside, the near-far pulse of sirens grew closer. A warm downdraft in the chimney brushed her cheeks as she leaned over to check the firebox. When she straightened up to screw the damper closed, old ashes that had somehow scattered on the carpet leapt up and kissed her on the lips.

Her sharp laugh was softened only by the silence between the siren calls. Her tongue rolled over the smoky residue on her lips. Leftover from winter fires, the ashes had lain cold in the firebox for months. But now they were on the move. And flirting. They had slipped on their shoes and gone out for a stroll.

She licked her lips again, hoping her mouth would give the ashes a means to speak. She knew that whoever had set the ashes in motion had not entered in the usual way. Yet only she knew of any other. But the ashes had little chance to come alive on her tongue. Not when she herself was as locked in silence as them.

With sirens shrieking ever louder outside, Viney bent down again to the fireplace floor. To listen, a body had to bend. Again the ashes leapt up, this time tickling her nose. She sniffed their scattered trail for any traces of their origins. But, giddy with trespass, they refused to give up who or what had carried them.

Instead she turned to the Tack Room's red leather booths for clues. Their curved and tufted cushions had embraced Stables' patrons for as long as she could remember. She leaned into one of the horseshoe-shaped seats while her fingers pushed and prodded its creases. But instead of easing open, they curled up tight as snails.

Massaging the leather did nothing to loosen the seat's stubborn silence. Even the booth's table resisted. As she pushed the table aside, throwing off its cloth for a better grip, she noticed a fresh stain. Then the raw wood promptly bit her.

She chewed at the sliver, then spit it out onto the floor. Those plain pine planks had always been sensitive. Years ago the original mahogany tables had grown weak from use and instead were replaced by the much cheaper boards, carefully disguised in fine white linen. The pine would nip at her waist and scratch her palms whenever she cleaned. Over time, she had learned to pack her apron full of old diapers for padding.

The booth creaked as she unfolded a diaper from her apron pocket and reached into the buggy. As she poured conditioning cream from a can and let her fingers press their questions, the red leather slowly gave way.

A cigarette burn on the booth's seat softened then collapsed against her cloth. Rubbing the charred lips, her fingers worked the burn, caressing the hole with white cream that turned pink, then red like the leather around it. *Tellmetellmetellmetellme,* she murmured, pressing her ear against the seat as if to a sea shell. Determined to coax the leather speak, she lifted the diaper and poured more cream.

The leather sucked and sucked at the diaper like a teat. The burn, now healed, begged for her imprint. As she pressed her finger into its new skin, a cool draft drew her eyes to the mantle. The top of her head grew warm, then hot. Loving cups from forgotten races again pointed their elbows at her. They knew only that she remembered. Yet she never spoke of those races, or what they had meant to the Stables. For that, the loving cups would not forgive her. Some day they would be abandoned to a trash heap, but for now, while they still had a chance, they took every opportunity to complain of her neglect.

Sighing, she fished a bent Old Gold out of her apron pocket, struck a match below a Stables' matchbook horse and rider, and leaned back into the booth.

As smoke from the Old Gold fingered the air above her, her memory, like the restless Tack Room air, stirred just enough to remind her of all that had been lost. Only scattered remnants remained. She remembered a stain. A burn. And ashes on the move. Ashes from a fire she herself had not lit, had never wanted. Then and now, ashes the only things she never bent low to love.

Licking her fingers, she pinched the spent butt, dropping it in her pocket. Easing herself up, she studied the carpet back towards the fireplace. Smoke continued to drift into the Tack Room as more sirens approached. It had taken her years to learn the difference between oven smoke and grill burns, stove flames and deep fat fires. This time it was the deep fat.

As she bent over the ashes once more, voices filtered in from the kitchen: the dishwasher with the cowlick who pretended not to speak English, Sarah on the salad counter, Opal working entrees. Mildred barked at servers and firemen alike to stay out of her way while she kept the lunch prep going. But not Billiard's voice, never Billiard's. As owner, he always managed to be away when the fires started. So was Mrs. Parkerhouse. In fact, in the eight years since she became manager, she had yet to show her face to Viney, or to anyone else, for that matter, except Billiard. Some of the Stables' staff believed Mrs. Parkerhouse didn't exist, that she was just someone made up by Billiard, who could divert blame to her for anything gone wrong.

Underneath the ashes' runaway laughter, she heard another, fainter voice. She untied her apron and flattened her ear to the floor. A high-pitched whinny put her nerves on alert. Groaning, she lifted herself and followed the sound back towards the kitchen. She found herself pausing in front of the former Wine Room door.

The Wine Room had been razed decades ago, leaving no visible traces except a door that led to nowhere hidden in the wall panels. Back then, after the horse barn had burned to the ground, everything had changed almost overnight. Drinking wine was no longer the closed-door pursuit of an inside crowd; instead, the speakeasy quickly shed its red light reputation to become an elite dinner club. Viney remembered every detail of the Wine Room. Not even Mrs. Parkerhouse, who was rumored to study the Stables like a bug in a bottle, knew of its existence. Instead, she focused on preserving the restaurant's plantation-style legacy, treating its seamier past as a short-lived exception to its stately rule. Viney was another relic of that past that Mrs. Parkerhouse ignored.

Standing before the Wine Room's long-forgotten door, Viney wondered why the ashes had led her there. As the private study of the Stables' first owner, a select few had been admitted, with only Viney, thin and tall, in a uniform starched to an inch of its life, bearing trays of wine and spirits off limits to the rest of the speakeasy.

That door never would have admitted A&P buggies loaded with silver polish, light bulbs, and diapers innocent of pins. Not sewing needles impaled on paper packets, nor a fistful of keys bigger than a baby's head. And most certainly not sneakers with smashed heels, nor a bargain basement Women's XXX. But as she stood now, slack-jawed, before this portal, the scattered ashes gathered themselves together. She stared, disbelieving, as they formed the ghostly gray outlines of hoof prints.

*

For as long as she can remember, horses have given Baby Divine her direction, starting with her daddy's Morgans. The Morgans long for their life down in the Low Country, their dainty hooves a poor match for North Georgia mountain roads. But they are in love with her daddy and so take him wherever he wants to go. He won them on a bet during a moonshine run to Savannah and drove the team home in darkness for two days straight. That way, no one would question why a black man was handling fancy horseflesh and a high-brow carriage on his own.

Listening to the bridle bells jingle each time her daddy leaves the mountain, Baby Divine concludes that she, too, began her life in a place other than Rabun Gap and one day is destined to leave it.

That day comes when an old Appaloosa carries her across the Carolina border. Her mama and younger brother, who drive ahead in a borrowed wagon, have given up on her daddy and instead are turning to her mama's people in Snowbird.

The sudden demand for moonshine once Prohibition began had made his trips home shorter and the time away longer. He even hired a neighbor to run his still while he was gone. For a long time, her mama said nothing. She never argued or raised her voice to complain. She traded the bolts of silk he brought her from Savannah for calico and advised her children to save the nickels he flipped into their waiting palms for shoes instead of horehound and licorice at the store in Dillard. The last time Baby Divine saw her daddy, he was dressed in trousers with a knife's edge crease, his dark face aglow. The Morgans lifted their heads and whinnied into her ear. "Next time, you coming with me," he told her mama as he kissed her deeply on the lips. She fixed the pins holding up her sleek, black braids as he waved goodbye.

Early the next morning her mama walked off and came back that afternoon with the wagon and the Appaloosa. She started loading everything from inside the cabin and directed her children to do the same.

"All these years, I say nothing about him leaving," she said to no one in particular. "I say nothing so that he will come back."

"Mama, why can't we go live in Savannah?" Baby Divine asked.

Her mama's eyes clouded over. She always reminded Baby Divine that her green eyes are from her Papaw's kin, along with the freckles and red hair. Mama's eyes, however, mirror those of her people, dark and smoky like a mist before dawn; her skin is like burnt copper, and her hair straight, black and shiny as a pond.

"We cannot leave," she replied, her voice curt. "Others left long ago with the soldiers, but our people stayed. How can your tongue leave your mouth behind?"

With each armload of quilts, pots, and clothes, Baby Divine listened for the telltale bells. But when it comes time to leave, it is the old Appaloosa, not her beloved Morgans, whose spotted rump carries her away to the land where her Mama, Mamaw, and all the kin who have come before still cling to the woods and valleys that the People have known as home.

That same Appaloosa puts her back on the road a few weeks later. She isn't expecting to leave and doesn't have a destination in mind when the Appaloosa appears at her Mamaw's cabin door one morning wearing a blanket and rope halter. She simply gets on. She has learned from her daddy to trust the horses. Different than people, money, or things, horses offer themselves purely; they will take her wherever she needs to go.

"Baby girl, you done born with the caul," he used to tell her. "You see what other people can't. Just like the horses. They don't see with just they eyes. They don't listen to no words. They see with they skin. The caul that seeing skin. Girl, you born Divine."

Because the Appaloosa is old, it takes three days to cross back into Georgia. She doesn't mind its lazy habits, which suit her own inclination to dawdle, daydreaming about the Morgans and her daddy's Low Country beginnings. She hunts fiddlehead ferns, day lily buds, dandelion greens and scotch broom flowers, and chews them slowly as her mama has taught, to release all their vital juices. She sniffs the air for signs of rain and compares the growth of jewelweed from one side of the valley to another.

On the third day, she arrives back at her family's cabin. She goes inside and hangs a raven feather over the door jam with red curls she's pulled from her own scalp, leaving it as a sign for her daddy that she has not *forgotten. Then she slaps the Appaloosa's rump to send it off. As she rubs the sore spot on her scalp, a man pulls up with a team of bays.*

"You live here?" The man squints down at her, his head cocked. His eyes are glassy and his stare cold. Instead of answering him, she smiles at the bays, who stomp one hoof, then another, in the dust. Bound in their bridles, they are eager for some of the new grass next to the cabin. She whistles softly, and their ears shoot up. She squares her shoulders, and the bays, both mares, lick their lips for her to approach.

The wagon creaks as the man shifts the reins into one hand. The wide wagon, his tall-heeled boots, and, of course, the bays, practically shout his lack of acquaintance with the highlands. The stiff way he turns his neck and the tension in his back give away his purpose.

Like many men, he has been lured up the mountain by moonshine. The man's pink-turned-brown skin tells her he's been some time on the road. Before her Daddy started peddling his moonshine in the Low Country, men came to Rabun Gap from farther and farther away, hauling off bigger and bigger loads of that pure liquor that sold on the promise of visions. The ones from farthest away were always surprised by his looks. Instead of dungarees, her daddy wore trousers with a knife pleat down the middle. Her mama refused to iron those pants, but her daddy wouldn't let her anyway. He also carried the charcoal complexion and buttery skin of a people born deep in sunshine. He acted as if he owned a kingdom, not just a backwoods still and hardscrabble where nothing grew except jewelweed and clover.

While her daddy spun stories about haints and horses, card games and duels, she occupied herself by studying his listeners. For the most part, they ignored her except to comment on her red curls and green eyes.

"Sister, you either blessed or cursed, but you ain't gone unnoticed by the good Lord," they'd say.

They always turned their attention back to the moonshine. The angels that spoke through the alcohol made it possible for her to observe them without fear. Though she herself had never traveled farther than Snowbird to visit her mama's family, she can easily imagine the kinds of places these men have come from by watching them swap stories around the still.

Eyeing the bees' nests clustered around the cabin door and the tin shingles askew on the roof, the man shakes his head, then spits under the wagon's wheel.

"I knew I shouldn't a listened to that fellow. Scotch-Irish bastard sends me running up here, expecting a dime for every penny I get." His eyes linger on Baby Divine's moccasins then follow her calico dress up to her face. He rubs an arm across his eyes as if waking from a long sleep.

"Damned if you ain't colored," he says.

Baby Divine scratches the bays' foreheads. The man says it as if being colored is unusual, but also distasteful. She knows that compared to most people in Rabun Gap, she has unusually bright skin. Both her parents attribute that to being born in a caul. She remembers that place between the womb and the world, and the ruby light the caul cast, even though her mama contended it was only her daddy's story she recalled. He liked to tell her how her name rose like a fountain to his lips as soon as he saw her. "Baby Divine," he said, and every time he said it, he smacked his lips.

She feels the man's eyes on her as she turns away to pull grass.

"Don't you talk, gal? You dumb or something?" As she feeds the bays, the man lays the reins on the seat then reaches into a satchel for a pouch and a newspaper.

While her daddy always praised the power of talk, her mama's example was on the lessons of silence. Baby Divine adored her daddy's stories, but it was silence that she practiced with her mama. Silence is protection, but also respect for Higher Powers, which is why her mama would not call her by her given name. Instead, she gave Baby Divine a plainer one, to show the ancestors her child is not vain. Her mama called her Sister, while her younger brother tagged her Spud, like the muddy red potatoes with yellow flesh that they dug out of the ground each fall.

Had this man known anything about silence, he would understand that the only thing that keeps her there with him is his horses. Unhappy with a long journey that was about to leave him empty-handed, he turns to her, flushing her out like a grouse.

"I speaks when it called for," she answers.

"Hoo, you a sassy one, ain't ya?" he replies, leaning back on his heels and waving his free hand as if about to fall.

He tears off a piece of newspaper, folding it along the bottom. Then he pinches a wad of tobacco from the pouch and sprinkles it inside the fold, keeping an eye on her.

"Well, maybe I ain't come for nothing, after all. How old are ya, gal? Sixteen?"

The bays whinny nervously. She doesn't blame the horses for bringing him. He is a fearsome man, and they must obey. But she isn't sure if she should go with them. Between the horses and her silence, she doesn't know if she has enough protection against the story that his face and hands are telling. Yet she also knows the horses need her courage, just as she needs their guidance now that she is about to leave all that is familiar behind.

He licks the newspaper edge and rolls it tight between his fingers. The cigarette plunges in and out of his mouth. To finish it off, a match licks its length then ignites one tip into flame.

She hears the tobacco cry out, trapped within the printed world that burns. The hoarse voice of tobacco mingles with horses' sweat so the sound has a smell and the smell has a sound. She follows the smoke with her breath, inhaling: Ahahahah, ahahahah. *Smoke moans through the cracks in his calloused hands. Then exhaling:* Eeheeheeheeh, eeheeheeheeh. *Between wiry blonde hairs erupts the scent of spoiled hay. The bays' nostrils shriek and the whites of their eyes rattle as smoke stirs the wildness held back by the bits in their mouths and the harnesses on their heads.*

Smoke whispers in the horses' pores and fills their lungs. It embraces one shoulder blade, then another, until all four of their shoulders lean forward as if to leap ahead and run. Smoke fingers their tongues and lips for all they have to say.

Hold still.

Smoke settles into floorboards where boots have agitated the wood's grain to smooth. It rests in tiny cracks in the reins and between the sunburned knuckles that hold them. Everywhere something is open or missing, smoke finds a place to spread itself. Ahahahah. Eeheeheeheeh. Ahahahah.

Finally, from out of the smoke, the answer-that-is-not-an-answer comes to her, something sensible that makes no sense, that will knock him off the path his story is following. "Mister, I am in a powerful hurry. My mama, she need some thread to patch things."

His eyes dart to the holes in the cabin where the shutters used to close, then settle on the collar button of her dress. A question surfaces in his eyes, but the smoke blows backwards and blurs them until he forgets what he wants to ask. Eyes watering, nose running, he pulls out a rag and blows, then stuffs it back in his pocket.

"Get on, then," *he says. He holds out his hand.*

The wagon creaks beneath her as her hand disappears into his, big as a bear paw. His eyes follow the next five buttons down the front of her dress as he shakes the reins.

For the next mile, she weighs whether to agree to the age he has assigned her, ignore it, or offer another. The bays trot restlessly, as if fearful of something in the woods. Every now and then one or the other rolls back an eye. When Baby Divine opens her mouth again to speak, he starts to pull back on the reins as if to stop, so she holds her tongue. Sensing his attention turn away from them, the bays ignore the reins and pick up their pace. He grumbles, then, glancing at her, lets the reins relax. The bays settle back into a trot.

He drives her the whole three miles down to Dillard in silence. There, he steers the wagon into a grove of pines spitting distance from the mercantile. The bays flick their ears at the lone mule hitched to the porch. She starts to tell him she doesn't have any particular birthday, now that her daddy is gone, thinking the truth might stop his story. But when he clamps his bear paw on her shoulder and growls, "You're not a girl-child, you're a she-wolf," she realizes her lack of birthday is now a hazard.

"I'm 12," she says. It isn't a lie. That's what her daddy said the last time she celebrated a birthday. Her mama never fussed over birthdays, and she lost track of how many she'd had since then, since her daddy wasn't around to remind her.

The man stares at her as if she really is a she-wolf and drops his hands abruptly.

"Go on and get," he mutters. "You didn't get no ride from me." Which is true; it is the bays that have driven her, not him.

As she climbs down into the red dust, the bays snort and shake their heads. She wants to rub their muzzles one last time, but the man starts cursing and searches for his whip.

"The hell if you think you can go wild on me. I'll show you who's in charge."

She clicks her tongue a few times while the man twists and turns, reaching for the whip but coming up empty-handed. The bays' ears perk up then relax. The man shakes the reins hard, but the horses now set their own pace down the road towards Clayton.

Baby Divine begins to wonder if she will ever go back to Snowbird and her mama, brother and Mamaw. But she clings to her daddy's trust in horses to take her beyond what she already knows. Like her daddy, she cannot live without them. They are her "seeing skin"; without them, she is lost.

Where the bays left off when they dropped her in Dillard, a mule takes over, moving her farther away from that corner of the world where two mountain ranges hug a valley that hasn't changed since the first People appeared. The mule carries her down to Clayton, stopping outside the post office next to two Percherons hitched to a wagon full of seed corn.

While the mule nibbles, she covers herself with the hard yellow kernels, trusting the massive yet gentle Percherons not to give her away. She hears the driver shout curses at the mule before taking up the reins. The Percherons shake their heavy harnesses as if to acknowledge the extra weight, but the man, distracted, seems not to notice.

For a long time, all she feels are the hard, dusty kernels pressing against her. If she breathes too hard, corn dust blocks her nostrils or kernels fall into her mouth. Sweat binds the seeds to her skin. The corn slides up her legs and pushes against the place her mama said her two bodies, earth and spirit, join as one. Her mama hinted that at some point she will have to cover over that place, to keep the evil out. But as a girl, it is important to keep the opening clear. Her two bodies are joined by one bone that forms around a woman's hole, allowing her spirit to move even as the life within her stays safe inside.

The seeds press against every pore, every crease, every curve, every hollow. With each bump and dip in the road, the corn rattles and hisses. Corn dust muffles her ears and eclipses her eyes. At times, she isn't sure if the darkness that creeps over her is shade or a blackout brought on by the heat. At these moments, she clenches her teeth and sucks air so hard it whistles. She chews stray kernels, letting them soften in her cheek before grinding them to their core.

Hours later, the wagon stops. She hears the brake squeal and the seat creak in the midst of voices and movement. A loud, hooting sound, like an owl a hundred times over, echoes in her corn-stifled ears. Light shines through the hulls in her eyes. She considers how to leave the wagon without notice.

After the first, long Hoo-Hoooo, she senses the voices and movements turn together like a flock of blackbirds. The Percherons stomp their hooves. Another hoot comes, with the same results. By the third one, she slips out of the corn and under the wagon into the safety of its shadow.

She has heard stories about Tallulah Falls and the big gorge that slices the land open, the river a silver thread far below. Hawks and eagles spiral on air currents up and down the rocky walls. Her daddy has met city people there sometimes to sell them his moonshine, watered down and dressed up in bottles labeled "tonic." He has told her about their clothes, city clothes that are strictly for show. He said they came for the air and water. Their skin is pale like mushrooms on rotting wood. She wonders how they could possibly reach water so far away in the gorge.

Her first glimpse of Tallulah Falls is between the bushy fetlocks of the Percherons, who continue to stomp with every Hoo-Hoooo. Instead of the gorge, she sees steep slopes of pine and rock. Many feet move around the wagon: dusty boots, bare toes, high heels, thick soles, thin soles, feet bigger than the biggest fish she's ever seen, trim ankles criss-crossed with straps of leather. Her own feet are callused by hours of walking alongside the Appaloosa, whose bony body could not bear her weight very long. And then there are the Percherons with their iron-clad hooves, stomping along with the Hoo-Hooos.

Suddenly a screech pierces the air so loud she has to cover her ears. Its thunder travels up and down her legs. Black Wheels roll past one Percheron leg then another, then grind to a halt. Smoke heaves out of a chimney. The wagon creaks as the Percherons shake their heads. She holds her breath, hoping they will not forget where she is.

This is as far as the horses will take her. She knows that, just as she knows the Percherons are eager to haul their empty wagon up the mountain and rest in their stalls with a bag of mash. Their huge heads graze the ground as if to signal her to go. They point to the Black Wheels where all the feet are going.

She leaps out from under the wagon. She doesn't care where she is headed as long as it is away from the Black Wheels.

A man's shiny shoes appear next to her feet. She looks up, narrowly missing his blue coat and stiff white shirt. With jowls like raw pie crust and a biscuit cutter hat, he asks, in a strangely musical voice, "And just what would your hurry be?"

Had she been less frantic, she would have laughed. Sometimes her mama would give her and her brother leftover pie dough, and they would shape fat little men with pale arms and legs that stuck out from their bodies, just like his.

Panting hard, she replies, "Ain't no more horses."

"Aye, well, it certainly seems that's where things are headed." The biscuit-cutter's voice takes on a kindly tone. She searches eyes bright like a blue jay's wing. "You know," he clears his throat, looking away, "first the Iron Horse and next the automobile. That'll be taking over these parts in no time."

She looks around and notices other wheels besides the Big Black Ones, spoked wheels alongside the wagons'. Glass keeps back the wind, and roofs give shade. On the side of one vehicle she reads, "Tallulah Falls Mineral Springs Resort," yellow on the black door. She wonders about "resort," which she recognizes from Mama's primer as an action, but not as a thing.

The man clears his throat. "You'd best be moving along if you expect to find a place to sit." He points to the end of the Black Wheels where people are still climbing inside.

"Iron Horse?" Baby Divine asks. "That what you call it?"

The man's frown cuts deeply into the pie dough jowls. "Certainly. Isn't anyone who doesn't know that."

So the Percherons have not been wrong, after all. Baby Divine follows the man's arm to the end of the Iron Horse, where smoke waves overhead. There, she catches a glimpse of the gorge and thinks she hears water falling. But it just as easily could be the Iron Horse, rumbling in anticipation of the journey ahead.

She never does see the falls. What she does see are miles of tracks, just like the ones she stands on as she tries to figure a way inside the Iron Horse. Another biscuit cutter frowns over passengers outside, taking slips of paper from their hands, as they board at the very end of the Horse. She stands there staring while a line of people give up their paper one by one. When the biscuit cutter throws her a frown, she takes off down the side of the train opposite where all the wagons and motor cars wait, in search of some other opening. Then she hears the sound of water splashing and crouches low under the Horse to find its source.

When the Iron Horse Hoo-Hoos again and begins to move, she balances herself over the hole she has come up through. It smells of piss and is dotted with dried dung but otherwise is clean, nothing like what lay at the bottom of her privy back home. The walls around the hole close in so tight she barely has room to stand or move. She crouches down to watch the tracks race past, to keep her mind off the heat and stink. A knock on the door finally shifts her inside the narrow aisles of the Iron's Horse's belly. She trades places with a man in overalls, who lets her exit before he squeezes past and closes the privy door. Inside the train, people stand clutching bags and boxes and sometimes a chicken or two, all with the same sun-weary faces, crowded by feed bags, wooden crates, and piles of mail.

Nobody's eyes raise a question. Everyone looks as if they already know her. She finds a sack of mail to sit on and watches the highlands disappear into rolling, piney hills.

When the train finally stops in Atlanta, she gets off with the others but then hangs back on the tracks, listening for the sound of water falling. Another privy hole invites her into the belly of another Horse. This time, when she opens the privy door, she enters a bigger car with more people, still standing but without the company of sacks, crates, and livestock. Unlike the last Horse, biscuit cutters pace inside, asking for papers. Seeing the fear on her face, some of the passengers guide her back into the privy and close the door, huddling around it until the biscuit cutter has passed.

For two days and two nights she listens to railroad ties go ka-chunk ka-chunk underneath her feet. Finally a proper seat comes to her on an Illinois Central someplace out of Alabama. After the first biscuit cutter passes through, she opens the privy door to one bright wooden bench winking right at her. She curls up in its lap and falls asleep for two more nights and three days, waking only when someone covers or uncovers her as the biscuit cutters pass through.

Since leaving Georgia, she hasn't eaten a thing. A boy child maybe half her age, with red hair and freckles against clay colored skin and a nose like a fish hook, shakes her shoulders, then thrusts a biscuit into her hands. An older girl she takes for his mother nods from the window seat across the aisle, a straw brim shading two round, soft eyes. They are unlike any eyes in the highlands, where moonshine or determination is most likely to shine through. Nothing so soft, so butter-melty, as this girl's eyes.

She hasn't noticed the pain in her stomach until those eyes melt into hers. She wants to cry more than she wants to eat. Where was her mama now that the horses have taken her so far away? Until now, the steady clacking of the Iron Horse has reassured her like hoof beats. She matched her breath and adjusted her movements to the Horse's rhythm. Even with her stomach's first rumblings, the Iron Horse's rocking steadied her.

Yet tears come while the butter eyes watch, bitter like those she shed each time the Morgans took her daddy away. Bitter because her mama never let her go with the Morgans. Bitter because now that the horses have taken her, she has no mama, only horses. Bitter because she knows her mama will never leave Snowbird. Bitter because she is unprepared for butter eyes that melt into her own. Bitter because she never received such a look before. Bitter because she is receiving it.

The boy pats her arm and makes little cooing sounds, awkwardly stroking her sleeve.

"Why you crying?" he asks. "This biscuit ain't so bad."

He breaks off a piece of biscuit and puts it into her mouth. Against the roof of her mouth it is tender, leaving a smoothness on her tongue. Her mama's biscuits always scraped the insides of her mouth and had to be dug out from between her teeth. But this biscuit kisses her as it goes down. When she bites into the ham, it, too, is easy. Instead of stinging salt, her tongue meets juicy flesh. She has never had fresh meat, only cured, dried, and pickled. It never occurred to her to want any other kind. Her mama knew how to butcher a hog but insisted hogs were man's work and so refused to raise them. Her daddy was a city-born man and so did none of that.

She nods to the girl-mother as she eats the ham biscuit. Grinning, she nudges the boy with her elbow. His nose hooks up as he grins back.

"You a funny color," he says. "Where you from?"

She looks around, suddenly feeling many eyes on her waiting for an answer. It is true; most folks around her are a shade or two darker than she, except this boy and his red hair and freckles, the likes of which she'd never seen before.

"You funny looking," she says, and pokes him in the stomach lightly, the way she used to tease her brother.

"Uh-uh," he smiles, shaking his head. "I ain't red like you."

Then he slides off the seat and squeezes through the forest of pants and skirts to his seat beside his mother, who lowers her eyes as if embarrassed. But she's come to expect that most of the faces on the Iron Horse will be different than her own.

At the Alabama station, the biscuit cutters call out, "She-cag-oh. All aboard," and shuffle a crowd of shadow heads from one track to another. Only when she steps out into the hard light of, "She-cag-oh! End of the line!" does she realize how vast are their variations of color and how many people the Iron Horse carried. Only in her daddy's Low Country stories were so many people in one place all at the same time, but in her child mind, they all had her daddy's soft skin and long limbs.

The surprise of so many people makes her wonder where this river of faces will end, if, in fact, it does. She looks up at a tower with a numbered face and wonders what it is for. She-cag-oh. The strangest name she's ever heard. Someone thrusts a piece of paper in her hand. Chicago Urban League, reads the big print over a lot of smaller words underneath. Shi-cog-uh. Someone says something about a lake. She wonders if she can camp there that night. Wind tangles in her hair. She feels as light as the newspapers swirling over the tracks.

As she stands in the wind in She-cag-oh, the end of the line, or Shi-cog-uh, the beginning of a new life, she recalls those butter eyes. Until then, she never pictured any mother other than the one to whom she was born. Staying on her feet will be hard, but whatever falls she takes will be more forgiving with others' eyes melting into her own.

*

A slight wind lifted the smoke of another Old Gold up and away. Viney watched as the smoke tangled in cobwebs overhead before lowering itself onto old silver on the Tack Room's sideboard. Speared on the tines of gregarious forks, cradled by treacherous soup spoons, and sawed by toothless knives, the smoke continued its restless course, even as a black feather dropped from ceiling shadows and onto the samovar's belly.

As the smoke continued its travels, it revealed other signs of silent invasion. Chewed wainscoting. Dead moths in a water pitcher. The used condom under booth 13 marked by teeth as big as a coon's. Finally, the smoke led Viney back to the fireplace, where her eyes traveled up into the glare of a gallery lamp then down to a fallen harness on a tablecloth below. The smoke lingered over the hoof prints on the carpet formed from ashes and fingered their open-ended faces.

As she leaned into a booth, stinging pain spread like a root down her back. Something had changed, overnight it seemed. Like fireflies that suddenly appear in summer skies, the ashy hoof prints had lit up a door to memories she had long since forgotten, surfacing briefly and bright, like sparks over flame.

There had been a time when her vision was clear; her bond with the horses had made her "seeing skin" alive. But when the horse barn fire scattered them, afraid to ever return, she was lost. Without horses to guide her, she had no choice but to stay at the Stables. Without her seeing skin, she had tried instead to remember where they went by holding, rubbing, and breathing into the objects, spaces, and people she had known, hoping to spark a memory that would ignite all the others laying like ash inside her. For years, she had groped along in this way, touching one shard of memory after another. She moved with neither hope nor fear, joy nor dread, only with the certainty that someday she would remember, and that her beloved horses would return and once again carry her wherever she needed to go.

She clutched her back, panting and sweating, her spine pounding. Every day since the horse barn burned, she called out for the horses. Every day she struggled to remember that night in the barn, how it was she had emerged, a ghost covered in ash, but the horses disappeared. But the fire had destroyed all traces of that night, and with it, her seeing skin.

The pounding in her spine swallowed her, then the Tack Room, then reached out beyond the walls, so huge that she almost mistook the pounding as her own, too large to get outside of, too deep to follow to its source. The pounding connected her to memories invisible yet palpable, as she struggled in their shadowy grasp. The Old Gold's smoke urged her on into darkness so complete that her eyes soon failed her. Her panicked breath grew choppy and shallow as smoke, then darkness, quickly overcame her.

Chapter Two: Two Way

Each night as T.J. waited to deliver the last car to its owner, his thoughts formed more and more around the stable boys' destruction. One or two good knocks with a sledgehammer would smash those shit-eating grins, squash those bug-eyes to nothing.

Yet it seemed that nothing could remove the pair from their eternal posts--not teenage vandals, not thieves, not drunks, not hired help out for revenge. Whoever had dug the holes, poured the cement, and positioned their iron bodies had had Forever in mind.

For as long as anyone could remember, the two stable boys had greeted Stables' patrons just outside the main door. During speakeasy days, light from gas lamps had lit their moonbeam teeth while slummers from the city sidled between. Black jodhpurs exaggerated their bow-legged bows while their eyes bulged with panicked eagerness, as if the brass bridle rings welded to their black hands might suddenly be ripped away.

He hadn't always hated them so purely. Or maybe it was just the heat.

A black Caddy pulled up, the last in a long line for a last-minute funeral lunch. Inside his head, a tape played over and over: *It's the heat, it's the heat, it's the goddamn heat.* Nothing on that tape about the new uniform Billiard had given him. It weighed in at 20, no 50, hell, probably 100 pounds. *Grand, oh-so-Grand-with-a-Capital-G.* "Grand" was what Mrs. Parkerhouse had supposedly told Billiard, to justify the cost. T.J. had never been so hot before, but neither had his uniform ever been so Grand.

Nor did the tape say anything about the fire trucks blocking the driveway. *It's the heat, it's the heat, it's the goddamn*--and then another siren went off in the distance. T.J. mopped his forehead with a drenched handkerchief. This was more than the usual grease fire if other trucks were on the way.

Back before Bedford Heights had a name, fire trucks had approached with little fanfare to put out kitchen fires. Their tires did not spit gravel, and the firemen offered easy waves as they hauled hoses past the Big Willow around back. Later, their cigar smoke would mingle with his as they discussed some bit of nothing that, more often than not, made T.J. laugh. Eventually, the firemen were hitting up T.J. for hot tips for the racetrack. The fire out, the Stables' customers pacified, they all shared in the satisfactions of a job well done.

But these fancy new trucks roared like predatory cats, their shiny sides spiking sunlight into his eyes. Their tires hissed, hot from hauling so much equipment despite the short ride up Illinois Road. Rubber coats and walkie-talkies pushed through the Big Willow's branches while helmets paused only briefly to nod at the gold braid on T.J.'s Grand New Uniform. He was not sorry that the willow, having flourished under the piss of the famous and the infamous, did not easily open its arms to this crew. All of them, him included, now had the flashy new uniforms and equipment. But now they did their jobs like machines, or ghosts, putting on the show, but at a cost no bottom line could measure.

For some reason *(It's the heat, it's the heat, it's the--)*, his feet wouldn't budge when that last black Caddy rolled to a halt. It was as if his insides had drained out and his feet, like the stable boys, had hardened to where he couldn't move. Something had shifted. Something had cut loose. What his mind wanted, his feet no longer cared. They had stopped listening. Everything else moved, but with a sense of hollowness, like a scarecrow holding up the bosses' Grand New Uniform.

Two months ago, on a soggy April afternoon, Billiard, the latest in a decades-long parade of boss man-owners, had buddied up to T.J. by joining him outside for a smoke. Unlike his operations manager, Mrs. Parkerhouse, whom no one ever saw, Billiard professed to like to "meet my people where they worked." No matter the weather, he often lingered with T.J., narrowing his eyes at the traffic on Illinois Road and saying nothing. Sometimes he'd turn towards the empty pastures to the west where the thoroughbred race horses had once grazed, ask a question, then answer himself and thank T.J. for his "input." At other times, Billiard would stare up Central Avenue as he rehearsed his plans to become a Widely Respected Citizen of Bedford Heights and the South Bedford Sanitary District by running for district commissioner.

That day, as rain had dripped from the canopy, Billiard had almost smiled, his shoulders hunched inside a three-piece suit whose wide lapels dallied with current fashion. The Windsor knot on his silk tie was loosened just enough to reposition it quickly, should the need arise. Little about Billiard was casual. But at a time when both leisure suits and pin stripes strolled through the Stables' door, he aimed to be both classy and hip.

Billiard had fingered his jacket buttons open and closed. "What about these boys?" He pointed to the two stable boy statues.

T.J. hoped this was one of those days when the boss would answer his own question.

Billiard continued. "You must be sick of them," he said.

Rain collected on the canopy's edge then splashed in big, sloppy drops to the cement walk below. Dampness and dust collided with Billiard's Brut aftershave. Fresh aftershave at 3:30 in the afternoon at first had struck T.J. as odd, but then he recalled how Billiard was always on the way to one meeting or another.

Stalling for time, T.J. turned to stare back at the main door, where the stable boys' jackets reflected two red streaks in the copper veneer. In all his years at the Stables, this was the first time T.J. had noticed that the right stable boy hunched over slightly more than the left. Schooled in the double-talk of countless bosses, managers, and power brokers, he carefully weighed the pros and cons of giving an honest answer. But for once, T.J. sensed that what he really thought was, in fact, what Billiard wanted to hear.

"Yessuh," T.J. finally replied. The Grand New Uniform weighed a touch lighter on his shoulders.

That seemed to satisfy Billiard. He shook T.J.'s hand and slapped him on the back. "My man," he said. Boss man learns jive talk, T.J. noted. On his way inside, Billiard leaned over the stable boy on the right and peered into its face. "Shouldn't be too hard," he said.

The following Tuesday, T.J. was greeted by two stark white faces where the black ones had been. His first reaction had been to laugh. The stable boys' white shirtwaists and cuffs had blended into the white of their necks and hands, making them short-sleeved and bare-chested. Their lips and teeth blended with their skin, obscuring their obsequious grins. Later he found out Billiard had allowed his long-haired, sandal-wearing son to "modernize" the pair, covering up whatever racial guilt he may have harbored with a quart of Sherwin-Williams 132. T.J. stared at them the entire afternoon. Even so, he could not quite grasp their transformation. Their hair was still black, their eyes coal, but their smiles no longer aroused ambivalence. Now he flat-out hated them.

Or maybe it was just *the heat, it's the heat, it's the goddamn heat.* He pursed his parched lips and whistled.

Lenny ran out from around the west side, his head twisting one way, then the other, his mouth flapping open like he'd just been robbed. Tall, lanky Lenny, whose whip-lean body shifted with the wind. No steel to his spine, instead just one long spring that would sometimes leap into action and then, just as quickly, recoil. His neck craned towards the main door while his legs carried him on a collision course with the Caddy. From under a teeny-tiny Afro, he squinted until, at the very last moment--*heat, it's the heat, it's*-- he spotted the Caddy and the passengers waiting inside.

Lenny was his wife, Mildred's cousin's boy, raised mainly by his mama and Big Mama. T.J., having raised only daughters, filled in now and then as a daddy, taking Lenny to the park lake to fish, helping him pick out his first car. When a position came open at the Stables, T.J. asked Billiard for Lenny, thinking of him as his successor.

Until then, the notion of passing on his knowledge had never occurred to him. He knew a lot about working the door, about playing and beating the odds that he suddenly realized would disappear when he left the

Stables. It never mattered to him before, but now, staring that possibility in the face, it did. He knew how jobs could steal from you, but he also knew how good work, work that you could put your heart and soul into, paid back more than a pay check. It gave a body respect. It gave a person a self-worth.

Anyone gone begging for those things, he thought, *it be Lenny.*

Lenny stopped just before his knees met the Caddy's grill and by some miracle kept the rest of himself from buckling over the hood. Adjusting his cap slightly, he strode, stiff-legged, to the driver's door, which, T.J. noticed with some satisfaction, he opened crisply. Then he disappeared on the passenger side. T.J. saw a flash of light and something stirring inside. Before he knew it, Lenny had flung himself into the driver's seat and roared off, leaving three people standing in a cloud of dust.

Dazed by the flashing lights and the fire engines' hum, the trio looked as if they might stay there forever until the man gripped one woman's arm while the other woman took the first one's elbow, and together they shuffled towards the main door.

*--the heat, it's the heat, it's the goddamn--*All of a sudden, the tape stopped, nothing, no sound at all, not even his heartbeat, buried deep inside the Grand New Uniform. Maybe because he was right where he was supposed to be, ready to open the door. Or maybe because the heat had suddenly disappeared. He shivered as a cold breeze preceded the three mourners. Deep inside the Grand New Uniform, however, he felt nothing at all. His feet anchored him like lead weights to the silence within.

Once upon a time, the stable boys had put patrons at ease. Women patted their tight black caps and giggled, calling them *too cute for words*. Men pissed in their faces, laughing at moments when no one but T.J. would notice. When he saw how much the patrons liked them, he made sure the pair was always spit-polish clean. As long as the tips rolled in and patrons patted him on the back like one of their own, he could put up with those shit-eating grins. Others might be fooled by the grins, but he wasn't; he and the stable boys were survivors.

But overnight their black faces had changed to white. Not the pinkish-beige of most white people's skin, but the bluish tone of a bed sheet or a dinner plate. It struck him as a most unnatural white. No matter that the black had been as unnatural as shoe polish; no one had ever flinched at that. But now tips were down, no doubt in part because of white faces where black ones were supposed to be. Even the Grand New Uniform could not change that.

All three patrons that Lenny had left in the dust were dressed in black, with two gray heads and one white. They stared at their copper reflections in the door as they approached. Like everyone else these days, T.J. figured they wouldn't tip a doorman. People didn't want to depend on anyone else anymore. Doors were supposed to just fly open by themselves: Auto-magic; No Body Need Apply.

When they reached the canopy, T.J. leaned into the handle (to his amazement, his feet still would not move), and pulled the door open. Out of habit, he held out his left hand, palm up. Once upon a time, patrons saw the open palm as an opportunity, not as begging. If they wanted the inside track, they greased the palm. It wasn't just about getting what they wanted. It was code for busting the Man's chops. For surviving and thriving against the odds. The game was rigged, no matter where you stood. Even for the Man himself.

Never in a million years would he have guessed what happened next. The stable boys might as well have been black for all these people noticed. The middle one, an ancient woman with hair like a dandelion gone to seed, stopped dead and stared at him. Him: brown eyes, pork chop jowls, teeth yellow like old piano keys, and a salt-and-pepper-but-mostly-salt head of hair under the Grand New Hat. But what she saw was not even close to that. It couldn't have been, because she just *(it's the heat, it's the heat, it's the goddamed--)*
cried.

He gripped the copper door like a shield. In over 40 years at the door, every possible insult, every compliment, every despair and raucous joy had been flung his way. But this little old lady's tears shook him to his bones, coming from a body likely to crumble in a strong breeze. *Who she crying for?* he wondered. Then he remembered the funeral luncheon.

Her eyes rolled up under parchment lids as she buckled under the slight weight of all those tears. Her crying set his Grand New Uniform to quivering. He wanted, urgently, to cover his ears, but duty kept his hands on the door while his mind journeyed back to his family home in Mississippi. He pictured a rocker on the porch, fishing poles against the wall, and thought how sweet retirement seemed. He had once vowed that he'd die at the track or at the Stables' door, unless he beat the odds and won a fortune. But now a shotgun house, a smoke on a porch sofa, and a fishing hole in view of it all never looked so good.

He shook his head, as if trying to wake up. Had the Grand New Uniform drained the last bit of feeling from him? Why wasn't he trying to soothe this sad old granny?

Just as he opened his mouth, the younger woman spoke up.

"It's OK, Mama." Two gray heads arched together over their elder's white one. "He's just a *man*." The younger woman tossed a hurried apology over her shoulder as she and the man hustled the older woman through the door: "Sorry, she's from the Old Country. She's never been this close to a Negro before."

He let the door go, took off his Grand New Cap and fanned his salt-and-a-little-pepper hair. What kind of person? he asked himself. He might have been saying it out loud, or it could have been deep inside the Grand New Uniform, he didn't know, and he didn't care. He tried it another way: What *kind* of person? and another: What Kind Of Person?

The weight of the Grand New uniform never felt heavier than at that moment. For once, he'd let down his guard, stopped his bobbing and weaving, his dance at the door. He had seen a woman old enough to be his mother—and that was pretty damn old, had his mother survived—in pain. Sad at the loss of a loved one, he'd assumed.

There was always that porch to dream about, but the fact of the matter was he was just tired, tired of fighting people's everlasting ignorance. It was time for someone else to take on the fight.

What Kind? The question kept coming. This time, though, he had an answer. The Kind to unstick his feet long enough to move out of *the heat, it's the heat, it's the goddamn heat!* and into the foyer.

Funny how life always telling you the truth you don't want to hear, he thought, as he stepped into the cool air inside. *She done seen a ghost instead of me.*

*

From his early years on, T.J. has a passion for beating the odds. His mama doesn't much like it, but beating the odds is a game she understands. Ever since she stepped off the Illinois Central and into the streets of Chicago, she has taught her children to do whatever they must to prevail. Running numbers for a bookie isn't the kind of work T.J.'s church-abiding mother has hoped for her youngest, the only northern-born son out of four. But numbers are in his blood.

Back in Sunflower, Mississippi, she subscribed to the Chicago Defender *with egg money and read it out loud in the small parlor of her parents' house. She bought the paper from porters who smuggled it onto trains that roared through the tiny town. The news was incredible: A Negro couple in Milwaukee wins an anti-bigotry suit against a Chinese restaurant that refused to serve them; Negro neighborhoods in Chicago run their own elections; black baseball teams attract a national audience.*

But the most astonishing story of all was a front-page photo of black men swarming a train in Alabama.

She read the caption solemnly: "The exodus from the south has caused much alarm among Southern whites, who have failed to treat them decent. The men, tired of being kicked and cursed, are leaving by the thousands, as the picture above shows."

The train trailing smoke became for Angel Fair and her family an image of departure both chosen and definite. The iron rails that had cleaved their mail stop town into two separate worlds of haves and have nots would carry them to a place where the tracks finally met.

According to the Defender, *Chicago folks were smart, and, even better, they were organized, eager to seize opportunity after generations of denial. Angel Fair asked her pastor to write a clergyman listed in the classifieds to verify the* Defender's *claims of plentiful and good jobs, new schools being built every day, and, best of all, no whites breathing down their necks.*

When the good news came, the family agreed they would either leave together, or not at all. Grandmammy claimed she was too old to be uprooted, yet even she, recalling the eager, anxious faces of hundreds of former slaves awaiting passage, gave in.

From the shiny new Illinois Central train, Angel Fair walked straight under stone arches big enough to shelter the whole town of Sunflower. The station's clock tower, as loud as 1000 firecrackers, had struck the hour her family arrived. She took it as an omen. When a handbill proclaiming, "No charges. No fees. We want to help YOU!" was thrust into her one free hand and a Chicago Defender *was waved in her face, it seemed like God Himself had arranged for her family a prodigious welcome.*

That handbill assumed a place of honor on the chiffonier, where it remains through T.J.'s early years. Mounted on a clean rectangle of cardboard, it professes a catechism of urban living, courtesy of the Chicago Urban League: Be on Time; Do Not Urinate from Porches; Keep Your Household Tidy and Your Children Clean; No Loud Conversations in Public. On the back side is advice on work to be found and assistance with housing. Whenever any of her children act less than they should, Angel Fair points to the handbill and reminds them to take pride in themselves.

Thomas Jefferson witnesses this newly minted pride forming itself throughout his childhood. South Side residents own and operate their own restaurants, department stores, laundries, bakeries, boot and shoe repair, livery, auto, banking and insurance. Madame C.J. Walker's cameo-like face dominates the streets. When he is old enough to let go of his mama's hand and follow his daddy and older brothers and cousins, he begins to see another side to his neighborhood. There are the storefront businesses, like those that sell chitterlings and collards raised in Gary, and fresh stew meat from back o' the yards. Then there are the hidden businesses behind the raw pine walls.

Policy is a game of their own making, run by and for the South Side. Almost everyone there is a player except serious church-goers, though even the preachers sometimes praise wealthy game makers whose front-end businesses keep money in the neighborhood. As long as prosperity reigns, almost everyone is willing to countenance, if not actually play, the game.

Angel Fair is well acquainted with policy but neither discourages nor encourages it to her sons. However, she deplores the street-corner drawings that take place every day and hurries T.J. away from such spectacles. Instead, she abides by her preacher's example. A practical man, the preacher vilifies policy's preying on the poor and desperate even as he praises the economic self-reliance that policy provides. He exhorts his flock to care for the downtrodden so they will not be driven to bet their last dime on million-to-one odds.

Despite his mother's vigilance, it doesn't take long for T.J. to discover policy for himself. One day while studying the jujubes and Mary Janes in the confectioner's case, T.J. looks up to find the owner, Mr. Shephard, staring at him. Usually, the candy store man is too busy with other folks crowding his counter, talking about "wheels" and "books" and elbowing each other for little printed slips of paper. But now Shephard, whose eyes bulge out in perpetual surprise, ignores the little group buzzing by the door and instead asks T.J., would he like a nickel's worth free.

"You just head on over to the hardware." Mr. Shephard's smile is slow and easy. "Then come on back, and I fix you up, you and your friends, too."

"Mama don't like me going no place she don't know about," T.J. replies. But the real problem is what to do with all that candy. No matter who he gives it to, no matter how many oaths of secrecy his friends might vow, he knows Angel Fair will hear about it. And if she doesn't hear about it from him first, she'll wear him out. He wishes he were bigger and older like his brothers so she can't cut a switch on his behind.

Shephard holds out a small roll of paper. A round seal of wax stamped with two S's secures the end. T.J. runs the whole three blocks thinking that if he moves fast, no one will notice him. He drops the roll on the hardware store counter and waves both hands over his head at the clerk, who frowns, then looks the seal over. T.J. is already halfway out the door when the clerk calls him back.

"Go on back. We don't take no slips up front."

As he pushes through the swinging door that separates the counter from the front, he sees his own, startled face in a mirror hanging next to a curtained doorway. Too scared to look for long, he only just peeks at himself, as if the mirror is Angel Fair's eyes and, if he is quick enough, she will not look his way.

Around back, T.J. discovers that there is another side to this mirror. When he reaches the back of the store, he is surprised to find that he can still see the store's front through a window where the mirror would be hanging. The mirror on his mother's chiffonier only has a front; its cardboard back faces the wall. But behind the hardware store mirror, T.J. learns another catechism, one that eventually eclipses the Urban League handbill enshrined on his mother's mirror: pay off cops to keep the game alive; policy stations take their cuts first; Irish and Italians who run the gin and beer get paid to protect the game; find your "hot" numbers through spiritual advisors.

The hardware store owner grunts as T.J. hands over the roll of slips. A table full of spectators crowds closer for a look.

"That Death Row playing right well. I caught $8.50 on it last week. My brother saddled a gig on it this week and caught $10," says one man sitting at the table.

"I missed out on that book," replies another man reaching for one of the slips handed out by the store owner. "It made me miss my mother's name once. I dreamed about her—she dead—but instead of playing her name, I played the Death Row. Her name fell out in the first sixes. Shit, I would be a rich man right now if I'd a played my mother's name."

Sighs, grunts, and one excited yelp follow as slips are passed out and studied. T.J. tries to add the columns of numbers on the slip, thinking they resemble his arithmetic tests, but the columns are too long, and there is no line at the bottom for the total. And then the slips are on the floor, where they join other slips that scuffle and slide under the men's feet as they continue their restless talk around tin cups of coffee and clouds of smoke.

T.J.'s eyes widen at the stack of five-dollar bills the owner is counting. "I ain't never seen so many dollars before," T.J. gasps. "How you get all that?"

By the way all the other men are joking and smiling, by the slips of paper and chalkboard with numbers scrawled in columns, and by the tobacco smoke that hangs over them like a cloud, T.J. guesses that hardware isn't the source of all this money. In fact, no one is paying any mind to the pipes, lumber, and boxes of nails stacked around them.

The owner laughs. "Here," he says. He wraps a five-dollar bill in a piece of brown paper. "Take it on back. Say." He stares at T.J.'s heaving white suspenders. "You run real good. You looking to keep running?"

He tells Angel Fair that Mr. Shephard has given him the candy after running an errand to the hardware. He knows he has seen something he shouldn't when her eyes move up and down his suspenders as if he has soiled them so bad they'll never come clean. Then, when she sighs, he realizes that this is something big, so big that he can't tell her, even if she already knows it in her heart.

He picks out the Mary Janes from his pockets, her favorite, and gives them to her. He knows their sweetness will last the longest.

*

T.J. couldn't shake the sense of despair that hovered around him and his Grand New Uniform even after the trio departed. So he cracked open the main door and whistled out to Lenny, who was slouching past the fire trucks, a tall, skinny kid among huge, menacing beasts, an unlit cigarette dangling between his lips. When he didn't respond, T.J. put his fingers to his lips and whistled again, struggling over the roar of the trucks.

Finally, Lenny swiveled his head towards the main door. Flipping off his cap, he wiped his forehead with a sleeve. Then, replacing his cap, he fished in his coat pocket, pulling out a red Stables matchbook, and lit up. His hands cupped the flame against the breeze, the tiny tongue of fire flickering like a dare as the firemen loaded the trucks to leave.

"What's up, my man?" Lenny walked into the canopy's shade. "Them stiffs all in?"

"I expect so." T.J. cleared his throat and spit on a stable boy's foot. "Stay here and keep an eye out, you hear?"

"Your old lady wanting you?" Lenny grinned. Lenny had never called Mildred anything but Aunty until he started working at the Stables. He used to call T.J. "Uncle Man," a name begun when Lenny was small, and T.J. used to tell him, "You the man." Now he avoided calling T.J. anything at all.

"Take that fag out your mouth," T.J. grumbled. "Never mind where I'm going. And stop slouching. You ain't never going to get nowhere if you look like you carrying a load."

"Next thing you going to tell me to smile." Lenny kept to his slouch, grinning.

"You know it." T.J. wasn't in a mood to argue but he wasn't in a mood to take Lenny's sass, either. He opened the main door and stepped inside the foyer. "You never know when somebody be watching."

The mirror that stretched the length of the foyer masked a secret passage that T.J. was certain even Mrs. Parkerhouse, who everybody thought knew everything about the Stables, did not know about. No one besides T.J. knew that that mirror looked two ways, as it had since speakeasy days, when its sole purpose was to help those inside watch out for raids by cops.

Old hinges groaned as T.J. tugged on a hidden door panel. The panel opened to the secret passage that ran parallel to the two-way. Fortunately, no one else was around to hear. He reminded himself about oiling the hinges; he didn't want to give away this one last secret to Billiard. The long, narrow space smelled like rain and old shoes. T.J. fumbled for the string that turned on a single bulb overhead. At the end of the passage, which had once allowed spotters to bypass the lobby door and tip off bosses before the cops came crashing in, another hidden panel opened into the lobby

The passage behind the two-way wasn't a place to linger, but it had become that for T.J., who spent more and more of his spare moments tucked away from public view. Inside was as bare as a burial vault. Only a small transistor radio perched atop a bar stool interrupted the emptiness. He picked up the radio and pressed it to his ear then settled into a satisfied slump on the stool as the first race was announced. Staring out the two-way, he kept one eye on the main door, the other on the lobby's. The radio's reception wasn't great, but it was enough to follow the race.

Ponies in the second race were jammed down the home stretch when, at the far end of the foyer, the lobby door opened. T.J. jumped up from his stool and searched the two-way for signs of Lenny outside the main door. But Lenny was gone. Turning back towards the lobby door, T.J. knocked into the bar stool. The radio thudded to the floor. It used to be he could hold five different bets in mind and still keep an eye on the door. Nowadays his own bets were the only ones to keep track of. His days as track tout and gambling advisor were long gone, but that didn't make his door job any easier. In fact, it was harder and harder to stay sharp on more than one thing at a time.

He half-hoped it was Lenny coming. As T.J.'s successor, it was time Lenny knew about the two-way. But he also hoped it wasn't; Lenny should have stayed where he was told.

T.J. never would have expected Viney to come through that door. She rarely showed her face anywhere around the Stables these days, and certainly never in so public a space as the lobby. Weeks might go by before T.J. laid eyes on her. Even then, all he might get by way of a greeting was a silent, preoccupied nod. But for Mildred, who still considered herself Viney's best friend, he could have easily forgotten her.

In her raggedy apron and beaten-down Keds, Viney shuffled halfway down the foyer towards the main entry then turned back around to face the lobby door. T.J. fought the urge to shoo her off, caught between curiosity and horror at her inscrutable actions. As if parking herself in the middle of the foyer wasn't bad enough, she started rummaging in her apron. A cigarette pinched between her fingers, she lit up.

Her neck swiveled slowly, and her eyes narrowed, as if alerted to some far away sound. Without the two-way between them, she would have heard him breathing so hard that he wheezed.

Mildred had said more than once lately that her long-time friend's mind was "holey." And while she didn't look especially spooky, Viney standing there for no good reason spooked the hell out of him.

The lobby door creaked open again; Viney's lips plunged into a frown. She blew out the match, licked the tip, dropped it in her apron pocket, then took a long drag on her Old Gold as T.J.'s thoughts leaped to the race results. He'd bet a small fortune on the third race, but that would have to wait. Viney took another drag while his heart pounded deep inside the Grand New Uniform.

Long ago, he would have done anything to protect a young and no-sense Viney. More than once during the Stables' heyday as a speakeasy and racing stables, he had run interference between her and male patrons with an eye for female flesh, equine and otherwise. He often sensed trouble before it ever showed its face. The night of the horse barn fire, he knew without anyone saying so she was in that barn; like him, she would never abandon her passion for the horses.

But over the years, the larger her body became, the more she seemed to disappear. When he did see her, her hands were always busy, rubbing, dusting, wiping, shining. Like she didn't know how *not* to touch. The Stables continued to shine under her care, but she, well, she was rubbing herself out of existence, a shadow haunting the edges of daylight. He hardly knew her any more, could barely remember the last forty years they shared at work. Mostly he remembered the past, before the fire that had changed their lives for good.

But what was she doing here, now, exposing herself to whoever happened by? And not only exposing, but blocking the way?

His legs tingled with the urge to rush out, save Viney from the stares and scorn any patron was bound to show her. The old impulse, he noted, still lived. So did the impulse to take care of the patrons. But just like earlier, his feet stayed put. The stable boys had converted him into one of their own. All he could do was grin and bare the ugliness about to come.

His teeth sawed his lower lip as the door creaked closed. Besides, he told himself, it was too late to try and move her without giving his secret away. He might no longer know how to protect the innocent; he may have lost the dignity of his daily work; but at least he still had knowledge of things no one else knew, that kept him close to his passion for playing the ponies.

Two gray heads and one white began their slow passage down the foyer. T.J. swallowed hard. What were the odds that the same three who came late would be the first to leave? The three inched forward, slow as a distant memory. Dandelion Head's raspy coughs rattled her thin, black chest.

Viney took another drag, ash dangling half an inch long. Smoke curled up from her lips to her nose then blew straight into the ancient woman's path.

Even he was aghast. Her whole life, as far as he knew, Viney had never harmed a living thing. Never deliberately defied a soul. And of all the people to suddenly stand up to—could she have picked anyone more helpless or pathetic than this pale, doddering elder so far from her native soil?

His eyes quickly scanned the scene. The hidden panel nearest the main entry was still ajar, exposing the two-way's passage. He could hear the radio muttering face down on the floor where it had fallen. If he tried to close the panel, the rusty hinges would squeal. Still, he wagered the trio would ignore those signs in favor of Viney, who, broader than a linebacker, was now blocking their path. Her stained calico dress and smashed down heels would add to her frightful attraction. They'd have to pass her single file, if they passed at all. The way Viney just stood there, elbows out, blowing smoke, he had his doubts.

As the trio approached, Dandelion Head's earlier tears echoed in his chest. The only other time T.J. had seen anyone with skin as white as hers was an albino man years ago, on the Cicero Avenue bus headed to Hawthorne Race Track. Even though the man had gotten on at 45th, worn a fro, and had the features of a brother, he drew sharp looks from some of the passengers. "Vanilla fudge," said a teen boy, just loud enough for the man to hear.

"Sharp tongue, dull wit," shot back an elderly woman, gray braids crisscrossed over her delicate head.

Then one of Angel Fair's lessons, murmured throughout her life, came sing-songing into his head: *Fire and water, fire and water, keep them apart or one kill the other.* Dandelion Head's mouth gapped open and closed like a hungry fish. Her escorts' gray heads arched protectively over hers. The idea that this frail old thing could kill anything made no sense. And yet his muscles tensed, ready to lunge. He hadn't expected Viney could do any harm, either.

Sweat rained inside the Grand Uniform. Viney stood solid, smoke swirling around her, as if conjuring herself into a ghost. A haint, Angel Fair used to say. His hands shook, and the fringe on his shoulders shivered. He knew he ought to do something to keep the two from colliding. But he couldn't bring himself to move. His secret kept him locked in place as the radio announced the third race to the floor.

*

Angel Fair no longer holds his hand to cross the intersection crowded with Saturday morning shoppers. Instead she steers him with her voice across 47th Street. It used to be she took him along to keep an eye on him. Now she wants him to show her the best shops and advise her on whom she can trust for a fair price.

It began with gummi bears, Mary Janes, licorice whips, and Wrigley's Spearmint gum, the latter for his daddy's bad digestion. But soon he is running for the game itself, learning from the men who crowd Shephard's counter what books to play, what numbers will catch, and how many legs to bet. Shephard allows T.J a dime play per week for all his running between stations, every day of the week except Sunday. Angel Fair draws the line at Sundays.

"All I ask is one day unhitched from the dollar sign," she says, crossing her heart. "Just one day without worrying about getting ahead or behind."

"Nothing stands still," his daddy replies. The worry never leaves his face, even on Sundays over Angel Fair's fried corn, meatloaf, collards, and biscuits. "Faith is about the future."

The policy players know all about the future. The next play, the next dream book, the next two-legged bet will make them all rich, so that they will own the wheels, pay off the cops, and be the Big Men on the South Side. Their dreams are fueled by the Defender *and the* Chicago Bee, *with stories of Negro millionaires and businessmen who have beat the odds and sit at the same tables with white men from the North. It's a fever that T.J. catches and from which he never quite recovers.*

On one of those Saturday mornings, now that he no longer holds her hand, he leads the way for Angel Fair across 47ᵗʰ Street. Either she doesn't see him, suddenly lost in the crowds of shoppers, or she doesn't yell loud enough over the motors and horns, hoof beats and bells clogging the busy street to warn him away from the reared-up hooves of a huge white horse.

His feet freeze to the road, though it is spring and the air has lost its chill. He has no time to think of anything but those monstrous hooves, mere inches from his head. But thinking doesn't loosen his feet, make room in the tight crowd for him to run away. Yet somehow those iron-shod hooves do not come crashing down on his head. Instead they dance away, backwards, into the crowd behind. Only after those hooves finally return to the ground does he see the policeman's face, pink and blotchy like raw sausage meat, his eyes narrowed and aimed at his own.

"Watch your step, boy," says the officer. But the crowd closes tight around him. The horse begins again its high-strung dance, this time with no room to move. Then a hand on T.J.'s shoulder whirls him around to face what has gripped him.

He stares into Angel Fair's still-as-stone face. Her eyes are fastened not on her son but on the horse, who now licks its lips and bows its head. Her shoulders are square and her spine straight and solid as a tree trunk. The crowd transmits her mood, as if roots are running from her feet beneath the road's dust, carrying a current of fire. They close in around the horse, muttering and shaking their heads. A one-legged man lifts a crutch and aims it at the uniform above him. The officer tightens the reins, draws the horse's head around to its rump, then squeezes through the slight opening the crowd reluctantly allows.

"Mama."

She does not move until the horse with its careless rider is well on its way. But the sway in the ruffles around her high, white collar reassures him that she is listening.

Finally, she releases her grip on his shoulder. "You know that man?" She nods towards where the crowd has closed over the path cut by his horse.

"No'm. Well, maybe. I see lots of police coming 'round the wheels."

"He got it bad for you, child. You watch out for him, you hear?"

"What I supposed to do?" Now not only his feet are moving, his whole body shakes as if overcome by chills. "Mama, what do I do?"

"You got eyes and ears. Don't let anything the Man does escape your notice."

"But what if he don't want me to see?"

She turns her full gaze on him like a spotlight. "What kind of son am I raising who won't use what good the Lord has given? Doesn't matter if the Man wants you or doesn't want you to see. Maybe he thinks you don't, but you do. You make sure you do. And don't you forget. The reckoning time will come by and by."

His eyes wander briefly to State Street Fresh Meats and Poultry *lettered in red, vaguely hoping he might catch one more glimpse of the colossal white horse. But quickly his gaze returns to Angel Fair and the coal black light of her eyes. Later memories do nothing to displace this vision of her, luminous and indestructible, even as the street trash can fires they pass on the way home devour the discards of the day.*

*

Later on, he would still be wondering if he could believe what he saw or if, like a racehorse, he was simply spooked by what he didn't. Was it *the heat, it's the heat, it's the goddamn--?* Maybe the two-way had confused him? Like Angel Fair, Mildred, too, believed in ghosts. He had always thought that was because she'd come from the South. He, on the other hand, believed in numbers and equations. But even he had to admit that *something* was going down, right before his eyes. Something was in the air, the way it sometimes was before a big race, when a horse with good breeding and numbers and a solid disposition all of a sudden got spooky at the starting gate. Someone up in the stands might have whistled a sour note, or a leaf could have blown across the track. You could never tell what a horse was sensing; you never knew what might bring on a panic. He didn't believe in ghosts, but he did believe that horses paid attention to things that humans didn't.

What he remembered was Viney's neck as it pulled forward in a finish-line stretch. Two gray heads and one white paused as she flicked long ash into her palm. She closed her fist, then opened it again and held it out. The ashes formed muddy rivers in the creases of her palms. Viney's green eyes stared into Dandelion Head's blue ones as she lifted the ash higher, as if offering something both terrible and true.

Dandelion Head coughed while smoke from the Old Gold coiled around her. Blindly, she tapped her cane until the tip neared the toes of Viney's Keds. As she coughed again, she fell against the younger woman, who cushioned the elder's fall against the two-way where T.J. stood, only a thin pane of glass between them.

Blood vessels webbed her translucent scalp. Her hair was little more than scattered clumps of lint. With each cough, he held his breath, certain that her bones would crack or that she would split in two. His hand raised itself to the glass, formed a fist, ready to knock a warning to Viney to ease up. But that would only scare the old white woman even more.

The younger woman struggled to right herself and her elder, but another, even stronger, cough propelled them towards the entry. There, the old woman clutched the brass door handles and doubled over, wheezing. The man hurried over to assist.

T.J. saw his opening. He eased himself through the hidden panel and shut it. The hinges squealed, as they always did, but did not give him away. He glanced at Viney, who stood facing the entry, smoke curling up her nose. She held herself so still that he wondered if she was really there, or if he was simply dreaming her. He could smell the smoke, see it in the air, even imagine her chapped lips on his cheek, as if she were Angel Fair come to bless or blame him. But Angel Fair had been small-boned and dark, with fine features. She was always immaculately dressed; a woman of spirit, she wore white well into old age. Yet she had an earthy side as well. She butchered her own chickens, even in Chicago, claiming they tasted better if they didn't know they were going to die. Viney, on the other hand, was large, raw, and shiny as a copper penny, dulled only with age. No two women could be so different. Yet for some reason, when he looked at Viney now, he saw his mother's straight-on, unflinching gaze. It was a gaze that penetrated well beyond the two-way.

T.J. caught sight of himself in the mirror, his skin ashen and his knuckles fat with arthritis. Wrinkles on his forehead held up the cap on his head. But he was still a little kid in love and terror before Angel Fair's powerful gaze.

The ancient one crumpled up like a too-loved doll in the arms of the younger woman and moaned as if in a dream. The younger stroked her hair, murmuring in a comforting tone.

T.J. hurried to them. "She doing ok?" he asked, genuinely worried. Images of more sirens and flashing lights, this time of an ambulance, filled his head.

The younger woman smiled wistfully, shook her head. "She thinks she's seen a ghost," she sighed. She turned her gaze to T.J. "She sees a lot of things the rest of us don't." She sighed again. "Dementia," she whispered.

He offered to bring a glass of water. The younger woman translated while the elder spoke. "Her mother died when she was very young. To this day, she cannot recall her face. No photos were ever taken of her, as they lived in a remote village in the north. All she knew was that her mother had green eyes. Everyone who knew her spoke of them with admiration. They were green as moss deep inside the forest.

"She saw those eyes as she passed the long mirror just now. At first she couldn't believe it. All these years, she longed for even the slightest memory of her mother. And now, it finally came to her, as she herself is approaching her end." The woman paused. Her voice caught as she continued, "Now she can die in peace."

"Glad for her." T.J.'s voice was hoarse. The older woman nodded, her eyes clear and content.

"She's had a lot of excitement for one day," said the younger woman. The old one clutched the younger's black sleeves with fingers as bony as bird feet. T.J. picked up her cane and gently closed her fingers around it. The cane trembled then resumed its slow progress forward.

"Grateful to you, sir," the man said as T.J. closed the door behind them. Lenny hustled to bring their car around.

When T.J. turned around, Viney was gone. He checked behind the two-way to see if she might be waiting there. The radio was off, upright on the stool. Next to the radio was an open Stables matchbook. The air smelled like metal polish and smoke.

He'd bet a fortune on the long shot, across the board and to place, but as insurance had also bet on the chalk horse, the track favorite, to win and show. After what he had stood to lose from the long shot, he didn't mind breaking even; sometimes, on a bad losing streak, he even welcomed it. He surely welcomed it now. Over the long haul, breaking even was often the best a body could expect. The odds were never in a player's favor. It was losing that kept so many in over their heads until they lost everything. The reckless ones wanted it all, or nothing. But Angel Fair had taught him patience. He might never win, and he was too good a handicapper to lose it all, but sometimes just staying in the game mattered more than winning.

T.J. picked up the matchbook and was about to put it in his pants pocket when he noticed marks on the inside cover. He fumbled in the Grand New Uniform pocket for her glasses, holding the match book in front of his race. For a moment, he thought he saw a racing form in miniature. He blinked and it disappeared. His glasses, he realized, must be at home. He held the match book even closer. Again, a form. This time, though, the race results were clear. The chalk horse had won. Automatically, T.J. calculated his take. Blinking again, the match book returned to its inscrutable marks.

Later, he would check the results against what his age-addled eyes had tried to tell him. It wasn't just wishful thinking; the chalk horse had won. He hadn't lost his shirt. But for now, he pulled the light string and stood for a moment in the dark, staring through the two-way at the empty foyer. Even from inside the Grand New Uniform, a chill penetrated the heavy cloth, its raw breath reaching the emptiness within. And now that that tape playing in his head had finally stopped, the silence was truly startling. For a moment, he thought maybe he had died. And then he wondered who on earth would think to look for him here, in a place he was the only one on earth to know about?

He picked up the radio and put it into a Grand New Pocket so deep it reached the top of his leg. His sensible Florsheim oxfords scraped against the cement floor in their predictable shuffle. Everything seemed at once so heavy and yet so eerily light. As he pushed the two-way panel closed one last time, he heard a ghost's voice repeat, over the hinge's protests, "Grateful," as if saying so might make it true.

Unlike that old woman, every time he looked in the mirror, the only eyes he saw were his own.

Chapter Three: Pasture

As I slogged down the gravel drive, I covered my ears and lowered my eyes. Fire trucks had lined up at the front entrance, sirens shrieking, lights catapulting off the Stables' painted brick. Few cars stood in the parking lot, a good sign—I'd have time for coffee before lunch rush began.

Growing up in Bedford Heights a mere block away, I had learned to expect fire trucks at the Stables. Not a month would go by without the familiar sirens and lights jolting everyone in the neighborhood to momentary alarm. But like the local air raid siren at the clinic next door, whose readiness for nuclear attack was periodically tested, most people stopped listening after the first jarring seconds. Though some solemnly predicted the Stables' inevitable demise, as certain as the Second Coming, many regarded the restaurant's longevity as a reliable forecast of its survival, as if the place would never burn down.

Still, the sirens were painful to hear, especially after more gin and tonics than I could remember the night before. Fortunately, the sirens finally stopped as I approached the entrance. But the lights kept twirling and swirling off the trunks of old cottonwoods lining the drive, prodding my stomach to twirl and swirl in kind. So I closed my eyes, trusting that I knew the way well enough to stay on course and, with my hangover-heightened senses, would hear any traffic in time to move.

The phone had rung this morning while I was still asleep. My parents had been in bed when I got home, so they had not seen me slip in. That might explain why my mother had woke me to take the call from Joan, the head waitress, the same Joan who, only hours before, had been shit-faced and weeping in her beer.

"Morning dearie," Joan chirped. "Mind coming in a little early today? We got a funeral lunch booked last minute."

This voice did not match with last night's Joan of the slinky champagne dress and see-through shoes, working the Star Dust's dance floor like a pro. This voice was full of sunlight, bouncing and breezy, not hazy with Seagram's and cigarette smoke. Two weeks ago, when I came in for my first week's schedule, she had been brief and to the point, as business-like as someone wearing inch-long eyelashes and who-knew-how-many gold chains around her neck could be. But last night had changed all that.

After grunting my assent, I hung up to face my mother's worried stare. "What?" I grumbled.

"What time did you get in?"

I shrugged while mentally calculating. I remembered midnight at the Star Dust, dancing with everyone and no one. Joan's breakdown. Sharon's arm under mine as we stumbled out the door, Mary Beth yawning behind us. Half an hour back down 75th Street, with the smell of leftover Brown's chicken in the front seat making me want to puke.

"Pretty late," I said finally.

Her eyebrows pressed together but she said nothing. Instead she disappeared to the laundry and returned with my uniform.

"I washed it for you yesterday."

"Thanks."

"What kind of baby shower goes on that late?" Whether this was a real question or simply my mother's way of airing her suspicions, I simply offered yet another shrug.

"Some people couldn't get off work until late," I replied, hoping she forgot that the Stables was closed on Mondays.

My mother smoothed the uniform's permanently pressed polyester before handing it over. "Be careful," she said by way of a blanket warning.

I wanted to call Joan back and cancel. But I couldn't. I had to go to work, or my mother would know just how crappy I felt.

In less than 30 minutes, I was out the door, walking up the street I had known my whole life, rubbing my eyes and squinting into the glaring sun, still wishing I had called in sick. Yet at the same time, a nervous anticipation crept in. Relations had changed—not just with Joan but with everyone at the Stables.

Stumbling on the edge of the ditch, I opened my eyes to regain my balance. To ease the ache in my gut, I glanced to my right, away from the churning lights and already intense June sun towards flush green pastures neatly fenced in white. In 19 years, I'd never seen a single horse there. Not that I expected to. I no more associated the Stables with horses than I did White Castle with royalty. In South Bedford Sanitary District, close to Chicago's sewage canals, amidst brick bungalows and frame houses huddled like refugees outside the city limits, horses were rare.

The pasture stretched down Illinois Road so far I couldn't see the end of it. The grass there was always mowed, although never as short as the lawns and park strips that lay like emerald napkins under the chins of neighborhood houses. Unlike the vacant lot kitty corner from my family's home, I rarely ventured into the pasture, which occupied a loftier world. Like a great green eye, the pasture stared dispassionately through the white fence that announced it as more than a vacant lot. It was tended to, watched over, *owned*. That in itself made it less interesting.

In contrast, the vacant lot, called "prairie" by the neighbors, was a dumping ground for lawn clippings, dog feces, empty cans of Old Style and

Miller High Life, and a seemingly endless supply of pop bottles to be cashed in for nickel deposits. I could sneak over and thrash through tall forests of milkweed, toe the ashes of fires started by neighborhood toughs, and watch finches dive for seeds on drooping sunflowers. Broken glass beckoned like jewels; I had to mind each step or risk slashing the soles of my Keds. The threat of tetanus, stitches, and rat attacks from within fortresses of rotting grass only amplified the allure of this place.

Yet the pasture still occupied much of my internal landscape, not as a place to explore and test out but as an obscure presence without character, like older adults without children who radiated a watchful dis-ease, wary of childish journeys across yards, over fences, into alleys, and through gangways. I sensed the pasture was interested in me, hovering around the edges of my attention, but I did not return its interest. While its white planked fence beckoned easy access to those of us used to scaling four foot chain link fences, and its lush turf whispered the allure of open spaces, such invitations raised apprehension, the way the laps of elders, unsoiled and intimidating, offered a place to merely sit and behave, with parents closely watching.

So I grew up in sight of this pasture, sensing its longing yet unmoved to respond, although I was crazy for horses. *National Velvet* had struck a chord in girls like me, endorsing our desires for soul mates. I had read *Black Beauty* and all the Misty books, convinced that horses were noble creatures that suffered at the hands of adults, and only a child's tender touch could redeem them. But for years, my contact with horses was limited to sad, bored Shetland ponies at Brookfield Zoo's Children's Park. That lasted as long as my legs didn't scrape the riding ring's dirt. Sometimes in the parking lot at Scottsgrove shopping center, ponies appeared, chained to each other like inmates, forced to pace hot asphalt in circles while white-faced clowns hawked rides and raffle tickets. I'd break away from my parents and rush up to the ponies, dying to engage my beloveds in a profound *tete-a-tete*. Yet their eyes remained glazed, my lilting voice more shrill than kind to their limp ears. Their heavy heads dared me to cheer them up. The bits in their mouths blocked their feeble attempts to chew, saliva frothing from their lips like that of senile old aunties.

Still, I was desperate to befriend a horse, any horse, and learn its secret language. Their mangy coats and drooling mouths did not dissuade me; their flaws only spurred my indignation at their adult keepers. I longed to ride with my best friend, Sheila Kelly, hooves pounding like a tribal drum beat, our respective manes flung back by the wind. Sheila took lessons every week at a riding stable near the forest preserves and wore boots with tall, squared-off heels and pointy toes. I had pictured myself in flat-soled white go-go boots until Sheila patiently explained how the heels kept your foot in the stirrup and the pointy toes were to kick the horse to make it go. I vowed to forego the pointy toes and search for go-go boots with taller heels.

But when I approached my mother about learning to ride, the look she gave me was as flat and uninterested as the Shetland ponies treading circles in the dirt. She reminded me of what had happened when I was three years old when, at my father's company picnic, a horse had stepped on my Buster Brown sandal. She had fussed a great deal, removing my white ankle sock and fishing oblong ice cubes out of the cooler to wrap in a washcloth and press against my toes. I had been surprised more than hurt; not even a bruise surfaced, but my respect for those huge creatures had swelled overnight.

Over time, I stopped asking for what others treated as dangerous folly and instead grew careful in what I revealed. Like the horses I longed for, I coded my desires in the twitch of an eye, a shoulder's roll, the muscular rhythm of legs and hooves flying across the ground.

Eventually these desires grew into feverish dreams that followed me in my sleep, sometimes inscrutably distant, other times so near and quivering that their joy was almost unbearable as they followed me through the caverns of adolescence. Yet at other times, I pursued them, swearing allegiance to wherever they might take me, so long as it was beyond Bedford Heights and those sewage canals carrying others' discarded and broken dreams.

As I stared into the pasture's green eye, I caught glimpses of these dreams, prowling restlessly between blades of Kentucky bluegrass. Captured by their strange, dark shapes, I felt destined to go wherever they would take me.

A plume of smoke curled out from the Stables' west side. Lenny was leaning against the wall, decked out in his doorman's uniform. His legs stretched out so far it was as if he was holding the place up, and his cap slouched down over his eyes. He stared at me; I looked away, fast. Until last night, he had been just another uniform, one face among the dozens I saw each day as I served martinis and mashed potatoes and prime rib au jus. Now it felt dangerous to look too long, as if he could tell, in one brief glimpse, everything about me, even more than I knew myself. Or maybe I just didn't want to see what might be in his eyes.

"Morning." T.J. nodded, his reliable smile spread across his lips. He held the door as if I were a customer, not a waitress. Nothing had changed. I was still Earl's girl from across the street, come home from college for the summer.

"Morning," I replied.

I couldn't help lingering on T.J.'s face. Was it just me who wanted to crawl into a dark room and not wake up until sunset?

Normally that would be the extent of our conversation, until the end of my shift. Then he would say, "You take care," and I'd reply, "You too," and be on my way down the drive. But he must have sensed the slight shift in my stride, my curiosity trying hard not to reveal itself.

"You have yourself a real fine day," he said, and winked. Later I wondered if he would have been so hospitable had he seen Lenny round the corner like a train gathering speed. As the door closed behind me, I heard him stomp his cigarette into the ground and mutter a curse or two.

*

Storefronts on this block have no lights in their windows. Heavy black security gates seal off most doors from view. Only a Pabst Blue Ribbon sign in neon blue flares out from the undistinguished darkness.

"Where is everybody?" asks Mary Beth. The three of us, Mary Beth, Sharon, and I, stand at the back of the brand new Oldsmobile wagon that Sharon has borrowed from her father. Although the curbs are lined with parked cars, it seems no one else is on the street, and certainly no one to greet us, strangers to this place.

"You sure this is the place?" I ask.

"It better be," Sharon replies. "I'm not parallel parking this boat again."

The Olds dimly reflects light from the nearby corner. Only the streetlights interrupt the night. As I take in more of our surroundings, I begin to notice shadows moving between the lights. Some collect in small groups beneath their unblinking gaze.

Sharon unlatches the rear door and eases it down flat. She crawls inside and starts shoving the huge, gift-wrapped box towards Mary Beth and me.

"Ugh, this thing weighs a ton," she grunts. We each grab a corner and pull until the box is standing upright on the sidewalk between us. Pink babies float in a yellow sky before my eyes, clutching blue and pink umbrellas. I am tempted to comment on Sharon's choice of paper, but now is not the time. Somehow we have to haul this baby crib (assembly required) all the way to the other end of the block. I tell myself at least the silly wrapping, not to mention the excess weight, might discourage anyone from stealing it.

When the traffic stops at the light down the street and silence steals over the block like an exhalation, a long, low whistle winds its way towards us. At first, I am too preoccupied with balancing the bulky package to care, but after the second whistle, followed by a litany of "Hey Babies" and "Hot mamas" and other Mms and Yeahs, we three, in unison, pause for a look.

Three shadowy male figures, one skinny tall, one slight and short, and one wide plus bulky, stand together at the streetlight's edge.

"Keep going, keep going," Mary Beth whispers tensely. *In her pink overalls and yellow t-shirt underneath, she is the most covered up of the three of us. Sharon's halter top slides suggestively above her butt-hugging jeans. But I feel most exposed in a thin cotton sundress with nothing but hip-hugger panties on underneath. Every slight shift in the air raises goose bumps on my arms and tightens my barely covered nipples.*

"Oh God, I hope they're not on drugs!" Mary Beth swings her head hard, shifting her brown pony tail back over her shoulder.

"Some mighty fine ass over there. I like to get me a piece of that," a voice croons.

"Squeeze between them sweet cheeks, oh baby. Squeeze me, baby, squeeze me til I ain't got no more to squeeze," says another.

A third voice follows, but it is low and muttering, vaguely complimentary and threatening at the same time.

"The only drug these guys are on is testosterone," cracks Sharon. I laugh, glad to release some of the tension that's been building ever since we crossed Western Avenue. Growing up, my parents used to take my brother and me, in the days before shopping malls, to Western, where we'd shop at Wiebolts and Goldblatts and Florsheim Shoes, and the Sears with hot marshmallow caramels at the candy counter. My mother had grown up even farther east, past Ashland Ave, only a handful of miles from Bedford Heights, yet I never laid eyes on the place she once called home. Whatever lay east of Western was clouded with murky cautions by family and neighbors about "those neighborhoods."

Now that we have crossed that border, those vague threats have taken on a shape and a sound that snares me in what First-Year Psych calls "fight or flight." Only in my case it is more flight than fight. But Sharon is all fight, and since she is the driver, I have no choice but to go along.

Under her breath, she mutters to Mary Beth and me, "If anything happens to that car, my dad will kill me."

"Forget the damn car!" Mary Beth hisses. "Those guys are following us."

Mary Beth is right. As we stop in front of the blue Pabst sign and peer into the dark glass for signs of life, the shadows across the street have left the net cast by the corner light and are on the move. As we ease our load onto the weed-clogged sidewalk, the voices start up again, only closer this time.

"Party time, oh baby let's party. Look where them fine asses going." "Look like an invitation being issued: We going downtown." "Get down, downtown, we gonna boogie down."

"Gross," says Mary Beth. I hold the outer door open while Sharon and Mary Beth lift then drop the package inside a darkened vestibule. Still

*no signs of life, but Sharon acts so certain this is the place that we aren't
about to turn around now. I just hope we don't have to load the present
back into the car.*

*Before I let the outer door go, I search the shadows one last time.
Hopefully they will leave us now that we're inside. But I look at them just
the same, in case they keep following. Without knowing for certain where
we're headed, I can't plan our escape, but at least I can keep an eye on our
pursuers.*

Sharon manages to wedge the package inside in just such a way
that it leaves enough room for the inner door to clear it. As I face the glare
of fluorescent lights and the blare of "Brick House" from the sound system, I
hear from the now-silent street a familiar name call out.

"Care-o-lion."

But before I can figure out how the shadows know my name, Mary
Beth shoves the outside door shut, and Sharon, excited, is urging us on into
the Star Dust's booming light.

I recognize T.J. despite the plaid sports coat and floppy fishing cap.
His smile is as broad as always, only here, with a drink in front of him and a
bar full of cronies, his whole body hangs looser, easier, on his aged yet solid
frame. Perched on a bar stool at the corner seat, he can easily survey the
whole room while minding the comings and goings at the entrance.

"Well, now," he says. His sandpaper voice strokes my ears. "You
young ladies can take that package on back then get yourselves something to
drink." He points to the rear of the bar, which is clogged with people
milling around a mountain of brightly colored packages, then to a banner
drooping over a mirror behind the bar: Ladies Night Ladies Half-Price. He
slaps the bar softly, chuckling. "Quite a crowd tonight, quite a crowd."

I follow his eyes as they scan the long, narrow room. The bar runs
the length of the room on the left, with long tubes of light parallel overhead.
A woman with a tiger lily blooming from her tidy afro is busy pouring
drinks. A mirror reflects scattered faces of those seated at the bar. Most are
of older men, like T.J., who presumably have staked out these particular
seats for years. A group of women hold down the far end of the bar, one of
whom I recognize as the guest of honor, Opal, huge and glowing pregnant,
one hip perched on a stool.

A dance floor, complete with a mirrored disco ball dangling from
the ceiling panels and tiny white Christmas lights strung along the walls,
struggles against shadows that swallow most of the right side of the room.
Only a pinball machine in the far corner offers any help. Even in that
dimness, I can see the dance floor is packed.

Sharon, Mary Beth, and I murmur our thanks and heave up our
load one last time to the back. Faces turn and stare as we pass, none that I

recognize until we reach Opal, who is deep into laughter with two other women from the Stables. The three of us wave briefly then head back to find a seat at the bar.

Before we can settle on our stools, Tiger Lily has slid cocktail napkins in front of us and waits, with raised eyebrows, for our orders. Once we order, she moves with grace and style, no gesture wasted. Unlike many bartenders, she does not flirt, and the men do not try, though she is striking: Caramel skin, full, round hips in white dress slacks, and of course what I take as her trademark tiger lily tucked against her sleek skull.

"Thanks," I say. She nods, regal. She knows who she is. I look around to see if anyone else is working the bar or the door. With a crowd like this, anything can happen. But only Tiger Lily, and by default, T.J., appear to be minding the store.

I elbow Sharon, nodding at the banner. "Ladies half price. What a bargain we must be."

She stares at me for a moment and then bursts out laughing. She shimmies her shoulders, her halter hugging her unbound breasts, and raises her arms up like Zorba the Greek. "Whoo-hoo. Party time!"

Mary Beth, sitting on Sharon's opposite side closer to the back, merely hunches over her whiskey sour, unmoving except to lift her glass and lick pale brown foam from the rim. Abruptly, the music stops, and in the pause between songs, I hear the crowd's buzzing voice and the bells and beeps from the pinball machine, and settle in for a night of people watching. After a moment, the music begins again, easing into a slow dance that clears the floor of all but a few couples clinging to each other like life rafts.

Just as I start to get a handle on some of the dancers, voices raise near the front door.

"What you boys want here?" T.J. is saying.

"We don't need your permission," retorts one of the three guys standing before him.

"Think again." Pausing, T.J. turns full around on his stool to face the trio behind him. Then he continues. "I don't know them." He points to the two on each end of their line.

"My man, they cool." That voice again. I lean back away from the bar for a better look. "I tell them, you come to the Dust, my man T.J., he take care of you," says the middle guy in his best too-cool-to-be-uptight voice. I know I've heard that voice before.

As the music swells, their words are lost, so I concentrate on getting a better look. The one closest to me is small and wiry, edging around his friends like a nervous little dog. An oversized slouch cap covers most of his head and darkens his eyes underneath. The middle one is tallest, his arms hanging loose but the rest of him tensed, like a spring only partially uncoiled.   Farthest away and nearest the door is a dude with Schwarzenegger biceps and a shaved scalp like Kojak. Of the three, he has the most presence, his body dense like a tank, arms angled from his shoulders due to the huge muscles in his arms and chest. His neck nearly disappears into his shoulders. He reminds me of Mr. Clean, but with an edge, dressed in a tight black t-shirt and blue jeans that look painted on.

"Don't make me sorry," I hear T.J. saying as he swivels back around to take a long, careful gulp of his draft. Just when I'm sure I'm going to hear my name again, I curl into myself, staring at my gin and tonic, as if it could make me disappear. Instead, I watch Tiger Lily pour three shots of Jack Daniels and hand them over the bar. The middle one, the one whose face is closest to the lights, hands over a twenty. I inadvertently catch his eye, and he grins, his front teeth crowded and overlapping, turned inward in ways I wouldn't expect from such a big talker. But it's those inward-facing teeth that give him away.

"Guess who?" I nudge Sharon and Mary Beth.

"Shit," says Sharon. "Was he rude out there or what?"

Mary Beth can only gawk. She sucks one ice cube then another, spitting each clean one back into the glass with a clink. Tiger Lily raises her eyebrows with each clink, and Mary Beth shakes her head no in response.

"Dr. Jekyll and Mr. Hyde," I say, thinking of Lenny's squeaky-clean image at the Stables. In the two weeks since I started working there, he has barely said two words to any of us, even Sharon, who is gregarious to a fault (and earns the tips to prove it). The few times Lenny has been inside, everyone treats him with kid gloves. Mildred downright dotes on him, saving him choice bits from steaks and prime rib, even giving him precious cocktail shrimp forbidden the rest of us. The kid could do no wrong. Now I know otherwise.

The disco bass pounds like a mechanical heart yet still pulls me magnetically into its beat. But it's too soon, despite the tube lights overhead that are unkind to us who stay within their reach. Every freckle on my bare arm, the slight scar over Sharon's left eye, even Mary Beth's thin lips cannot escape the notice of their merciless gaze. The shadowy side of the room, where the dancers whip around, precise and intent on each shift of balance, beckons. Still, I cling to my bar stool, an island in a sea of unnamable dangers, even as I long to embrace the more forgiving dark.

*

"Hi there," Joan greeted me. "We got a big crowd coming." She handed over a stack of fresh-from-the dryer napkins and pointed to the seat across from her.

Usually, if I shared a shift with the two other "college gals," we sat together, apart from Joan and the veteran waitresses who worked the Garden Room. I'd never actually seen Joan do prep work like this; as head waitress, she was usually off somewhere else, posting schedules, talking to Billiard, flirting with Ernie, the bartender in the Winner's Circle Lounge. Right now, it was just Joan and me in the Derby Room. I wondered who else would be coming.

Her face looked the same as it always did, which made me realize how much makeup she used. Like a mask, it covered all the swollen redness from last night's tears. Her hair was perfectly in place; fat curls like Polish sausages piled up on her head in a crown. She made no pretense to follow the "natural" look that was hot at the moment. Her red hair came out of a box, and her blue eyes were framed in long, black eyelashes straight from Walgreens, along with Yardley Blue Shimmer eye shadow and Iced Pink lipstick.

When I was ten years old, I wanted to look just like her. She wore her uniform dress hiked up her short, plump thighs, as if mini skirts were still in style, the way I used to roll my Catholic school skirt way above my knees, against school regulations. But now, I hadn't even bothered to shorten my Stables' uniform even though it hung well past my kneecaps. It seemed like too much trouble for just one summer's work. And anyway, my mother hadn't offered to re-hem it.

I started folding, the warmth from the clean cloths pleasant against the Derby Room's chill. "Quite a party last night," I said, not knowing what else to say. Joan was maybe only six or seven years older than me, but we were worlds apart. Sharon had heard she was married, living in Bedford Heights with her husband and six-year-old son. Yet working seemed to mean more than just a paycheck to her. She was sassy and flirtatious with everyone, from the "suits" who ran up checks in the hundreds of dollars, to Rose, the service bartender for the Garden Room, to the high school boys who bussed our tables. Yet she was also sensible and earthy, showing me the ropes of getting food out to the tables on time. She drove a sporty car, wore pounds of gold jewelry, and never apologized for any of it. Until last night, I assumed her ambitions went no farther.

Joan put down her napkin and looked at me, her eyes wide and, now I could see, webbed in red. Later I would swear I saw tears welling up, but at the moment all I could see were the blue eyes softening and the hard edges of her mask crumbling ever so slightly. And then she laughed, a gorgeous, full-belly laugh that had me laughing as well.

"Hey, you guys," Joan's attention was already at the doorway. I turned around to face Sharon and Mary Beth. "Join the party."

*

The more I watch Joan, the more confused I become, especially now that the house lights are off; only the tiny white Christmas bulbs and spots behind the bar offer any light, besides the "Big Mama" pinball way off in the corner. Even after the music ends, men keep approaching her, stroking her arms, patting her ass, bending her neck like a willow branch for a kiss. Their hands touch hers, over and over, until I am sure something more than caresses is passing between them. But it is dark, and it is late, and I am a stranger here, though she, quite clearly, is not.

I didn't see her when we first came in. Maybe she wasn't here yet, or maybe she was hidden inside that gyrating crowd on the dance floor. She is wearing the same gold chains, thick and thin, short and long and every length in between, that she wears with her Stables' uniform, along with her scarlet Southern belle curls and I Love Lucy eyelashes. But these familiar details take on a different air here, where such excesses seem less a Bedford Heights' housewife's fantasy, or even a wife's plea for attention from a withholding spouse, and more like icons of feminine power, from the clingy champagne-colored dress like Marilyn Monroe's "Happy Birthday, Mr. President" costume to the clear plastic heels reminiscent of Cinderella's glass slippers. Unlike those fragile predecessors, hers look strong enough to hold up to any man's misstep.

"What's she doing?" Mary Beth hisses. "Letting those men paw her like that?"

Mary Beth has an irritating ability to ask the right question at exactly the wrong time. Tempted to comment on her quaint choice of words, I instead turn my attention to the other dancers. Several are Garden Room waitresses. Like Joan, they live in or near Bedford Heights. Some are older; some divorced. They are all dancing with men who, like them, appear to be Star Dust regulars. One I recognize as a Tack Room waiter at the Stables.

"Weah's yo white women at?" *Sharon mugs, stealing a line from* Blazing Saddles.

Mary Beth slaps her on the back. "Shhh! Don't start anything."

The real question is where are the white men? *Certainly not among the Star Dust regulars. The women, on the other hand, span a broad spectrum of tones, from Mary Beth's porcelain pale to Opal's Devil's Food brown. The lighter faces dominate on the disco floor while the darker ones cluster at the back near foil pans heaped with fried chicken, Italian beef, mostaccoli, potato salad, and slaw. Sharon, Mary Beth, and I occupy the border between the two groups, glued to our seats at the bar, as women circulate between the dance floor and food, and men between the bar and the women.*

A quick inventory of Stables' staff provides at least a partial answer. Besides Billiard, the owner, the only other white men on staff are

Ernie, the main bartender; Hal and Al, the maitre d's; and high school busboys who rarely stay long enough for servers to learn their names. Had Joan invited any of them?

After two gin and tonics, I search for signs of a restroom. Reluctantly, I leave my stool, draping my shawl over it to claim later.

T.J. sees me looking around and waves me over. I cross my arms, though the room is hot. Feeling my nipples under my sundress, I suddenly feel self-conscious. At the U, I never gave my bralessness a second thought. Here, it seems to communicate something much more direct—and not necessarily welcomed—as I feel more than see three pairs of eyes follow me to T.J.'s side. What I do see is Joan being spun in and out of the arms of all those eager men. Just before I look away, I see her slip her fingers between her barely covered breasts, in that gesture of all female movie spies hiding crucial evidence. But this gesture was not directed to her mesmerized male circle. Instead it was quick and clean, more in line with the brisk, business-like Joan I had met my first day at the Stables.

Sharon swears on the ride home later that it is slips of paper tucked between Joan's breasts. "Telephone numbers," she nods knowingly. Maybe that's what the other women are saying, too. But at the moment, all I see are two wide blue eyes fixed on the door, as if waiting for Prince Charming to walk on through.

*

Our trays shouldered, we three college gals traveled down the winding halls, grimly determined to get through this lunch. We had agreed no one should go into the Lincoln Room by herself; the work was too much to face alone, especially with a room full of blonde-headed foreigners. But together, the task became bearable; with each trip, we relished our small bit of progress.

During the many long trips between kitchen and banquet, I perused the paintings scattered on the walls: The little girl in the red Caroline Kennedy coat; the faces of two horses, one red and fiery, the other angelic white, promising both innocence and ecstasy; and inside the Lincoln Room, those commanding equines, displayed by magisterial owners or posed in pastoral settings. Far from the romantic Mistys and Black Beauty orphans of my childhood, in their haughty eyes, I was the object of pity.

Yet the allure of their attentions was so powerful I met them at every chance, in the breathless moments between one plate and another, one heartbeat and another, between footsteps and silence down the dim hall. Eventually it dawned on me that our diners were under the same spell. What I had mistaken for their foreignness were in fact their attempts to appease these haughty looks, as they sang and called out, performed brief skits and little jigs, and told jokes and somber stories. Their equine hosts looked on regally, even righteously, though with a touch of fear, as if their very existence depended upon the passions of their onlookers.

*

"How're you doing, little lady? Can I help you find something?"

Brut aftershave assaults my nostrils as I set my third gin and tonic next to T.J.'s beer. A fresh cocktail napkin appears just in time. Tiger Lily is quick.

"How ya doing?" I reply. Although I think of myself as neither little nor a lady, I can't bring myself to ask for directions to the toilet.

"Them boys bothering you?" He jerks his chin towards Lenny and his friends huddled next to the pinball machine. They seem to make a point not to look my way.

"No, they're ok." I sip my drink as Joan does the bump with one very animated dude.

"I don't want no trouble here," he says in a low voice, the emphasis on "I."

"No trouble." I uncross my arms and let the sundress relax over my chest. As Earl's girl, daughter to the man who smokes cigars and shoots the breeze with T.J. in the evenings, I am being watched out for. But protection is a double-edged sword. I think of my father, with his cigars and chit chat--his way of keeping tabs on "strangers" like T.J.

"How's that dog of yours?" T.J. melts back into his easy, Sunday-afternoon-at-the-park tone. My father sometimes brings Daisy, our Weimaraner, on his visits to the Stables. I am certain Daisy scares T.J. but my father laughs off any such idea. Still, my father has this little game. He drives down the Stables' L-shaped drive to avoid the stoplight at Illinois and Central, slowing the car as T.J. approaches, to make him think we are customers. When T.J. sees it's only my father, he always laughs as if he's been fooled. Maybe he has. Then he leans into the window that my father rolls down so they can talk. But when Daisy is in the car, T.J. stands back and waves us on.

"She's fine," I answer.

"That dog like none I ever seen."

"She's a good dog. Wouldn't hurt a flea."

"Good looking dog." T.J. nods.

"My father hunts her."

"I hear she real good."

"You like dogs?" I lean closer to T.J., warming up to this sudden intimacy. This is the longest conversation we've had in my two weeks at the Stables.

T.J.'s eyes turn away, glassy and distant. I worry that I've offended him, until his eyes return, intensely bright, looking at me straight on.

"That's a good dog," he says. "A good one."

My bladder insists I move on. This time I am rewarded by the sight of a doorway at the back of the bar, next to the food table. "Nice talking to you," I say, thinking about how my father would say there are good ones, and not so good ones, and how sometimes you had to make sure the good ones stayed good.

"You a model?" says a low voice behind me. I turn away from the pinball machine and Sharon's excited grunts. A tall man in a leather jacket and tinted aviator glasses wets his lips as if about to say more.

"Model?" I laugh. What a lame come-on, yet part of me wonders if this guy might not surprise me. So much has already surprised me tonight. I turn back to Big Mama, her name splashed in fat, drippy lights arched over the pinball's playing field. Sharon slaps and shakes the machine to keep the metal ball from disappearing down the hole between Big Mama's legs.

"That red hair, them long legs—girl, you don't fool me. You already modeling."

I jump when a stack of quarters on the pinball's glass tumbles over as Sharon pounds it with her fist. The quarters reserve a space for others waiting to play. But with so many people milling around now, it's hard to tell who's player and who's spectator.

"I don't think so." I absorb myself in Sharon's battle with the metal ball. Lights flash, bells ring, buzzers sound as she racks up points for her play.

"Baby, I got a studio around back. I'd love to take some photos of you."

Even in the heavy smoke, I can smell this guy's leather jacket. I try ignoring him, but the leather smell creeps closer. He's taller than me, and I'm pretty tall, and right now he feels a whole lot taller, and bigger, crowding my space. Then I turn to face him, grasping for the right words to refuse him.

His leather jacket makes me sweat just to look at it. I am sweating, even without my shawl and only this thin cotton between me and the air, which has heated up as more people have filtered in. His hat's visor shadows his already smoke-tinted glasses. He's the creepiest guy I've seen all night, yet I choke on what ought to be an easy rejection. His camouflage gives me second, even third thoughts, as to his motives.

I lift up on tip toes and crane my neck, searching for T.J. But with this crowd, he is too far away to hear me call. Not that I would. This guy is taller, younger, and likely bold enough to ignore any warnings from an old man.

"Sharon," I mutter into her ear.

"Hang on." She's in the middle of a play so can't be distracted. I look around for Mary Beth, but she has disappeared, probably keeping the food table company. Last I saw her, she was gobbling mostaccoli like a miracle cure.

Leather Man takes my hand and won't let go. This time my whole body freezes, unsure of how to extricate myself and not cause a scene. Somehow causing a scene seems worse than having to touch this guy's smooth, soft hand.

"Let's go," he murmurs into my ear, as if such talk will convince my captured hand to surrender.

A fast song comes on and people rush onto the dance floor. I break away and join the crowd. Leather Man, however, follows right behind. I start dancing, freestyle, any which way, just to put some distance between me and those smoke-screened eyes. What a sight we must make—me flopping around to the crisp bass rhythms, him standing there in the middle of the floor, waiting for me to finish.

Then from behind, someone grabs my elbow in mid swing.

"Let's dance," says a familiar voice. This time I let myself be moved away to the other side of the dance floor.

In the midst of all those gyrating hips and swinging arms, I am once again speechless, trapped between relief at not having to outright refuse Leather Man, irritation at Lenny's macho take-over, and fear of not being able to keep up with his disco moves.

He takes the lead, me unused to being led, except for slow dancing with aged uncles at wedding receptions. Otherwise, my moves are strictly 60s freestyle. I hope he won't try any of those aggressive John Travolta moves, pushing and pulling and twirling his partner like she's his puppet on a string.

But compared to some of the other males on the dance floor, Lenny is more tentative, waiting for my reaction before making his next move. When the song ends, I see Leather Man waiting next to the pinball machine that Sharon has now turned over to the next player. He stares at me; I squeeze Lenny's hand and whisper into his ear, *"Let's keep dancing."*

He leans backwards as if about to fall over, a sly smile on his lips. His eyes follow mine back to the pinball corner. He keeps smiling.

He doesn't smell like anything but himself, thank goodness—clean, a little sweaty, warm like the air around us. He is taller than I expect, with shoulders that curve in slightly, both protective and shy. As he smiles, I catch sight of beautiful teeth, strong and white, their inward turn reassuring, even endearing. I trust this, even as I glance into his wide eyes. His skin is smooth and unblemished, as if he's passed adolescence without the usual scars, and up close his hair looks much softer, more like carded wool than *the Brillo pad I'd imagined. He wears a pic in the back—some vanity there, wanting to keep his hair just right.*

As luck would have it, the disco takes an R&B turn as Earth, Wind, and Fire sings out "Shining Star," a song I actually like. His hands are comfortable around my waist and in my hand. I am content to linger in the rhythm of his breath, his lean, boyish torso arching back and forth towards mine. His breath on my bare shoulders makes me want to snuggle closer. Yet I can't quite relax. I feel him asking with every shift and turn of our bodies, What next? And I fear once either of us opens our mouths, this magic will vanish.

As the song ends, I spot my shawl still draped over the bar stool near T.J. It beckons to me like a safe harbor, but also like a needy infant crying for the security of a shoulder. Near the entrance, Lenny's two friends high-five each other, then point at Lenny and give him the thumbs up.

"Hey Caroline," Lenny murmurs with a lilt in his voice. He says it, Care-o-ly-in. Do you care or are you lying? A tease, a challenge. Do I care?

A slow song begins. According to the black and white clock over the bar mirror, it is nearly midnight. It is a stark, simple clock, like those on Catholic school walls. Couples pair off. From the corner of my eye I see Joan draped over a man who slides his hands up and down her spine, smoothing her dress like a second skin. When she lifts her head, I see mascara dripping down her cheeks like those sad clown pictures in our neighbors' living room. Then Mary Beth catches my eye, staring at me, mouth open. Maybe she hasn't yet recognized Lenny. Does she even notice him at the Stables, pampered pet of Mildred, T.J's right hand man?

When I return my gaze to Lenny, his eyes have taken on a harder edge. "I'm tired," I say. I scan the room one last time; Leather Man is gone.

Lenny nods slowly, deliberately, not taking his eyes from mine.

Just before the stroke of midnight, I break away, returning to my shawl. T.J. grunts what I take as approval—or maybe simple acknowledgement of my return. I watch as Joan hangs on for dear life as her partner traces her curves over and over, right there under the sparkling white lights, as the clock's black hands join together over the 12.

*

Thoroughbreds looked down their patrician noses at us from behind gilt frames as we hustled trays of roast beef into the Lincoln Room. Not content to fasten condescending looks on our feeble bodies, they pursued us with thunderous hoof beats up and down the Stables' halls. At least that's how it felt to me, hauling heavy trays on unsteady shoulders, with two servers even less experienced than me. Lack of sleep, thirst, heat—any number of factors could easily explain my obsession to escape into a dark corner and curl up to sleep, as I'd once seen Delores, another Garden Room waitress, do. Caught between one world and another, between the wee hours at the Star Dust, and the bizarre spectacle of a hundred blonde, gray, and white heads chanting in a language I'd never heard before, I struggled not to lose myself in the strangeness of it all.

After turning over this job to us college gals, Joan had disappeared to work a private party by herself, leaving us to face the head cook, Mildred, alone. True to form, Mildred had flamed us with her opening, "*How* many plates you need? A *hundred*? I don't think so. Uh-uh. We ain't prepared for no *hundred*."

Sharon, Mary Beth, and I had stood before the steam table, our heads bowed before au jus, melted oleo, and soup du jour, repentant for a sin we had not yet committed. We all knew how Mildred dealt with the fickleness and uncertainties of food orders; once through her initial tirade, she'd dig in and do the job, as long as nobody talked back. Problem was, we didn't always know what counted as back talk. Returning a rejected piece of meat might, on some days, be punished by long delays to replace it, ensuring a lackluster tip. At least parties like the funeral lunch had the tip written into the bill, so we were in no hurry to deliver, except as Mildred dictated.

With the last of the plates finally dished out, Mildred straightened her black wig and peered at us over the counter. "Ya'll up late last night," she said, less a question than a statement of fact.

I glanced over at Sarah behind the salad counter, now busy wrestling scoops of pink ice cream out of ten-gallon tubs. Word traveled fast.

"Oh, *yeah*," Sharon moaned dramatically. I followed suit, rubbing my fists into my eyes for effect. Mary Beth merely blinked, dark circles under her eyes enough of a statement to set Mildred clucking sympathetically.

"I fix you gals some breakfast." Mildred spread her wrinkled hands on the counter's hot steel and hunched further under the heat lamps for a closer look. "Y'all finish up, and I make you some eggs and toast."

"Quite an honor," Joan's voice drifted over our shoulders.

Usually any special requests for food were met with scorn. "You get it the way the menu say," the cooks would spit back, their way of teaching new hires not to ask for too much. But to be offered food off the menu, that was unheard of, even for veterans like Joan, who usually got a much friendlier reception.

With the last big tray teetering on my aching shoulder, I could only choke out, "Fine," before thunder hurtled me back to the Lincoln Room and the eyes of horses intent on having their way.

*

"Y'all getting enough to eat?" Opal asks. She is radiant in the ways pregnant women are said to be but usually aren't. Her face is moist but not sweaty, the color of coffee with a touch of cream. In the Stables kitchen, she is overshadowed by Mildred, choir to her preaching, backing up her witness with nods and affirmations. Visibly pregnant, Opal is not uncomfortable. Instead, she gains energy from her oversized belly.

"Plenty." I rub my belly before I realize what I'm doing. Opal laughs, rubbing vigorous circles into her own.

"This what come later." She jerks her chin towards Joan and the other waitresses locked in hot embraces.

Rose and Sarah laugh behind me. "Oh Lord, why do it have to feel so good at first and end up feeling so bad?" says Rose. Rose wears circles of rouge on her sagging cheeks, along with dark red lipstick and blue eye shadow, what I imagine she wore as a young woman in the 1940s. Waiters from the Tack Room sometimes cross the kitchen to flirt with her when orders in the Winner's Circle Lounge are backed up. They always get their drinks right. If Rose doesn't like you, your drinks come out wrong.

"Women just like bitches in heat," Sarah chimes in. Sarah and Opal often exchange such observations between Sarah's post at the salad counter and Opal's on the grill. Now Sarah shoves Opal's shoulder playfully and says, "Why didn't you listen to your mama and keep that nickel between your knees?"

"You think I don't want this child?" Opal shoves Sarah back.

"Not saying you don't want it. Just maybe that you want Roy's hootchie kootchie more." They all break up, laughing. I laugh with them.

"What about you?" Sarah tugs at my shawl. "You getting any?" The most I've said to Sarah until now is to ask for salad dressing or a shrimp cocktail. But I am less embarrassed by talking about my sex life than I am at the prospect of discussing Kyle. I picture him in his apartment, hunched over a makeshift brick-and-board desk, a statue of Ganesh on the left, a photo of his mother and father in Indian holiday attire to the right. Like his studies or his worship, sex for him is pure ritual. Little about him is spontaneous. That's what I first found attractive.

But thinking of him now as a "hootchie-kootchie man" propels me towards a lie.

"Ever hear that song, 'Don't Advertise Your Man'?"

"Ooh, she got herself a hot one!" Sarah hoots.

"Girl, you are wicked," says Opal. She wipes her face with a paper napkin, her smile a beacon in that dim corner of the bar. But her smile clouds with worry as Joan teeters over, dress sagging, feet unsteady in their transparent shoes.

"He didn't show." She starts to sob. "That bastard promised he'd come."

Opal and Sarah catch her as she collapses, then lead her to a chair next to the gifts. As Joan continues to cry, Opal and Sarah roll their eyes, as if Joan is a distant relative they are compelled to tolerate, if not love.

Tiger Lily cocks her head from behind the bar, pointing to Joan. Opal replies, "She just need to cry it out."

While Opal and Sarah rub Joan's back and murmur, Rose stays seated on her barstool, something like pity and disdain, along with a certain knowingness, holding her aloof.

I wrap my shawl more tightly, despite the suffocating heat. Part of me wants to understand what I am seeing, and another part prefers to stay in the dark. Sarah returns my gaze, saying, "You play with fire, you get burned."

I can't stand to see those black streaks down Joan's cheeks, so I snatch a cocktail napkin from Tiger Lily's stack. A glass of water appears before I open my mouth to ask. I crouch in front of Joan, who sits with her head between ring-studded hands, dab the napkin in the water, and, careful of nails as polished and sharp as fine cutlery, wipe the smears away.

"Son of a bitch," she mumbles, shaking her head. But she lets me keep wiping.

"You ok?" I ask. Sarah and Opal take turns massaging Joan's shoulders.

"He gave me a Monte Carlo, you know."

"Who?" I look to Sarah and Opal, who click their tongues.

"That son of a bitch. He promised. He promised." Joan starts weeping all over. I reach for a fresh napkin and begin blotting again. Underneath her makeup I see light brown freckles, some crow's feet tracked around her blue eyes. "Caroline." She says it with a long "i," but it's the closest anyone besides Lenny has come to saying my name.

"What, Joan?"

"Tell that son of a bitch to go fuck himself."

I don't ask any more questions, my stomach suddenly queasy, gin and mostaccoli locked in mortal combat. Lights from the pinball machine flash red and green across the dance floor, where only one couple is left dancing, hanging on for dear life. Opal and Sarah start to gather up the leftover food and stack presents as Tiger Lily wipes down the bar in earnest, clearing off the few remaining glasses. Mary Beth is asleep in the corner, *her head pillowed by a pink and blue package, while Sharon has disappeared, into the bathroom, preparing, I imagine, for the long drive home.*

I pat Joan's back and wipe her cheeks again. She seems so old and world weary, her head hanging between her knees. This spooks me. How could only six years separate us?

"Tell me," I say. Opal slides a chair my way. Rose leans forward like she's heard it all before yet can't wait to hear it again. Sarah sighs and gives the foil covers one last turn. "Tell me all about him."

*

Breakfast was my least favorite meal; I often skipped it. Eggs made me want to puke. As much as I wanted the funeral lunch to be done, I was not looking forward to breakfast at the end. If the eggs are over easy, I thought, I will surely throw up.

Not to leave this last detail to chance, I gambled instead on Mildred's good will. "Could you please make mine scrambled, with pumpernickel toast?" I asked timidly and smiled, the way I did when the prime rib was too rare and the diner has already taken a bite.

Mildred glowered at me then turned back to the grill. Flames shot up through blackened metal as she flipped fat burgers and capped them with buns. As she plated the burgers, she glanced up again and said, "Ain't you got work to do?"

As I turned to leave, Joan breezed past me behind the counter and headed straight for Mildred. I envied her that; if any of us college gals stepped foot behind the heat lamps, our heads met a verbal chopping block. But experienced servers like Joan slid plates of split rolls under the broiler and retrieved them themselves, without repercussions from the cooks. In the easy way that Joan and Mildred now spoke, Joan smiling, Mildred steadily nodding, punctuating their talk with "Uh-huhs" and "Ain't that sos," I sensed a deep understanding between them.

When I returned, along with Mary Beth and Sharon, to claim our promised meals, Mildred was just setting them on the counter, steaming hot.

"Scrambled, just like y'all like them," she cooed. Had I inadvertently spoken for all three of us? I looked to Sharon and Mary Beth, who sighed and lifted their plates to their noses. "Perfect," Mary Beth beamed.

The last plate left had pumpernickel toast. A quick check confirmed that the others had white.

"Y'all good girls," Mildred nodded.

In the Derby Room, hidden away from other servers winding down from their shifts, we three ate in silence. I had planned to give my meal to either Sharon or Mary Beth, swearing them to secrecy. But when I sat down and watched them spear soft bits of yellow, I was persuaded to at least one bite. How bad could it be?

The eggs and toast turned out to be the perfect food after all. Tender and creamy, the eggs were cooked in real butter, not the oleo routinely ladled out. The toast had just the right amount of butter, too. Mildred surely had the magic touch. Even the Derby winners staring down from the walls seemed to envy our satisfaction.

Chapter Four: Kitchen

In the Stable's kitchen, something was always burning, or had just burned, or was on the way to being burned. Days, weeks, months would pass without flames, yet smoke lingered like an unwanted kiss. On the walls behind the deep fat fryer, greasy black stains loomed like huge hand prints. Smoky endearments whispered through the back door where scores of smashed cigarette butts lay. Even after the dishwasher's breath blew steam clouds into the air, the reminders of smoke never disappeared. Instead they retreated, until the next flame reached out with charcoal plumes to brush the walls with its shadows.

Lenny had lived with smoke so long he couldn't smell it any more, even as he couldn't remember a time without it. It was always on his mama's breath, mixed with mouthwash when headed out on a date. The iron skillet she used to fry catfish and Italian sausages always reeked of it. She never used soap on that skillet, claiming that would ruin the taste. Instead she scrubbed it with cornmeal that turned black and greasy. When he ate her cornbread, he sometimes wondered what lay inside him that its gold would scour clean.

The doorman gig at the Stables agreed with him; he was rarely without a smoke in hand. Its sinuous body slid into his nostrils and curled up behind the soft hollow of his throat. Most of his time he spent waiting for lunch and dinner rushes to gear up or wind down, leaning against a brick wall, with only a little lip of roof to keep him dry when it rained. T.J. kept the canopy for himself, his protection from all the sky might hurl at them. Late nights sometimes Lenny would join him for a smoke, fishing out his Luckies while T.J. dragged a match to light his thick, black cigars.

His first day on the job, Lenny had lit up right next to T.J. Late morning, lunch rush yet to start, he'd barely taken a drag, no cars in sight, before T.J. started bossing him: "First rule: no customers see you smoke."

It wasn't the rule Lenny objected to as much as it was T.J. thinking he had to say so. Lenny was about to walk off for good when the first car of his career pulled up the drive.

All Lenny knew about being a doorman was what T.J. had told him, and that wasn't much. What else anybody expected was a mystery he had assumed he'd figure out soon enough. Working for tips was new, but here T.J. had proved a valuable source. For years the man had bragged so much on the big ones he'd landed that Lenny could recite the scenes by heart.

T.J.: You gentleman waiting on your ladies tonight?

Customers: We're waiting for ladies alright (laughter). We're tired of twiddling our own thumbs (more laughter).

T.J.: I can tell you are gentlemen who want only the best. Excuse me while I wipe that dirt off your fine collar. Me, I can spot a good piece a horseflesh a mile away. I can tell what's going to run and what won't leave the gate. And I am not afraid to put my money where my mouth is.

Customers: Oh yeah? Anything running today?

T.J. (holding out his hand): I ain't no palm reader, but I do got a clue.

T.J. had mastered the art of asking without asking. But it was one thing to memorize the lines, something altogether different to produce them. Since Lenny wasn't counting on the Stables for the long haul, he decided in that moment before he walked off to just listen and let T.J. feed him his lines. That way, he'd never have to pry himself loose from those fine, thin twists of smoke that marked all those idle moments as his alone. What he hadn't figured on was how much he'd want those big tips for himself, nor did he figure how much his act mattered to those who gave them.

*

Hanging around his homies, Murth and Sugar Butt, the show is about not putting on a show. Not supposed to act hungry for nothing. Be cool. You want something, act opposite. Otherwise, some bad-ass whip your sorry self for being weaker than rock solid.

Somewhere along the way he forgets that not wanting is not real, it's just his show. Now T.J. comes along and reminds him, No, you hungry, boy, and if you ain't hungry, you better get hungry, and quick, if you going to survive. His first month at the Stables he thinks T.J. is Bojangles, all shuck-and-jive, massah this and missus that. But T.J. turns out to be a wilier dog. He knows about wanting and hunger and can play them better than even the ponies he bets on. His show doesn't mean he's not hungry; it's about doing the dance to get fed. You don't deny you want something; instead, you mix it up, show some style, flash a few white ones and say, Thank you very much, while you serve up shit on a platter.

But still, he knows T.J.'s show is being pulled, replaced by new shows courtesy of the Brothers: No dancing around, no playing games, no making nice, just demanding what's your due. Lenny admits T.J.'s show is good, real good, but the problem is everything's changed, is changing, and even Lenny can see the old show's ending. But that end isn't here yet, and that isn't going to help him, right here and now. One way or another, a man has got to eat.

His mama: You hungry, baby? Like she died and gone to heaven if he says Yes. What you want, baby boy? You want a mess a chicken, maybe some smashed taters and gravy? Anything you want, Darling. She gets a rush cooking for him then watching him eat. She tells him, You so skinny the food run through like a drain pipe. How come you so skinny when all the meat stick to my bones, and your daddy done like that, too? She sits across the kitchen table and watches him shovel spoonfuls of gravy and forkfuls of pork speared with greens. She never eats until after he does, as if he might stop eating if she starts. He never has to think about sharing; she eats whatever he leaves behind. It is always more than she wants.

But now he is a working man, and she doesn't cook for him on nights he is on the job; Mildred Aunty promises to take care of that. When he does, finally, come home, his mama waits up to see his tips, lick her lips, wait for the stories to start rolling. She doesn't have to ask him; she gets hers and then some. She starts wearing fancy hats and bragging to anyone who will listen that her son is a man who loves his mama, loves her so much that her burdens are now lighter. She has raised a man. Halleluiah.

Still hungry, but his mama's cooking for him is now mostly done. Mildred Aunty has taken over. It's a natural move into the kitchen's smoke where Mildred Aunty stands each day, stabbing sides of beef, plunging chicken parts into boiling oil, stirring pots of soup so big a body might fall and turn into goulash. Ghoul-ash is how Mildred Aunty says it, grinning, knowing exactly what she means in that. From his mama's Camel straights to the Stables' deep fat fryer, he can't escape the smoke, not if he wants to eat like a man.

He thinks of Murth, who lives on Vienna Red Hots and Polish sausage from Gyros King, always eating on the fly, so much food to keep those weight-lifting muscles bulked. Murth is never at home, never anywhere but in the hood, roaming. If his mama ever cooks anything for him, Lenny doesn't know, so Murth takes to the streets, nickel-and-diming his way to a full belly. He never wants to eat sitting down, just pays his bread and stands at a counter to woof down three dogs and a quart of ice tea, maybe some fries, skipping the slow ketchup just to get that food down quick. Like a shark, always on the move.

*

Two o'clock, lunch rush over, Lenny headed straight for the kitchen.

"Child, you better be hungry cause I got something for you." Mildred Aunty greeted him, wiping her forehead with her apron as he turned the steam table's corner. Steam rose thick and moist like fog after a summer storm.

"You got something for *me*?" He still thought of her as "Aunty" but now that he was doing a man's job, it seemed juvenile to say that. He didn't dare call her Mildred, and "Sister," what the other cooks called her, was too much like church talk. Besides, the way Mildred Aunty ran that kitchen, she was more Preacher than Sister, maybe even the Devil himself, cracking ribs and hacking meat with a cleaver as big as her head. Her black wig sat crooked over her crazy grin as she ordered Opal and Sarah around, that same grin spreading as she stirred the ghoul-ash and split lobster shells with bony, gnarled fingers. He considered calling her Sugar and even Big Mama, but the former was too familiar and the latter something he worried might get back to his own mother, who maybe didn't want to be usurped by a cousin, but on the other hand might be relieved. So he stuck to calling her nothing. She seemed not to notice, or at least didn't say so.

"Who else but you, sweet boy? Come here."

A bloody sliver of beef dangled between her fingers; Lenny tongued it into his mouth and chewed slowly. He tasted corn and that sweet metal that came from blood boiled clear.

"Something leftover from that funeral party." She piled a plate full of already-sliced-up beef, mashed potatoes, and peas and pulled up a stool for him. He slid the top button of his uniform out of its tight hole and tucked a napkin into his collar. A knife and fork showed up on the counter next to his plate; then two shrimp, shells off, magically appeared. He looked up to catch Mildred Aunty's sly smile. She enjoyed those small crimes against Billiard's orders. For big things she'd still challenge him straight on, but for petty rules, petty crimes were her answer.

A hurricane fan at the back door blew the sweat off his face and neck. Even steam from the steam table bent away from him, back towards the dishwasher's fog. Opal was busy shelling shrimp near the walk-in and Sarah was grumbling about her aching feet and that dog of a husband who wouldn't give her no peace. The steam made everything a little fuzzy around the edges.

Lenny knew he was her boy. Not even T.J. had it so good. She'd hand over T.J.'s dinner plate around 8 o'clock, and they'd sit together, alone in one of the empty banquet rooms, eating mostly in silence. But Lenny she fussed over. Fussed and fussed. *Child, I save you this little bit, open up now, let me see you eat it. Just like a baby bird. Open up, honey, take this here bite, I make it special for you.* She found out his most intimate likes and dislikes, right down to the thickness of the radish slice in his salads: *You don't like them thick-sliced ones? Child, you don't have to eat nothing that don't sit well by you. Let me make it right.* Even his mama, dedicated to pleasing his taste buds, had never fussed like this.

He never thought he was picky until Mildred Aunty started that itch. She called him spoiled and stroked the back of his neck when she said it. She fed him shrimp, something folks said not even Mrs. Parkerhouse ate, against Billiard's orders. "Don't tell nobody," she'd whisper. But everybody knew.

Almost everybody. He was biting into the second shrimp when he saw her. The hurricane fan blew back the stray strands of hair that had worked loose; she squinted as if staring into bright sun. But in the jungle steam and smoke clouds of the kitchen, she could pretend she didn't see him, see the forbidden pink flesh trapped between his teeth. Not that he cared if she saw him. But he did care if she didn't see him, devouring that prized shrimp.

Then, all of a sudden, the wet floor threw her balance off, her arms waving to right herself, her pen flying out of her hand onto rubber mats next to the dishwasher. She tiptoed over, careful not to slip again, then bent over, bit by bit, until she reached the floor. Even through the steam he saw the dishwasher man's grin as his eyes slid over her hips, shoulders straining for a better view.

Lenny hadn't expected blood to rush to his face, nor his arms to tighten and his hands to clench. Hadn't expected angry words to flood his thoughts, unbidden, sounding just like Murth. Murth, who marked his turf with spit and the tight hairs he set loose from his head. Chicks make you crazy, man, Murth would say. Which was exactly why Murth went after them.

And then she smiled at the motherfucker, who didn't even try to get the pen for her but instead hung back to watch her rising ass. Was she messing with him? *Look but don't touch*--was that the message?

Mildred Aunty interrupted his thoughts. "Forbidden fruit taste sweeter," she said under her breath. She whacked the cleaver so loudly that the dishwasher man jumped, dropping a tray full of silverware. Undeterred, Caroline headed towards the counter, head down against the hurricane fan's wind, arms out at her sides, elbows bent like a scavenging seagull.

"Mildred?" she asked.

He speared some prime rib, dragging it through the mashed potatoes before raising his fork to his lips. He chewed slowly, deliberately, as if savoring every bite. In fact, he could barely taste it.

"What you want?" Mildred replied.

Caroline's elbows pointed at him, hot pink under the heat lamps. His eyes slid away, to the walls, the floors, anywhere but her.

"Could you--?"

Mildred kept chopping, her eyes on the bones she was breaking.

"--I was hoping--"

"Hoping and wishing won't get you nowhere." *Whack.* Pieces of bone clanged against the empty pot.

"Can I have some more toast?"

Mildred kept pitching bones into the pot, harsh music. A grin tightened across her lips. He knew the signs. She was working up to a major scold.

"You the only one or them other gals want some, too?"

He couldn't believe it. Mildred was fussing over her.

"I think Mary Beth took off. Joan--"

"She don't hardly eat."

They looked at each other and smiled.

"Pumpernickel ok?" Caroline asked.

Mildred stomped over to the walk-in. Lenny kept his head down, eyes locked on his plate. All of a sudden his princely meal was reduced to leftovers. *She* got something fresh-cooked, to order. What *she* wanted.

And no fussing.

"I got something for you." He couldn't believe he said it. The words kept pouring out of his mouth, filling up the silence between them, like cool water clearing out the smoke and steam. "Something you want." He patted his pants pocket.

She took the bait. "How do you know what I want?" She leaned closer. Red curls fought loose from her tight-pulled hair.

"I just do," he crooned.

"I bet."

"OK, what you want to bet?"

Hands waving in front of her face, she laughed. "I didn't mean it that way." She cupped one hand to her mouth, still laughing.

"You lying, Care-o-lyin."

"So what do you think I want."

The walk-in fridge door slammed shut. He heard Mildred's heavy breath move behind him before the hacking resumed.

Patting his pocket again, he held two fingers to his lips and sucked his breath, hard.

Caroline turned red. "You think I want that?"

"I don't just think, I know."

Mildred smacked her lips, two, three, four times. "You going to eat that prime, or I toss it?"

Lenny pushed the plate away.

"How's that dog of yours?" Mildred asked as she picked up the plate.

Caroline brushed a hair from her eyes, stifling a yawn. "Daisy? She's fine. You know her?"

"Fine-looking dog. Smart, too. Sit, speak, roll over--what all your daddy train that dog to do?" Mildred chuckled.

A cough rolled up his throat; he started gagging. Mildred slapped him on the back until he stopped.

"You OK?" Caroline asked nervously.

"Just something stick in his throat," Mildred answered. She leaned over and growled low in his ear: "Pride." Plucking the toast from the oven with her bare fingers, she turned to Caroline. "Your daddy know his business, for sure. That dog so trained it sit forever waiting on his word."

"It's really his dog," Caroline said.

"Pretty, too."

"That's what everybody says."

"Always do what it told."

Caroline sighed. She ran her fingers across her scalp until they caught on the band in her hair. With one hand, she twisted off the band and with the other, she shook her hair loose. He didn't know his mouth had dropped until he felt Mildred's glare. He shut it quick, hoping Caroline hadn't noticed.

"My dad's good at giving orders," Caroline said finally.

Mildred busied herself with plating the toast. He knew once her radar was switched on, there was no turning it off. What was her deal about "college gals"? Being white wasn't it—in high school there were plenty of white girls, and brown, and even a few yellow ones. Everybody dated, curious about the other "flavors." Mildred was just old fashioned. Just because Caroline was college didn't mean she wasn't curious.

*

This cat ain't got no tail
It don't know how to hiss
What claws it got no man can see
But it sure know how to piss!

How low-down muthafuckin bad can they get out there on the corner? Him calling out: I got the meat you dying to eat/ I make you full/ you ain't no fool. *Murth's silence egging him and Sugar Butt on. Nice girls never hear the real nasty stuff. The bad, low-down, trashy stuff that make you drool like a fool.*

Three white chicks in the hood. Their shoulders raise up; they hunch together like birds. The station wagon door flops open. Daddy's car, all shiny and new. They pull out a package so long it takes all three to hoist it. Across the street, he and Murth and Sugar Butt keep on signifying. How low down can they go? But these chicks are too scared to even look up.

That's cool, Murth says, smiling. His smile is a shadow crossing his lips, a ripple in the air Lenny feels more than sees. The same smile comes when he is about to hit somebody or cut a killer deal. That smile says what's his is his, and he ain't shy about taking it.

Just where we want em, Murth's grin is saying now. Sugar Butt jumps around, acting confused. He thinks doing the dozens is hot, but what does he know about college gals in station wagons toting packages a mile long? Murth wants to scare them a little, so when he finally goes over, they can ooh and ahh over his tight pecs, fight for his protection.

Something about all that loose red hair gets to Lenny. She's tall and lanky, what his mama says he is. Thin but not skinny. Wide ass but not fat, riding not high, not low, just right where it should be. Good legs, long and lean, like she walks, maybe runs, to keep strong. He can see them through that thin dress, her whole outline a shadow in the street light. Her hair, loose, shoots out every which way.

Murth is watching him watch her, his smile gone. His eyes narrow and his forehead sinks into his brows. But Lenny knows once inside the Star Dust, tonight is his show. He is Murth's ticket; the college gals are his stable.

Inside, Murth starts muttering about chicken, staring at Lenny like his eyes are pure fire. TJ gives them the look: Don't mess up my re-cre-a-shun. *Until now, Lenny has had no cause to go inside the Star Dust. The Dust is T.J.'s hang out. But when Lenny found out some of the Stables' servers hang there, Murth went after him.*

"You been holding out on me, muthafucker."

"No, man, they ain't nothing."

"Don't give me that shit. White chicks don't come here for nothing."

Murth made him promise to take him. "No more holding out," he says, jaw twitching. Anything on Murth that moves, beware. Nothing moves unless he's riled. Or humping a piece. Lenny caught him in the act once, in an alley. Murth wasn't just moving, he was shouting. Didn't care who heard or saw. Flat against the brick wall, the chick looked stone high.

Inside the Dust, it's no back alley humping. Murth can't connect without Lenny showing him the moves. And the right moves now are no moves at all. It's all about waiting for an opening to show. But waiting is not Murth's game. Sugar Butt is happy to wait for the leftovers. But Murth can't stand still. He doesn't care how he looks, as long as he lands his piece. T.J.'s warning tones him down some, but he tries his stuff on one chick, then another, before coming back to Lenny and Sugar Butt.

"Them some cold bitches there," Sugar Butt says. "They freeze you out like the North Pole."

"No bitch freeze me out," Murth answers. "I just come back for my blow torch." He points at Lenny. "Go blow, muthafucker."

"Chill, man." Lenny waves the bartender over. "Three shots of JD."

Murth keeps drinking after the first shots go down. He can't just wait. Shark that he is, he has to keep moving.

She has a thing for backbeat. He knows chicks who'd laugh at how her hips fly all over the place and her arms flap loose like rubber. The beat takes her body parts and scatters them all over the floor. Yet something else has gotten hold of her that catches him off guard. The other chicks have cut loose, some hanging on dudes, some dancing in big circles spread out on the floor. But not like this. Not wild.

Finally, his opening comes. He even slow dances her to an R&B tune. Then, suddenly all her parts fit together, a little stiff, maybe, but together they flow, clear and true. He reaches for the small of her back, feels her melt into his touch, feels his hand deep inside her skin, and the lights around them fall into his sky. But when the music stops, she is all over the place again, and this time, her wildness will not wait for him.

*

The laundry room smelled of bleach and spoiled food. Piles of soiled tablecloths, napkins, and kitchen towels rose up in one corner, stacks of clean in another. The washer and dryer looked on silently. The smell of rotten food had followed him from the kitchen, down the hall past Mrs. Parkerhouse's office and now joined the other smells inside.

He counted on Caroline coming back to the kitchen to drop off her plate. Besides the business office, the laundry was the only place he knew where they could be alone.

"Hey!"

At first she didn't hear him. He said it again, louder: "Hey!" Mildred might hear, but right now he didn't care, as long as she couldn't see him.

Caroline looked around, as if not sure the call was to her.

"Come on." He waved his arm. Glancing across the hall, he noticed the business office's blinds were drawn. That meant Mrs. Parkerhouse was out, or busy. At least that's what everybody said it meant. He hoped they were right.

She frowned, looking around the kitchen. "What?" she hissed.

He pumped his arm towards the laundry room door.

"Here?" she said. "What if—?"

"Nobody can see. C'mon." He patted the joint in his pocket to prove his point.

She set her empty plate in a tray full of dirty dishes. This time the dishwasher man was gone, and she managed to keep her balance as she started tiptoeing across the flooded floor, lured by his promise of smoke.

*

He's seen fires before. Houses burned, stores and businesses crumbled. Part of life on the South side. It happened. But this one is bigger, much, much bigger. Ten years old. Smoke thick in the air. Not sooty smoke from chimneys. Not tobacco smoke from the front-stoop-squatting, lawn-chair-sitting grown ups gossiping. More like the chemical smells from the janitor's closet at school.

Gossipers' heads turn towards black clouds that spread and spread like monster fingers, from the same direction his mama said his daddy lived on the West side. Then the heads turn again, like birds in a flock, this time towards the lake and downtown. Dark clouds take on a spooky red haze well into the night. Nobody goes to bed. Everybody is either shouting or crying.

King is dead.

He remembers it was like this when Kennedy was shot. Only people weren't mad, just sad. King is like the president to him. He wonders how he should feel. He didn't know then and he doesn't know now. He just knows this man was shot down dead. Everybody else seems to know how to feel but him.

Nobody sits inside. It's too cold, but a little shivering is better than listening to the television's lies. Instead, they hunch over transistor radios. Telephones ringing inside bring more news. The mayor says people are shooting each other, looting and stealing in their own neighborhoods. That's what the morning Tribune tells them, too. Front page photo of warehouse fires and a cop car bashed in. Cops pour in to save people from themselves.

They all know who the protection is for. Damen Avenue businesses are on the line.

Morning comes and nobody has gone to bed. Boxes of donuts, cups of coffee and juice get passed around. He is sore from sleeping in lawn chairs, tired from all the sirens and radios blaring. He asks his mama, Will the smoke get us, too?

No, she says, and pulls him to her legs. But her eyes are dark with worry.

*

That red hair waved like a flame, dancing in the steamy air. He patted his pants pocket. Still there.

"So what's your surprise?" Her voice was skeptical, impatient. He had to move fast.

"I'll show you." He opened his arms to guide her inside the laundry room, then pulled the door halfway shut. That door was never closed all the way. He didn't want to rouse suspicions.

Even with the dryers off, the room was hot as hell. No a/c vents, just a fan in the corner near the ironing board. Sweat broke out on his lips. His face flushed. A mistake? he wondered.

All that red hair going wild in the heat.

"Jesus, it's hot." She pulled her hair up off her neck, then let it flop back down. She looked around. "So this is where the laundry fairies work?" He must have given her a weird look because she laughed sheepishly. "That's a joke around the house. You know, like when you don't see something get done. My mom says we all act like fairies keep the house clean." She turned towards the clean stacks. "Wow, look at all these napkins. I'd kill to have these during dinner rush. Delores stashes piles in the banquet rooms."

"I got a stash."

"Oh yeah?"

He reached in his pocket, breathing deep. The joint was perfectly rolled, tapered on either end. A huge gamble. He knew that. He hadn't expected to play these odds, hadn't even planned to get high. Unlike Murth, he didn't like going to work stoned. Plus, one look at him and T.J. would be able to tell. And the smell. He'd come home and his mama would know and kick his ass for risking his job, the only one that had any future.

But he'd let Murth slide it in his pocket anyway, remembering T.J's stories, how he was always bragging on the big tips. "Give people what they want," he'd say, sly smile tightening his lips. Lenny watched as the Stables' barmaids came to the door on slow nights in their hot pants and thigh-high riding boots, a flash of metal exchanged between their hands and T.J.'s. T.J. didn't deny that he liked to mellow out on bourbon when business was slow. The barmaids left after their shifts with men in pin-stripes driving Monte Carlos who T.J. said tipped big. Part of the business. Get people what they want, and they give you what you want.

Murth's joint could have maybe landed that first big tip. He didn't know where Murth got his weed, but he never seemed to run out. Sugar Butt egged him on to take it: "This is your *job*, bro." Acting like the pimp he was.

"Dessert, madam?" Lenny smiled his best English butler smile and, holding out the joint, bowed ever so slightly before Caroline.

"J-E-L-L-O?" She sang the tv jingle then laughed nervously. At least they had commercials in common.

Two dances and fending off a homeboy at the Star Dust were surely worth something to her. At the very least, he hoped she wouldn't narc on him. The rest was just a guess. If she had the shit to come into the hood, get drunk, and dance with him, then maybe, just maybe, she liked to get high, too. Hippie chicks usually went for weed. Didn't college gals get high? And how about that low spot down on her back? Did she remember when he'd touched it?

He cocked his head with that puppy look that chicks liked. Still holding out the joint. His heart felt far away in his fancy uniform, like fast trains running deep inside his chest. He reached in his other pocket for matches. Her face turned redder by the second. Something behind him, out in the corridor, was ticking. Or maybe it was just the blood in his ears. He silently urged her to take the joint. Instead her mouth moved, her lips like worms cooking under a magnifying glass. He watched them twist until the sound of her voice caught up with his ears.

"Oh shit. I should have told you--but then how could I--"

Still holding the joint, matches in hand, a circle of coolness eased down around him. The train in his chest slowed. She was scared. His breath slowed down in one big exhale. He knew what to do with scared.

"Shhh." He put the joint back in his pocket, the matches in the other, and pressed one finger first to his lips, and as she kept talking, to hers.

"--boyfriend at school--"

"Shhh."

Nothing at all was still about her, her arms telling one story, her hands telling another, and her feet telling something else altogether. Too many minds in one body. But up close, her green eyes held a steadiness like light in pond water. Her lips were flat and pale, but her hair drew his hands. *Like moth to flame.*

*

T.J. had showed him how to bait the hook. They bought nightcrawlers from a toy-sized shack at Marquette Park, where T.J. liked to fish on weekends. Lenny bragged to his friends how he'd hook one end of the worm first, in the fat of its tail, then twist its body into an S and pierce each curve through the metal. Girls shook their heads and slapped the air when he told them, but boys debated the merits of the technique. They snatched storm-drenched worms from sidewalk puddles and tried to replicate Lenny's lessons on safety pins.

Hook baited, the whir of line over water drew him to a still place somewhere between the play of light on the pond's surface. Blink, swallow. The bobber drifted aimlessly past the floaters in his eyes. When he tried to talk about why he liked fishing, it sounded boring. But it wasn't. Instead, inside the water, everything gained a certain intensity. T.J's cigar smoke snaked up to the moon. Weeping willows poured into their own reflections. Little kids in the distance chased soccer balls into the clouds. Below, fish magnetized into arrows pointed at the hidden hook. When the red and white bobber finally disappeared, he'd jerk the pole back and up to set the hook, T.J. murmuring approval.

He remembers that still place, but nowadays only smoke can get him there.

*

Her head eased back into his waiting hands, his fingers traveling through her thick, red curls. He scanned her eyes, waiting for that flicker below the surface. The rush of heat through his limbs tightened his grip. His breath grew fast and shallow. Something coiled within threatened to burst forth. Her eyes were wide and cool, almost indifferent, it seemed, to the flames that circled her head and flickered in their mossy depths.

Incineration

Obliteration
Incarceration

He brought his eyes so close to hers he lost sight of her, then surrendered to the smell of her coffee-soured breath. He took her lips in his, circled them with his tongue, once, twice, again. He knew he was crazy. She didn't move, didn't even breathe. He started to feel a sickening spin, and out of desperation he pulled her closer, his hands pressing the small of her back. Their bellies met, as they had at the Star Dust that one, brief moment. This time he held her there, afraid to let go, afraid not to.

Something like a ripple, water or flame, air or earth, moved through her skin. Her hands found the big, padded shoulders of his uniform and pressed them until they met the bones below. She was kissing him back. An intense heat tore through his blood. He had to stop, now. He heard voices crying out in pain, spectators to his annihilation, or maybe victims themselves. Was he a witness or a victim?

He started pulling away, but her hands weighed down his shoulders, cool, steady, and absolutely sure of themselves. She kept kissing him back, slow, deliberate, testing for results. His eyes were closed but he could feel her eyes open, looking directly into him, through him, asking how the parts fit together, the speed of his heartbeat, how many layers before emptiness-- the kinds of questions they asked in sophomore biology when they cut the frog open, panicked and exposed. She froze him with that stare, and now she was moving in for the kill.

Another ripple, down her back this time. He tried to move his hand away but she slid her hips to keep it in place. Now her hips were moving, slightly. He stroked that small place in circles, tiny ones at first then bigger and bigger. Her hips moved against his. The hard, gold buttons on his uniform pressed into his stomach, nearly his groin, into hers. The weight of the jacket was now too much. Too many layers between them. He stroked her chin with his free hand, then started to release the buttons from their tight, new holes. She was helping him. He unfastened one, she the next below. Still that cool, assured movement, only now she was in a hurry, too, which made him slow down. *SLOW DOWN!* Somebody was shouting this somewhere outside, or inside, he couldn't tell. He didn't care. He'd heard it all his life. Somebody was always telling him to *SLOW DOWN!*

He flung the jacket on the pile of soiled linen behind him, a grand gesture that made her giggle. He kissed her again. This time her tongue was inside his mouth first, wiggling like a worm on the hook. Now he had her. Now she had him. Her pelvis rubbed against his until it ached. He let his hand slip from that small spot to her ass, the left cheek. Right then, he just about lost it. No way he was going to let himself come in his pants. So he shifted his attention back up to her shoulders and fumbled for the zipper pull at her collar. From the effort of trying to pull down on the zipper, keep his tongue and pelvis moving, and shimmy the other hand up and down her spine, his eyes forced themselves open a crack. Light poured in. He shut them but the light kept coming. He saw red throbbing under his eyelids. Sweat stung until tears formed. He realized he was soaked right through his underwear. Sweat had drowned his eyebrows and was making a play for his nose and mouth. When he opened his eyes again, everything was gray and distorted like water, fog--or smoke.

She moaned and forced her breasts into his.

He heard the laundry door swing open. *Shit.* The goddamn door was open. He kept stroking her back even as the smoke-fog overcame him. All these ghost eyes came streaming into the grayness. Big, round, horsy eyes, like those portraits in the lobby. Eyes that looked at you not straight on but from around the sides of their heads. Bulgy, fearful, black, vacant eyes floating in the cloudy fire that engulfed him now. Here and there he had heard the stories. There had been a fire. Some horses had struggled. But the fire had kept on coming.

This weed more than Murth tell me, he thought as the floor shivered under his feet. Pounding, throbbing horses reared up, leaping, falling back and collapsing. *Not the trip I want.* Too late; he was in it now. Then he remembered: he hadn't actually smoked.

She clutched his shoulders and hung on like death as he pressed her to his chest, only thin cloth between them. In the distance he heard someone cry out. He opened his eyes wide past her red hair and mossy eyes and met the eyes of another. These green eyes were on fire, lighting a tarnished copper face both ancient and familiar. A corner-of-the eye uncertainty—had he seen/not seen this face before? A face that sent both a blessing and a warning. Somewhere he had seen it before, yet he could not remember where. So maybe he had not seen it, or maybe he had in his dreams?

Either way, the effect straightened him up. He closed his eyes. His hands drifted down to rest lightly on her hips as he exhaled. Her hands and breath followed his. This time his kiss was soft and slow. Hers mirrored his. He sighed, both disappointment and relief. Those green eyes had unnerved him.

He opened his eyes, blinked, and saw the laundry room door was closed all the way now. The gray air cleared. The smell of bleach and spoiled food returned. Caroline was pulling her zipper back up from where he'd edged it down.

She drew her finger down his lips and sighed. "Too dangerous," she whispered.

He wanted to shout, *What are you afraid of?* But he knew. He already knew. The smoke had shown him horses overcome by fast-moving tongues of flame. He had heard their screams. He didn't believe in ghosts or visions or whatever those flaming green eyes had flashed at him. But clearly someone was watching; to ignore them was at his own risk.

He took her face into his hands and pressed the freckles on her nose with his finger tip, lightly but firmly. She let him, watching his eyes move over her face like headlights in fog. She opened her mouth; his plunged forward to meet it. Like a drowning man, he could not tell up from down. Either way he moved, he was lost.

Part II

There is this cave
In the air behind my body
That nobody is going to touch:
A cloister, a silence
Closing around a blossom of fire.
When I stand upright in the wind,
My bones turn to dark emeralds.

---James Wright
"The Jewel"

Chapter Five: Rose Garden

Shadows hung heavily inside the Stables, like breath trapped in an old bottle. Over the years, some shadows had grown so distinct that Viney had taken to giving them names. Some names she found inside the Webster's Pocket Dictionary she carried in her A&P buggy for that purpose. Other names invented themselves from syllables that fused into sounds and shapes that pleased her tongue. Constability, for one, was a shadow that lived in the lobby under the reservation stand and whispered to the maitre d's. The kitchen had its shadows as well. Buried within the deep freeze, Come Again cried out from between ancient layers of frost. Early in the morning or late at night, she often heard Futility murmur, *Never touch the bottom* from within moldings carved in grapevines along the Garden Room's ceiling, distorted by many layers of paint.

Shadows in the Tack Room were especially dense, since little light entered there. Hunched inside the arms of silver loving cups, Effluvium brooded over the Tack Room's mantle, humming at a pitch only jilted lovers could hear. While aged beef filets courted even older pools of snifter-bound brandy, and stiff tablecloths softened in hopes of attracting mahogany walls, Effluvium presided over anniversary dinners and betrothals, first dates and clandestine affairs. Whatever doubts lay in lovers' hearts Effluvium stirred with fumy fingers, giving witness to all fluctuations of affection with an equal impassivity.

But perhaps the most potent of all were the shadows newly returned. Long after the parking lot emptied, after the moon had risen and traveled the night sky, yet still far from the first stirrings of dawn, ash-filled hoof prints crossed that abandoned ground where shadows grew as thick as the dust that now claimed it.

Something, without a doubt, had stirred the air from its apathy, and along with it, memories Viney feared had been lost. If only she could survive the remembering.

"Viney?"

She wiped sweat from her face with the day's last diaper then stuffed it into the A&P buggy as she wheeled it into the laundry room for the night. In no other place could the buggy rest undisturbed. Few entered that room; as if by some invisible force only those in urgent need of clean or desperate to rid themselves of stain were granted a brief audience within.

Like the two new ones. Black and white, light and shadow, piling on each other, gathering their storm. Together they sparked. She liked that.

It had been so long since sparks had found their way inside the Stables. She remembered: Sparks.

Cool came quickly once the dryer's load whirled to a stop. Laundry was often the last chore for the night, when she would mound piles of newly stained linens and take satisfaction in the neat stacks of clean. Scouring stains and weeding out worn cloth she saved for early morning, before the small room baked in the dryer's heat and the washers agitated for hours on end. Evenings were about emptying the clean and making room for the next day's loads. But tonight the last loads would have to wait.

"Viney?"

Down the hall in the kitchen, she heard the dishwasher race to catch up with the night's remains, its moist heat fingering through the laundry room's door. She turned to leave the buggy behind when she met Mildred's stare.

"Ain't you hear me?" Mildred's forehead pressed down on her brows.

"I hear you," Viney replied. "I just forget."

"Forget? What you mean, 'forget'? You forget who you are?"

"No, I be remembering." Mildred shook her head like a horse dodging a fly. Viney continued. "Why you call me that? Why you call me 'Viney'?"

Mildred's black wig slid back and forth across her scalp as she scratched her head. Her eyes emptied, sunk deep in shadow. Viney sighed and looked out across the hall to Mrs. Parkerhouse's shuttered windows. No light leaked through the shutters' slats; she and Billiard had left for the night.

She couldn't blame Mildred for fussing. All these years, and Viney never saying anything until now, like she was saving it up to throw in her face. Truth was, she was just now remembering. Mildred's naming her way back then had been nothing new. Her whole life, people had called her names of their own choosing, for purposes they thought she should claim as her own. Her mama had called her Spud, to protect her true self from evil. Her brother followed suit with Tater, and even her daddy had taken to calling her Skeeter by the way she lit around him whenever he came home. Mamaw she could count on to call her Child, sometimes adding Blessed if she was in a holy mood. For many since then, she was simply gal, until her bones disappeared into her skin, and after that she just became the Cleaning Lady. Only now that Mildred was calling out for her, and she wanting more than ever to simply disappear, had the question finally found her tongue.

She looked back at Mildred, whose chest had fallen as if asleep or hit hard.

"What you mean? You always been Viney," Mildred insisted.

"No, you the first to say so." Mildred had been the first at the Stables to ask Viney her name. At first Viney had refused to tell her, recalling the startled eyes of others who had asked the same.

But Mildred had pressed her: "Cat got your tongue?"

When Viney had finally answered, Mildred's lower lip thrust out, and her knuckles dug into her hip bones. "You want me to call you what?"

"Baby Divine," Viney had repeated. Mildred had shook her head. "The 'baby' part I got, but you, nothing but a slip of a gal, being called upon like the Lord? What your mama thinking?"

"Well, I'll be." Mildred now leaned an elbow on the buggy's handle. Sweat nested in her eyebrows and moistened her skin as she let out a long breath. Except for the dishwasher's jet sprays, the laundry room and hallway were quiet. "You let me name you?"

Viney nodded. Before the Stables, what people called her didn't matter all that much. Back home, everybody knew her name; she didn't have to tell them. Whatever else they called her didn't stick; they always knew who she was. But Mildred's name had stuck in ways she'd never expected.

By this time of night, the staff had usually scattered—out back for cigarettes, in the Winner's Circle Lounge to chat up Ernie the bartender, or perched on a good chair out of sight of Billiard, waiting for the last tables to finish. Only the small brown men who bussed tables and loaded the dishwasher busied themselves with work. But Mildred had stayed later than usual.

"I remember now," Mildred continued. "I remember clear as day. You looked to me like a growing thing, with no beginning, and no end in sight. Like a vine."

Viney turned off the laundry room lights and stepped out into the hall. Some nights she drove home with Mildred, and some with T.J. They never guessed that she might want to stay behind, with only the small brown men for company. Lately she counted on Mildred thinking T.J. would escort her and T.J. thinking his wife had already seen their friend home.

"You coming?" Mildred shook her keys, nodding towards the kitchen. Mildred always turned out the kitchen lights one by one, leaving only a dim light on over the stove. Viney would follow behind her in the dark, until they reached the back door, where Mildred would step aside for her to exit while she closed and locked the steel door against intruders, while locking in the small brown men--dishwashers and bussers--for the night.

Tonight, Viney hung back in the hall, hidden within its shadows. Overhead, feet shuffled and scuttled across the ceiling, prelude to a restless night. In the morning, she was often greeted by ruined dinners left abandoned at the stove, eaten up to their inedible char. She did not need to know the names of those who'd stayed the night to know that they were there.

"You coming?" Mildred asked again. In the heated stillness between the dishwasher's cycles, not a single sound rushed in to fill the void.

*

From the Iron Horse at the station, two blinkered mixed bloods draw her to their wagon. The butter-eyed woman from the train climbs into their buckboard then, looking down, sees Baby Divine standing below.

"You be needin a ride?" the woman asks. The mixed bloods have already stomped their feet in assent. They are bound to take her; it is lucky that the woman has sense enough to go along.

The woman directs a young man at the reins to give Baby Divine a hand up. Cut off by their blinkers, the mixed bloods give little notice to the noise, traffic, and smells swirling around them, yet they nod as she climbs on board.

"What's your name?" The butter-eyed woman has been the only one to ask since Baby Divine left the up country.

"Baby Divine."

"Come again?"

She says it again; the woman falls silent.

"That's a big name," she finally replies.

In back of the wagon, Baby Divine straddles a board with the butter-eyed woman's boy and the five young children come to greet them. She settles into the view from up high, searching for signs of the lake, where she still hopes to camp. The woman does not turn back to chat. Instead she fixes her eyes on the horizon. After a few questions, the buckboard children busy themselves with waving at motor cars creeping through the crowds.

When the mixed bloods finally stop in front of a hulking wooden two-story, all manner of motor cars, two-wheelers, and carts clatter past without end. The house stands shoulder-to-shoulder with dozens of the same. She senses that in this busy place, it might be days before the next horses stop. To make matters worse, the butter-eyed woman, who insists on "Celia," will not let her take to the streets alone.

"Sister, what would your mama say, me letting you run wild in such a place?" Celia scolds.

Baby Divine thinks it best not to mention that her mama has no notion that such a place exists and, like herself, would find a lake much more hospitable than these rickety old houses leaning this way and that. Her mama could not have imagined how forever busy, how caught up in its own business Chicago is. Later on, in the days she spends with Celia and her household full of kinfolk, she says so little about anything that at one point Celia asks her point blank, "Sister, tell me, are you touched?"

Recalling her daddy's stories about her birth, Baby Divine tells her the truth. When her daddy said, "Touched," his eyes lit up with pride. But Celia's eyes drop back into her skull, and she grows quiet.

"Don't you worry, sweet pea. We look after our kind."

Look after they do. She becomes one of some half dozen "Sisters" that occupy the house. But unlike them, she stays behind during the day while they join the men folk who go into the streets every morning to work. All she has to do is step out the front door, and one of the ten children that belong to the house runs up and takes hold of her hand.

"You s'posed to be watching me," the child would tell her. That is the "agreement" Celia has struck; in exchange for room and board, "Sister Baby" will look after the children. Celia proposed, and Baby Divine's silence did not contradict.

The two-story is never quiet; with ten children and nearly as many grown folks living under its roof, someone is always asking, arguing, loving, or crying about one thing or another. The human smells overpower all others, with so many bodies so close together, and only one tin tub for baths. Wet socks hang in every open space, leaching wooly sweat into fumes from boiled cabbage and stale onion breath. Opening a window invites in soot-soaked breezes full of rotten potatoes, kerosene, and manure. Getting rid of one smell brings on smells of another kind, of lye soap and damp rags turned sour as they dry. While cleaning is constant, from bedsheets to socks to undergarments to work shirts, the smells still linger, soaked up by crumbling plaster walls and egged on by coal spewing sulfur from the stove. With no interruption in this relentless march of smells, she is captive inside their invisible walls, unable to navigate the busyness that surrounds her.

The smells continue out the door, up and down the streets, into every crowded, drafty house, in the muddy spring streets choked with all manner of creatures. Close quarters are nothing new, her family spending long winters together in one small cabin, but there the land breathed, and a good airing, windows flung open, chased off the funk. Here, where smells have no place to go, they link arms and idly roam the streets, eager for the chance to overpower all others.

A few stolen ventures out into the streets convince her to stay close by. The alley behind the two-story is narrow, usually muddy, and stinks of all manner of foulness. She goes there only to empty the trash. While mules pull trash wagons past, she sees no place to ride with them except inside their filthy bins. But even there in the alley the horses eventually find her, when what Celia calls "golden apples" appear in the mud. Usually they disappear quickly, prized for their free fuel. Today, when she dumps coal ash to mix with the alley's dust, she sees these signs the horses have left behind.

At the alley's end, draft horses are hitched to a green market truck parked behind a café. They stand 20 hands high, towering over the tiny mules and the alley's narrow, dark lane.

Two days later when the draft horses return, Celia is home, sprawled on a bed, a wet rag plastered to her forehead. Now that the children will not be left alone, Baby Divine slips out the bathroom window and picks through the alley's mud, pausing briefly to greet the horses before boarding the truck. Their slow movements and steady eyes speak of long miles and heavy loads. They hold their heads up, confident in their strength, unafraid even of the fire bells clanging down 26th Street. It is early morning; they have a long way yet to go.

She climbs inside the truck bed and hunkers down behind piles of cabbages. In the dank, raw darkness, the faces of Celia, Mama, and Mamaw start circling the air around her. She ducks her head, trying with all her strength not to see their images before her. Scolding, dancing, crying, they demand she meet their eyes. Obeying their swirling voices, she lifts her head. Their eyes give witness to all the people they love whom they have already lost, and all those, like her, they have yet to lose.

She hears the reins snap and the driver's tongue click, but the draft horses do not move. Her daddy always told her that horses were her fate, that, like him, she could not help but follow where they led. But in that pause, the horses offer her choice of climbing down and turning her back on them, a choice that until now she never realized she had.

*

The key turned smoothly in the back door's lock, which clicked as it opened. Mildred had given up trying to coax her to go home and had left, locking her in. As she pulled the key out, others on the key ring jangled against each other, scratching at the door as if eager for release. Cuts had scarred the keyhole's face, deep and narrow like stab wounds; she wondered what could have left such marks.

Out back was where staff gathered to smoke and gossip, sometimes share a nip or pop a pill to ease the day's demands. She had waited all day for a chance to slip out, anxious to answer the restless shadows without drawing attention to what the shadows concealed.

Lingering in the door's threshold, she listened for the sound of hoof beats. After she'd found the scattered ashes in the Tack Room, the sound of the thoroughbreds' hooves followed her from room to room, mingling among the shadows, unseen and unnamed, thundering in the gaps between one world and another.

The steel door unbolted, she waited in the threshold, cool night air streaming on her face, hot dishwasher steam elbowing her back, embracing the two worlds she stood between, even as they pushed against the other, each struggling for a greater claim. She paused at the center of their dissolve, herself dissolving between outside and inside, cool and warm, starlight and shadow.

She pushed the door ajar just enough for night sounds to wind their way inside before the dishwasher's heaving breath rose up to overtake them. Surely some of the cooler night would reach through the steam and tap the small brown men on their shoulders. How could they help but follow her out into shadows that, like them, were forbidden to cross the threshold?

Once outside, she let the door fall shut then stood in the hard-packed dust. Next to the dumpster, rotten lettuce and cigarette butts greeted her nose. Mosquitoes hovered lazily around her, weak from long days with no rain. The security light above the door did not light up as she slipped out of range of its trigger. If she waited long enough, perhaps the small brown men would follow, speaking in their galloping tongue, slipping away into the night then returning, hugging brown paper sacks close to their chests. She pictured them smoking and drinking outside in the dewy air, pointing to her apron where the keys to their passage sagged against her knees.

Her eyes had no trouble finding the hoof prints she'd expected to find in the dust. They traced a circle into which they disappeared, reappearing on the other side. For years, the thoroughbreds had lingered as only a tightness in the air that left no marks behind. Now their hoof prints outlined the circle where the Rose Garden had once stood. She had almost forgotten the Rose Garden.

*

Everyone at the Stables is as desperate for distraction as she is to be alone. Out there on the flatness, on the edge of all things familiar, few of the workers have enough strength left at the end of the day to chase to the city for its pleasures, and even fewer the money to pay for them. So they lean on each other to make the boredom go away. But the more they lean, the more she pulls away. It's the horses she wants.

Never in her life has she seen horses like this. "Thoroughbreds," the stable hands call them. Unlike horses in the up country, they are bred with one sole purpose: to run, as fast and as long as their legs will hold out. They carry chests big enough to house a heart three times the size of her daddy's Morgans. But their legs look like match sticks compared to those breeds. And their tempers often get the best of them, so much so that the stable hands rely on her more and more to ease the horses' comings and goings. They are impossible creatures, with their huge chests and stick-like legs and fiercely tender hearts; they are miracles, dreams that drift just out of reach, defying all attempts to contain them.

Besides the pregnant mare, two young geldings and two older mares sleep in the barn at night. Only the stallion is left to himself in the paddock next to the tack barn, where he high-steps with his tail in the air, neck arched, displaying his powerful muscles. The two mares nicker to him in their stalls, lips twitching, and stomp their hooves. In the morning, they do not need to be coaxed out, only given plenty of room as they rear up against the halter and lead. Unlike the mares, the two geldings have no use for the stallion. They busy themselves chewing the stall door, or nibbling a groom's arms just hard enough to bruise but soft enough to count as love. The younger of the two, a yearling, will not let his legs be taped without a fight.

The pleasure she takes from the thoroughbreds is enough to carry her through cleaning the speakeasy all day and serving the patrons all night. She helps in the horse barn at dawn and dusk, the only times besides the dead of night that she has to herself. She takes care not to reveal to anyone else her bed in a far corner of the hayloft, hidden behind bales. She fears the stable hands will not trust her, witness to their sighs and grunts in the grip of hay, lacking any other mates but themselves. Since her first week, she has slept there, learning the loft ladder's predictable squeaks, how to blend the sound of her own movements with theirs, to listen to breaks in their breathing until she can be sure of her next step inside.

One night not long after she starts sleeping in the barn, she works so late in the speakeasy that the grackles have already started to twitter, and the sky towards the city has stained red. She has little time to sleep but is still eager to hear the day's first whinnies as she steps onto the ladder.

"I know you ain't lost, so maybe you are just stupid."

Two tall, worn and muddy riding boots point at her black-booted feet from behind the hayloft ladder. She freezes, skirt bunched in her hands. The trainer is always inside the stalls early, but never early enough to see her climb inside.

He clears his throat then spits, close to her boots.

"Then again, you got a way with horseflesh."

His name is Mudrack, and it suits him. His skin is yellow brown like the mud in rivers kicked up by storms. The stable hands call him Yellow Dog behind his back and speak in low tones about him.

She feels his stare before she sees it, two eyes empty as sky squinting above a mustache with the ends curled up. He holds her eyes for several breaths. Trespass is drawn in the lines on his face.

"I expect you better come regular now to help the boys out. But the less the boss man knows about where you spend your nights, the better off you'll be. And don't think this means your pay gonna increase. We can't afford another hand."

It turns out the stable hands are glad to have her among them. They build up bales for her in the hayloft so she might sleep in peace. After teaching her to smoke French-style, they teach her about tack. But Mudrack still makes her uneasy. As trainer, he has the final word. If he ever finds a reason to keep her from the horses, she expects that no fight will ever be harder.

*

The only other garden in her life had been a hard-scrabble plot of potatoes, squash, and beans her mama had called the Patch. Like the patches on a dress, or a bandage on a wound, the Patch had helped her family make do. "Garden" was strictly a Sunday word, when Mamaw told of a garden where the People had once lived. In the People's Garden, things grew but did not die; fruits ripened but did not rot; birds soared high and never flew down. That was before the soldiers came and forced many to walk the Trail of Tears.

The Rose Garden had looked nothing like Mamaw's Garden, just a straggly mess of thorns and branches heaped onto itself, taking on the attitude of wild roses that grew everywhere back home. Mamaw had burned and hacked at them, white, flat-petaled foreigners that smothered all natives within reach, as determined in her efforts as the roses were to spread. As long as she kept at them, the roses respected the lines she drew. But the Rose Garden roses had been small and pink, with raised petals and a delicate scent. Yet left untended, even those had grown wild, although they had never spread beyond their plot. The trampled soil around its edges had held no promise for growth.

Calling that mess a Rose Garden had made as much sense as calling the Stables a speakeasy; between the loud music and even louder voices, speaking had been far from easy. But much about the Stables back then had made no sense. Still, someone had loved it enough to pace its plot, scratch loose the dirt, and plant its roses in a ring. Someone had thought to place it out of casual view, out back near the Big Willow. Someone had sought shelter inside its thorny crown, taking solace from sweet blossoms with their wide-open faces. Why someone would abandon it and why it was still called a garden long after its time had puzzled her to no end. Gardens were tended to, not abandoned to their own wild reach.

Mamaw had tended gardens that she and Papaw raised in the bottomland they once owned. Papaw had had his own farm, part of what his grandfather from across the sea had claimed, clearing trees, burning stumps, and piling endless rocks into tiny mountains. More than just a Patch, their garden had supplied everything they could imagine. Mamaw even had flowers—purple iris in the spring, daylilies all summer, and best of all, fall chrysanthemums she had taught herself how to pinch back and fertilize for hardy blooms later on.

"Our circle was unbroken," Mamaw used to say. "We were not plagued by restlessness; we knew no want. If the Bible hadn't already claimed it, I'd say we lived in Eden."

But the War came, and Papaw, who swore he'd never fight for some rich man's cause, was taken off by gray-clothed soldiers and never came back. Mamaw moved back to Snowbird and the People, waiting for her child to come, surrendering their garden to the wildness from which it had sprung.

"Why don't you grow that Garden now?" Viney would ask.

"Such things as in that Garden don't grow here," was all Mamaw would say.

Perhaps for the same hidden causes Mamaw had hinted at, the Rose Garden was never revived. A fallen place, it could never be tended back to its original glory.

*

He plays songs about love, and they make her laugh. What does she know about love? His saxophone purrs late into the night, when dancers drink from glasses empty for hours or cling to each other on the smoky dance floor that sighs under the shuffle of their high-steppin shoes. Earlier that night, his sax spat fast, tight notes that put the dancers in a panic. She doesn't understand why they want to move like that, as if their houses are on fire, keeping time to the same restless rhythms they hear in city streets. But these love songs, rolling from the sax's bellflower mouth, tease her into their dark embrace. What does she know about love?

His name is King, and he isn't from any place particular, though his disappearing t's and lazy a's conjure her daddy's Low Country drawl. He's got the same dark skin that shines blue-black in the moonlight. She likes it best in that light, when he takes a break from the band and steps out into the summer night. While the rest of the band smokes grass in the doorjamb, she and King slip outside, back beyond the dance floor to the Rose Garden. She laughs when he stands there kissing her like the slow, round notes that have been kissing her all night. And she laughs when he tells her he plays only for her. He says the city slummers wouldn't know love if it split their sorry heads in two. But what does she know about love?

Every time she gets down on her knees to squeeze between the rosebushes, she wonders what other man would crawl after her, let thorns snag his clean white shirt and scrape his slicked-down scalp.

"Some garden," he says. "I seen weeds better looking than this old heap." And then he kisses her, bellflower slow, as if to prove again how much she's worth it. Even she can't quite reckon it: kneeling in dirt, crawling through thorns, just to tangle themselves together so she can't tell where her skin ends and his begins.

*

The Big Willow's branches swayed just beyond where she knelt, tracing in the dust the upside down U's that circled her. Overhead, an airplane lowered its landing gear among stars blinded by street lamps. Air conditioners buzzed and brakes squealed in the distance as traffic lights at Illinois and Central blinked in mindless rhythm. But inside the circle nothing spoke, too deep in its darkness to show the shadows that claimed it.

Raising up, she paced out the circle, remembering the soft grass it had once held inside its thorns, not prairie thatch nor bluegrass, but a fine, light blade top heavy with seed. "Our circle was unbroken," she whispered to the night. But now, nothing but broken. Shadows chained together against the light, against anything that might bring back what had once rooted in this dust.

*

Other bands have played on the Stable's stage, but King and his players play hard, like their lives depend on making just the right sounds. Their music speaks in a secret code that makes her want to stop and think, or shake it all off, answer with shoulders, hips, or belly. The last thing she is supposed to do is stop serving, clearing, and cleaning, and call back to those sounds. So she keeps doing what she's supposed to, only now to their rhythms, mindful of their pauses, caught up in the sway of her hips as she picks up one glass and puts down another.

From the beginning, King catches on right away to her moves. While he plays, he stares out from under smooth eyebrows while urging her on with his own hips and chest. After a few nights of this, he calls her over to bring him some water. He lifts the sweating glass from her hand like an eggshell, then tips his head back. Water streams into his mouth.

"Ahhh," he sighs, licking his lips. "Best water I ever set my lips to."

Her lips turn up to meet his smile before she knows what is happening. For the next few days, he asks her for more. Each time he takes a little longer to drink, edging closer towards the back door where the rest of the band stands between sets. Before she knows it, she has forgotten about serving, clearing and cleaning. And, it seems, so has everybody else. The music has made them all forget.

*

Back then, she would have gladly left the Rose Garden to its tangles. Its flowers couldn't feed her, nor did its chest-high bowers offer any shelter. It certainly lacked the prolific order of Mamaw's long-lost garden. The fact that others had still called it a garden had not been enough to tempt her into its thorns, until one night, weak cries deep inside had startled her. Dropping to her knees, she had crawled in the dirt until a small opening had appeared. Six calico kittens, eyes barely opened, had squirmed in the tall, seed-heavy grass that formed a circle around them.

Stretched out on her belly, she had watched their mouths struggle open and closed, their tiny bodies quivering as they mewed. Overhead, the rangy branches had reached over themselves, forming a canopy that shielded them all from view. The grass inside, especially tender for having never been cut, had cushioned her chore-weary head and whispered her to sleep. Had the morning dew and horse flies not found her, she might have slept the whole day through.

She could have never tended that garden, as Mamaw and Papaw had tended theirs, as the People had their own. She could not recover what had never been hers. And had she tried, she might have lost the only place where she could finally hear, in the kittens' cries, in the grass's green breath, in the aching arms of the roses, her first and only true name, the one that no one but her Daddy had dared to speak.

Kneeling now again in the dust where the roses had once grown, she remembered their thorny love circling her heart, each beat piercing more deeply, until the distance between where her heart ended and the thorns began finally disappeared. She remembered, too, the pause between one beat and another, one thorn and another. Without that pause, the thorns could never have held her as closely as they did.

Reaching from her knees, she traced and retraced the *U's* that marked where the Rose Garden had ended and where it had begun, calling out their sounds as her finger followed them deeper into the dirt. Calling and drawing, dirt drifting into air, until the distance between dirt and *U*, garden and shadow, then and now, dream and daylight, dissolved in the threshold between the thoroughbreds' fire and their shadows, reaching back into a world long departed yet still reflected within their flickering eyes.

*

She and King lay together, face-to-face in the grass. Sweetness from the roses surrounds them, at least until the next set begins, or the band drives off in their rusty model T, barreling toward another backroom or basement where gin freely flows. The grass is cool with dew. He likes to rub his face in its long blades like a cat, loosening the sweat and smoke on his skin. She likes how the grass makes him smell like green hay, a scent that lingers long after he has gone.

He teases her about bringing him here, where he has to crouch like a dog to miss the thorns. But he says he doesn't mind going low so long as she goes, too.

"You better not mind. No place else to go," she says.

"Where you sleep?" he asks.

"No place you want to," is all she tells him.

"Why won't you come away with me?" he asks, like he does every time he returns.

"Ain't no room," she always answers, but that's not why she won't go. Not that there is any room in the Model T, though King has said he'd buy his own wheels and drive her wherever she wanted. If only she'd leave the Stables, that "plantation-come-north," he calls it, she'd be free to roam, live out of a suitcase, see the country. Instead, she makes him take to his knees every time he wants to see her.

"You mighty cruel," he says, running a finger between her eyebrows.

When this makes her laugh, he groans like a beast then pins her shoulders to the ground. Crouched above her, he rolls his eyes back and barks like the mad dog she is always telling him he is. When she holds her hand up over his mouth, he tries to bite it, then, with a sigh, falls onto his back.

"I don't expect you ever pull yourself up." His tone starts as a tease but falls off quickly. They both hear it. They've argued this before. He tells her that working for the Man, eating his food, sleeping under his roof, will get her nowhere. A new day has come, but to taste its heady brew, she's got to break free.

"Maybe so," she says, tucking her head under his chin, a gesture both sweet and stubborn. She feels his eyes on the back of her neck. He has scolded her before for living low like a slave. "You ever hear of a house girl? Massuh piss on the floor then make you smile when you wipe it up. Give you that fancy uniform so his eyes got something to feed on when his hands too busy with other things. Next thing you know, him or one of them slummers find a reason. No, boss ain't about to save your ass. Fact is, he think it good for business."

What she knows about slaves is even less than she does love. Her daddy never knew that life, though he said his daddy did, but he was long gone by the time she came around. And her mama's family never knew it at all. In the hollows above Rabun Gap, people didn't talk much about it, and when they did, they blamed the big plantations. Hill people like them didn't need all those slaves. They took pride that that shame had not stained them. She learned not to ask how her daddy's daddy could be from those parts and have lived his younger years belonging to someone else.

King can't help but tell her about living low: picking cotton his family did not own, sleeping in a shotgun shack with two rooms, five pegs on the wall, one for each person to hang his clothes, and newspapers pasted over the split log walls to keep out the cold. He tells her this with a catch in his throat, as if he still loves what he now says he hates. The hate pours out

*when he comes to the swamps where he sometimes hid at night to avoid
being strung up and left for crow bait.*

*"No manhood there," he has said. "The minute you start feeling it,
they come looking to cut it out."*

*In his half-formed teeth, she sees a small boy still running, afraid to
let his manhood catch up. She wonders what if she told him the truth, that
she doesn't know about slaves but she does know living low, low enough to
hear worms turn in the ground, to smell possum breath in the dead of night.
That for her, there is no other way, which is why she sleeps in a hayloft
instead of the Stables' attic, where she has her own bed and washstand.
That living low means she can only find her rest in horses' breath below her,
their dreams tangling with hers. That she cannot leave them, having
traveled so far to answer their call. That life in a "horseless carriage" is no
life at all. That for her, living low is living.*

*But she also knows that until she met King, she was just alive.
Before now she could not see the steady twists in her life without his restless
leaps to show her the shape hers was taking.*

*"Maybe so," he says, softly mocking her words. He kisses the soft
spot on her skull where Mama told her Spirit entered the body and where,
when the time came, would leave again.*

*She holds him down there to let him know his manhood has finally
caught him.*

*

The steel door creaked open, just wide enough for spit to fly
through and join the cigarette butts scattered on the ground. Brown fingers
grasped edges that now softened in moonlight. Lucky for them, the dew had
only begun to collect itself, the night air still moist with intent. Lucky, too,
that tonight the door had opened when on most other nights it locked them
in.

The fingers retreated as the small brown men slid out carefully,
hugging the wall, careful to temper the hinges' squeal as they moved. Backs
hunched and feet shuffling, they raised their hands to their eyes, careful to
avoid the security light, wary of any shadows other than their own. Then, in
the trampled dirt, they kicked up cigarette butts, gathering them in open
palms, pinching likely prospects like fruit.

Brushing the dirt from her knees, she stood to greet them. Startled,
they drew back, huddling closer together, a knife point between them
glinting in some distant source of light. Inside her apron pocket, keys
clanged together, answering the knife's fierce edge. As she fingered the
keys, their sounds unfolded the men's hunched backs, sorting their shuffles
into steps that closed the distance between her feet and theirs.

Their voices picked up where her keys had left off, rolling notes that raced past her ears. All three she knew by sight, a few among the dozens of back door hires who'd passed through years of scraping and rinsing, cleaning grease traps, pouring water, and filling ice bins for meal time rush. They had seen her, and she them, but like shadows, they had stayed within their own dark worlds. The one holding the knife bore scars on his face: pock marks that the moonlight carved out in rough craters. The knife she recognized as Mildred's, razor thin, with a fine point good for scraping delicate fat from veal and liberating sole from its spine. Moonlight told the story of those marks and that night, but what finally came to her mind were the gashes that marked the keyhole inside like a pox. She realized then that moonlight was nothing new to men who picked locks with stolen knives.

The voices dropped from three to one, heading straight towards her inside the circle of *U*'s. One man pointed, first at her, then back at himself. "Sue numb ray," she heard him say.

She shook her head and shrugged. "What you want?" she asked. Whenever Mildred needed pots cleaned or ice hauled, she spoke her own tongue. Servers were split on whether the small brown men understood English, but Mildred dismissed that question. "If they want to work here, they understand," she'd say. "It ain't just words they be tending to."

The man pointed back and forth again. "Sure nome bray," he said. "Quaint oz." He pointed to the man on his right: "Robe-air-toe." He pointed to his left: "On-hello." He pointed to himself: "Gober-all." He pointed back at Viney: "Yew stud?"

Her teeth parted, leaving an easy gap between them, and her lips curled up in the corners. "Baby Divine," she answered. She almost laughed out loud; it had been that long since she'd heard those exact sounds.

"Bobby Dee Vayen." All three pointed at her, wagging their heads.

The security light switched on, freezing them in the light. They scanned the dark for signs of life, but only a few leaves danced in wind that had picked up as they spoke.

"Say it again." She held her hand to her ear and leaned forward.

"Viewest row numb ray Bobby Dee Vayen."

"Yes," she said, her eyelids drifting down, small slits of brown light filtering through. Inside their small brown dreams she was more than herself, more than them, more than the threshold between them. Inside the Rose Garden, the small brown men were more than themselves, more than the soil that nurtured wherever they stood. The keys in her apron pocket sang to the men's departure, until they disappeared altogether into the Big Willow's arms.

When they returned, hugging brown paper sacks just as she'd imagined, they opened a can and passed it over the *U's* that stood between her and them. Her fingers wrapped around *Pabst Blue Ribbon*. Old Golds stood up inside their cellophane name and offered themselves to the Stables matches the four of them held out for each other. Inside her apron pocket, keys jingled as she searched for the Bun candy bar she'd saved all day. She held out her hand for the knife that would slice its tawny roundness into four particular bites.

*

The players groan and moan and suck their teeth when she passes. They crowd the doorjamb so she has to brush against them when she wants to go outside.

"I smell chicken," says Chester. His right eye drifts up to his skull whenever he gets excited.

"Chicken dinner being served," Hines replies. When he plays horn, his cheeks get so big they almost explode.

Lou and Gizzard sniff the air, noses roaming as close as her neck. "Here, chick, chick," they sing, one low and mellow, one brassy high.

She hasn't yet gotten used to being looked at. While the slummers pretend they're not staring when they are, the band boys go wild like she's put a spell on them. Their bloodshot eyes float in clouds of smoke.

"You junkies back off," King interrupts. "This ain't no chicken, this here a Queen. Mind yourselves."

This makes them all laugh til they start choking. Hands fly out, elbows knock against her chest, and she is stuck until they straighten up and let her pass.

"Queen, he says." Hines won't let her go. He rubs his cheek against hers so slow and smooth that King stops laughing. "More like kitten, King Man."

"Here, kitty, kitty," Lou and Gizzard sing, still in tune.

"He looking for a Queen for his King but he done found himself a kitten instead," Chester says, shaking his head like the worst has come to pass.

"Robbing the cradle, man," Hines says, rocking arms bent at the elbow.

She hopes they'll tire of this game after the first few trips through the back door. But they like it more each time she passes, as much as they like the sharp, weedy smoke from the fat rolls they pinch between their thumbs and first fingers.

"Give me some of that," she demands, grabbing Chester's wrist. He almost drops the roll. King grabs her wrist just as she's ready to take in a deep drag of smoke. Lou and Gizzard's laughter jumps up ten notches.

"He don't want the Queen to meet Mr. Gauge and blow," Hines keeps jabbering. "Don't you think the Queen can decide for herself? Your Royal Highness, what is your pleasure?"

Chester bows his head below her waist, holding up another roll.

She stares at King's hand on her wrist, then into his eyes, bloodshot like the others. He smokes as much as they do. She can tell when he has just had some; his hands drift like a lazy river, and he moves as if he has all the time in the world. He must see the question in her eyes because he drops his hand and turns his head away.

Lou and Gizzard keep up a chorus of "Ooos" until King waves them off and they stop. She takes the roll and sniffs it, once. The smoke enters her nose and mouth before she can take the next breath. She hears its voice, high-pitched like sunshine, sees its body, full of colors: blue, orange, yellow, green. It curls inside her throat like a cat with claws out and burns inside her nose. On the middle of her tongue she tastes moldy hay.

She hands the roll back to Chester, who right away draws on it. "That weed got designs on you," she says. They laugh so hard, even King, that Chester drops the roll. She doesn't return their laughter. She doesn't tell them what the plant told her.

Later in the Rose Garden, King won't look at her straight on. When he buries his head full of shiny, slick hair between her jawbone and neck, she feels him deep in her spine. She presses down hard on his shoulders so he will give all his weight over to her. But she has already spied his shackles through the smoke.

*

Long after her companions had gone inside for the night, she stayed in the circle, retracing the *U*'s, unable to stop her finger from touching those shapes as they crowded close around her. The deeper she drew, the closer they came, until the distance between them had all but disappeared. Their open mouths cupped her as she poured herself inside; her single, pointed finger inscribed them ever more deeply into the ruined soil. *Without hope or expectation. Surrender to lost, finger its shadow. One shapes the other.*

The keys in her pocket jingle as she moves; she moves to their jingling; they call back and forth, and as they call, the dew gathers on grass far from their reach, answering with its growing buds of wet that bend the blades. Blind stars blink their answers from behind the streetlight's fog, invisible pulses that the keys cannot ignore. When dawn bleeds fire over surrounding rooftops, hoof beats answer the throb in her chest, pounding until the distance between their thunder and hers has dissolved, and her skin is the ground on which they tread, and their hoof beats the force through which her skin must cut to be whole.

In the pause between thorn and flesh, that threshold of what is and is not, the thoroughbreds have been waiting, but until now she could not touch them without risking their flight. Bred to run at the slightest touch of a whip, they did not know how to stop running when flames answered their calls to be set free. Running was breath; running was muscle; running was the only way they knew to reach the pauses that told them they were alive. Every last thing deserved to know its own life. Despite hope. Despite desire. Despite the flies that circled what has fallen, dreams too distant to be claimed as dreams.

She knew they could not help but run; it was what they knew to do. She was their pause. She held the circle, remembering the thorns and the petals, and the shadows that showed the way. While they ran, she held their thunder as they reached for the silence that brought their memories back to life.

*

In July, the roses lose their blooms, too hot to form new buds. In the back room at night, only slow tunes get danced to. Inside the Rose Garden, their dance eases, too, now that their rhythms have merged. What used to require big, swift strokes to find the sweet spots in their play now takes the lightest touch: tongue tip on jawbone, pinkie curled over open lips.

She never knows where King goes when he leaves. They never talk about him staying. As soon as Hines blows the car horn, he crawls out of the Rose Garden and jumps onto the running board as the motor car grinds off down the drive. She isn't even sure he sleeps. He talks about joints on 35th and State that never close their doors.

"You got to come hear these jim-jam-jumping cats play," he begs her. "And when all the slummers and homeys wore out, they ask me to jam with them." He cannot go a night without playing.

"Got to give them their fix," King grins. "Gin they got most anywhere, but only the Stables and the Sunset Café got the Hopdog Five."

She cannot go a night without horses. Secure above the sleeping thoroughbreds, she is content when King leaves. But back inside the Stables, by day scrubbing floors he walked on, wiping down walls where his smoke still lingers, washing glasses that his lips may have touched, the restlessness of his rhythms overtakes her. As she empties Barnwell's chamber pot, scrapes soot-scarred pans in the kitchen, bleaches lipstick kisses from white napkins, the memory of his notes pierce every pore, accepting nothing less than surrender.

He still asks her will she go away with him, but now he says it as if he has all the time in the world, and she the same to answer. And even when she tells him no, he still seems content.

"You know you hooked," he drawls. "I know it because I can feel it in me, and if I can feel it in me, then I know it's in you. You hooked, baby girl."

She has grown so used to his ways that some mornings when she sneaks up to her attic room to wash, she sees his eyes in the cracked glass that is her mirror. She can't get away from his eyes following her around, and she doesn't want to. Back home she never stared like that at herself, not intending to look as much as just catching a flash of eyes, teeth, and hair in a still part of a creek or pond. But with King's eyes staring out through hers, she cannot help but look.

Beloved, it is his whole self, not just the sights, sounds, and smells of him, but the insides of all that, his skin alive inside hers. She inhales his heady sweetness, revels in the senseless beauty of those sounds that keep reaching, reaching, reaching, arching over themselves in a joyful heap, pausing only for the next long breath, without hope of ever untangling.

"I hear you," she whispers, pointing to her chest. He sighs, lays his head down where she has pointed. That his music is inside her seems enough to last the night.

A storm rolls in one night, its thunder exploding in time with the Hopdog Five's beat. She roams the back room with a tray full of empty glasses, lightning lighting up the pasture through the open door out back.

She never knew a place could get this hot. Mildred says Mississippi is ten times hotter than this. But then there is the cold. "You think this hot, just wait til the cold," Mildred says. "Wind like to freeze your tongue, shut your eyes with ice. Snow pile up higher than a motor car."

Between sets, the band stays inside. At the first break, they crowd into a corner where lamplight barely reaches. But Barnswell sees them, grabs hold of Chester's elbow, and steers them towards slummers who pass silver flasks their way. "Good for business," Barnswell tells King, slapping him a little too hard on the back.

King's mouth curls down as Barnswell hand-shakes his way across the room. Once Barnswell's black coat disappears, King fixes his eyes on her. Thunder shakes the walls so hard that lamp shades scatter shadows on the ceiling. Before she can answer, some city women circle him, cigarettes drooping from long black holders. King smiles at them, but his jaw is throbbing. The women laugh, their arms stretching out towards him. The quieter he gets, the closer they come, restless moths to his bright flame.

Those silky women, draped in velvet and fringe, drop their heads back to bare necks and laugh from deep in their throats, hungry laughs that cut and cry. But she cannot keep standing there with a tray full of empty glasses. She fixes her eyes on King. He loosens his tie and wipes his brow. His eyes narrow like a cat before it hisses. The women crowd closer still.

She disappears quickly into the kitchen to rid herself of her load, hoping Mildred won't notice the lightning flashes in her eyes.

After the second set, the storm has eased, but the rain stays steady, drumming hard overhead. Barnswell tells King to join him in the Wine Room. King waves over the other players, but Barnswell cuts him off. Just King. Hines, Chester, Lou and Gizzard don't hide their frowns. King nods at them slowly, like a very old man, then follows Barnswell out of the room. Barnswell cocks his head for her to follow.

King is so tall he has to hunch through the doorway. In his spotless suit and stiff white collar, he makes Barnswell's guests look like they slept all night still dressed. Hovering over the others' pie-dough faces, King's shines coal bin black. Next to their potbelly waists, his is whip lean.

"Good sound," the guests say to King. "Where'd you get your style?"

Her starched white apron whispers against her thighs. King won't look at her, even when he hands him a glass of bourbon. His eyes can't find a place to settle. Inside this sealed-off room, within the amber light of glass-beaded lamps, she and King are strangers.

The smell of leather is strong: shelves of bound books; chair and sofa; a riding whip laid at the base of a lamp. Thick, soft rugs absorb their voices. It is cooler here than other rooms. She feels air stirring but can't locate the source. The room is otherwise sealed tight. Even thunderclaps are muffled. But somehow the air keeps moving, the way it did deep inside up country caves, where no wind could possibly follow. Her mama had never heard of such a thing, but Mamaw knew. She said even caves have to breathe, and when air outside fails them, they find it deep within.

Ash breaks loose from a big, fat cigar and falls to the rug. The mustached man holding the cigar keeps on talking. Barnswell jerks his chin at her. She bends over before the rug's wool is scorched.

As she straightens up, a yellow-haired man, the youngest-looking one among them, says, "Do that again." The cigar-smoker raises his brows, then grins big like a boy with his hand in the honey pot.

She feels before she sees King's body tense and twitch all over. Barnswell busies himself with a squat, gray man who has already gulped his first bourbon and now helps himself to a second. The cigar man takes a long, slow draw, drops his head back, and blows a stream of smoke that bounces back off the low ceiling. Then he flicks the drooping ash and grins again.

She breathes in slowly, inviting his smoke into her lungs, letting it travel up and out her nose. It speaks of sea breezes and salt air, of soft hands and strange rhythms. Her mouth waters. Then the faintest scent of scorched wool finds her nostrils and quickly fades. The smoke falls silent.

Tomorrow she will take Barnswell's mustache scissors and trim the burn, brush it out with a whisk broom. But for now, she turns to check the bourbon. The bottle is almost empty.

"Gal." The yellow-haired man's voice stretches the "a" long and hard. She empties the last of the bourbon into the squat man's glass then reaches into the liquor cabinet for another bottle of Kentucky Gold.

The dull throb of rain overhead comes to a halt. She unfolds the small knife Barnswell keeps in the cabinet and eases its blade, no longer than her thumb, around the bottle's throat. Once the seal is broken, she lays down the knife and starts picking off the wax.

When she was a small girl, she plugged her daddy's moonshine jugs with corks while he sealed them with beeswax. He never let her open those seals.

"Once you open them bottles, you let fly all kind of things. Once it's open, it's out there for good."

Mamaw added that that brew was called spirits for a reason. "Good or bad, they take over if you don't take care."

Once the neck is clean, she picks up the knife, stabs it into the cork, then twists hard. She glances at King, whose chest pumps as if about to explode, the way it does when his music climbs so high she doesn't see how he can ever get down. The difference now is that he is climbing hard, like he's pushing a big stone ahead of him.

"I'm talking to you, gal," the yellow-haired man snarls. This time Barnswell stops and turns, head jerking back and forth across the study. The yellow-haired man points at her while he says to Barnswell in a familiar drawl, "Is all your hired help this uppity?"

Barnswell's collarbone rises, threatening to bust out of his shirtwaist, one of a dozen he sends to Chicago every week to be cleaned and pressed to an inch of its life. "I beg your pardon?" he asks. His eyebrows squeeze together so close it looks like they are one. Barnswell's big belly and height cast large shadows over the younger man's thin gold shine

The yellow-haired man's voice catches just a little. "I told her to clean that up." He points to the ash near the cigar-smoker's shoe. "I'm just looking out for you."

"Indeed." Barnswell squints at the yellow-haired man then down at the floor, curling his lip. "Gentleman, if I may, please permit me to direct you to the ash tray." He turns back to his conversation with the squat man, whose lips have frozen in a pucker.

But the yellow-haired man won't give up. "It's your place to lose," he says. "You think you're the only game in town? I've got news for you, B.G. I know you're in up to your neck. You haven't had a winner yet, and you've got just one prospect coming up. On top of that, the Oak Lawn track deal fell through, so now you have to drive your stable all the way to Hawthorne. Who do you think is going to keep you afloat?"

Barnswell's face turns from ash to blood. The squat man clicks his tongue sympathetically. "Shelman, this is a sporting man's club, not a trading floor. You're welcome to stay if you share our passion for the track. If not, T.J. will be happy to bring your car around." Barnswell's chest falls back to normal size. Pointing to her, he says, "Viney, kindly take care of our guest's miscalculation."

Instead of bending over, this time she crouches low, out of the yellow-haired man's reach. In the cigar-smoker's shoes she can see her face, blurry like a ghost's. The only sound in her ears is of her fingers scratching the rug, hunting for gray ash, then patting down what little is left behind. The rug returns her pat with its soft wool. King's eyes draw hers with their fire, tell her she is supposed to care. Even if, like him, she doesn't say a word, only chews her lip and tenses her chest, she is still supposed to want to refuse. She is supposed to be afraid, answer like horses when the whip strokes their flanks. She is not supposed to want to be low.

For a moment, the crash she hears is just the storm returning. But when the light dims, and she looks up to see King's hands squeezing yellow-hair's neck from pale to purple, she knows this storm is inside, and she is in its middle.

She stays low, as she always has during storms, the soft rug and the ground below it receiving her crouch. Looking up, the men are all giants, too large to notice what calls from below, too fixed on the lines each wants to draw to notice anything but what might cross them. From her crouch, King seems perhaps biggest of them all, as he puffs up his chest and presses forward against the air. When he looks again at her, his eyes call out for her to follow.

His throat strains with the roar that twists his mouth. Before the other men gather their wits to stop him, he releases yellow-hair, now choking, to the rug, to his ashy stain. King doesn't look at her as the Wine Room door flies open from his giant's touch. But she can see amber beads turn to water on his cheeks before he begins to run.

*

She remembers that night; she stayed in her attic room for the first time since she arrived. The storm had passed, but she wanted only human breath around her, to sleep on cloth instead of hay, as King would have her do. Like the cat who resettled her brood in the barn, she wanted to stay among her own kind for a while. Later in her dreams, he is running; he is running because she stays still. She stays still because he runs. What she sees in his running is his stillness, the pause in his breath that gives his breath shape. What she sees in her stillness is her running, the movement that molds to the stillness that holds it. If this is love, then she will race to hold it close, as close as the dream of him racing to be still.

Chapter Six: Laundry

For days I did not see him. Unseen from the front door, absent in the kitchen, he seemed to have simply vanished. Until then, I had paid little attention to his comings and goings. Perhaps he had always been so invisible? Then my desire took over, conjuring hopeful fantasies: He was waiting for me, in that small, airless room, hoping I would find him.

In the contours of his desires I found my own. I fell in love with the spread of my hips, the slope of my back, the freckles that littered my arms and face then stopped suddenly at my shoulders where my breasts poised, pale, mounded with pink nipples like tongues. I marveled at the eruption of red-gold hair where my thighs met, and wondered if other women's mounds were as thick and dense as mine. I savored the unlikely scent of wild onions and baby powder under my arms. I loved my legs with stubble; I loved them smooth and slick with scented lotion. I loved the yellow crusts of sleep in my eyes when I woke, flicking them away with a tender hand. What was previously repulsive, embarrassing, untidy, unclean was now a source of fascination, a mark of individuality. What was once attractive was still attractive, only now because of, not in spite of, its flaws: one hip riding slightly higher than the other, one breast a little lower, one eye a little droopier, teeth a little more crooked than the cover girl look I'd come to assume as my ideal. The mirror became my lover.

If only the mirror had been enough. I could have stood before it for hours, locked away in my parents' house late at night, exploring all he had revealed. But of course, the mirror could not shape itself around the curve of my neck, the arch of my thigh. It could not show me how to feel what I felt: shapes, contours, textures; shades of light and dark and all tones in between.

I could imagine the delight that Joan and her Star Dust crowd would take if they knew. Maybe what I wanted wasn't so different than them, but I wasn't about to tell them, even if it meant I would have to beg for steak knives from their secret stashes or take their late tables for the rest of the summer, pay back for keeping myself a mystery to them.

I eavesdropped on Mildred and listened for T.J. to whistle for him, waiting for clues, watching for signs. Was Mildred fixing his special plate or Opal letting loose some idle gossip to Sarah, or even Rose glaring at me with special intent? Just when I was almost exhausted from all the guessing, one afternoon Joan called me into the bus station that doubled as her office.

I sidestepped the overloaded bus tray on the verge of avalanche as she handed me my next week's schedule. Bored, or maybe just tired, her blue eyes stayed flat and disinterested.

"I know I'm late," she said. "That's why the hand delivery."

From behind the service bar Rose snorted and fussed about some drink order gone wrong. Schedule in hand, I stood silently facing Joan. A few seconds passed before Joan glanced up from her scribbling, one penciled eyebrow arched. The steamy kitchen had soaked me with sweat, but inside the bus station I was chilly. I rubbed my bare arms, shivering.

I didn't know his last name; I had no idea where he lived, where he'd gone to high school. I obviously didn't know his schedule. My own was so erratic--split shifts on some weekdays, sometimes a Saturday night, mostly Sunday afternoons when old folks came for bargain dinners—that he'd never figure mine out. I ached from my own ignorance. In that moment I was certain Joan knew everything. But as I started to form a question, I suddenly doubted she knew anything.

Ice cubes clinked in the cooler below me on my right. The Bunn coffee maker burped a halo of bitter steam behind her. Surely anything I asked would seem a mere match flame compared to the bonfire that was Joan's life. *No big deal*, she'd shrug. *Happens all the time.* That in itself was a scary thought. Did everyone at the Stables eventually find themselves haunting the margins of the permissible? It depressed me to think that my life, too, could be that desperate.

My eyes returned to the schedule in my hands. She'd copied it for me on ruler-lined paper, the kind that left confetti edges when ripped out of spiral notebooks. I'd used them from high school to freshman year in college, when I discovered legal pads and their precise perforations. Below the coffee pot, the black curtain that concealed extra coffee filters and foil packets of Perry Brothers coffee stirred slightly as Joan turned back to the schedule in her hands. The soft folds behind her sturdy legs reminded me of the confessional booth at St. Albans, its dark fabric muffling penitent voices and penances thus proffered. The dim walls of the bus station similarly urged me to confess: his slow mouth; the rhythm of his hand; his soft, buoyant hair. Confess, and she would absolve me.

"Joan?" Her face stayed as flat as the oil paintings that littered the Stable's walls. A mask, it had settled, unlike that rare night at the Star Dust.

"Hm?" She stared past me to Rose, whose snorts had transformed into baby talk. She had a thing for the salesman from Lundi liquors. I had pitied her, old and faded, flirting with a man maybe half her age until I overheard Delores comment on a new outfit and hairstyle Rose was wearing one Saturday night. "I'd dress sharp if I took kickbacks, too," she sneered. Coming from Delores, who cached steak knives and napkins, I was at first skeptical. Then again, who would know better? It wasn't the first time I'd confused flirtation with business.

"Do you know--" I didn't know what I wanted. His phone number? She'd tell me to ask Mrs. Parkerhouse, who of course would be wary of releasing that information. Somehow I hoped that, with a wink and a nod, Joan would know what I wanted without saying so.

"Darlin, come on over here," Rose called out. "This boy think he got something you want."

Joan's glance pierced me as she murmured, "Later." The bus station collapsed into darkness. My skin was pimpled with goosebumps from standing so long in the cold. The dining rooms were always at least twenty degrees cooler than the kitchen. The trick was to keep moving in the dining rooms, then creep slowly around the kitchen to preserve the cool, while at the same trying hard to look unrushed in the one and busy in the other.

Steam smacked my face as swinging doors gave way to the kitchen. I shivered again, the chill fleeing my skin. I willed myself invisible, counting on clanking dishes, hot clouds of spray, spoons banging against pots, humming refrigerators, and hurricane fans to conspire with me. Loose-limbed, eyes straight ahead, I strode towards the bleached scent of clean.

I was working a split shift that day, so I had a built-in excuse to visit the laundry room: I'd need clean napkins for dinner prep. The blinds to Mrs. Parkerhouse's office were half way open and the lights were on. I was tempted to peek inside to see if I could spot her and add my own story of a sighting to the gossip pool. Instead I slipped inside the laundry room before anyone inside the office noticed. Heat from the dryers hit me full force, a sudden shift from tropics to desert. This time, the hot air proved so stifling I could barely breathe. A chemical cloud burned my nose and lungs.

I knew I could, at least momentarily, interrupt the cleaning cycle. Surely he had had a similar thought when he called me inside that day. I could switch on the fan, pull the dryer doors ajar and halt the washing machine's hollow chug. For a moment. That's all we'd need. We hadn't known, that day, that's all it was, an interruption. The cleaning would go on as before, savaging any bit of food, skin, saliva, the wastes and residues of the body and all that nourished it, drowned, broken, bleached, scorched, and pressed back into shape for another round of use. The mechanisms were in place to wash us out of each other's lives for good.

I closed the door, all the way this time, and locked it. I reached behind my neck for the zipper pull and listened to plastic teeth part the track that bound them. The metal hooks and eyes of my bra unclasped and fell to the cement floor in a heap. My fingers slid along my hips, under the elastic band that held my panty hose close, and pushed it down to my knees. I stepped out of my cloddy nurse's shoes, one slow foot at a time, and released those empty outlines of my legs to the floor. Standing in the heat without anything between me and it, I felt its full weight upon me. Awful as it was, even the heat had its limits.

My eyes watered from the chemical air. Hot and stagnant, it clutched my head in its vise. In one moment, moist heat pulsed from the washer; in another, my pores shrank from the dryer's hot breath. Sweat beaded my chest and dripped down my forehead and nose. I breathed deeply, taking in the sour food, the burning air, the relentless motion of the cleaning machines. I felt suddenly, inexplicably tired. A pile of soiled tablecloths offered itself for rest. Napkins flung themselves against the dryer's glass porthole like doves in a storm. I watched them rise and fall in the darkness within. The washing machine hissed then shook, in the last throes of its final spin. I listened as it bumped and squeaked against the floor, grew dizzy as the napkins rose and fell purposelessly inside the dryer's single eye. My ears started to buzz.

Had I come to be cleansed? The mechanisms of renunciation were fully in place. No coincidence, then, that our first real touch had taken place here, the only place either of us knew to go. There had to be other places, but we had had no way of knowing where those might be. Who could we trust to help us when no one was supposed to know we were together? The irony was that probably everybody did.

I resisted laying down with the soiled linens. Instead, I drew circles in the sweat on my chest, licked salt from the soft hairs above my lips. As sweat rose up over my skin, it cooled me. I closed my eyes halfway as napkins inside the dryer flew across my vision. My eyes drifted, neither following nor resisting their soft movements. I breathed in bleached air and breathed out decay. I let go of the belief that I could, with the flip of a switch, stop all that had been set in motion before me even as I embraced it: the slow wrench in my lungs; fevered skin; machine pulse; clean and tidy; with the flip of a switch, automatic salvation.

Yet where did the torn, used-up, threadbare finally go? Who decided when it was time? Every time I passed, the laundry room was always empty of those hands that kept it going, even though the washer and dryer never stopped working.

My head started to swell. My bones melted until I was nothing but muscle and nerves. His touch low down my spine. The machines couldn't clean that. I pressed my hands to my head, feeling what he must have felt, the bush of curls a luscious tangle. Enough to get lost in, maybe for good. I traced the thin stem of my nose, its fleshy bulb and wide, horsy nostrils. I tongued my lips, thin and tender like new-born flesh. I cupped my breasts. Their compactness pleased me. I marveled at their soft, full underbellies, the convex slopes to my nipples, which swelled softly to their wrinkled peaks. Even the red flecks that my mother called birthmarks pleased me. I held each breast from below, assessing their weight, but unlike scales and other instruments, I felt rather than saw their true measure. I felt my hands as his. Their strange familiarity.

And then I reached below, between my legs, one soft layer, then another, slowly parting. One hand cupped within the other, fingers gliding. Without words, they knew where to go. Without sound, except my breath, to guide them. The washing machine bounced crazily against the cement floor, a distant, dull thud, water gurgling in the drain below. Heat that had pressed so hard against my temples suddenly broke out all over my body into voluptuous blooms of sweat. The napkins flapping in the dryer's eye ended their long flight.

From the fluorescent lights to the yellow stains on the walls to the iron that pointed its nose at the ceiling, everything in this small room was suddenly hungry for touch. Napkins lay·in quiet stacks waiting to be folded. The gingham-padded ironing board begged to be smoothed. The clock rimmed in black like a schoolteacher's eyeglasses ticked off seconds like a metronome. All sounds filtered against this steady, mechanical drone, even the abrupt jiggle and pop of the door handle, and the whoosh of sensations from the world beyond.

The world beyond. The world beyond. It had not occurred to me that someone might have a key to the door. I had thought that when I locked it, as I did my bedroom door at home, I had shut out the world. But as keys chimed and the handle rattled, I steeled myself, naked and alone, for the shame sure to come.

Even so, hope lingered that it was him who held the key, that sheer passion could conjure such serendipities. The key ring bristled as the door opened, the hand within brown and freckled, its grip firm but easy. My own hand reached out, palm up, the weight of all those keys and all they could open irresistible even as my eyes cast down, following a thin stream of the washer's foam as it swirled into the narrow floor drain.

My panting exchanged with her labored breath. She mumbled words like an incantation.

My hand reached out for the key ring, like the brass ring on a merry-go-round, the kind of thing I'd read about, but had never actually seen. I pictured my hand, freckled and bronzed from summer sun, inside that ring. Its bristly keys did not frighten me; passion made it possible to believe this woman, this large, lumbering woman, was holding them for me. Wasn't her hand as brown, maybe browner, than mine? Didn't we share the same freckles? And weren't those green eyes and red hair reflecting back my own? She was a much older, wiser, world-weary vision that held the keys to my future.

Pocketing the keys, she bent over, slowly, and grabbed a pile of clean napkins. She continued mumbling, nodding her head. Then the reality of her finally sank it. The reality of me, naked, flushed, and exposed, came crashing down on me. My hands fumbled to cover my genitals and breasts. But it was too late. She had seen it all.

Excuses rose readily to my lips, but her piercing green glance stopped all words from forming. And then she spoke.

"Bout time," she said. She turned to go.

The door closed as if from a great distance. The keys again angled, and the lock clicked back closed. In what wasn't said, I learned something about the order of the Stables that until now had seemed without order. At the core of my new-found passion had emerged a woman with green eyes and red hair pulled so tight she looked about to explode.

Chapter Seven: Lobby

Eight o'clock on a Saturday night, Lenny stood in the lobby, drenched and miserable, while Hal, the maitre d', glared from behind the front desk, and Billiard, busy on the phone, spoke in hushed, urgent tones. Al, the other maitre d', was nowhere in sight.

Rain plunged recklessly off the rim of Lenny's cap, his uniform soaked from the thunderstorm that was now pummeling the Stables' roof with hail the size of ice cubes. While water pooled around the new Florsheims he'd just spent two days' pay on, a piercing shriek penetrated the surrounding hush. The siren on top of the township building next door was working itself into another high-pitched wail before its shuddering collapse into silence. In response, the fringe on his epaulets swayed like hooked worms. His chest swelled with panic, and his breath grew shallow.

When hail had first hit the canopy where T.J. stood, dry but somber, Lenny had choked out, "What *is* this shit?" Now that question kept circling in his head. In all his 19 years, he'd given little notice to the natural world. Living in the city, he just stuck his head out the door to decide if it was a t-shirt or sweatshirt day, or in the winter, whether to dig out a coat or make a dash through the cold. The sky where he lived was squeezed out by three-flats, billboards, and street lights so tall they almost disappeared; he had to rely on his skin, nose and ears to judge what the weather might bring. Rain storms had once meant splashing shin deep in flooded curbs while some old person warned about getting sucked down open manholes. He didn't remember hail, only its winter cousin, sleet, that turned sidewalks into ice rinks for playing Slam the Man, a street version of hockey for kids with no skates, pucks, or sticks.

Back in '67 neighbors had stood around shaking their heads after big storms had torn through the suburbs that spring night. They had swapped stories about legs with skates still attached found under the rubble of a roller rink, and rows of ranch houses resembling Viet Cong villages after an air raid. The longer he listened, and the more Colt 45 they drank, the number of tornadoes to strike that day climbed, and the more extensive and bloody the damage became. By the time his mother called him inside (reminding anyone who cared to listen that this child had school in the morning and would not be drinking malt liquor any time soon), the tornado count was up to 20, with everyone arguing over what counted as one. A tornado, they said, had to actually touch down. Sightings alone were not enough; hitting the ground made them real.

T.J. had stared from under his dry cap and replied, "You done seen it before. You just forget what you seen."

That had only made Lenny's gut churn harder. Elbowing T.J.'s arm out of the way, he had opened the main door and started up the foyer. He wasn't fool enough to wait for some killer cloud to come tear him into pieces.

"Go back where you belong," Hal hissed at him. Billiard turned his back to them both, twisting the black phone cord around his shoulders.

If only he could hear beyond the blood ticking in his ears, see past Hal in his plaid Howard Cosell jacket and calculating eyes to get to one of those Jimi Hendrix moments, when people's bodies turned to cellophane and their thoughts floated around them like clouds. Hal's thoughts would appear as parallel columns of Risk and Benefit, ratios signifying odds, long, winding rows of strategies and bottom lines and, hovering over it all in big chalkboard letters, The Problem, with Lenny's face directly below. But then, as he contemplated these strange, unsettling signs, the siren kicked back into gear, shattering the lobby's silence as it rose to its ear-splitting zenith.

Billiard slammed down the phone and barked at Hal, "Who the fuck does Ed Krakowski think he is, running that damn siren?"

"There must be laws—" Hal answered solemnly.

"People don't need a goddamn air raid siren to tell them a twister's on the way!"

"Of course you're right."

"Damn right I'm right. Just because the next town over got slammed way back when doesn't mean they have to run a siren for every goddamn warning."

Lenny's thoughts hitched themselves to a stray tune playing in the back of his head. Lyrics poured in, fending off Hal's columns and ratios and bottom lines, Billiard's bulging eyes, and the siren and storm pounding inside and out:

Elimination, condemnation, procreation.

At that moment, it seemed no matter what he did or didn't do, the song was telling him: *You're fucked.*

> *Constipation*
> *generation*
> *elevation*
> > *privation*
> > > *mutilation*
> > > *recreation*
> > > > *libation . . .*

to the evils of the

world

He recognized the Stevie Wonder tune he'd heard on the car radio that afternoon, driving up 75th Street, something about a pastime paradise on a day as hot as hell. Now, at the very moment when he could least afford to let such words fly from his mouth, the music insisted he improvise further, as if the words and sound had a destination in mind, and he was bound to follow.

> *Citation*
> *Mutation*
> *Proclamation*
> > *Exploitation . . .*

to the evils of the world

It wasn't even a song he'd paid much attention to, but its rhythms and rhyme resembled the dirty dozens he and Sugar Butt and Murth often traded, what the old folks called signifying. Yet the words that music brought to him now, as he stood dripping in the lobby fending off Hal's evil stares, insisted he remember and know: this is who you are. Odd that they came at a time and in a place where nothing around him told him anything about himself. There in the lobby, the eyes in old officers' portraits stared past him to a place where Lenny did not exist, while a brass-studded sofa dared him to sit down, and hounds framed over the fireplace tore their prey to shreds. Behind him, the tall mahogany desk that stood between the maitre d's and the public like a bank teller's booth cautioned, Stay out! maintaining a small, screened-off world that judged who would be admitted, where, and how.

Everything in this hushed-up place spoke of the absence of himself. With the great weight of its silence on his shoulders, he struggled to hear something that might give him a clue as to what he should or should not do to save his ass from the storm. But only the music responded.

> *Copulation*
> *Population*
> *Rotation*
> > *Salutation*
> > > *Recreation*
> > > > *Salvation . . .*

To the peace of the world

And then the siren started all over again.

*

In grammar school civics class, Civil Defense lessons describe a different siren, a harsh buzz cutting off the radio's music followed by a mechanical voice announcing: "This is a test of the emergency broadcast system. . . . This is only a test." And until his civics teacher walks them up and down busy streets, pointing out yellow signs stamped "CD" in bold capital letters with black triangles wrapped around, he never thinks about what emergency he is supposed to prepare for.

"These yellow signs mark a bomb shelter inside. Metal drums of water and canned goods are stored there. In the event of a nuclear attack, the shelter will provide enough food and water for at least two weeks for the number of people noted on the sign," says the teacher.

"Are you scared?" blurts one of the girls.

"If you are prepared, you have little to be afraid of," the teacher calmly answers.

They watch films in which school children hide under their desks, hands locked behind the backs of their heads while a sing-songy voice trills "Duck and cover," as if it's all a game. Air raid sirens provoke this strange behavior. The only other time he's heard such sirens is during the black and white movies his mother watches, where people speak in sharp, urgent tones as if the world is ending. She likes movies about World War Two because her daddy had served, and she had loved him better than life.

He and his friend, James, sit under the stoop at James' house: their own fallout shelter that they won't have to share with nobody no way no how. For days afterwards they dissect "Duck and Cover."

"You see how big that cloud get once they drop that bomb? You can't tell me hiding under my desk going to save my ass," Lenny says.

"Know how much dynamite you need to match one nuclear bomb? 23,000 tons. And picture this. The craters they leave are big enough to swallow a city," James says in his somber, ministerial voice. He is a studious boy with thick black frame glasses like Malcolm and red hair to boot.

"I knew it! I knew they be lying to us."

"Why do you think schoolteachers lie like that? They're supposed to tell us what's true."

Lenny loves when James sets up these slam dunks for him.

"So we stay inside, out of trouble, no stealing, no fights, no screaming and crying. We stay inside and die instead of going out and fighting for what we deserve."

James steeples his fingers under his long, sharp nose.

"They want us to believe we can survive. If we've got hope, then we'll believe their lies."

Now Lenny is the one nodding. He crawls out from under the stoop's darkness, letting the hot June sun scorch his head.

"I hear them sirens, I know where I'm going."

"Uh huh," James stands, brushing bits of leaves, weeds, and dirt from his jeans.
"I steal me a car and drive away from that sound fast as I can."

*

Between siren blasts, air vents coughed while water hissed through unseen pipes. The ceiling above him echoed a bellowing thunder, shaking the walls with each blast. The sky was about to fall down on their heads, yet all these people at the Stables cared about was business as usual. When they turned on their sirens, he figured he had two choices: duck and cover, and be a sitting duck; or run as fast as his legs would take him and hope the killer clouds didn't catch up.

Hal kept glaring at him from behind the front desk, blocked in by Billiard who paced with the phone cord stretched from desk to wall. It was only a matter of time before Billiard hung up and freed Hal to clear Lenny out, or Al reappeared and did it for him. In the meantime, as he stood there, his whole body shaking, whether from chill or the siren's blast, he knew didn't want to turn into a story for the neighbors to shake their heads over. He didn't want to become a number in Hal's Cost Benefit columns or ratios or bottom lines, and he certainly didn't want The Problem solved, if resolution meant his face disappeared for good. He didn't want to be the fox in the hound's path, or whatever caused the general's frown, or the untouchable brass studs tucked inside the sofa cushions. He didn't want to be any of this, but what he *did* want, he couldn't picture.

Over the empty fireplace, the general's pale eyes held no reflection of whoever stood before them. Lenny wondered how many had passed before those eyes and survived their powerful stare. Those eyes had never doubted what was theirs.

Behind the front desk, Billiard sucked in his side-burned cheeks, now staring at Lenny, sweat beading the creases in his brow. Unlike the general's eyes, Billiard's stare was more calculating, less personal, but also impatient.

That stare froze him, iced him so bad his breath stopped. He didn't belong here. Not just the lobby, but HERE, this gig, these people, this world where he was next to nothing, no, *was* nothing. Billiard kept staring, but it was as if he wasn't seeing Lenny, more like seeing past him, through the walls, and into some other place where men on phones were shouting orders at each other. No doubt Billiard wanted to be the one shouting the orders. Lenny, it seemed, was just another distraction that Billiard's laser-like glare cut right through.

Far off sounds grew clear as he stood, unmoving: the low hum of conversation; glasses clinking against each other; shouts to the dishwasher for more of one thing or another. Boozy laughter rolled in from the Winner's

Circle lounge. But more than any sound, what captured his attention was the silence underneath it all. In the midst of so much noise, how was it possible to hear the potent hum of no sound, unless he was losing his mind. Was he losing his mind? Rigid with fear, frozen by the awful silence around him, it seemed not only possible but likely. His mind was slipping into a void. Soon, he was sure, his eyes would follow. Even if he still wanted to run, his feet likely would refuse him.

*

"You run, you dead," they say now that the fires are out. At the high school, the protests after MLK's killing had been peaceful, but in neighborhoods to the north and south, people had taken to the streets. Teen-aged boys shot down cold, they say, although the big newspapers only report how many are arrested. No one knows for sure who, if anyone, has died. Like an explosion, it is impossible to gauge exact outcomes.

"The last thing a person ought to do is run," James says sagely.

But when sirens are going, running is the only way that Lenny's legs will move.

*

The ceiling thunder stepped up its steady rumble and broke out into a stampede. The Jimi Hendrix moment he had wished for finally arrived; the horses that followed the ravenous hounds leapt through their picture frame and were now on the loose.

Billiard blinked as if the thunder woke him from his pissed-off day dream. "What's up with you?" he said, irritated but only that. He looked down at the desk, shuffled some papers.

"Gotta go," Lenny said. At least he thought he said it; his lips were moving and the words flew out. No, the thunder had waked him up, too. Billiard kept staring as Lenny turned 90 degrees on his heel. He had no idea where he was going, but he knew he had to move before Billiard ordered him outside.

Billiard was crazy. They were all of them crazy, just standing there, waiting for the sky to fall on their heads. But that was nothing new. People were always ignoring the warning signs, too caught up in making a buck, too easy about past safety to realize the real shit about to hit the fan.

A flicker crossed Billiard's eyes. His mouth twitched, or at least Lenny hoped that's all it was. Mad or amused, he couldn't tell. Billiard's jaw softened. He jerked his head in the direction Lenny was facing.

"If you got to go, you got to go. Don't wait on me to tell you."

He didn't have to piss but was glad Billiard thought he did. Up until now if he'd had to relieve himself, it was out back under the Big Willow or late nights staring at the whitewashed brick of the west wall, the moon beaming overhead. On the streets with Murth and Sugar Butt, they always pissed in alleys. They made jokes about hitting the can. "We don't just say it, we do it," Sugar Butt liked to say. He'd perfected the art of doing his business without looking like he was.

Billiard might think the storm had scared the piss out of him, but he didn't care. He got the go-ahead nod. Hal hunched his plaid shoulders and ignored Lenny as he swept past the front desk, wet uniform coat flapping.

His old-man Florsheims walked him firmly past the men's room sign, out of sight of Billiard and Hal, then turned a sharp left. Smells of smoke and grease and the clatter of dishes guided him toward a dim door. As he pushed it open, and lights pressed back into view, the Stables suddenly lost its power, and every light in the building failed. A collective gasp swept through the kitchen.

Shadowy forms raced through the dishwasher's steam. Dim light filtered in the back door, now propped open, since the air conditioning, never much good when the power was on, had now shut off completely. An eerie stillness lay over the place. Between hushed laughter and sighs, he heard refrigerator and freezer doors suction open and closed. Couples twisted together in embrace, moaning and giggling, their arms reaching out as if for invisible treasure.

His first thought was, What would Murth and Sugar Butt do?

"Nobody can see nothing, so grab yourself some booty." Sugar Butt would spread out his arms, palms open, beseeching, as if his whole life depended upon what Lenny would do. If the tables were turned, and Sugar Butt had his chance, Lenny figured he'd be too busy rubbernecking everybody else to actually do anything himself. By the time Sugar Butt would have decided what to do, the storm would have passed, the lights would be back on, and he'd be standing in the middle of the kitchen slack-jawed and empty-handed.

Murth was a different story. As Lenny's eyes adjusted to the gloom, he thought of the two places where Murth would head. The more likely place would be the service bar. He'd sweet talk Rose into looking the other way while he helped himself to shots of Stoli. But the other, more serious place was the business office, where the cash was held. Picturing Murth skulking about that dark, airless room, feeling his way to the safe, he realized he didn't really know how far Murth would go. Dealing a little pot, some PCB, even some coke now and then wasn't much compared to outright theft. Everybody knew drug laws were stacked against people in the hood, but burglary was another matter. When the stakes were so high, would Murth take the greater risk?

His second thought was that these kitchen people were just as crazy as the bosses up front. Didn't they know the sky could fall on their heads while they were scarfing mint parfaits and boiled shrimp and groping each other on the salad prep counter?   Instead of looking for shelter, they were looking for a good time.

His coat had soaked through to his t-shirt; even in the heat he was shivering.   His muscles urged him to keep moving, remembering Hal and Billiard behind him in the lobby.   No doubt they'd soon be recruiting staff to calm panicky patrons.   All Billiard had to do was flash his perfect white teeth, the ones that Mildred Aunty claimed were capped, and diners would tuck their napkins back onto their laps and stare into the glass-hooded tongues of the dining room candles, feeling safe in their host's reassuring gaze.   They could enjoy their prime rib and crème de menthe liqueur and go home with romantic memories of dining in the dark.   Even if a more savvy man demanded that his Cutlass Supreme be shielded from the wind, Hal and Al would tell him, in smooth, low tones, that everything possible was being done, meaning, of course, that nothing was possible except to wait the storm out.

Inside his pants pocket, the Camel straights were a little damp but likely smokeable. Smokers had already collected near the back door.   Why not stand hunched over with them, rain whipping in gusts outside, defying the rules that forbade them from smoking inside the kitchen?   If, like them, he pretended nothing was wrong, then maybe nothing bad would happen.   Or he could join the shadows inside, try to forget that the sky was falling by grabbing whatever was at hand, slurping, sucking, moaning, groaning his way to escape?   Was this what it boiled down to—pretending, forgetting, hoping for the best when the worst was hurling itself right in his face?   Was this what people inevitably did when there was no place else to go, nothing else to do but wait and hope that in the natural course of things, the darkness would blow over, by and by?

Outside the wind was a train roaring at full speed, while rain blew level with the ground.   Everybody acted as if it would all pass soon enough, for some maybe even too soon.   Maybe they knew something he didn't, the homie who barely noticed if the sun was shining. But then maybe they were just too bored to care.   Maybe they weren't any different than the bosses, believing it more important to act like they would live forever even if a roaring train was on track to shatter their world.

*

The first brick flies through storefront glass while he is standing on the corner.   Other boys quickly surround him.   They are just a few years older than he, yet physically they are decades apart: broad chests, strong arms, powerful legs.   In their hands, a bottle becomes a grenade, a rock a bullet. Adults are shaking heavy heads, or shouting angry cheers, but unlike the adults, these boys are anything but sad or mad.   They are smiling, even laughing, egging each other on. Walls crumble and fire licks their backs, yet their eyes brighten as uniforms blare in bullhorn monotones to stop what they are doing and leave the street NOW. They are quicker, more nimble, and they know all the shortcuts, even when only rubble is left for sign posts. They love the chase; for the moment at least, the odds are in their favor.

He is too young to be mad or sad like the older folks. He sees grown women crying on each other's shoulders in the middle of the day and wonders what he should be feeling. The question alerts him to the tight spot in his gut, where scared and sad churn in a volatile mix. He feels the loss that everyone else is feeling but doesn't understand it for himself.

Someone hands him a brick and shows him a window full of vacuum cleaners: "We take this place out so bad nobody ever put it back together again."

The brick is cold. His wrist hurts just holding it. In the window he sees his reflection backlit by a fire behind him. The boys want him to smash the window where his image stands, inside the only world he knows. They tell him he can do it himself, or get out of the way because somebody is going to do it if he doesn't. Now the tight spot in his gut gives way to pain, and he clutches his stomach, brick and all. The rough brick presses against his tender belly until he moans and wakes himself up, alone in his dark bedroom, bolt upright, sheets tangled at his feet. His stomach is still heavy, like he's swallowed that brick.

*

He wanted to cry out, beat his fists in the air against the unfairness of his own ignorance, not knowing how his life had brought him to this nightmare of a storm. Once more, the siren outside began to sound. He covered his ears, but the sound bit through. The wind screeched through the back door so hard even the smokers scattered. A high-pitched whine shrieked between the siren's rise and fall. Everyone was suddenly still.

His fingers crushed the remaining Camels in his pocket down to powder. He could do something: run away, find someplace to hide, steal whatever pleasure he could and hope that he survived. Or he could do nothing. Fighting was no option; how fuck could anyone fight something like a tornado?

In light of everything going on around him, nothing seemed the better choice. Unlike the rest of them, he would meet the roaring train, eyes wide open.

*

James' eyes are wide as he asks, "Ever play with yourself?" They are sitting under their bomb shelter stoop. In the sun it is so hot their sweat dries right away, but under the stoop's shade, their foreheads grow damp.

"You mean like playing cards or soldiers, that sort of thing?"

James steeples his fingers and pushes his glasses up his nose in that way that means his mind has gone deep. James scares him sometimes going deep like this. Other people steer clear or make fun, or, like Old Lady Bourbonhead, wave charms to ward off his Evil Eye. But it's what's scary about James that draws Lenny to be his friend. James liked to say, "When you stop thinking about it, nothing's really scary. We're so good at thinking scary we wind up believing what we think."

"I'm talking about feeling good, man," James replies. "Like skyrockets blasting behind your eyes."

"What you be knowing about that?" Lenny says, gripping one knee to his chest. Around the school playground, the stories run from conjuring voodoo to going blind or even losing a hand. He's been tempted, in bed, waking from a dream when all that heat would surge through his legs and his hand automatically moved to hang on to the feeling. But he feared what would happen once he started, and that was enough to keep him from going any farther.

"I read a book."

"Get out of here."

"No, man. I am not lying. I'm at the library, checking out the shelves like I always do and I see this big black book--"

"They put that in a book?"

"Everything is in books. You just got to know where to look. Anyway, I find this book. Mostly it's a lot of big words like doctors use but then the pictures—"

"Oh, man, pictures? You killing me. Somebody take pictures of that?"

"—and this book says that it's natural and normal and even good to do. They say 'to release sexual tension.' Those the exact words."

Lenny unfolds his knee. His head is swirling. His stomach is lead. He smacks his head against the stoop in his mad scramble to leave.

"I don't know nothing about no 'sexual tension.' You talking voodoo, man. You don't know what you conjuring there."

James nods a little as he drops his steeple into a salute.

Lenny follows James' eyes to where Lenny's thing is as straight as a flag pole. He grabs himself, trying to cover up, but he only gets harder.

"Just think of the worst thing that can happen. Picture it so clear in your mind like it's really happening. Then watch it happen. It's never like what you think."

*

He couldn't picture whether the train roaring past was outside or inside, or both, but wherever it was, it had suddenly eased. His breath ballooned in his lungs, and a deep stillness surrounded him. And then she was next to him, standing in the back of the kitchen. The swinging door to the hallway he'd just hustled down flapped behind her.

She squinted, smelling like warm pond water, red hair straining against its clasp. Chewing the end of her braid, she looked like his six-year-old cousin with the "good" hair, who, against all protests, would pacify herself with her own thick curls.

His chest puffed up like Superman, and his well-muscled arms circled her thin shoulders. Silky tones rolled off his tongue, awash in honey and gold, from a not-too-distant place where the light was about to return. He ached to fly with her, limp in his arms, to some place absent of grasping hands and reckless tongues, and save her from a force greater than himself.

In the stillness before the storm's next blast, he could picture the ceiling tear away, and everything around them begin to spin. His body and hers whirled up into the greedy vortex that flung them across the sky to become someone else's horror. Then a voice boomed, laughing and defiant, as the scene quickly faded: *I am your worst nightmare.*

"There's got to be a better place," she said. "Someplace safer than this."

Of course she would think that. She believed in such a place. "Look at them all acting like they know something. They don't know shit," he said. He could only believe the worst.

"Oh, they know plenty." Her voice was strained.

"Say what?"

He could not see, only feel, the green vibrating in her eyes. How long had it been since they'd stood together, pressing their hands to each other's skin, feeling his arms through hers, his lips through hers, his hair and nose and mouth through hers? Touching her to touch himself to touch her again. With each breath, something had changed; they had conjured something else between them.

"They forget they're only human," she said.

"So then what *do* they know?" His worst nightmare could very well be her dream; his dream might be her worst nightmare.

He could feel more than see the smile stretching across her face, the even white teeth, moist gums, fine lips. They were acting out a story whose ending they took as final: *I am your worst nightmare.*

"They have their secrets," she replied.

"Damn straight."

He wanted to kiss her right there in the kitchen, in the semi-dark of that powerless room, but something within resisted making her part of the scene under way, the mindless grabbing and groping in the dark. He could wait. That much he knew. Unlike everyone else, he could wait until the time was right. *I am your worst nightmare.* There was power in that. *When you stop thinking about it, nothing's really scary.* Even when the sky fell down, as he always knew it someday would. *Then watch it happen. It's never like what you think.*

And then the walls began to move.

Chapter Eight: Coat Room

Every dwelling holds forgotten space. There is always more room than we think. In dreams I've wandered through spacious houses as rooms kept appearing, some between existing rooms, some even between floors. Each time through, I found yet another room, as if these rooms existed somewhere between new discoveries and remembered pasts. In the remembering, they are somehow also new, and in their newness, they are nonetheless familiar.

As Lenny and I scrambled to protect ourselves from the tornado's fury, we stumbled onto the coat room. It was there what I knew and had forgotten blurred with what I never knew. The moment we crossed the threshold, both calm and dis-ease greeted me. The musty smell of old wood was overpoweringly familiar, yet until now, I had not known that room existed.

Although my mental map of the Stables had not included the coat room, I had been certain inner rooms existed. I had strained to remember rooms where I had never been. Such rooms held out the best hope for shelter. I had taken it on faith that they, in fact, existed.

That is how I reached the heart of the Stables.

My confidence that inner rooms existed buoyed me enough to take Lenny's hand and start moving as the tornado's locomotive roar slammed into our ears. Once out of the kitchen, I slid my hands along the dark hallway's wall, feeling for the doorknob I hoped was there, while Lenny followed, his stale tobacco breath hovering just over my ear. At the first doorframe, I grabbed Lenny's hand to touch what I'd found. Then, when the knob yielded and the door opened, a strong sense of homecoming overcame me, despite the fact I couldn't see a thing.

*

"Basement," she says, and that's all I need to hear. On the way downstairs, she dips two fingers in a brown glass jar full of holy water and shakes them like the miters used by priest for holy days. I know she is blessing the house against its ruin but the gesture strikes me as somehow blessing the storm as well.

I take to the basement reluctantly. Being inside, away from windows, is enough safety for me. The damage that can happen is something I glimpse briefly on the news. Even then I never really pay attention. Destruction never happens in Bedford Heights, or anywhere else nearby, so I believe those sorts of things just don't happen here.

But that day changes everything. Distant sirens blare into the night. I watch the news and argue with my sister over where the tornados struck and how many hit. My dad brags about beating a tornado home, driving well over the speed limit down 75ᵗʰ street. My sister and I later guess that same twister razed the roller rink where a Girl Scout troop like mine had gone for a field trip. I sit glued to the Zenith while special reports that I never used to care about roll in: death tolls and fires and broken gas lines and power outages. My mother makes TV dinners and lets us eat in the living room with snack trays, something she ordinarily does not allow. I listen to figures and facts, watch camera footage with new-found excitement. The thrill of it quickly flips into a stomach-churning fear the next day when yet another storm erupts and the sirens start all over again. I am the one to prod my sister and father away from the window to join my mother in the basement keeping vigil with the transistor.

Anything I read, see, or hear about tornadoes from then on magnetizes my attention. I become a walking encyclopedia on the subject of severe storms and safety: Seek shelter in the southwest corner of the house or building; go to a first floor or, if possible, basement room; inner rooms with no windows are best when below-ground shelter is not available; open windows slightly to ease internal pressure caused by the tornado's vacuum force. Like a bomb, our house can blow up from all the internal pressure if we don't take the proper precautions.

*

Eventually my eyes adjusted to the darkness as wood paneling, a countertop, and a Dutch door leading to, I assumed, the front desk, appeared. The smells reminded me of my grandparents' former home, a brick foursquare on the south side. My grandmother had hung old fox furs with the heads intact and musty woolens in a cedar closet underneath the huge oak staircase. I wondered if the Stables' coat room also held in its embalming grasp similarly ancient and gruesome relics. But before my eyes could confirm such suspicions, my nose had already fine-tuned its assessment of the coat room's smells. Here they were less stagnant and sealed off than they were old and porous, as if very old trees whose powerful breath had condensed for decades still lived in that small, unfrequented room.

In the presence of these ancients, I felt strangely comforted, a distinctly different sensation than my grandparents' house, whose wooden floors and banisters sagged under the smells of Ben Gay, scorched coffee, and Beaman's pepsin gum. Yet behind the deserted counter, where empty wooden hangers hung on vacant racks like bones, the thought of all those secrets in the shadows set me on edge. The hangers knocked hollowly against each other as I ran my hand across them, shells of a by-gone age, dozens of them still waiting for the garments to complete them.

In that sphere of ancients, Lenny's breath stayed constant and close. His rain-drenched clothes released their moist odors, and for a moment I was uncertain whether I was outside or in. In the dark, the outlines of his hair hovered higher than I remembered. In his wet coat, he seemed broader, more substantial, even as he wheezed slightly, trying hard not to cough and thus give us away.

The locomotive winds reached their climax; sounds of breaking limbs and twisting metal filtered through the darkness as we stood, breathless, and listened to the storm. We had searched as hard as we could for protection; whatever happened now was out of our control. I had no reason to believe that we were, finally, safe, but surrounded by all this old yet vital wood, that was how it felt.

He must have absorbed some of that steady old strength, too, when he said, in a low voice, "You ever pray for something that don't ever happen?"

Prayer was the farthest thing from my mind at that point, so it startled me to think that it was close to his. What if this was it? What if, despite our best efforts, we were swept away? What then? That was a question whose answer I could not imagine. But when I looked into his eyes, illuminated by some distant light, I knew he had already imagined the worst, perhaps many times before now.

"No," I replied. It wasn't completely a lie. Few things seemed urgent enough to pray for without promptings by nuns, priests, and parents. Prayer was something you did for people who were suffering in ways that you could not help except to pray. But as I got older, when I suffered the pains of being a little too red-haired and a little too pale, with too many freckles, a little too wide in the hips and too small in the bust, I did not hesitate to call upon the Higher Powers for help.

"I pray my daddy come home."

"What happened to him?"

The wooden panels creaked faintly like a rocking ship. Something stirred overhead, perhaps debris flinging itself at the roof, although the sound struck me as more slow and deliberate.

"Nobody know."

"You must miss him."

Lenny paused, his head lowering. "Never met the man."

For a moment, the eerie stillness that accompanied his words amplified the wood's enfolding solidity. The darkness emphasized the room's function as a closet, a place rarely entered, with only select items stored within—to hide away, to stow out of everyday view, to confine within a chosen place. As we stood facing each other, I pictured the racks around us full of heavy, dark coats swaying on those sturdy hangers, holding the subtle imprints of their keepers in the bend of a sleeve, the smell of after shave and hairspray, the shapely scrolls of hair caught in the fabric's nap. Into this room these potent traces had been entrusted, the protective shells that embraced the wearers' secrets, desires, and dreams.

"But you still care?"

"I be hearing about him since day one. How much I look like him, act like him." Above us, the roof continued its slow, deliberate clatter, although the random bursts of wind and debris had settled, as had any sense of urgency. Whatever had come had now left the Stables in its tempestuous wake. Yet with this revelation, Lenny's expression seized me with a similar urgency, only stronger, as if I'd caught him in the act of undressing, his look both pleading and angry.

I focused instead on his uniform, which hung heavily from his shoulders, wider than the wooden hangers behind us. The fit, now that I had a chance to study it, was tailor made, unlike my own uniform, which I'd had to purchase ready-made at a uniform shop. The sleeves met the shoulders exactly where they dropped. The sleeve's hem reached just below his wrists, touching the fleshy saddle of his palms. The trousers broke perfectly above the curve in his polished shoes, the pleats razor-sharp even where the fabric bent. Obviously a great deal of care had been taken in outfitting him for his job, even down to the crest on his hat, a shield with the Stables' trademark horse and rider emblem stitched within.

This impeccable uniform seemed at odds with the face I was trying hard not to meet, framed in neatly trimmed hair, whose inward-turning teeth belied unease with the uniform's perfection.

I gazed down dumbly at my scuffed and battered shoes, sorry sisters to his princely polish. I could no more imagine a life without a father than I could one in which I devoted my life to servicing the whims of a pleasure-seeking public. What had I been thinking, bringing him here, as if I had the least clue as to what he really needed?

"I'm sorry," I began. I tugged at my collar, as if to choke off the words I was fumbling for. "I had no idea. What was he like, your father?"

He looked past me into the gloom. I instantly regretted the question.

"They say he tall, kind of smooth, both in looks and ways. Get along with everybody. Everybody like him. I got his eyes. They call him Moony because he got this far-off look even when he talking right to you."

The distinctly nasal voice of Hal, answered by Al's sharp baritone, drifted through the Dutch doors. My thoughts returned to the tables I'd abandoned. I stood to lose an entire night's tips if I didn't get back to work. Saturday was the biggest tip night of the week. Nearly everyone wanted to work Saturday nights, but as a "college gal," I was scheduled only when a veteran was off. I'd run away from a full station—three two-tops, a pair of six-tops, and one table of four—with some pricey orders already placed. The six tops were guzzling Tangueray and tonic like lemonade, and all three two-tops had ordered surf and turf, and filets. One table had even ordered a bottle of wine (nobody in Bedford Heights ever ordered whole bottles of wine). I had looked forward to my best night ever. With the lights out, and the kitchen stopped dead, at least I had an excuse. I checked my watch. What seemed like forever had been only a few short minutes.

The lure of a good night's take was more difficult to give up than I'd imagined. The low ceiling, plate glass windows, and northeastern location of my station in the Garden Room was perhaps the most exposed area in the restaurant, yet even the storm could not finally deter me. For weeks, I'd blistered my hands on hot plates, washed grease and smoke out of my hair every night, took flack for flubbed orders from Mildred, Rose, and Sarah, added up checks incorrectly, wore out my face with tight smiles and "Have a good evenings." After all the heat and headaches and insults, I was ready for some payoff; those tax-free tips would earn me three times the minimum wage and make coming home for the summer worth it. So far, nothing had made coming home worthwhile. Now it was time to cash in.

If he hadn't already, Lenny was bound to see the shallowness that marked my life. I'd been raised to believe that bad things didn't happen to good people. But that had changed as I got older and began to figure out that the inverse was more likely true: good things happened to bad people. It was the good ones who more often than not were the losers. What I hadn't yet figured out, and what Lenny reminded me of, was that I wasn't sure whether I was a good one or a bad one, or what, if anything, lay in between?

*

Kyle is one of the good ones. Now I have the longed-for steady boyfriend, who calls me exactly twice a week. I admire Kyle, even look up to him; that is a big part of my attraction. I meet him my first semester. On my way across the Quadrangle to find my friend's dorm, I suddenly stop in the middle of the walk, squinting, and in the process nearly cause him to run into me. After he rights himself from our near-collision, he asks me where I am headed then walks me to my dorm's door. On the way, he chats easily about his major. He is a junior; his home is in Bangalore, his interests in communications technology and the good it can do for his country.

I dread every lull in the conversation, tongue-tied over what to say to this elegant, dark-haired stranger whose British English makes my Chicago flatness sound coarse and even backward. My instant impression of him is of a greyhound, with his long, straight, finely-chiseled nose and brown-black eyes aimed at his goal. Even in casual conversation, his coiled anxiousness to bolt ahead cannot help but surface in the sure, steady movements of his trousered legs and muscular haunches. Compared to his refined demeanor, my awkward silences and halting questions are no match. I feel only great relief, even gratitude, to leave him at the door. It never occurs to me that he would have enough interest in a dazed and disoriented freshman to later seek me out. The next day he calls my dorm room. I recognize his perfect English instantly, and since then we are together.

The summer is our first time apart. My father insists that I return home to earn and save as much money as possible, and thus relieve him of some of the burden of paying for an education in art history that he senses is somehow right for me but not entirely sure why, given that the career opportunities are next to none. I see no reason to tell my parents about Kyle, and since his parents live in India, I do not wonder too much whether he has told his about me. I prefer the anonymity; once the gates to parental approval are opened, there will be no hiding our obvious differences, differences which we rarely speak of, and when we do, we regard as charming idiosyncrasies, not serious divisions. In fact, he is more British than Indian, having grown up in Birmingham and only in his later teen years returned to Bangalore with his family, who maintained their Western ways back home.

Over the summer, I want to be the one to make the calls. Kyle keeps late hours, so I can call while my parents are asleep and thus preserve us from prying parental questions and embarrassing pronouncements. But he has started a summer pre-graduate internship off campus and so maintains irregular hours at uncertain locations, as he visits communications centers all over the region. I do not want to admit to him that I don't want to disclose our up-until-now secret relationship, even though I suspect he has not revealed it to his parents for similar reasons. But to openly admit to that would cast everything between us in a new light. Instead I let him call me at times we prearrange each week.

The first time my mother answers the phone and hears Kyle's clipped and proper voice, she offers, after I emerge from my bedroom, that he sounds like a professor. I do not disagree, and that is how the lie begins: Kyle is a professor with whom I "connected" that spring and who is now including me in his research this fall for archiving the ruins of an ancient Greek temple. My mother, whose education ended after high school, since marriage and children were her assumed aspirations, never tells me what she thinks of me taking hour-long calls from a male professor shut up in my bedroom. She briefly mentions him to my trade-school educated father, whose retort is simply, "I hope this means she'll make money."

With Mondays as the only days that the Stables is closed, that is my day to visit Kyle. Though his time is restricted, and we can spend perhaps only an hour together in his un-air-conditioned third floor walk up before fleeing to the leafy terrace of a local coffee house, I find myself even more admiring of his commitment to his studies, including his ability to strike a sensible balance between his developing professional life and our emerging relationship. He maintains a rigorously structured schedule; while I typically have been more spontaneous, over the last year, I have come to admire his self-discipline even if I fail to adopt it for myself. Living in Bedford Heights, I have moments where I want to jump in my mother's Impala of an evening to see him instead of enduring an endless stream of game shows and sit coms. But I manage to restrain myself enough to even read ahead for next fall's classes, my first steps towards self-discipline and a more structured approach to my future.

*

"I love your eyes," I blurted. Until then, we had not yet put any of our feelings into words. With that declaration, I had crossed into new territory.

The muffled voices and movements outside the coat room grew louder and more insistent. Despite the easing of wind outside, the steady pacing continued on the roof, as if part of me was pacing overhead, silent observer to my unspoken desires.

"They say he a ladies' man." He searched my face for a reaction.

I did not hesitate in my answer. "I can see why."

His smile spread slowly; the way his lower lip caught on his inward-turned front tooth made him all the more adorable. Either my eyes had adjusted, or more light was coming through because I could see his face clearly now, down to the thin pink line peeking out from inside his lower lip. As I continued to stare, other things around us came into focus. The portrait of a horse, one of those full-body profiles that celebrated a champion's physical beauty and strength, caught my eye. Curiously, its face was turned towards the viewer, breaking the smooth line of its spine.

Cool air grazed my arms as the low chug of motors pulsed in cooling vents somewhere in the room. I closed my eyes to try to shut out this distraction, but it only intensified. Coat hangers knocked against each other lightly; the machinery of the Stables was springing noisily ahead into the interrupted night.

Opening my eyes again, I discovered the thoroughbred's head aimed right at mine. Its nostrils flared and the white star on its forehead glowed.

"You hear that?" Lenny said.

"The ceiling?"

"Yeah. Like somebody walking around up there."

"You heard it, too." It wasn't a question.

"Sound like they right over us."

"You think they hear us?" The steady knock worked up to a chaotic pounding, as if a bag of bowling balls had been dropped overhead.

"Weird shit, man."

"Probably just some downed branches, don't you think?" I offered.

Part of me wanted to make this sudden intimacy disappear. I wanted a rational explanation for why blood was surging to my face and throat, my heartbeat was in a competition with the noise overhead, and the gentle clink-clink of the hangers was almost too delicate to bear. But then again, the last thing I wanted was to explain away such sensations. The "weirdness" had to be more than that. At least that's what I wanted to believe.

Shaking his head, Lenny took off his cap, ran his hand through his hair, and set the cap back on carefully. "I got no clue what's going down here." He brushed off his lapels then straightened the gold braid hanging from his shoulders. He tugged his trouser creases back into place.

"You in there, son? Come on out, now." Three knocks on the door revealed T.J.'s position outside the men's room down the hall.

"Don't go yet," I said. The thoroughbred dipped its star-kissed head and waited, as still as the pause between each short breath I took. "There's a lot you don't know about me."

His brow furrowed, and he tucked his chin, staring up from under his elegant cap.

"Uh-huh?" His teasing smile spread as quickly as the thoroughbred's starlit face faded behind him.

"I mean, you told me such personal things, and I wanted—"

His fingers found a loose strand of hair near my face and followed the shape of its curl before gently tucking it behind my ear. "No lyin, Care-o-lyin?"

I blinked, and Lenny was still there, his moony eyes shining soft light on his face, now clean of all cares. I blinked again, and it was equine eyes staring back at me, their eerie orbs jutting out from the sides of their head. Again, and two bright moons, twin reflections of star light. And again, star light aimed itself between my restless eyes, as if it knew that looking straight on at such beauty would be too much to bear.

Chapter Nine: Derby Room

Why Mildred had picked this shoebox of a room, with its tight tables and no windows, for their dinner hours together, he couldn't quite figure. Until about a year ago, the room was a walk-in closet, but after the new banquet addition took off, Billiard decided to cash in on the Baby Boom's endless celebrations and remodel the closet for dining. The other banquet rooms, those for rehearsal dinners, baby showers, first communions, graduations, and anniversaries, had lots more room to stretch out, spread legs, lean back. But here he could barely squeeze himself into his seat. Not that he was one to complain. But lately the cramped quarters were more noticeably cramped. Either he had grown or the room had shrunk, but in any case, the space was now past tolerable.

He had just filled her in on the day's reactions to the stable boys as he scooped up gravy with a strip of fat from his t-bone. Tuesday was steak night. Mildred had it figured out. The week's beef shipment came Tuesday afternoons, and with the walk-in jammed with tenderloins, prime rib, and New York strips, she reckoned no one would worry about a Saturday night shortage. She herself rarely touched beef, preferring pork and organ meats. "Trophy meat" she called those big slabs of stockyard beef that had made the Stables a local landmark. Still, T.J. stayed sanguine about his weekly steak, and Mildred never gave him more than he could comfortably consume.

Her lower lip thrust forward in that fiercely thoughtful way that had always captured T.J.'s respect even as it warned that somebody, present or not, was about to receive a dose of the Truth and Nothing But. T.J. smacked his lips, chewing fat to gristle. His visceral appreciation of her cooking usually pleased her. But tonight, Mildred merely shook her head.

"A sign," she said. Her nose drooped, as if sniffing something decidedly foul. Her eyes squinted like mail slots. "They scared of seeing white faces where they expect colored."

"Why you think?"

Head bowed, Mildred stirred her soup slowly as if reading a divination. "People crazy, that's all."

"Tips are off. Them white faces sure be making people nervous."

"You think them statues what making people nervous?" she asked.

"No."

Gravy had separated into shiny pools of grease and lumps of flour where the last bits of fat lay hidden. What T.J. had once thought about the stable boys suddenly didn't make any sense.

"Whole economy's in trouble," he conceded.

"Still, they ought to trash them things. Ain't nobody nowadays even know what they for," Mildred replied.

"Take a jackhammer to bust them out of the ground."

"That ain't much, considering all the trouble they be causing."

T.J. pushed against the table until his belly barely touched the edge. "Won't be no more trouble," he said. His eyes wandered to a plaque engraved with Derby winners' names and dates that hung on the far wall. Empty brass plates waited for the names of new winners. Dark oil portraits of the horses punctuated red fleur-de-lis walls. In their proud postures and regal profiles, the Derby winners were poised to accept much more from life than simple offerings of apples or oats.

Mildred held similarly high expectations. She didn't hesitate to serve the Stables' best food on her and T.J.'s plates. Yet for some reason she chose a room where he could not fully enjoy it.

The Derby winners' eyes followed him with sly anticipation. Being a winner of the Derby won you a gilt frame and a name on a plaque but also for some the peak of a career that had nowhere to go but down.

One thing about winning, he thought as he stretched his arms overhead. Make you less willing to lose.

*

He works the late drawing for the Streamline wheel at 35th and Indiana. A lot of policy men spend their time in the clubs at night, but he isn't much for music. He's all business. He's also promised Angel Fair he'll finish high school, so the midnight game is the only one that won't interfere.

"I didn't tear my folks away from home for nothing," she tells him the day he takes the policy writer's job. "We came for schools and you are going to finish, even if I have to take you there myself."

He's been inside policy for so long now that Angel Fair's worries have had lots of time to grow. The longer he does it, the more she wants him to get out. "Dirty money," she says.

To which his policy men inevitably respond, "Ain't no such thing as clean money."

Dirty or not, the money is good and it keeps him in school. He can buy his own shoes, books, pens and tablets. He can even give his mother something for the table each week. He sees what choices his father and brothers have had. Daddy is gone to the Armour plant ten hours a day, six days a week; two of his four brothers work in factories. One is a bellhop at a fancy downtown hotel. One can't find steady work so he does odd jobs, sells newspapers, and writes letters home for those who can't. Angel Fair claims schooling came too late for them. The youngest in the family, T.J. is her biggest hope.

As long as his "dirty money" gets laundered through good uses, Angel Fair keeps her worries to herself. In the meantime, T.J.'s education goes beyond Wendell Phillips High School. Black men are starting their own businesses, clean work like Angel Fair insists on, but with policy money. Edward White is a friend of his uncle (from the same part of Mississippi) who starts a paper company supplying rolls of white paper to policy wheels. And then there are the "dirty" businesses: the policy "advisors," dream book writers, incense sellers vending oils, powders, roots, herbs and candles. T.J., however, is more scientific, like truly successful businessmen must be to get ahead.

He is good at math, no surprise since he's been tracking gigs ever since he can remember. Between his family's cautions and his own calculations, it doesn't take long to see how the odds are stacked against them. A dime bet has odds of 7000 to one. But he figures he can gain better odds with the right tips from other insiders. Problem is, everybody else thinks the same thing: an inside angle is key. This leads them to experiment with hocus-pocus, assigning numbers to dreams and using dream advisors, something he swears he won't do but does anyway, losing his lunch nickel for a week straight to pay for a dream book that the writer "guaranteed."

He started in policy by accident, when shopkeepers with second-floor wheels snagged him to run between stations. He is fast and likes to run, and their payments of pennies, cookies, crackers, and sweets are luxuries Angel Fair can seldom afford. He soon catches on to where other stations are after he learns to read their signs in the windows: "4-11-44," a popular number combination, "All Books," or just "Doin Business." Then he is tapped to pick up drawings slips from near by. Later, one manager makes him a clerk. He picks up bundles thrown onto the street from pick up men's new coupes and rushes them inside for the drawing. He even gets into the station's scrapbook, charged with the task of pasting in back drawings. His scientific mind, along with the station manager's savvy, has him tracking winning gigs, narrowing down the odds from out of sight to slightly less impossible.

On his 14th birthday he finally gets a chance to write policy. He stops playing gigs himself and instead plays to other people's hopes, putting together plays on paper and collecting tips from those who hit. He has learned from tracking gigs in the scrapbook what plays have better odds, information that helps his popularity grow. Writing policy comes naturally to him; it is almost too easy to gain people's trust. The game is rigged from the get-go. Most people lose; few win. Yet players insist on following the rules. So, despite the odds, or perhaps because of them, he is careful never to cheat. The game itself may cheat them, but people trust him to play fair.

The last task of his policy-writing day is the one Angel Fair dislikes the most, drawing numbers from the wheel. She doesn't like him staying out that late, claiming it will cloud his head for school. A barrel-like contraption full of rubber-coated, numbered pellets, the wheel goes on public display for each drawing, so no one can claim any cheating goes on. He and the other midnight writers have to be there when the numbers are pulled. Sometimes the station manager asks the writers to draw.

"I'm learning more doing business than just talking about it in school," he says to Angel Fair. He has seen the inside of more businesses on the South Side than if he had taken up shoe shine or newspaper delivery. He knows who is who, how to keep a store going or even just the appearance of one to front a wheel. Most importantly, he knows what people want. "I'm doing a service," he argues, to which Angel Fair sniffs and straightens the doily on top of her chiffonier. That's a line he often hears around the station, one he's not sure he believes, but not sure he disbelieves, either, especially when they start talking about keeping money in the community, that part of the city where only black folks will live. Policy supports churches and their ministries, not to mention brings businesses into neighborhoods that would otherwise go without. Our money as good as anybody's, they say. Downtown, white people hadn't yet figured that out.

"You are still sleepy eyed when I send you off in the morning," she replies. "And just when do you study?"

"They don't give us no homework, Mama."

"Well, let me give you some right now. Start saying, 'They don't give us any *homework' or I'll wear you out."*

In this, Angel Fair sounds just like his teachers, some of whom are white. He knows he'll get trashed if he talks like that to policy men, but sometimes, to impress the cops, he does. The cops, too, have their own way of talking, nothing like the schoolteachers, but they still slap him on the back, spouting Irish curses of approval.

About the sleepiness, she is right. He can barely hold his head up through first period, especially when Mrs. Lynch reads The Odyssey *out loud. At least she tells them what she will ask on the tests. But napping in class is the least of his problems. The longer he stays in school, the less real it seems. Policy is real. Working and earning wages is real. Learning how to run a business, keep customers happy, and grow a stable of players is real.*

What does, finally, keep him in school, is his scientific mind, that part of him that knows the difference between playing a guessing game and knowing how the game is played, what is at stake, and how to improve your chances to take less of a risk. He learns about the stock market, how groups of people can share risks for the sake of greater gains. He learns about accounting, how keeping track of expenses and income, and balancing books can have more power than a handshake. Statistics are nothing new but he's fascinated to learn new formulas that extend his mind's reach. He even learns from Shakespeare, despite the old-fashioned language, and hears themes from policy wheels echoed in the plays: Policy barons who live like kings and fight their enemies (in this case, white law makers who call for raids before and after elections to "clean up" vice), only to be foiled by a tragic flaw or fate; young princes who dabble in vice but rise to their true station; and of course the comedies of errors committed on a daily basis by those who play the wheels.

School learning sharpens his ears for the wisdom of his policy men. "Same as the stock exchange," says Miguel, a Cuban immigrant who claims policy is beholden to Spain for its existence. "The white man take your money, give you piece of paper with a big, fancy name, and you gamble for your luck. Your stock go up, you make money. It go down, you lose. At the race track, same thing. Policy no different."

Miguel, as it turns out, thinks South Side policy is penny ante compared to the numbers game in New York. His real passion, though, is for the track. He laughs when T.J. asks him if it is cleaner because it is legal.

"Legal, no legal, it don't make no difference. Sometimes it legal, sometimes no. Depend on who get elected. Races get fixed, horses drugged, jockeys lose on purpose. But, my friend, at least with the race, los caballos have the final say."

Miguel has a different way of looking at things. T.J. thinks it has to do with being Cuban, but Miguel claims he is a poet at heart and isn't the least bit embarrassed to say so. "Policy nothing but sitting around a dark room, your fingers turning white from chalk. You bet your one-legged gig, two-legged gig, hope the legs bring you a hit. But when you go to the track and bet on the four-legged ones, there is a chance that things can turn out different. You yell and scream, jump up and down, like you running it yourself. Policy, you can keep your policy, pulling little black numbers out of a barrel!"

When T.J. finally rides the streetcars out to Hawthorne Park one Saturday with Miguel, he realizes why he never trusted poetry. Blinded by his romance with the horses, Miguel has overlooked the scientific splendors of wagering. There are the statistics: records of previous races, bloodlines, weights, classes. In addition, a whole new world of horse talk--gaits, track conditions, temperaments, riders, seasons, race distances--opens endless possibilities. Such talk reminds him of overhearing his father talk to his uncles. They had had some mules and a horse or two down south. The mules they used for plowing and pulling wagons, but the horses they rode, sometimes to far-off counties to join up with other Negroes to race in open fields. They bet whatever "shugah" money they had, sometimes even more than that. But mostly it was an excuse to get together. T.J. remembered his brothers talking about it like a big picnic.

The first few wagers he loses. He bets purely on guesses—a horse's name that holds a certain appeal, a lucky position at the gate, whatever strikes his fancy. But later that changes when Miguel pushes them through the grandstand crowd to the rail, where the horses are led to and from the paddock, paraded past bettors before being loaded into the gate.

"You see how they walk?" Miguel says, nudging T.J. with a skinny elbow. "I don't care what the tote board say. If the horse ain't ready, he going to show that. See," he says, pointing to a dapple gray rearing up on its hind legs, "he supposed to be a big deal, but today, he not going along with all this. And there," he points to another horse, chestnut, "look at his eyes dripping gunk. He not feeling so good. But this one." He lifts his arms over his head, excited. "His record not so good so far, but he only run three races in his life, and he hate the sun and the rain. No sun, no rain today. We better put some money on this one."

Miguel doesn't just bet to win. He bets to place and show. He bets trifectas, across the board, sometimes betting on the same horse, sometimes betting on two or more in the same race. In policy, the more complicated the bet, the higher the odds. But here, Miguel has it figured to spread out his losses. The odds on the tote board are just a starting point for him. In policy, nobody even talks about odds except the ones who make money off the players. Odds stacked against players mean policy men will keep steady work. But at the track, figuring a bet can start with the odds, but statistics and horse flesh turn bare numbers into real chances, chances that keep Miguel winning enough to keep coming back for more. Looking at the whole field of horses, instead of just one, changes everything.

After the last race of the day, Miguel takes T.J. to the horse barns. He knows the Spanish jockeys, men even smaller than Miguel. Many of them limp and carry scars. They curse at each other in casual, friendly tones. Miguel passes a flask and offers them cigarettes, and they invite him and T.J. to join them in their "parlor," a barn-like building where horses and jockeys put on their silks before a race.

The smell of damp horse hair and green hay hits T.J. even before he enters. He has to dodge the affections of a billy goat, which has a taste for the straw hat in his hand. Miguel slaps the rump of a pony no taller than T.J.'s waist to clear a space for them to sit.

"Amusements for Los Dios," Miguel says, sweeping his arm around the room. "We, too, are their playthings." The jockeys laugh and pound him on the back.

T.J. is tongue-tied by the strangeness of it all. He has always been able to talk himself into or out of any situation. But now he can only hang on while the conversation races along. He's never ridden himself, never even gotten that close to a horse except the old nag that pulls the rag man's cart. Standing at the rail that afternoon, he found himself drawn in by the jockeys more than their mounts. He couldn't believe his own eyes, how they sat with knees bent to their chests, barely touching the horse's back, and made it through that meat grinder of churning hooves and crashing bellies without falling off. He finds out later that sometimes they do fall. Watching each race, he held his breath so long that Miguel had to remind him to let go.

The jockeys speak Spanish, so T.J. waits, looking around the "parlor" until Miguel interrupts to fill him in. Miguel asks them about the day's races, the horses they ride, their training, habits, likes and dislikes. The jockeys' voices change when they speak of the horses. They speak faster, with more emphasis. Their jaws loosen and their eyes grow round. Their hands fly in the air around them. "Los Dios, Los Dios," he hears over and over. Finally, as the jockeys light up Miguel's cigarettes, Miguel fills him in.

"You see, no matter how good the jockeys ride, los caballos are what count. You got a good horse, don't matter much who ride him. The horse decide what he going to do out there. All they do is whisper in his ear, maybe yell sometimes, too, to show their power. Give the whip but not too much or you make the horse mad. Just like Los Dios, you know? You do a little dance, cry a little, sometimes beg and plead, to get the attention of los gigantes."

The jockeys fall silent as a white man in gray trousers and striped blue and white suspenders leads a horse in one door and starts across to the other. Miguel lets out a low whistle. This horse is huge, towering over its tall handler. Its glossy hair and silky mane speak of constant care and attention. It tosses its head violently in front of the men, as if objecting to their stares. Its front hooves lift up then crash to the floor so hard T.J. can feel the dirt vibrate under his boots.

Miguel points out that the horse's legs are still taped. "This gringo, he going to call mis compadres to take off that tape." He grins, shaking his head. "These gods are not always kind. But sometimes they listen to sweet talk. Even this one, who still got his balls." Miguel starts to whistle, so low T.J. can barely hear it sitting right next to him. The stallion stops kicking and lifts its ears up, snorting. The handler wastes no time in pulling the horse along.

T.J. is large for his age, but he feels small next to this huge beast. Yet when he looks at Miguel and the others, he feels very, very tall. As if reading his thoughts, Miguel says, "You Americans grow too big for your own race. You need us little people to ride for you."

Miguel's eyes flicker between brown and black but do not waver. Even his slow smile cannot drain their dark depths.

It is a long, slow walk back to the race track gates to catch the streetcar. Miguel goes up to one bettor after another, whispering about the horses slated for tomorrow's races, just enough to make them reach into their pants pockets. "Daisy Junebeetle been tearing up the track," he says. T.J. recognizes the name; it is one the jockeys had spoken of earlier. "She a little off today, got some sore muscles from sleeping on the ground. She be ready to run tomorrow, though. That how it is with her, some days slow, other days she can't wait to go."

Sometimes, the bettors greet him first, like old friends. Their hands are out before Miguel opens his mouth. "We hear Reverend Charles got a stone hoof," one says. "What do you know?" Miguel never says he doesn't know. Instead, he talks around the question and tells more and less than the questioner asks for. He has a story to tell, one that puts him in the center of all things Horse. He makes sure everyone he meets knows him in this way.

By the time they reach the streetcar, Miguel's pocket sings of many quarters. He pats his trouser leg to smooth the musical bulge on his thigh. He hands one to the streetcar driver, who looks at him like he's crazy.

"For my friend, too," Miguel thrusts his head towards T.J. The driver growls, "I don't give change," to which Miguel responds breezily, "Keep it, my friend."

"You land a trifecta?" The driver's tone softens.

"My friend, mi trifecta today, su tomorrow."

The driver waves him off. "Just what I need. Another stinking tout."

"You are so much mistaken, my friend. I speak to these horses myself, and they tell me their secrets."

"Here's a secret, for you, pal. If you don't get your black ass to the back of the car, you're gonna have to ride them ponies back to your greaser shit hole."

Miguel shrugs and starts to push his way through the people standing in the aisle. When he and T.J. are out of the driver's reach, he calls out, "Keep the change."

T.J. doesn't even have to see the driver's face to know he is aching for a fight. Black men get tips, they don't give them. He wants to ask Miguel if it is worth three whole nickels just to get somebody's goat. But when they reach the back rail of the car, and Miguel runs his fingers through his pomade-slick hair, smiling, T.J. already has his answer.

*

"Billiard say Mrs. Parkerhouse find a man to put the black back where it belong," T.J. said finally, in answer to Mildred's long, waiting stare.

He wiped his mouth and plunked the napkin on top of the gravy-stained plate. Mildred made pan gravy for him and nobody else. Everyone in the kitchen would kill for her gravy, but no one ever wanted to put it on the menu. "Too down home," Mildred would sniff. Only after the napkin's corner touched the leftover gravy did T.J. remember how she was always after the bus boys for mixing napkins in with the dirty dishes and soiling them beyond salvation. He folded the napkin neatly and laid it on the plate's edge.

Her fingers clutched a soup spoon and eased it to pursed lips. Her black wig tilted forward, resting in a wrinkle in her forehead. Without her wig, her hair was as patchy as a baby bird's feathers, but few besides T.J. knew that her good hair days were over. Mildred told anyone who listened that she wore it to spare her natural hair from all the grease each night. Still, she did not want people knowing that she'd lost her "glory." For Mildred had had amazing hair in her day. Thick, wavy, shoulder-tumbling hair. But old age and a vicious case of shingles had ravaged it. Every night before turning off the light, he kissed her balding head, remembering the heaven it once brought him.

She had quarreled vehemently with the hair loss at first, fussing and fighting with it late into the night. No matter what potions she'd mixed or bottles she poured onto her scalp, her hair kept shedding. Her practicality finally led her to see wigs as a boon--hair that curled and dried itself without following her into bed and making her sleep miserable.

"She can put the black back, but it never did belong," she replied.

Wednesday night was swiss steak smothered in onions, tomatoes, and peppers. Pan gravy, of course, in that orangey color that only she could make. It looked good, smelled even better, but when he raised it to his lips, he found he had no appetite.

When a person was so sick they couldn't even look at food, Mildred always knew how to bring back their appetite. No one ever refused her cooking. One of the frustrations she suffered at the Stables was that people often asked for the wrong foods, foods they expected would make them happy, satisfying some deeply held desire, when in fact all it did was stir up discontent. Next time, they would want two olives in their martinis, a bigger steak, more pepper in the chicken batter, parfaits with not just mint, but hot fudge, too. Nothing they picked ever truly satisfied. Not only was she unable to advise diners on the best foods for them, she also couldn't fix what a person needed because more often than not, it wasn't on the menu. She had long ago resigned herself to working within set limits.

While Mildred busied herself sawing at a ham hock, he forced himself to take a bite. He didn't want to upset her, preoccupied as she was with Viney of late, calling her mind "holey" and her appearance "possessed."

She had always been reclusive, but now she was nearly invisible, disappearing a little more each day. Just the other day, in a rare moment of despair, Mildred had turned to him as he was falling asleep. "What I going to do? She slipping away, and nothing I do or say get to her," she sighed.

The meat was tender, falling apart on his tongue. His mouth told him it was tasty, but he could not enjoy it. If he was standing out back next to the trash bin, he'd probably savor it more than in this small, over-cooled room where every eye blink, every finger twitch was weighted with some dark thing he couldn't name. Until lately, he'd always fancied himself a spectator to the Derby Room's decor, but now he harbored a distinct sense of being the one observed.

The Derby winners stared down their long equine noses, casting disdainful glances. The red fleur de lis throbbed, their bodies tense and graceful. Crown molding that marked where ceiling met walls cut a clean and measured boundary that struck him as painfully precise. Though a new room relative to the rest of Stables, the Derby Room retained an aged quality. With so little space to circulate, people's breath clung to the wallpaper, the ceilings, the brass plaques with the creeping tarnish. The red carpet's dancing horse shoes sparked a friction in the air. The whole room was frozen in one big inhalation, having expanded to its limit and now unable to release that breath. The horses looked on knowingly.

Trying his best to keep the annoyance out of his voice, T.J. put down the silver fork and asked his wife, "Don't this room make you want to get up and walk away, and keep walking till your feet wear out?"

Mildred knitted her forehead in that way she reserved for those confusing beyond belief. Behind her, the eyes of the horses multiplied, reflecting him trapped inside his Grand New Uniform. That uniform could not erase his 65 years, working the same damn job when he could have left years ago. Inside that Grandness a young man still stood, still expecting to beat the odds, each day looking forward to another chance to win bigger than his bloodlines and breeding had forecast.

He recognized himself, standing in the shank of the evening, with patrons who plied him with big, black cigars, trading tips on the next day's races. Back then, he had subscribed to one rule for himself: don't bet on what you can't see. He used to park himself at the walking ring before each race at Hawthorne, sizing up not only confirmation, but also a horse's mood and attitude, those things that the track program and his stats book couldn't tell him about a horse's performance under particular conditions. But that didn't stop him from giving blind tips to others. In fact, he had gained a reputation for picking winners through his more "scientific" approach. But when it came to his own bets, if he couldn't be there in the flesh, studying what a horse's markings might say about its personality, or how it reacted to abandoned mutuel tickets swirling in an updraft, or whether its gait was perky, nervous, or angry, he rarely placed a bet without at least a surrogate pair of eyes to call in what they'd seen. In this regard, he was stubbornly old-fashioned. Only a few trusted track cronies knew his predilection.

For years he had never bet the Derby, even after television cameras made it easy to study the ponies from home. He objected to TV dictating his view. But one year his friend Stanley, a bellman at the Drake, drove down to Louisville and phoned T.J. from a pay phone just before the race to tell him what the paddock had revealed. Between Stanley's sharp eyes, the pre-race broadcast, his ever-present stats, knowledge of the field, and a strong hunch about the yearling's name, he won a bundle on Carry Back, whose ugly feet had dissuaded neither Stanley nor himself from placing all their money on the colt to win.

T.J. scanned the Derby plaque for Carry Back's name, feeling oddly wistful. His bet on Carry Back had won him enough to never worry about a pension. He and Mildred would have enough to live as they were used to living, no more but no less. The future had been fixed for them both at that point. Until then, he had thought little about such a far-away thing as old age. He and Mildred never spoke of it. They tacitly understood that they would work until they could work no more, and whatever happened after that, they would trust in providence. But to have a future determined by a bond market and to live according to a plan was a strange thing. That big question mark that had hung over their lives was replaced by that future, one he took pleasure in imagining what it would be. Yet the more he imagined, the less content he grew. Surely, he thought, their labors amounted to more than church suppers and fishing and that back porch on the pond in Mildred's family's acres down south. He and she would create no burden for anybody else, but beyond that, what would they have?

That had been the biggest purse he'd ever won, and that was already 17 years ago. Since then, he was glad to just break even and not lose what he'd risked so much to gain. Since the Derby win, he'd done all right protecting his winnings and even adding a little, but nothing matched the thrill of when he'd had nothing much to lose except his reputation for making other people winners.

He watched her calmly chew shreds of ham hock and realized that to her, this room was just one among many where they could go. But to him, it configured the choices that had led him here and now refused to let him go.

His encounter with Billiard a couple of months earlier still dogged him, despite Mildred's insistence to let it go. For once, Billiard had invited T.J. into the office. He knew he was supposed to be honored. But *supposed to be* and *was* were two very different stories. He knew which one held the most truth, but the other kept trying to dictate its own.

The leather and brass-studded chair Billiard pointed him to had groaned as he eased between its arms.

"Doctor, them lawn jockeys be scaring people," T.J. had begun.

To T.J.'s relief and puzzlement, Billiard had agreed. A desk drawer opened; one hand rummaged until two cigars appeared, torpedoes between his fingers. T.J. slid one forward gingerly then sniffed it end to end.

"Cuban?" he asked.

Billiard nodded. His face flushed hot pink as it always did when he was pleased with himself. Although T.J. seldom had trouble gaining such contraband for himself, he admired Billiard for securing this prize. More than likely he knew an importer with obscure connections to Havana. T.J., on the other hand, depended upon the extravagances of customers.

"People don't like change, T.J." Billiard struck a match, squinting past the flame to meet T.J.'s eyes. The desk drawer whined as he elbowed it closed. Stacks of papers pushed back at T.J.'s chest as he leaned into the flame. The overflow paperwork from Mrs. Parkerhouse attested to how rarely Billiard used his desk.

"We're here to take their minds away from change," Billiard continued. He tipped his head back against the edge of the chair. Smoke rolled from his mouth then curled up to the bare bulb overhead.

"Them two ugly mugs make people nervous. Bad enough when they were black." T.J. bit off the cigar's tip. Billiard had chucked his into a trash can under the desk before lighting up. Had they been outside, T.J. wouldn't have thought twice about spitting. But inside, even the bare cement was out of bounds. Billiard, all settled back in his big chair, was not about to offer the trash can. So T.J. plugged his cheek and kept smoking.

"Even David owned that they look bad," Billiard said. He went on to explain that he has only been trying to teach his "bleeding heart son," a young man who favored porkchop sideburns, platform shoes and t-shirts littered with popular sentiments such as "Eat Me" a lesson in human behavior.

"It's all about the past," Billiard concluded. "That's the draw. Other restaurants bank on novelty and trendiness. But we're in the business of making people believe that nothing has changed. Stability is the name of the game."

It didn't take a genius to see where Billiard was headed in his thinking. No change was the best change as far as he was concerned. Even T.J. wasn't sure what would happen if the stable boys were taken out for good, although that was a risk he was willing to take.

T.J reached inside his pants pocket. "Best hire somebody that knows what he's doing," he said. He honked into a handkerchief as if sounding the final notes of the discussion. Billiard straightened up abruptly as if an alarm had gone off.

"Mrs. Parkerhouse's lined up a damn good antiques man. Restoration, repairs, you name it, he does it."

The cigar see-sawed between T.J.'s fingers as he listened. Billiard's shoulders returned to their slump as he leaned back into the seat, cigar clenched between his teeth.

T.J. couldn't erase suspicions from his mind despite Billiard's explanation. The longer Billiard sat staring at the Cuban scissored between T.J.'s fingers, the more T.J. was tempted to ask the Big Question.

His lips had already formed the "W" to his "Why?" when shouts from the kitchen interrupted them. Billiard stood, dropping his Cuban on the floor and grinding it out with the heel of his Italian lace-ups. He gave T.J. an odd little salute before he turned to leave.

T.J. winced at the wasted Cuban, then relieved himself of the plug in his cheek with one big spit. A little extra water to make sure the fire's out. Ashes from his stogie dropped onto the stacks of papers. He didn't wipe them off.

Later that week T.J. overheard Billiard tell yet another version of the botched paint job to one of the Sanitary District commissioners as they stood smoking in the parking lot late one night. Billiard recounted how, upset by his son's amateurish work, he wanted to "dump the little nigger boys altogether, " but at the last minute Mrs. Parkerhouse talked him out of it, arguing their value as antiques.

"And then T.J. here comes in," Billiard said, pointing towards the canopy where T.J. stood while Lenny retrieved the last of the dinner rush's cars. T.J. let his chin drop into something like a nod, acknowledging the two men but keeping his distance. "Even he hates the white paint. Who would a thought? Not only doesn't like it, but wants the old faces back."

Even his Grand New Uniform, with its epaulettes and fringe, and padded linebacker shoulders, could not shield him from the eager-to-the-point-of-panic eyes of the stable boys. T.J. spit into gravel dust while the two men laughed until they choked on the smoke of their smuggled Cubanos.

*

Spring 1968. 5000 National Guardsmen, 8000 U.S. troops, and 12,000 Chicago cops are on call to the city's west side while Bedford Heights holds its breath. Smoke from the fires isn't visible there, yet everyone at the Stables claims to smell it. The Defender prints pictures of the city's West and South Side streets transformed into ghosts of World War Two European rubble, ghosts that never quite faded from sight or mind. The Tribune, on the other hand, is what Bedford Heights is reading. Instead of war-torn Europe, they see photos of looters and read accounts of white bus drivers who "heroically" rescue black and white passengers from rioters' rocks and bottles.

Driving west on 75th street, he is stopped by guardsmen on his way to work. Oncoming drivers seem to grimace as he nears Bedford Heights. Maybe that's how it's always been, he thinks. Or maybe that's how he is feeling, leaving his home of nearly 40 years unattended while schoolchildren march in the streets and black mourning banners fly next to the American flag all over the South Side. Or rather, his South Side. He learned long ago that what other people don't want, they call yours. All of a sudden Billiard is asking him, "How're things in your neighborhood?"—the first time he's ever acknowledged that T.J. has one.

As the West Side burns and the South Side agitates to spread the fire further, suspicion blooms into full-fledged hatred, hatred from which he and Mildred have previously been exempt. Before then, neither he nor Mildred have ever been accused of any wrongdoing during their years working in the Heights. They have been the exceptions that prove the rule. April 4 changes that.

The talk in Bedford Heights, the talk T.J. isn't "supposed" to hear gets louder. Now it is as if they want him to hear. As if they know that for years Mildred has kept a photo of Dr. King next to Jesus on his mother's chiffonier. Or that four years earlier he let marchers for fair housing use his garden hose to cool off. Or that he plans on voting for Bobby Kennedy, should he get the nomination. Or that he likes to fish at Marquette Park every now and again. Or that when letters to the editor in the Defender agree with Stokeley Carmichael's argument that black men and women have a right to defend themselves against white aggression, he has a hard time finding any counter arguments, though he considers himself a peaceful man. What he isn't "supposed" to hear, then, is how it is King's fault for agitating people in the first place. What did the commie expect? And look at how those people are acting now that their leader is gone. Proof enough it's their own fault they can't ever get ahead.

They let him hear because he is one of the "good" ones. He is like them—decent, hard-working, responsible. Like them, he has little patience for those who are always leaning on others, pointing the finger of blame instead of taking responsibility for themselves. They can say these things to him. He is not one of "them." He is the exception that proves the rule.

*

As he lit up his after-dinner cigar (Kentucky, not Cuban tobacco), Mildred studied his plate. He'd tossed the spent match into the plate's center before realizing he'd used it for an ash tray.

"That meal didn't suit you." She pointed to his plate, emptied of all but a puddle of gravy.

"What you mean, darlin? I eat every last bit you done serve me." His calm words sounded false as soon as he spoke them. He tugged the ashtray closer and rested his stogie on the rim, careful to aim the smoke away from the table.

She shook her head sadly. "Don't recall the last time you ain't sopped up the gravy."

"Maybe it's time I start leaving some behind." T.J. patted his belly and tried to chuckle. Until now, he never thought of himself as carrying too much weight. He had a belly, yes, but he had always seen that as a sign of well-being. Skinny was for younger folk, or movie stars. He and Mildred were content to be well.

"Since when don't I know what and how much you need on your plate?" Mildred's face sank between cupped hands. "Since when you got to 'leave some behind'?" She folded her napkin into a neat square then reached over to stack his plate on top of hers. "First Viney, now you be disappearing on me."

"Disappearing ain't hardly the problem." He tried another, lame laugh. Mildred turned her head away and stared at the brass plaques of winners. "Tell me something." He leaned in as close as his belly would allow. "Out of all the rooms we got to sit in every night, why you pick the smallest?"

Her head turned sharply back. "Cause nobody come here, that's why."

"Since when you start caring about eating dinner alone? We eat with other people for years. Why all of a sudden you got to set us apart?"

Mildred sighed, setting her head back to rest on cupped hands. "I just do," she finally replied, pushing back her chair. Unlike him, she had no trouble finding room to stand.

That night he dreamed he was alone in the Derby Room, surrounded by the portraits of winners, his hands sprouting mutuel tickets for races yet to be run. The room was cold, like the walk-in cooler just off the kitchen. The entry had a steel door with a bar that slid across and locked shut. Like a piece of meat, or a corpse, he was shut away until the next stage of processing. His shouts drew no response.

How could anyone respond to his cries when he didn't know how to himself? He could not imagine turning his back on the track for a fishing pole and a porch down south. He and Mildred would be living on "the plan," with no room for extras except what the bond market allowed. At the same time, he could not imagine staying on at the Stables, catering to increasingly ignorant people. And then there was Lenny.

He wasn't used to caring so much how younger folks saw him. He had always placed more importance on them caring how he saw them. He'd tried his best to make that plain to Lenny. But now that Lenny was working at his side, Lenny reflected T.J. back to himself, and the picture was not what he'd expected. Now the emptiness reflected in Lenny's eyes, the same emptiness T.J. felt inside the Grand New Uniform, was almost too much to bear, his whole life wiped clean of consequence. Yet the only passage left for him to take was through that emptiness. Lenny, it seemed, was his only way out.

Part III

This dawns on me: no cloud is measurable.

Make mine cloud.
Make mine cloud.

> ---Marie Ponsot
> from "This Bridge, Like Poetry, is Vertigo"

Chapter Ten: Attic

The stairs creaked. As we climbed, I worried they would give us away. At least our shifts were over, so no one was looking for us. We could simply disappear and who would notice? The wooden steps sagged, my feet stumbling in their grooves. Groping through that narrow, dark passage, it struck me that many others had trod these steps before us. Lenny went first, eager for discovery, holding my hand as if to make sure I wouldn't change my mind. With no rail for balance, I had only his hand to steady me on the uneven, deadly steep steps.

"How'd you find this?" I asked him, stopping for a moment to catch my breath, hoping to slow him down. The staircase stood behind a door with no handle. I'd never noticed the door before. It looked like a mistake, a plywood panel hastily hinged to hide some broken-down space.

"That day we in the laundry," he said. "I seen it after you leave. When I come out to the hall, I'm just standing there, my eyes roaming. All of a sudden I see hinges, and I'm thinking, What the fuck? So I try it, even though there ain't no handle. And what do you know, it opens. Too dark to tell what is what, so I just stick my head in, and before I know it, I'm headed upstairs."

"You go all the way up?" I asked. He shook his head. "I hear them calling for me in the kitchen, so I have to go."

"You ask anybody about it?"

"Shit, no. Don't want nobody to know that I know."

I laughed. "Always thinking ahead."

"Damn straight."

"You plan this?"

"As much as I plan anything."

"How'd you know I'd come?"

"I didn't."

"So why do you think I'll go now?"

He pressed his thumb into my palm, flicked it like a tail. "You curious, Caroline."

"This is way past curiosity."

We took a few more steps until heat pressed down, my chest burning with its panther breath. His silence hung even heavier in the air. We had both passed curiosity some time ago. What was forbidden was drawing us out, directing us up this narrow canal, in search of its unspeakable source.

We kept climbing, feeling our way. My fingers slid against wood panels rough with flaking paint. The stairs were barely wide enough for us to pass single file. At the top, a corridor opened onto three rooms, each with their own, separate doorway. Moonlight filtered in from paned windows like quicksilver, painting everything a liquid gray. Here, too, the air was thick, almost immovable, like walking through walls.

Urine stung at my nostrils. Sour food desiccated on dirty plates. No mattresses, only abandoned blankets curled up like fetuses on the bare, scuffed floors. Another world up here, another logic, one of misery and survival.

"Not a rumor," I murmured. "Roberto. Angelo. Gabriel."

Lenny sighed. I squeezed his hand. "No place else to go," he said, shaking his head.

A slight wind carried in the smell of cut grass and exhaust. At the end of the corridor, moonlight shone on another door, solid and new. Unpainted, it offered a handle, unlike its counterpart at the bottom of the stairs.

He grabbed the door handle, then hesitated.

"It couldn't be any worse," I said.

He turned his head and stared at me as if he didn't know who I was.

The door opened easily. Inside, total darkness. We stood silently, apart. I waited for my eyes to adjust. After all the wretchedness we'd walked through, I could finally smell something clean. Clean and new. But also utterly stifling.

A closet," I said. "How far back d'you think it goes?'

"Let's see," he said, and took my hand.

One step, two steps, three steps, four. As long as the length of us, it was that deep. As I stretched out my arms, my fingertips touched the edges of shelves. There was just enough room for us to lay down or stand. Barely enough to stand—his hair flattened against the low ceiling.

As the moonlight caught up, the closet's offerings appeared. Everything was white—stacks of toilet paper, towels, tablecloths. Monkey dishes, cups and saucers, bread and dinner plates. Soup bowls. Aprons. Paper towels and Kleenex. In a tall apothecary jar, hundreds of Q-Tips in tidy, compact rows. Bags of cotton balls, boxes of powder puffs. The shelves were stuffed with this peculiar bounty.

"We never have enough monkey dishes," I said. "Why aren't these downstairs? And how come there's Kleenex here when I never see it anywhere else?" I couldn't begin to guess what the Q-Tips were for. "Why hoard when there's a need?

"And you the college gal."

I could feel more than see his smile in the hazy darkness.

"What a place," I sighed.

He brought his hand to my face and stroked my cheek, kissing me full on the lips. I reached for him, clutching his neck, and clung to him in the darkness. I was only too happy for him to relieve me of my uniform. I helped him do the same.

Layers of his smell rising as we undressed. Wondering, Do my smells unfold the same? Not to see him but to feel his skin against mine, his scent in my nose, to taste his tongue, hungry for his darkness. His hands urging my shoulders down but my legs wanting to stand. Wanting to stand with him. My hands reaching for his buttocks, gripping them, pulling them up and towards me, pressing him to do the same. The shelves biting into my shoulder blades, the bottom of my head, even my hips, sliding back even farther. His kick, and the door banging closed, urging us deeper inside.

His penis rising between my thighs. The shelves ending and my weight against the wall, hard, but his arms catching me, hands gripping my ass, holding me up off the ground. Thrusting back into him, my breasts mounding the curves of his chest. My left leg hugging his hip, relinquishing all balance. My legs splitting apart, allowing *too much* to move through my blood, my skin, my nerves, my pores. Giving over *too much* to his muscles and bones, his blood, mucous and breath. What has been hoarded a mystery no more.

Freedom. My bare feet flying off the floor, his hands gripping my hands gripping his. Feeling my dark breath inside his, giving his over to mine. This is freedom.

Chapter Eleven: Horse Barn

Viney still remembered which floorboards in the attic would give her away and which would keep her steps quiet, despite so many years and so much more flesh on her bones. She did not have to look to one side or the other to know that others were sleeping where she once laid herself down, with only blankets for their bed and buckets for their night soil. Instead, shadows drew her eyes straight ahead. No moonlight could reach them; no tongue could speak their name.

Even before her eyes adjusted to the darkness before her, she heard it. A new sound, like bones cracking or skin stretching as far as it can go. Only this sound didn't snap back to its old shape but kept turning into something new. A sound low enough to make the soles of her feet tingle, yet high enough to open the top of her head, so bright she could hear it bending through the corridor into doorways marked only by moonlight, could taste its eager odor on her tongue.

It was a holy sound. That she should hear it now did not surprise her.

Earlier that night, Mildred had offered her the usual ride home. Viney had shook her head.

"You going with T.J., then," Mildred said. It was not a question.

Viney stood quiet, holding her eyes steady as Mildred's bore into hers.

"You telling me you got another way home?" Mildred asked.

Viney shook her head again, slow and deliberate.

"You know I can't be leaving you here. No ma'am, I ain't about to do that." Mildred squared her shoulders. Her fists dug into her hips as she smacked her lips, her head and neck swiveling like an agitated mare. Only a few inches separated her face from Viney's.

"I ain't leaving," Viney said. Unlike the rolling tones in Mildred's high-pitched voice, Viney's remained flat and plodding, as if stating an obvious fact.

"You ain't going home?" Mildred asked, shaking her head as if to clear out cobwebs. She slapped the counter, its metal top echoing.

What loomed larger than Mildred's sweating face were the crickets out back, sawing at breakneck speeds. In fact, everything at the Stables lately was moving at a faster speed, following familiar rhythms but at a more frantic pace. The shift was small but noticeable. Mildred's sudden closeness made even the tiniest increase tangible.

"I'm staying," Viney said.

Mildred's jaw locked shut. Her eyes grew watery. As she spoke, her voice cracked.

"I done told T.J. my worries. I tell him, my girl's mind getting holey. I say that hoping it ain't true. I pray to God it ain't. But now you tell me you staying. Where you going to stay? Ain't no place for you here. Anybody can see that."

The same hollowness that used to drag down her mama's eyes had taken over Mildred's. It was a look that saw what was to come yet at the same time clung to the stubborn hope that maybe it would come a little more slowly, a little bit easier than it had before. And now, just as then, no words rose to Viney's lips to reach out, smooth over, build a bridge between them. Now, just as then, she felt the weight of her skin lift off her bones. What was different now was that she recognized that look, of having seen too much too fast, fearful of what all that seeing could do, how it could, in its contrary way, strike a person blind.

Tears drained from Mildred's eyes and did not stop, even when Viney, skin lifted off her bones, stepped forward and kept on going out into the night. By the time Viney came back inside, Mildred was gone, the back door locked, and as far as she could tell, the Stables closed down for the night. She looked forward to completing her nightly vigils in peace. The last thing she expected was laughter overhead.

She had stopped going to the attic so long ago it was a trial to remember the last time she had set foot there, in her former living quarters. Nothing upstairs had required her attention once the original Stables had been sold and she, T.J. and Mildred moved back to the South Side. Over the years, as owners came and left, few made more than a cursory visit to the remains of the Stables' old servants' quarters. Recently, however, interest in the attic had rekindled, as the word around the Stables was that Mrs. Parkerhouse had been spotted one evening stealing up the corrupted stairs. Shortly after, carpenters were dispatched, dragging up a hollow core door behind them. That in itself was not enough to urge Viney to make that monumental climb. Nor was this night's laughter enough, although it did give her pause. Only the hoof prints she found at the base of the stairs could compel her upwards, trusting that, despite the lack of light, they continued all the way up.

As she neared the shadows, the raw sound of new wood alerted her to the door before she saw it, the only room in the attic closed off from all the others. The brass doorknob cooled her palm as the door swung open.

Nothing disturbed the perfect dark around her. Clean lined the shelves inside --towels, toilet paper, dish cloths, typing paper, socks, underwear, dinner plates, and candles all uniformly untouched, despite the soiled blankets and ruined dinner plates scattered around outside. Even without a lock, even with so compelling a need as homeless blankets and splintered, worn floors, the clean remained virtually untouched.

What eventually filtered through her skin roared inside her like the night creatures she had come to know so well, breathed a wind so hot it was cold, turned itself inside out, then repeated its urgent circles. Moonlit rivers of sweat sprayed the air with smells of fish and frog, with all things damp and heaving, locked together in unshakeable embrace. Tentacles reached into air then melted into one solid trunk as they streamed roots deep into the closet's endless dark.

Slowly, as her eyes adjusted, she could see the heap of clothes that had snagged her feet, then two pairs of eyes above it staring back like startled deer. Swamp smells flooded her lungs and drowned her skin. Like a salamander, her skin breathed in the watery air then released it back to itself.

In the garden of Eden, Mamaw once told her, *God made Adam and Eve in His own likeness.* What was she doing, standing here among shame-filled clothes, while the two trembled, naked, before her?

She scooped up the pile gently, like discarded snake skins that, in less careful hands, would fall away in pieces. The clothes hung limp from her arms as she turned to go.

As she trod back through the attic's corridor, the moonlit bodies continued to sleep. Then suddenly four feet raced past her down the narrow stairs. Below, a door slammed shut. Outside, two voices rose up to the open windows where she had stopped to listen, each one's laughter colliding into the other's.

*

At night inside the Stables, bands still blow their horns and beat their drums while slummers kick back their heels. But not quite so many people come piling out in their fancy motor cars as before. She is glad to end her nights a little earlier, climb the horse barn's ladder before the birds begin their sun-greeting chatter. Her back hurts and her feet ache in new ways. She thinks about curling up in a ball and not rising until she's rested. Just as she's ready to release herself into the hay for the night, her skin starts to burn like tiny needles. A hunger for some unnamable something drives her out of the hayloft and into the pregnant mare's stall below.

Once when Viney was small, Mamaw wiped her mouth with the hem of her dress then took her on her lap. "You're a growing thing," she said, "and you need what growing things need. Here," she handed Viney a small metal box. "Go ahead and take some."

Viney pried the box open, lifting it to her nose and sniffing hard. All kinds of wonderful smells passed through her: rain puddles, moss, the fresh rot of fall leaves, wet rock inside caves, sweet decay from new-dug graves.

"I know what you been taking in. That's why I want for you to have some of mine. It's the best of what you been scratching for."

Mamaw pinched the black dirt between her fingers and tucked it into one cheek. Her empty fingers sparkled with mica dust.

"Most folks figure on the plants they eat to take in what they need. But sometimes that ain't enough. Sometimes we got to go straight to the source. And I know the best ones."

Until then, Viney hadn't thought much about what she put inside her mouth. The dirt, or whatever was in the dirt—rocks, plant rot, dead bugs and worms, dust from all over—was urging her to take it, lay it against the moist cave of her mouth. When the dirt was finished, she would move on to something else. Mamaw's keen eyes had found out Viney's secret and helped her pay attention to all the earth had to say.

Now that old hunger is coming back, and her source is Queen's Shadow's stall. Seeing the pregnant mare, hearing her, smelling her, even touching her is not enough to satisfy Viney. It helps that she is the only one Queen's Shadow will let near, trusting no one else.

Viney piles straw in the corner of the stall and keeps a vigil on her hunger, waiting for that moment just before the sun passes under the belly of the earth. Only then will she reach for that crazy quilt of smells that Mamaw had stitched for her so long ago, urging her to take what she needed, teaching her the generous ways of the earth. Like Mamaw, she is careful to keep her hunger a secret, away from daylight eyes. Her box is the night, that deep, soundless core that comes once stillness has fallen. That is when she lifts Queen Shadow's night soil to her mouth and lets her hunger have its way.

Every night before sleep comes for her, she listens to Queen's Shadow's breath for signs that birth is near. Viney must be there when the foal comes; Mudrack has made that clear.

"She'll try to trick you," Mudrack tells her. "Mares get so spooky, they don't want nobody around when they're foaling. She'll wait you out until you give up and leave and then the colt will pop on out."

The last few nights she has heard Queen's Shadow's hooves circling in the hay, pawing the horse barn's floor. The other mares and the geldings nicker and blow through their noses. Tonight, the circles are smaller, the pawing stronger. She hears the mare's body thump against the floor, her neck and withers ease down, get up, lie down, then get up again.

When Viney lifts herself to listen, Queen Shadow's hooves stop circling. If Viney eases herself down, the mare gets up. With this her first foal, she is not about to take a chance on humans, their hunters' eyes hovering over her exposed belly. No matter that Viney has spent weeks *standing in the mare's stall, combing her already perfect coat just to please her.*

The mare's restlessness stirs Viney's own belly, like cave echoes that bounce off one wall after another. This belly sense is new, just in the last few weeks. The bigger Queen's Shadow's belly gets, the more Viney can feel the foal turning in its mother's womb. Her own belly has gotten bigger, too, just enough to feel a downward pull whenever she gets up. Hidden underneath the man's shirt that T.J. has provided, her belly has drawn no one's notice. But whenever Viney enters the mare's stall, Queen's Shadow lifts her nose and sniffs at Viney's womb.

This night, when Viney enters, the mare is too agitated to notice. She licks at her tail, her eyes flashing white. Mudrack has said he wants to be there when the foal is born, but right now Queen's Shadow is kicking out at the walls, foam churning on her lips. Viney must stay close to the door to steer clear of flying hooves.

Finally, the mare exhausts herself and falls to the floor. Her stomach ripples with movement. The smell of urine hangs heavily in the air, mixing with fresh hay. Her coat is slick with sweat. She pants, exhaling hard.

Viney reaches for a bucket and sponge in the corner near Queen Shadow's head. The mare looks up at her, eyes dark, as if under a spell. She lets Viney smooth the cool sponge over her forehead, crest, and withers. As Viney works her way over the belly, she feels another ripple, its sharp stirrings inside.

The stall is nearly dark. Without windows, moonlight has nowhere to go. The heavy air is suffocating. Wet heat collects on her skin, drips down her neck and arms, between her breasts and thighs, gathering stray bits of straw on her bare feet. She has to feel her way down the mare's body, no warning signs to tell her if the mare will rise and thrash again.

Queen's Shadow kicks at her hip, as if to rid herself of the strange thing inside her. Viney manages to dodge the kick. Speaking in calm, even tones, she says, "This little baby trying to tell you something, Mama. Listen up now. You can't listen if you be lashing out like that."

With a sigh, Queen's Shadow's head falls back to the floor. Suddenly, her whole body tenses. A whooshing sound escapes from her hindquarters as she relaxes again. Viney strokes the membrane and fluid as it slides out into the straw. The mare raises up, her upper lip curled back, and sniffs with great concentration at what has passed through her. Viney sinks her fingers into the membrane, which breaks free with another push from the mare. Then a small hoof reaches forward into the still, dark air.

Mudrack had been firm, "You come get me the minute that mare shows signs of foaling." He sleeps in the tack shed across the yard. But the mare has wasted no time. If Viney slips out now, the foal will come on its own. Better that she stays. The mare has made it clear she wants Viney there as the foal slides out, one great heave at a time. Mudrack had warned her that the mare would try to stall while anyone was watching and wait until they left. But instead the mare has waited until Viney could reach her on hands and knees and watch over the foal as it breathes its first breath outside its mama's womb.

While the mare pushes and rests, pushes and rests, Viney sits back on her heels. She is now as wet as the mare, as the air, as the straw where the birth sac has broken. The heat grips them like a watery sac. She has to breathe through her pores like a fish through its gills. The foal is drenched, its hair flat against its bones like pond scum on a log. Its legs flail like a newly hatched frog. One final push and it is all out. It lacks for nothing; even its tail and mane are there, fully formed.

Something makes her bend over the exhausted foal and put her nose to its nose. Something makes her fill her nose with its newborn breath and to breathe her own breath into its perfect nostrils. She wants to know this smell, wear it, move inside it for as long as she has breath. A moist, heavy dampness that carries blood and hay and piss and spit in its breath. The smell of new skin and of dead.

The mare waits until Viney moves aside to start licking the foal clean. She licks steadily, carefully covering every inch of the foal's body, once, twice, three times. The umbilical cord lies in the straw between them, still connected by blood. She licks and licks until the foal has had enough. It shakes itself off and rises to its legs. The mare gets up, teats heavy with waiting milk.

Viney cannot help but feel pride in the foal's first tottering steps. Unlike the human babies she has known, the foal can see and hear her, stand on its own, and find its mother's milk within moments of leaving the womb. And also satisfaction—she is the first one the foal has touched, smelled, seen, tasted. Her voice is first to prod its ears up into a point. Her breath is the first it took.

This horse will be different than the others. This one is her Baby. She will raise it, and unlike the other thoroughbreds, it will run its heart out without being blind to what lies ahead.

By the time the sun has burned the sky orange, the mare and colt are standing together, sniffing, nursing, listening to the rafters creak overhead as the stable hands stretch their arms and legs to climb down to a new day. When they reach the mare's stall, they fall over each other, their shouts and cries drawing Mudrack out of the tack shed.

His yellow-brown eyes squint so hard the stables hands clear out. Viney alone stays, squatting in the far corner, picking hay from her hair.

"I couldn't leave her," she says, fixing her eyes on Baby's star-shaped blaze.

Mudrack grips the crop in his hand. His sideburns twitch as his jaw tightens. "You got a mouth, ain't you? That's what it's for. You supposed to use it."

"You say to come get you, but then you say she drop the foal if I leave. So I don't leave."

Mudrack walks his hobnail boots up against her bare toes. When he leans over, his gin breath fumes a sick cloud. He is the last person she figures to be taking a nip right now. Had he not been drinking, he might have heard the stallion stirring in the paddock, picked up the mare's restless paces, the groans of her final push. The stable hands often joke about Mudrack's uncanny traits. If they plan a party, Mudrack is sure to know about it, no matter how closely kept the secret. If a horse is off its feed or a stable hand out of sorts, he knows before anyone else. Nothing escapes his notice.

"Don't act dumb with me, gal. You got a mouth and lungs to yell with." He shakes the crop close to her face. "I got a mind to make you prove it."

She figures he knows as well as her that yelling was the last thing called for, horses' ears being fine-tuned things, and a pregnant mare's even finer. But for some reason, he wants to pin her in a corner, like the first time he caught her climbing the hayloft ladder, just to see what she will do.

Over Mudrack's shoulder, Barnswell's waxed-up mustache appears in the stall door.

"Oh ho, what have we here!" he bursts out, pointing at the foal.

Mudrack stares Viney down then turns to Barnswell. "Looks like we got us a fine horse colt," Mudrack says. "Sturdy as a rock, I venture."

Barnswell leans his elbows on the stall door's ledge. He nods to Viney, eyebrows raised, then turns his attention back to Mudrack.

"Dr. Harmkey already gone?" Barnswell asks.

Mudrack looks down at the boots that the stable hands joke will stomp through anything. Winter or summer, rain or shine, those boots cling to his feet through mud and shit, across bluegrass turf, and on into the red carpet inside the Stables. "I called him these last two days," he says, "and he told me to keep an eye out."

"Bastard! Too busy with his cattle and hogs. Just goes to show these hicks don't know a good horse when they see one." He presses his white shirt against the stall door and looks to Viney. "She stay calm, then?" he asks her.

She can feel without looking the heat rushing up Mudrack's face, his fingers tightening into a ball. She's just where he likes her, hunkered down in the corner of the stall, in that place where no kind of answer will do. Yet keeping her mouth shut won't do, either.

"Nature take its course. I just let it." She points at Mudrack. "I do what he tell me."

"Sounds like you had things well in hand." Barnswell pats Mudrack on his shoulder, on the brown serge coat that always covers his shirt sleeves. Mudrack makes a point to mark his difference from the stable hands with boss-style clothes, even if it means he does the dirtiest chores in them. "Next time, though, better wake me up. I'll give that two-bit vet an earful if he thinks I can afford to just let nature take its course!"

"May be time to make a change there," Mudrack says, his voice suddenly smooth. "Over to the track, they got vets that care about making winners. This here Harmkey just works out the basics and leaves the rest to chance. We could use somebody more scientific. We got lucky this time. Next time, could be different."

"You think we can get someone way out here?"

Mudrack draws a circle in the straw with the tip of his boot, then clears his throat and spits. Those rare times Mudrack has spoken to her, he sounds his cautions about horse doctors. "They get a piece here and another one there, but they ain't any good at giving you the whole picture," he says. He admits that Harmkey has a way with the Stables' brood, but when it comes to their moods and fears, he leans on tranquillizers to get the job done.

"Everybody's got a price," Mudrack says, staring into Barnswell's eyes.

Barnswell lifts himself from the door shelf and brushes off his shirt. "Find out," he says, his voice curt.

"I'll find out, all right," Mudrack says after Barnswell leaves. "We'll just see who knows the most about horses."

Sleep claims her quickly now, pinning her to the blanket across from Queen's Shadow until Baby's nose prods her cheek before dawn. Even when barnyard cats knead her stomach in the night, she cannot wake without a struggle. More and more, sleep wins out over all else.

She is the only one who mare and foal will let near, the only one Baby allows himself to be groomed by and to groom in kind, more fiercely courted than even Queen's Shadow. Each morning, she breathes in Baby's nostrils, giving him her full scent. Then she pinches a few strands of his mane between her fingers, working his neck, forelock to withers, while he nibbles the buttons on her shirt. He follows her around the stall while she mucks out old hay and lays fresh, hauls water and grain, and grooms Queen's Shadow with her favorite comb. By the time Mudrack and the stable *hands are up and around, she is whispering goodbye to Baby while he nurses at Queen's Shadow's side.*

When the new vet pays a visit, he can't get near enough the pair to do any good.   "I can tranquillize them," he shrugs, closing his black snakeskin bag, "but I have to get closer to do it."

Barnswell barks at Mudrack, "Tell him to give her the needle." He thrusts his chin at Viney.

"Pills would be better.   Any pills?"   Mudrack asks the vet, who pulls a vial from his bag.

"Put this in some oats," the vet says.   Mudrack grabs the feedbag off its hook and leaves.   Returning, he takes the vial and empties it into the feedbag.

"I'm done fooling around," he growls at Viney, handing her the feedbag.   She slips it over Queen Shadow's head and under her chin.

"What about the colt?"   Barnswell asks.

"Here."   Mudrack pulls out a hood from his jacket.   He tosses it to Viney.   "Slip that on him."

The hood is a sheet cut down and sewn up the sides.   It slides easily between her fingers.   She makes a fist under it.

Queen's Shadow shakes her head from side to side and up and down. The feedbag flops against her cheeks.   "She ain't taking it," Viney says, nodding to the mare.

"Damn!"   Barnswell yells.   The mare snorts and rolls her eyes. Baby's ears flatten.

"Put that hood on the mare," Mudrack tells her.

She releases the sheet from her fists and holds it up between her hands.   The sheet is smooth, stroking the ashy calluses on her hands.   She strokes it back, her fingers curling into the sheet's silk, first with one hand, then the other, admiring its flawless weave, feeling her roughness in its smoothness, her smoothness where the seams bunch up along their crooked path.   Plunging one arm then the other inside the hood, she pulls it taut, enjoying its caress on her forearms above her rolled-up sleeves.

As she pulls her arms wider apart, the sheet pulls back, and the seams show their gaps.   She tries to match her arm's width to the mare's head, but try as she might, the hood will not give way.   She can stretch it wide enough for Baby, but not for a full-grown horse.

"Too small, Thomas," Barnswell mutters.   She has never heard Mudrack's Christian name before.   "You were right the first time. That hood is better for the colt."

Mudrack stares out into the barn's aisle.   His jaw sticks out and his cheeks pull in.   When the vet snaps his bag shut, Mudrack blinks and shifts his eyes back to the stall.

"I've seen this before." The vet shakes his head. *"Once or twice, but it does happen. The foal bonds first with its human caretaker. Then the mare has trouble getting the foal to nurse. In this case, thank goodness, that hurdle is jumped, since this mare has bonded with your groomer."* He nodded towards Viney. *"In fact, I'd say she's protecting not just her foal but your groomer, too."*

"So how will you examine them?" Barnswell asks. *"What are the options?"*

"From here, the foal looks healthy, about the right weight, good posture, carriage, conformation. Beyond that, you'll have to ask your groomer. Your situation is psychological, not physical. I can't help you with that." He takes his bag and leaves, still shaking his head.

"Scientific, my ass," Mudrack spits out.

"And exactly what are you going to do about it? 'Let nature take its course'?" Barnswell says, his voice full of ice.

Viney holds the hood in her arms, welcoming its soft body against hers. Of all the cloths that could have been used, this was by far the finest. Still, no matter how soft, it would scare a foal as young as Baby to lose sight of it caretakers. Mudrack knew that as well as she. She used to trust that he had the horses' best interests at heart. Now, as he grew more desperate to prove himself, she had to rely solely on herself to protect and care for them.

Even at this young age, Baby's leg muscles twitch, testing their readiness. In his sleep, his limbs kick out aimlessly into the air, moving as fast as they can, his legs stretching so far all four hooves rise up at once. Already Mudrack is talking about when and how to break him. He, too, has seen Baby's restless legs and dead-set eyes, and is planning his first year on the track. The talk around the horse barn is that this is the one they've been waiting for. This is the Stables' winning number.

The tack shed is full of all manner of contraptions she has never seen the likes of before. Even the simplest halters and bits look complicated. And they are too big for Baby. Fortunately, there are blankets and rope. She picks up an Indian weave and rope no thicker than her little finger and heads back to the horse barn. Sunday mornings are quiet at the Stables, everybody sleeping off the effects of whatever spirits held them captive the night before

She is not surprised when she hears Mudrack behind her as she goes into Queen's Shadow's stall. If the creaking hinges on the shed door and the clanking harness rings hadn't woke him in the tack shed, then surely her ragged breath would have. Even with his eyes closed, sleep had no real power over him.

He stares while she holds the blanket to Baby's nose and sniffs it along with him. He keeps staring as she lays the blanket on Baby's back, his *flanks quivering. A sharp whinny escapes from his lips, and Queen's Shadow moves closer, her neck arching protectively over Baby's back. Mudrack's shirtsleeves bear wrinkles from where his brown coat has pressed them flat, and his suspenders carry shreds of straw from lifting bales. The air around him churns with the smells of a river bottom resurrected.*

He has always kept at least two arm lengths between them. Before now, there had never been cause to cross this invisible line. But now, as Mudrack steps closer, the line is crossed. She can't move forward or back, trapped between Baby and the man who would claim him.

"Teach me," he says, his foul breath carrying his words halfway between an order and a plea. His mud-colored hair sticks straight up like a rooster tail. He inches closer, his trousers brushing hers at the knees.

Her daddy was the one who had schooled her on how to listen. "The world be telling us all manner of things that most folks don't pay no mind to. So nobody can see what they is, who they be," he'd say. He taught her how to listen to the Morgans. "They tell you what's inside you, and you tell them what's in them. This way, both get bigger."

Through her, Mudrack is holding up a mirror to himself. Inside it, a river swells its banks, yellow-brown and thick, harboring branches and roots torn away in its current. "Whatever inside them be inside you," her daddy told her. "You feel something strong, that strong be you. You feel something weak, that you, too. If you listen, you know what I mean."

She is that fierce, onward flow that knows only it must keep flowing. She is that stink being swept loose in this drive to merge with something beyond itself. How could she not love this?

Mudrack raises his hands, palms out, both a blessing and a threat. "I can beat you, or I can beg you, but neither way is going to get me what I want. So I'll just say it straight. I ain't no science doctor, and I ain't no voodoo man, neither. Just show me how you do it. Show me how you get through."

The more he talks, the more his face loses its pulled-tight look. His shoulders roll back, then his hands drop down to his sides. In his eyes, the yellow-brown has sharpened to a clear, clean light that pierces her like a fine needle.

"Only way to get through is to listen."

Mudrack's eyebrows squint down into each other like two caterpillars courting. He crosses his arms and takes a step back.

"You mean to tell me this colt is saying something?" he asks.

Viney brushes off her trousers. "If you ain't already think so, you'd a been long gone."

"What do you want?" he whispers hoarsely.

Queen's Shadow knickers, her ears flattening. Her tail swishes, agitated, against the pine board walls.

Viney points to Baby. "I go where he go. I say how he and his mama get treated. I do what need to be done."

"Looks like that's what you aim to do regardless."

Her eyes roam the dark stubble on his chin and upper lip, dark circles like nameless shadows under his bloodshot eyes.

"Ain't no cure for this," she says, gently, as if to a newborn. "They take us over. We got to listen and do for them, or we lost. Can't live without doing for them."

He reaches out for her shoulder, but Queen's Shadow snorts and shakes her head until he lets Viney go.

"I hear you," he says, rubbing his fists into swollen, watery eyes. His thick tongue grazes his lips. "No cure for something that ain't a ailment to begin with." He turns and heads for the door.

"Lucky," she says. He swivels around to look back over his shoulder. Baby is nibbling her fingers on one hand while she rubs pieces of his bottle-brush mane through the other. He squints at her like she's a too-bright day. "We lucky not to believe in luck," she says as he heads out the door.

"You ain't one thing or another," Mudrack says. "Nobody claim you."

Since the new moon, he has been coming to the horse barn late at night. He waits until the hayloft has settled before he inches open the barn door then closes it right behind. Careful as he is, she still hears the hinges complain, smells the hay he stirs up with his thick-soled boots. Queen's Shadow nickers nervously until Viney lays a hand on her chest to calm her. Still, Baby saws his lips back and forth so much she has made a salve to treat the rawness.

If heat has a belly, they are inside it. She can't take a step without something creaking or cracking or crunching underfoot. Barnswell has ordered the stable hands to take their smoking off the property. She can hear them in the evening rustling around the tasseled corn that has already begun to turn yellow. Barnswell worries out loud that the wells will run dry; the stream that feeds the willow has already disappeared, and the cattails around the swamp have scattered like white feathers. The heat has held everyone so long and so close it seems like some other lifetime when water flowed.

Lit up with gin, Mudrack hasn't waited this evening for night fall to cover his tracks. Light is still creeping up the horse barn's aisle. Mosquitoes hover in the dusk, half-hearted, finding little water to draw them.

The stable hands are out having their smoke and smashing a few stalks of the neighbor's corn.

She backs up closer to the horses, putting herself between him and them, as she has before, but with no intent other than to ease him into their company. Little by little he has been closing the two-arm's length between them. More and more she feels pressure boiling up in that last bit of space. Tonight there is enough gin on his breath to sour what air remains. His yellow eyes are sunken and dull, dangerous in a way she's never seen before. He has left his brown coat behind; his shirt sleeves are rolled up above his elbows as if for a fight. Sweat shivers from the ends of his raggedy mustache.

"All about the blood. Ain't got the blood, ain't got no chance." As he stands there staring, his words hang in the darkness between them. They have a flinty edge that puts her nerves on notice. She isn't used to this sharp aimlessness from him. He has always been more steady, muddy crust on the outside, rusty crystal within.

He leans forward, the last bit of air between them disappearing along with the light. She backs up into Queen's Shadow, who whinnies nervously. She can back up no farther without putting the horses between them. And that she will not do.

"Shit!" he exclaims, spraying spit in her face. Startled, he backs off a little and looks down at his boots. "They put you in the race, knowing you ain't got no chance of winning but knowing you'll run because that's what you do."

She gulps a full breath, grateful for the space. Her shoulders, hunched up near her ears, roll back to their natural place.

He slouches over to the far corner, away from the horses and the stall door, and reaches up for a lantern on a hook overhead. "Shouldn't be in here," he mutters. The lantern clanks slightly as he lowers it to his side. "What in the hell?" The lantern drops from his hand and rolls to one side. He leans over, scooping, brings his hand to his nose. "What's this?" he growls. "Filthy, cocksucking—what the hell is this doing here?"

Fresh manure heats up her ankles even as a vague coolness drifts in overhead. She hasn't yet mucked out the stall for the night. The other thoroughbreds wait until the morning, but with Baby, the science doctor insists that "germs" should get no chance to spread sickness. Mudrack still can't believe that the vet has ordered the stall to be scrubbed up and down with bleach water every morning and the bedding hay to be boiled. Fortunately, Mudrack talked his way out of that one to Barnswell, but the stink of that order still lingers.

In the stalls across and next to Queen's Shadow, one gelding is scratching himself against the wall while the other whinnies his approval.

The chestnut mare whinnies back, and soon the stallion in the stall nearest the barn door starts his courtship knickers. "Damn," Mudrack says and kicks the manure, scattering it onto the hay where Baby had been sleeping. "Not enough these people got to win. No, that ain't enough to satisfy them. They ain't winners until they make everybody else feel low."

A catch in his voice softens her. Queen's Shadow and Baby seem to have heard it, too, for they quiet down almost instantly, while Mudrack sinks in a slow stink of gin to the filthy floor, unmindful of his white shirt sleeves or the trousers he takes such pains to press. She crouches, the muck around them heavy and sweet.

Across the gloom, she sees Mudrack, in his carelessness, has knocked over the lantern. That sweet, heavy smell is more than manure; kerosene has spilled out onto the floor. Now he is up to his wrists in the muck, frantically stirring fuel into the fresh manure. "Damn it all, now look what I've done. Don't just stand there. Help me dilute this fuel."

His shirt cuffs have disappeared in the pile. She thrusts her hands in along with his, her man's cuffs soiling themselves as well.

All of a sudden, the catch in his throat bubbles over into a wail, at first quiet, caught in his long, horsy nose, then gaining volume bit by bit. "Ain't worth it," he says, finally, sitting back on his heels. Both of them have added their own sweat to the stink around them. He leans to one side, reaches into a pocket, pulls out a tin flask.

"Science doctor knows a science-type trainer." He tips his head back to catch the last drops then carefully recorks the flask. "Only a matter of time before I'm out. They got you for everything else."

Even in the gloom that has settled in the stall, she feels the flare of his nostrils, his racing heart beat, the rigid muscles that bend his bones at sharp angles. She has watched the exercise boy, whip in hand, graze the stallion's flanks when the thoroughbreds fell into a just such a state, fear about to overtake the flow of their stride. The neck strains, the stride shortens, the eyes roll up to show their whites. One side fighting to break with the other, the other side racing to stay joined. That the whip would not settle the matter in one, clean wrist snap surprised her when she first started to watch. But over time she understood how the jockey was clever not to force a final outcome. Instead, he let the whip's leather dance on the horse's rolling flank, a hint of predator claws enough to play on the thoroughbred's panic without losing the flow of its stride.

Mudrack, though, is on the verge of stumbling. She has heard so many stories of thoroughbred legs snapping like twigs during races, their bloodlines favoring this weakness over less agile, but more dependable limbs. She has yet to put jockeys' whip wisdom into practice, but Mudrack, now sitting down in the manure, is pushing her to use all that she knows before fear shatters the flow of his good sense.

Her fingers curl and spread out like tails, snaking towards his right shoulder. She feels the strangeness of his shape, like a tight, new bud before it blossoms. Her fingers guide themselves by his hard breathing, reach his starched-to-a-fault shirt, limp now in the swarming heat, and start to brush in quick, strong strokes behind his heart, as if her fingers are four legs running.

Breath comes as if through her pores rather than her nose and mouth. Two-arm's length is left behind in a hazy before, *and* now *is a space she must steer without light. He is a creature unlike any others. Despite his horse-like ways, he is a mystery to her. Only his misery is familiar. She knows what misery requires.*

Her fingers race across his shoulders, a landscape of rock, roots, and wind. But before she can inhale once, he shoves her away, hard. The force is enough to drop her on her behind.

"Red-skinned witch," he hisses. His face is huge in hers, so huge it almost disappears in the gloom. "You can work your hoo-doo on them horses, but not on me."

Something about the in-between light, not quite darkness, keeps her from ducking his mud-colored arm as it cocks back then speeds towards her, fist at its helm, until she is knocked flat on her back. But the same not-quite-darkness alerts her to Queen's Shadow, darker than what surrounds her, rearing up, so she can roll away from under the mare's hooves and into a broken-up bale.

"I know what you are," Mudrack is on top of her, shouting. "Wearing them man clothes. You put a goddamn spell on me."

In the pauses between his hard breaths, she hears Baby screaming. Queen's Shadow snorts like a train engine at full blast. Far off, a stable hand's laugh somehow finds her shit-soaked ears even as the snap of buttons flying from her flannel shirt pounds her like gunshot at close range.

His knees pin her between them so she can't move away from the sound of her shirt ripping, nor from his gin breath cooling her bare chest. She can taste the horse shit even before it enters her mouth, covers her eyes, clogs her nose.

"This is what you are. What we are. You and me both." He thrusts his hipbones into hers, bone knocking bone, with just a thin stretch of cloth between them. "Low down, dirty, shit-eating cunts."

The hum in her head is so loud it shakes the whole stall, until Queen's Shadow kicks out with her rear hooves, and Mudrack is holding his chest, laying flat on his back.

"*Science doctor say we unnatural.*" A laugh shoots out while he's still on his back. "*Got that, gal? You and me, the mixed breeds, unnatural. Thoroughbreds what count, not us.*"

It is all she can do to keep Queen's Shadow from stomping him into dust. Baby has stopped screaming and has collapsed in the corner, exhausted. The harness on the wall calls out for her to lead Queen's Shadow out to the pasture so she can clean up the stall without Mudrack stirring things up again.

At the sound of the harness jangling, Mudrack is on his feet, searching his pockets once more. Queen's Shadow starts snorting all over again. Mudrack pulls out a fat cigar and bites off one end. A box of matches follows.

"*This is what they dole out when they are done with you.*" Tobacco pierces her nostrils in sharp, bitter tones, more mysterious than the roll-your-owns the stable hands provide her. "*Well, I got news for them. They can clean themselves up, call the gin joint a 'supper club,' get some fancy-looking people with some fancier-sounding titles, and act like they legit. But I'm the only one who can get these horses to run like they should. Them people can't have it both ways. They can't keep using people up and spitting them out and expect them to lay down and take it.*" He strikes the match. "*Let em burn in hell.*" The matchbook, unlit, slips from his hand to the ground.

It is so dark now that the one match looms large before her. Its flame doubles inside his eyes, and in the eyes of Queen's Shadow, whose snorts have changed from long, throaty shouts to quick pants of fear. The light freezes Viney, stock still in her black boots and suspenders. Her pulled-back hair has fallen and spreads across her cheeks and shoulders in tight waves. Her breath freezes, too. Every last bit of her is focused on that match flame, as if by holding it still in her mind, she can hold it still in Mudrack's hand and let it burn out to its natural end.

He stares back from behind the match, a hard squint. "*Purging is the only way. You grit your teeth and burn it out. That's the only way.*" The cigar sails smoothly into the flame, which bites its tight-rolled body. Mudrack shakes out the match, holds it to his tongue, then releases it into the muck-soaked hay.

She bends over to snatch the spent match as he walks out of the stall, stiff and ceremonious. The last she sees of him, the cigar is pinched between his right thumb and forefinger, and his head is bent forward, pulling a blind load like a mule.

They find a human skeleton in the ashes, along with those of the thoroughbreds. That ought to prove she is alive, but instead she struggles *with the conviction that those bones belong to her. She was supposed to die; the barn door was locked, and but for Baby, she would have slept too long to ever wake again.*

She still hears the talk going on around her. The stable hands stay on a few more days to clean up, and when they stop for their smoke, their talk revolves around another stable hand who disappeared that same night, along with Mudrack. They argue different stories about what happened, including a "lovers' quarrel" between the two men just inside the barn door. But the stable hands' words pass through her like smoke. Nothing they say convinces her she did not die with the thoroughbreds. The barn door was locked. She knew no other way out.

The stable hands find the latch in the rubble, still locked shut. When they ask her how she escaped, she answers them by staring through their charcoal-striped faces. Since the fire, she can see through solid objects as if they were light, like the picture show she saw once on the South Side. You could wave your hand in front of the picture-throwing machine, and it would be covered with pictures. She can see things both as solid and as rays of light. When she sees the world in that second way, she can move through anything, even walls. So if she is dead, and she thinks she must be, she feels an unexpected relief in this double vision of things. Now nothing in the world can contain her.

*

The two laughing voices led her back downstairs. On her way outside, she stopped in the laundry room, arms full of their clothes, and set the machine to fill while she sorted through them, more by feel than sight, having left the lights off to do her work. One pile lights: long-sleeved shirt, shorts, bra, panties, slip. One pile darks: trousers, dress. One pile leave-alones: red jacket, black hose. She scooped soap in a cracked coffee cup with no handle and poured it into the warm running water, letting it run over her hands. Then she bent down, breathing hard, and picked up the light pile, releasing it into the foaming tub. The lid slammed itself shut. The laundry room's door hinges wheezed behind her as she eased herself back into the kitchen.

Even without a full moon filling the sky, she knew where they would go. The grass grew a little greener there, a long, rectangular patch that was always a little ahead in its height, fed by ashes below the turf. But for the moonlight, it was the darkest spot anywhere.

She stood in the back door, palms pressed against the doorjamb. Lights from nearby houses had been switched off hours ago, leaving only distant halos from streetlamps and porch lights to crack the absolute dark. An owl hooted, paused, then hooted some more. Mouse feet skittered in the dust. Just beyond the pasture's whitewashed fence, lightning bugs flickered like flames, scattering themselves over the grass in ragged bits of brilliance.

She did not see them. She did not have to to know they were there, lying together in the exceptionally long, green grass. But unlike their storied forebears, they would have unspoiled clothes to step into when the garden was no longer theirs.

Chapter Twelve: Big Willow

For years, it had been his favorite pissing spot. He liked to think his water had helped the tree swell to its huge reach, wide enough to dust the Stables' eaves. Working outside as much as he did, it was a blessing to have a place to stand. In the old days the stable hands had had the choice of a broken down privy or a stolen piss against the barn. At night, they had the whole pasture to piss in, but nothing to piss against. The Big Willow gave him that.

With Bedford Heights so built up over the years, and so much traffic clogging the roads nearby, he had had to give up the quiet shelter of the willow and go inside to do his business like everybody else. Not that he minded on those days when the air was cold enough to freeze his johnson. But when the weather was cool, and especially when it was hot, nothing eased his soul more than the leafy hair of that big willow tree brushing against him while he stood, listening to the breeze rustle its drooping yellow branches. It didn't bother him that he was staring straight into the kind of switches that Angel Fair used to use on his behind. She'd had to go to some trouble to get those switches, since the only trees around were next to big houses on Grand Boulevard, a considerable walk from their three-flat. In fact, seeing those limbs again was a comfort, like her hand brushing against his cheek, a hand that, for all its upright firmness, was as warm and enfolding as a hot cup in winter.

On those nights he couldn't talk himself into going straight home, he stayed back just to relieve himself against the willow's heavy bark. It was one of those nights, hot and steamy like the hottest nights down south, that the notion came to him; he would keep Lenny late and show him where the famous and the lowly had mingled piss and smoke, something unheard of in this day and age, tell him the stories of what had brought them all together.

But when the time came to bring Lenny around, he found himself scrambling for some reason to persuade Lenny to stay and listen to his stories. After all, Lenny had his own spot staked out on the Stables' west wall; he didn't need the Big Willow for a place to stand. T.J.'s shoulders sagged a little more underneath the Grand New Uniform as he considered how Lenny likely would cock his head and lower his eyebrows as T.J. told about pissing with Charles Lindbergh and sharing a smoke with W.C. Fields. These were dead men in history books that Lenny probably hadn't even read. Or if he did, it was as The Past, a time that meant only shuck and jive and minstrel grins and too poor for shoes. The past was the past. Lenny wasn't the only one to think so.

But T.J. clung to the thought that he had to offer more than stale gossip and old dreams. *Angel Fair, don't let me down.*

*

Angel Fair is nothing if not steady. The burn from the willow switch spreads evenly across his backside. She never hits him out of anger or passion, but in an even, dogged rhythm that somehow brings the chaos inside him to a halt. Even though it hurts, the switch somehow always calms him. But this time, it just seems sad. He is already taller than she is, and stronger, too. They both know he doesn't have to suffer her licks. He does so out of respect, but also not without some guilt. He's fallen in love, and little by little, that love is taking him away from her, from the South Side, from the life she's imagined for him.

She finishes with a loud, "Huh," as if her last breath has escaped. When he turns around, he half expects to see her lying crumpled on the floor like an empty flour sack. Instead, she is still standing, the switch hidden inside the folds of her considerable skirt. Dressed in one of the high-necked white dresses she's worn ever since he can remember, her brown eyes swim in white pools of fear.

"Those horses bring the wrong element around," she says firmly. She still wears her hair in a knot on top of her head, looking much older than the women who go to beauty parlors to relax their short-cut hair. Sometimes people mistake her for his grandmother. Her face is smooth and her eyes clear, but her old-fashioned style speaks of times past.

Her attitudes follow her style.

"I can't help it," T.J. says, holding his palms out in appeal. His fingers are still sore from gripping the chiffonier. While Angel Fair swung the branches, he stared into the eyes of his family in their traveling clothes, captured in a framed photo, into their straw hats and shiny clothing: determination and hope in Angel Fair's face, his father's quiet, downcast look, his brothers barely older than babies, and uncles and aunts crowding the scene. As he took his licks, he found strength in his family's presence, even as he felt their disapproval of his new, more "modern," ways. He is glad for the chiffonier behind him now as his mother speaks.

Angel Fair's eyes flash as she answers, "You can always help yourself."

Until he starts going to the track, he believes that, too. With policy, there is a clear line between gamblers and numbers men. The gamblers throw nickels and dimes at a chance for more, no matter how slim a chance it is. They have no other. The numbers men make their chances. But do

*either love the game? Love hasn't been on T.J.'s numbers-man mind; what
has been is getting ahead, making Angel Fair proud and himself flush.*

*At first, he puts off Miguel about watching horses train. He wants
to be scientific, study the charts, learn about breeding and blood line
success. He doesn't need to go deep inside a world where the only black
faces are placing nickel bets at the window or mucking out stalls out back in
the barns. But Miguel lures him out early one Saturday, when the streetcars
are empty and the drivers too sleepy to nod them aboard, promising T.J he
won't be sorry.*

*They sit on bleachers next to the exercise ring, rubbing arms for
warmth. What happens next lingers like a dream. A huge black horse
walking past. Those muscles, their ripple and glide. That chest as big as a
truck. And that single, side-glancing eye, staring down from its heavenly
heights. Fixing him with a look that says, All glory to the race.*

T. J. like a flea waiting for his chance to hop on.

*One man holding a stopwatch, the rider crouching high on the
horse's back. The sight of this horse, straining to be released, rider gripping
the reins, digging in his heels, leaning into its ears. Making it wait, as it
would at the gate, as it would on the track for that moment it longed for, not
before, not after, but now. Ready now.*

*Let him go. Let him go. T.J.'s breath grows shallow. His heart
beats against his chest, squeezing his lungs and gut. Too big, too big. His
heart is set to explode. If they don't let this horse go now.*

*And then, they are gone. Hooves flying across the dusty ground.
Not just a manner of speaking, not touching earth. On the far side of the
track, making the turn, gaining speed. And would keep going but for the
reins, the rails, the rider's shifting weight. But for that, running forever.*

*The stop watch has clicked off. A frown creases the watch man's
face. "Again."*

*But they do not let the thoroughbred run for long. He is forced to
hold back. Will not let him feel the full measure of his power. For the race.
It is all for the race.*

*

He couldn't put his finger on it, but something was different about
the boy. Like he already knew what T.J. wanted, even before T.J. knew
himself. Lenny didn't put up a fight about staying late. He didn't ask why
he had to walk over to the Big Willow. And when they got there, instead of
complaining about the mosquitoes, he unzipped his fly and let out a big sigh.

Like he'd been doing it all his life.

"Man, I been waiting for that," Lenny said. He zipped back up and
stretched his arms over his head. His Grand New Uniform sleeves drew up
to his elbows as his hands pushed aside willow limbs to make room.

T.J. wanted to ask him where else he took his Stables' pisses but thought the better of it. He didn't want to act like the boy had no sense. Instead he asked, "Been saving it up, now?" Lenny had always been sort of shy when it came to his personal goods. Years ago he'd had to show the boy how to grip himself properly at a public toilet, not that two-fingered sissiness his mama let him get away with.

"Putting it off make it feel so good when you let go," Lenny said. Even in the Big Willow's shadows, T.J. caught the light playing in Lenny's eyes. His cap was off, and he was running a hand through his noticeably fuller afro.

"I imagine you got some practice with that, then?" T.J. tried to smooth over the quarrel in his voice between curiosity and disapproval.

Lenny took the bait. "Ain't just practice." His grin egged T.J. on to ask more.

T.J. chuckled like he was amused, not worried. Just the other day, Mildred told him about a pair of black stockings she'd found in her big bone pot that morning. T.J. had clicked off the possibilities in his mind. Now, Lenny's bragging narrowed the list down even further. He didn't discount bartender Ernie, but Ernie wasn't the kind to mess around on greasy counters and funky floors. Ernie picked women who looked like what was between their legs was as tidy as their painted-on faces and sprayed-together hair.

"Getting some, now, are you?" The wistfulness that came over him all of a sudden was surprising. There was a time when that kind of attention mattered maybe more to him than tips. He was new to it all back then, and so he thought those sidelong looks and whispered words were promises he could count on, licking him, petting him, rubbing and brushing and oiling him up and down with their eyes, fingers, mouths, breasts, hips, legs, toes. Grooming him to give them what he had, *all* of it, no holding back. They weren't asking about the latest hot tip at the track, and they knew nothing about horses or racing. They didn't seem to want anything from him but *him*. Not work, not money, not gossip, not even goodness. No expectations except that he want them back.

"White chicks be crazy, man." Lenny shook his head ruefully, but his smile said otherwise. "Know what I mean?"

Now it was T.J.'s turn to unzip himself against the Big Willow. He didn't realize how much he'd been holding in until he let loose a long flow that lasted a good minute. He'd been too preoccupied with what to say to the boy to notice his own water build up. He was grateful for the interruption; he hadn't expected the conversation to go this way at all. He had expected he'd face a struggle to convince Lenny that staying on at the Stables, as he did, was a worthy pursuit. But now Lenny was turning to him as someone who might know things he wanted to know, somebody with a past he might find value in.

Funny how it took a "white chick" to make him ask.

"Son, if you only knew." Not just about crazy white chicks, but about a life at the door, a life going by the wayside, soon to be forgotten. Who would remember it, pass on even a little bit of what he'd struggled so long to learn? Angel Fair had known how to pass on what she knew, and as much as she could of his daddy as well, and their family and their family's family, and back on into Before Memory. He had had to learn to listen not just to her words, but to what was inside them. Problem was, he was no Angel Fair, never was, never would be. He didn't know how to tell what he knew, enough for Lenny to climb inside his words and feel them like T.J. felt the willow branches against him now, right down to his root.

He zipped up slowly, his thoughts weighing on him, burdening his movements. Lenny surprised him by reaching past into the Big Willow's trunk. From inside, he drew out a bottle, flat and rectangular like a hip flask. He unscrewed the lid and offered it to T.J. In the moonlight, T.J. could make out a Seagrams 7 label.

"I bet you bagged some booty in your time," Lenny said, his voice low enough to be almost reverent.

T. J. barely heard him. He couldn't get his mind past where Lenny had hidden his "booty." All these years it had never crossed T.J.'s mind to store his secrets in the Big Willow's crotch. Just propping it up against the branches would have doomed it. Between stable hands and squirrels, and rowdy patrons sneaking a little whatever outside, he'd known not to try to hide anything there. So how was it that Lenny did, right under his nose? Surely T.J. wasn't slipping. His tips were, but that was the fault of the white-faced stable boys, and Billiard had sworn to correct that, even if he hadn't, yet. He knew this tree like the back of his hand. But maybe that was the problem. He saw it too much to really see it anymore.

He took a swig then returned the bottle to Lenny, waving him closer. "What you got going here?" he said gruffly, almost to himself.

"Man, you could fill that thing up with a hundred pints of 7 and still have room. Rotten to the core."

Later T.J. would wonder at his reaction. It was just a tree, a goddamn tree, after all. But his heart seized up for one, dim moment. He didn't recognize the tears forcing themselves out of his eyes. Then disbelief set in; he had to touch it, feel for himself what lay inside Lenny's offhand words.

The bark gave way like a rusted-out carburetor. Even after weeks of heat, the wood deep inside still felt damp. He realized it was not rain he was touching, but sap leaching out from the wound. The hole was wide enough for two fists and so deep he couldn't feel the end of it. Lenny had it right: "Rotten to the core." The heart had disappeared without T.J. ever seeing a thing.

He heard the *sploosh* of whiskey smacking the mouth of the bottle, Lenny's lips licking themselves by way of answering. Somewhere between the roar of tires on distant pavement and the far-off hum of streetlights, he heard an owl call out, once, twice, three times. Or at least what he imagined was an owl. It had been some time since he'd actually heard one. Crickets sawed away in the swamp that had just about given up on itself, and a frog or two belched out for a mate. It all stung him, hard, the way skin feels when you rub it awake. Tingly and alive but aching to get past that. The ache would pass but the hollowness would stay.

A nudge to his Grand New Uniform epaulet. The bottle clinking softly against the gold metal button that secured the silky braid. "C'mon, man." Lenny's voice, of course, like from the other end of a long tunnel. "A little grease to the wheel."

T.J. shook his head. What was he thinking, anyway? Lenny already had it down, "grease to the wheel." In a few months, he had grasped what T.J. had learned by trial and error over many years. What was he worried about? He turned to Lenny and let out a big sigh.

Rotten to the core.

"Look, son." Lenny instantly dropped the grin and lowered the bottle down to his side. T.J. had never called him "son," careful not to confuse the boy about who his real father was. "I'm not saying this job be perfect. And the things that turn you on right now, down the road they what going to eat you up inside. But other things stick with you. Like this here tree." He tugged on a branch like a girl's pigtail and searched Lenny's face to see if he was listening. Lenny's hat had returned to his head, and his visor shaded his eyes. But T.J. could feel his stare.

"See, this big willow been here a long time. It done seen everything and everybody come and go. It don't miss nothing, young and old, ugly and handsome, rich and poor, famous and nobodies. You ever hear of W.C. Fields?" Lenny shook his head. "Back then, he a movie star, when movies first start talking. He come by this tree one night, asking me will I 'join him for a smoke?' He tell me everybody think he this hard-hearted man because of what he be in the movies, but that how he like it, so nobody know how he really be. He give me this stogie about as big as my head, and we smoke, take a piss, while everybody inside off doing they thing."

T.J. paused to give Lenny a chance to react. All he heard was Lenny's Florsheims brush restlessly against dead leaves.

"This be a place to stand," T.J. concluded.

He couldn't bring himself to put it in the past. But it was only a matter of time. Mrs. Parkerhouse, if she wasn't already, would be on the Big Willow like a spider to a fly. Lie-ability, libel-bility, those lawyer words for paying up the wazoo when something bad happens to patrons.   Not to mention the ultimate hoodoo, "bad press."   She was the one who made such a fuss about "historic preservation" but that was about buildings, not where they stood or what they sheltered, or even who they spoke to.

"Not for long," Lenny declared solemnly, almost apologetically.

A big, old breath cut loose from T.J.'s lungs before he could stop it. Just like the air escaping from the brakes of those shiny-sided fire trucks grinding down the gravel drive. He didn't blame Lenny for speaking the truth. But hearing it out loud like that made it too real. What it also made real was how many times T.J. had come to the Big Willow for answers to questions he never put into words. He couldn't exactly say he'd forgotten that because it was not something he ever realized he'd done in the first place. Only now, in this young man's presence, a boy about the same age as he was when he first came to the Stables, could T.J. know this had ever happened. It was like a door had opened to a new place that was the same as the old, only different in how he saw it.

"Don't get me wrong, man," Lenny kept talking even as T.J. leaned a hand against the Big Willow's trunk and dragged a Grand New Uniform sleeve across his dripping forehead. "I appreciate all you and Aunty done for me. And I admit, when I first take this job, I think, I can't do all this "yes'm-ing" and "no, sir-ing" to all these stupid ass white people. I'm listening to my bros, who say I make more bread scoring a little weed here, a little angel dust there, and selling it to white folks looking for a party. And then I'm thinking, well ain't that what Uncle Man be doing all these years? He score a little of this and that to land the big tips. That what you always telling me, so I'm thinking, might as well stay in the hood with my bros instead of getting dressed in this monkey suit and perform for whitey.   But lately, I been thinking maybe I got more in me than that."

He couldn't blame the boy for believing that. *Whispered promises.* All T.J. had promised was that he'd have a steady job, and these days even that wasn't too certain, given people's inclination towards Auto-magic, opening their own doors. Lenny wanted a little Auto-magic of his own. Funny how Lenny's wanting that made T.J. see how the Big Willow had been his "magic" all this time.

"No doubt about that," said T.J. "But you see what you got in you *because* you got the job.   You stay with your friends, and you won't see nothing but tired and pissed off."

"Aw, man." Lenny tossed the half-full bottle to the ground, cap screwed on. Even in the heat of the moment he was careful to guard his pleasures. "That's the problem. You think opportunity is sucking up to white people, begging them for a little bit more of their pie? Maybe back then it was, but things different now. I'm going to take what's mine."

"Including your white women?" T.J. felt a strange tingling run through his legs and arms as he said that. One thing Angel Fair would not tolerate was carrying on with strangers, especially those that stood to do you some harm. As it turned out, he had fallen for Mildred when he was still young and so kept only a certain curiosity about the slummer women who begged for his eyes to swallow them. He suspected that that's all they wanted, just the looks, although some of the stable hands had sworn otherwise.

"You think this the first white chick ever come on to me? I get them any time I want."

"And just what do you want?" T.J.'s voice was sounding farther and farther away to himself, like he was falling down a deep tunnel.

"Somebody who accept me for who I am. Not be trying to change me into something else."

T.J. let the Big Willow take all of his weight as he leaned into the tree. His head argued, Stand up! but his knees got the better of the argument, softening beneath him. For a moment, he worried the willow would collapse under his tremendous load: *Rotten to the core.* And it was a huge one, no doubt about that. But the tree managed to hold up. The strange thing was he never realized how often he'd come over the years to do just that, never quite saw the compassionate heart that invited his questions and murmured answers that always managed to set him at ease. And now, just as that door to the past was opening to him, the price his neediness had extracted from that tree was revealed as well.

Rotten to the core.

If it wasn't so painful, he would have laughed. Instead, he pressed one hand against the Stables' coat of arms sewn over his heart on the Grand New Uniform. Lenny kept jabbering away about being a "natural man" and "not putting on a show" and "not caring what other people think." T.J. heard everything he said, but it sounded like baby talk, baby talk he could understand, but baby talk just the same. It wasn't nearly as interesting as the swatch of moonlight that had come up out of the south and now bathed the Big Willow in its cool brightness. Nor was it as interesting as the wind that kicked up from out of nowhere, and the white-dressed Angel Fair with the fiery eyes calling out for somebody she said she was missing something fierce.

He opened his mouth to answer her, but words were useless. Instead, he gathered up the ball of pain rising from his chest to his throat and breathed out. The wind snatched it up and took it who knew where. Then he gathered up the warm light in his gut and turned it on like a spotlight to where Angel Fair still stood, hands cupped around her mouth, leaning forward with the effort of calling. Suddenly she stopped, moved her hands to her ears, and stood up straight, waiting. Moonlight caught the smile that spread across her shadowed face.

Thunder shook the ground below his feet. Lenny's baby talk cut itself off; fear flashed in his eyes. "You hear something?" Lenny asked nervously.

T.J. breathed hard, struggling to find a breath long enough to carry his words out into the air. "Just watch," was all he could manage to say. Even before the thoroughbreds came running out across the former cornfield and crossed over to what remained of their old pasture, T.J. felt an enormous gratitude. He didn't have the words to tell Lenny what it all meant, what to carry with him, what to leave behind. The pain in his chest gripped him harder. Could he even hope that Lenny would see what he saw, listen to the inside of his words?

Seven of them altogether. They ran from the south, like they were made out of moonlight, but kept running, seven horses in one, tight-moving body. At the pasture they were greeted by a white clapboard fence that they cleared effortlessly. Cleared it without jumping: just ran straight through, as if the wood was *rotten to the core*. The way the Big Willow now gave way to his hands pressing so hard in search of a place to hold himself up. But then the tree gave way; his knees buckled.

"Uncle!" Lenny cried out. He hovered over T.J., blocking the moonlight, the flow of horses running to the west. T.J. waved a weak hand, managed to grunt out, "Over there."   Angel Fair waved back solemnly before calling out again to T.J. The thoroughbreds wheeled around like a school of fish and started thundering back towards the pasture where the barn that had burned once stood.

Look, boy. But words had abandoned T.J. Even Miguel, the poet bookie, could only say so much to show T.J. what he meant when he called the horses *Los Dios*, worshipping them with his prayers of curses and praise. This was it; this was the race. How many people ever got the chance to see it from the inside? They ran through his blood. They ran with his heart. He had spent his whole life trying to keep his love in sight.

Angel Fair flashed her brilliant smile at him once more. The black stallion raced full-out past her, no holding back, as if her smile fueled his ecstatic pace.

"Uncle!" Lenny's sharp voice shattered T.J.'s ears. Lenny was tearing at T.J.'s Grand New Uniform, thrusting each gold button with the raised lion head through too-tight holes. If he could have laughed, he would have. Lenny had it all turned around. He was missing the show of his life.

T.J. may have been overcome by their power, but the horses were what drove everything. *Everything.*

He gathered his breath for one last, insistent command: "Go!"

Lenny squinted like he hadn't heard but followed T.J.'s gaze, twisting himself around. He snapped back towards T.J., fear and disbelief in his eyes. T.J. closed his eyes. *Enough. No more rotten to the core.* The last thing he saw before he passed out was Lenny running into the moonlight, running as if he thought he would catch one of those horses for himself.

Chapter Thirteen: Walk-in

"Hey," Caroline whispered.

Cold air spilled out from where she stood, holding the heavy, latched door ajar. The cold felt good on his sweaty face. Lenny took off his hat to let the cold find his head.

"What you doin?" he asked. Her lips were a strange, purplish color, like a stiff's. At first he thought it was lipstick. Then he remembered she didn't wear any. He had to say something to her about that. He only saw her in her uniform, and out of it. Except for that one night at the Star Dust, he hadn't seen her out on the street.

"Waiting for you," she said, and pulled him by the arm inside the walk-in. Damp, sour smells hit his nose. Lining the walls were shelves stuffed with boxes, barrels, buckets, and jars. Two yellowed stalks of celery hung limp from between the slats of a wooden crate.

His gut reaction was, *Get out, now!* The pleasant chill turned quickly into teeth-chattering cold. At least he had on his uniform jacket. She stood shivering, rubbing her bare arms together. Her feet were soaking in a puddle of water or some other nasty stuff. He lifted his head; she must really want to talk, to stand here freezing.

These days, they waited to get together after their night shifts, when most everyone had cleared out except bartender Ernie, T.J., the lounge lizards who danced to organ music played by a waitress in hot pants, and the Mexicans fast asleep in the attic. Lenny and Caroline mostly dodged being public together, but sometimes, in the heat of things, they took the risk of being seen. And as things got more intense between them, the more risks they took.

Now was broad daylight, between lunch and dinner shifts, and the whole cook staff was prepping for the night. All he needed was for Opal or Sarah to barge in and see them. Didn't matter if all they saw was just him and Caroline talking. Besides, Mildred Aunty didn't want people wandering in and out of the walk-in for nothing.

Caroline read his mind. "They sent me for ketchup." She held up a glass jug sticky with red shit like dried blood.

He shook his head, confused.

"Prep work. They make us refill the ketchup, salt, and sugar bowls for the next shift. I'm the next shift, so I might as well do it right. Nobody can accuse me of not earning my 33 cents an hour." She returned the ketchup to the shelf.

"Thirty-three cents an hour? You shitting me?" He tugged on walk-in's handle until the door was almost shut. But he couldn't quite make himself click the latch all the way.

"Not including tips. They don't have to pay us minimum. Then they skim our base to pay the bussers."

"I never thought I'd say it, but girl, I feel like a rich man."

He reached for her arms and started rubbing hard. Her lips quivered and her head bobbed, but she stood still while he warmed her. "What you doing, standing around freezing like this?" he scolded. It felt weird to talk to her like this, in the cold, bright light of the walk-in. It felt weird just to talk. That wasn't something they did much of, if at all.

"I broke it off." She leaned over and stuck her hands in his coat pockets. He could actually see little clouds forming around her mouth. The thought of Sarah or Opal or even Mildred Aunty coming in now worried him less than the jars of pimento olives staring at him like bloody green eyeballs, the slab of raw meat hanging like a fist from a ceiling hook, and the rotten smells from leaning cartons of lettuce. Sarah and Opal would give him shit about black women needing their men, and Mildred Aunty would start praying over him to find The Way. All that he could handle. He didn't much care if even Billiard or Mrs. Parkerhouse saw them. It was just a job. What he couldn't handle was the walk-in itself. Damp, stinky, raw and funky.

"Broke what with who?" He put his hat on her head then stuck his hands in his pockets next to hers and squeezed them hard. The hot shine in her mossy eyes lied about the cold. His hat tilted on one side of her head, making her look small and girlish. Even in the cold, he felt himself go hard.

"My boyfriend."

"Come again?" He felt her hands go slack inside his pockets. He pressed harder to bring them back to life. The cold had stolen her to a far away place.

She tugged her hands out from his pockets then stuck them under her armpits. Her lower lip disappeared between her teeth. "Kyle. I told you about him." She frowned, almost scolding. "I couldn't wait to tell you. I stood here freezing my ass off just to give you the good news."

Pouty was a new one from her. At least he was on familiar ground with that. But the "boyfriend" stuff sent him scrambling. He didn't have a clue about that, but *pouty* was at least something he knew how to remedy.

"Baby, I can't keep up with all the men who hot for you." A start, at least. *Put it back on her.*

"Well, aren't you glad? I did it for you."

"Whoa, wait a minute. I don't recall asking you for nothing."

Now he was the one shivering. His lips were probably as white as the fat on that cow's carcass. He rubbed his hands together and blew on them, as if caught midwinter without any gloves. His hard-on was just a memory now.

"What I mean is...I'm free! I told him he wasn't good enough."

He saw her lips move, heard sounds come out of her mouth, watched her eyes shift from round, liquid emerald to a hard jade squint. Everything felt way too heavy; he was in a slo-mo movie, could barely lift an arm to scratch his freezing head. His knees ached; he searched for a place to sit, or lean. Over in the corner, behind the meat-on-a-hook, a few dirty crates of lettuce teetered in a stack. He motioned there with his head.

"I can't stay—Dolores—" she stopped short, catching his look. "OK, just a minute."

. . . *good enough.* He was good enough, and that appeased the green-eyed olives enough to stop them from staring back, eased the rotten-sour stink of too-ripe food, and the electric hum of the condenser cycling on and off with blasts of frigid air. Even the fluorescent lights overhead softened, while his mind chased itself for an answer, *Good enough for what?*

She practically sat on top of him, not much room on a lettuce crate. She winced at the meat hanging before them, a partial shield between them and the door. They weren't exactly hidden, but they wouldn't be the first thing somebody saw, either.

"Gross," she said. Then quickly, "Oh, I don't mean—"

"'S ok."

"It's just that I'm a vegetarian—"

He didn't think he could take in any more weirdness than was already crowding him in this small, stuffed, freezing space. "Right," he said abruptly. "I get you."

"You do?" she looked surprised, even a little hopeful. "I mean, I would have broken up with him eventually. But with you—" she ducked her head ever so slightly, as if scared at how he might react. He kept his expression steady, unmovable. When he didn't react, she sighed. "I didn't want to hold back anymore." She settled back against a box of Land o' Lakes butter, chin pressing into her collarbone.

News to him that she'd been holding back. Whether that was good news or bad news, he didn't know.

"So you all mine now, baby. That it?" He fell back on that smooth, high-toned voice he had learned how to use with the high school chicks, who fell all over themselves just to hear it. But as he heard himself speak, it sounded hollow and deceptive. He couldn't play on her feelings now without feeling them himself. He had thought she already was "all his," and now that he knew she hadn't been, he wasn't sure he wanted her to be.

"Are you?" she asked. Her eyes skated across the walk-in as she spoke, her voice sinking like cold air to the floor. She could barely ask the question, couldn't even ask it all the way. So that's what it was about. *The big C.* Commitment.

This, too, was familiar turf. From pouty to possessive. White girls, black girls, brown girls, yellow girls, they were all the same. And he knew just what they wanted to hear, what would get him what he wanted, *a little sugar.* Or at least that's what he was supposed to want. What his homies bragged and scrapped for. But that was before The Talk.

That night under the Big Willow, T.J. had made it easy for him to see what, until then, he couldn't admit to himself. Lenny had been holding back on his homies. Tired of the same old rap they all had about either *getting some* or bragging on the piece they had just bagged, he had kept quiet about Caroline. It wasn't enough they each went out and got their own. They had to have a piece of his, too. Murth and Sugar Butt were street smart, but T.J. had been around longer than the two of them put together. Nothing surprised Uncle Man. He had seen it all. If Lenny was going to rap on Caroline to anybody, T.J. was the one he could trust to listen.

"It's weird, man, but we *connect.* We just click, you know, turn the switch on and we be flying," he'd told T.J.

Still, Lenny had struggled to put Caroline into words. Even the Seagram's he'd stashed inside the Big Willow's crotch could barely loosen his tongue, yet T.J. had stood and listened. Lenny had heard his voice echo back from T.J.'s chest. The more Lenny said, the bolder he got. Hearing himself talk was a comfort.

He had leaned over T.J., dropping his voice to a whisper even though nobody else was around to hear. "It's *freedom*, man. When I'm with her, I can do anything, be anybody."

At that point, T.J. had slapped his hand to his chest. His eyes had shined too bright, and his breath came out in short, ragged chunks. Lenny had panicked, thinking he'd crossed some invisible line between them. But when Lenny saw T.J.'s eyes were fixed behind him, he turned towards the very things he'd been trying to describe but couldn't. A strong wind messed with his hair. Under his feet, the earth pounded. High-pitched cries tangled through it all. Bulbous eyes gleamed through the dark, and noses flared to take in the musky, damp sweetness that surrounded them. T.J. clutched his heart like a man deeply moved, tears of sweat rolling down his face. He urged Lenny on. "Go!" he had growled, not once, but twice. "Go!"

Caroline was standing now, staring down into his eyes. She had stopped shivering and now held herself still, like a runner at the starting line. All around her were huge open cans of tomatoes, green beans, and evaporated milk, jars of mayonnaise, and plastic tubs and tins. Every inch of shelf space was packed tight with enough food to feed the whole hood and have leftovers the next day. He checked an urge to turn the dead cow into a punching bag. It didn't stop him from wanting to punch something or someone, swing his way out of this cramped, cold place, away from her red hair, plain black dress, and funky stockings like the saggy, black monsters his Great Aunt Amy used to wear.

"Well, are you all mine?" she asked again, this time managing to ask the whole question. Now her hands found her hips, and her elbows shoved out like raw chicken wings, the skin pale and loose and pimpled blue from the cold. The stark lights overhead brought out the blue shadows under her eyes, blue veins almost black at her temples and in her hands, angled towards her crotch. Blue like the fat on the beef hanging next to them. Raw, butchered, stripped, the blue blood trapped in cold, dead flesh. That was the prize, what Mildred Aunty cooked and fed him like a prince. And he ate it without ever thinking of where it came from or how it got there, just woofed it down like a hungry dog. *Getting mine.* That was his due.

He recognized the black that covered Caroline like a sack. It had veiled Great Aunt Amy's face as she lay asleep in her coffin. It had bandaged Murth's head after he was jumped by a gang out roaming for crystal meth. Now it punched a hole in his vision, a dark blot on the raw meat hanging before her: a question mark; a tunnel; a doorway back to night, secrets, and lies.

"Are you?" She was back in the walk-in's doorway, holding the door ajar. The dead truth or the lie he could live on? "Mine?" Her voice dropped on this last word. She couldn't keep up the pushy attitude.

Funny thing, that hole. It was like another set of eyes on him. He could see himself through them, and also Caroline, the raw meat, the pimento eyes, all the things that haunted him. He could hear voices crying out from beyond the walk-in's cold white grave. Eyes that gave no light, that had no white, that took everything in and gave nothing back. They were in her pupils opening wide and closing; the drain hole in the middle of the floor; cracks in the ceiling; the pause before she left the ketchup bottle behind.

After The Talk, he had done just what T.J. had urged. He had run out behind the Stables, circling west to the pasture fence where he had sat countless times to smoke, and flung himself over it, insane with the joy of having no reason to do it. In the darkness that surrounded him, he had been *stripped, raw,* but tender, too. Sturdy shoulders lifted him as he began to run, not away but to join something bigger. Grass sprouted between his toes. Sweat bloomed on his skin, air stroking his whole body until he nearly burst.

After The Talk, the urge to run came more easily. Whatever panic used to spur him on had been swallowed up in the dark. He wasn't running *to*, or running *for*, or even *away*. He was running *with*.

The walk-in door opened. Caroline caught herself quickly to keep from falling over. In the doorway stood Mildred Aunty's friend, the cleaning lady. She mostly stayed out of view, keeping close to those places in the Stables where no one was at work. She pushed the door all the way open, slow and deliberate, squeezing Caroline against the shelves. As the lady entered, her eyes met Lenny's straight on. She reminded him of a turtle. Her shoulders were hunched and her eyes small and set far apart. Her head thrust forward on her neck as if testing the air. She moved so slowly she almost crawled.

He knew he'd seen her before, but until now did not recall the times she had appeared. He knew those eyes so well, and yet he had never really seen them. They had been a brief, corner-of-the-eye glance, something seen and forgotten in a hurry. The look she gave him now pinned him to his seat on the lettuce crate.

His jaw tightened, preparing to argue. *My business and nobody else's. Nobody hurt. Do it on our own time.* His arms crossed, hugging his gut protectively. *Don't make me feel bad when I feel so good.* But her eyes refused to leave his. It was a look that bypassed his brain and went straight to his blood. Her eyes burned green fire. He hadn't quite seen that before, only felt their strange heat. In her over-sized body her eyes were so buried deep that he had barely noticed them at all, put out of his mind right away. But now there was no mistaking that he had been seen. *Green fire.*

She must have been satisfied that he saw her because she then turned towards Caroline, who pressed her back against the shelves to stay out of reach. She shivered so hard she looked like she was crying. She lifted a hand to cover her wide-open mouth, but not before she let slip, "Oh my God."

The cleaning lady nodded, slow as mud, then shuffled over to a shelf holding a cardboard box with no label and plunged a hand inside. From inside the box came a crackle. She withdrew her hand and held out it out for them both to see.

Two squares of glossy brown paper leaned against her open palm. In block letters, the word, "Bun" gleamed white against yellow shading. She raised her hand up, urging them each to take one. Her smile spread quickly as she watched them. Her teeth were small, like a child's, out of place in her heavy, round face. She looked like she'd just told the best joke in the world and was waiting for them to respond.

Caroline got over her shock in a hurry. She straightened up, smoothed her skirt, and moved close enough to take one of the candy bars.

She smiled back, a well-rehearsed smile he had seen her give Mildred Aunty and the other cooks when her orders were up.

"My favorite," Caroline gushed. She pressed the gift between her hands like a prayer.

The cleaning lady stood holding out the second bar while Lenny fidgeted. Caroline might be relieved that the lady meant no harm, but Lenny felt cornered. She stood so still he thought she might never move, as if her movement depended upon his. Like a turtle, she could stand there forever. He almost bolted, but his manners got the better of him.

"Ma'am. Mighty nice of you, ma'am." He took the candy. The lady's fingers closed slowly around the empty space left behind, and her arm dropped back to her side. Something made him look over at Caroline, whose smile covered her face and whose eyes flashed the same green fire. She looked like she was going to laugh out loud. Her pale eyebrows raised up. The sides of her mouth pulled down tight as her eyes squinted. She was shaking, only this time not from the cold.

He felt a tickle in his gut. He bit his lip, afraid he was going to lose it. A snort traveled out his nose. To rein himself in, he forced his eyes back to the cleaning lady. His good manners would prevent him from laughing in her face. But she was already gone. He looked back at Caroline. Her mouth hung open.

"Do you think we insulted her?" she asked. Her eyebrows pointed stiffly down but her eyes moved like water.

"Did you see her grinning away? You tell me, who insulting who?"

"I've seen her before."

He felt strangely disappointed to hear this.

"Me, too," he said.

"You have?" Surprise pushed her forehead upward. "When?"

"You tell me." He stuck his hands in his pockets, stuffing the Bun in, too. If he didn't get out of that walk-in soon, he was going to fucking freeze to death. She wasn't making it easy for him to leave.

"Oh, here and there. She's the cleaning lady, you know." Her voice turned thin.

"I know." His disappointment lifted a little.

"Kind of like she's everywhere. Ubiquitous." Her lips pressed themselves together in a mysterious little smile. Her eyes bore hard into his. *She knew.* But she wasn't telling.

"Let's check out her stash," he said.

Caroline laughed. "I bet she lives on these things." She pulled the cardboard box out, bent over and sniffed. "I remember that smell. I used to scrounge for bottles in the vacant lots by our house. I'd go to Rexall Drugs with the deposit money and buy candy. Bun was my favorite. After a while, they stopped carrying them. I never knew why. For the longest time, whenever I went to the grocery store with my parents, I'd look for them. They disappeared." She took the box off the shelf and held it up, looking it over. "I wonder where she gets these?"

The box was unmarked. She put it back on the shelf. "I'm tempted to take more. You can't find these anywhere."

He bristled but said nothing. If he liked Bun as much as she did, he might have had the same thought. But hearing her say it out loud made that thought too real. *Like the only reason she don't steal because she don't have to.*

She sighed and turned her back on the box. "You comin?" she asked, her voice dropping down again.

"Look," he said. He had his hand on the latch. It was up to him to open the door. "I want to see you. Not here. Somewhere else."

She stood quietly, her skin flushed open like a flower. She was listening like his words were water.

"I want to *see* you. Not here, sneaking around at night. Where you live. I don't know what you wear, who you hang with, what you're like when you're not here."

He made himself study the panic in her face then the slow sadness as it shadowed her eyes. All this time he thought they'd been hiding out to save both their asses from being fired. But now he realized she hadn't worried about that.

"My parents would freak," she said flatly.

Any minute, Sarah or Opal, even Mildred Aunty, was bound to come into the walk-in. Or Delores would get fidgety for her ketchup and come after it herself. Or the produce guy with his delivery, or the meat guy, or whoever the hell else had a stake in this ice cube of a room. They would want to come in and do their business, and get the hell out again. As long as he and Caroline stood there with their hands on the door, all these people would be blocked. He and she would have to move.

Or at least that was the expectation.

Every action has a reaction, James used to say. He was big on chemistry. *That was the law of things. But when the temperature changes, action-reaction changes. Molecules vibrate at a lower frequency in cold. Things slow down.* He had walked into the walk-in warm, vibrating, alive. But now he was stuck, freezing his ass off, unable to complete the *action-reaction. If you can walk-in, you can walk-out,* he heard James' voice saying.

Competing with James' voice was that high, smooth voice talking overtime: *Baby, I don't care nothing about your parents. Just meet me.* But his lips had frozen shut.

She stared at her feet. He finally understood. *Chill,* James observed. That's why she dragged him in here. She lured him in on a promise and now was going to leave him, *raw, stripped,* hanging on a hook. Fine. But first she'd have to push him out of the way.

"Say something." Her voice cracked from the cold. She sounded almost mad.

He pictured frost covering his mouth, pale lips on a dark face. He almost grinned at the thought. But then he remembered: *Chill.*

That night of The Talk had changed everything. In the deep shadow of the night, he had known *ubiquitous.* He knew the cleaning lady had been there that night, had, in fact, been there all along. He did not have to go back to T.J., to the Big Willow where he lay clutching his heart. Even if he'd wanted to go back, he couldn't. The wind had shifted, the moon rose high, and the grass between his toes had gathered dew. Out of the corner of his eye, quickly, he'd seen her. And she had gestured to him to take all he had seen and to run with it, to run and not go back.

Still, he had held his breath returning to work the next day. Guilt and fear throbbed through his chest. Relief did not begin to describe how he felt to find T.J. standing upright under the Stables' red canopy. "Uncle Man," he'd said, the first time he'd used that name since he'd started at the Stables. He pounded T.J. on his uniformed back awkwardly, as he had as a child, his feeble attempt at comfort. "You ok?"

"Son." T.J.'s hand fell heavily on Lenny's shoulder. This time the gesture really felt like a father's. "For a while, I think I ain't going to make it. I'm thinking I shouldn't a sent you off like that. I ask myself, 'What if he ain't back in time? What if he don't come back at all?' I had to face the worst thing, see, and the worst thing was you be gone and I got to finish up alone. And funny thing, that was ok. You staying, you leaving, it all the same. Main thing is, you understand where I be coming from."

Confusion bloomed as he stared at T.J. Nothing was what it seemed any more. He had run with moonlight, just as T.J. had, just as he had said Lenny should. But his mama was always telling him, *you hear what you want to hear.* Maybe this time she was right. And now he felt ashamed for that.

"I didn't know—"

T.J. held up his hand, a frown on his face. "Course not. I realize that then. Can't expect you to know something you ain't never been taught."

"Your heart--?"

"I get these pains sometimes. They come and go."

Lenny had sighed. His uniform had felt much lighter. He hadn't realized how much weight he'd been carrying until it finally left his shoulders.

"Don't be telling Aunty." T.J. looked away as he cleared his throat and spit. Fear leapt up again in Lenny, but he said nothing. T.J. had ended all discussion.

As he stood staring at Caroline, he kept his hand on the door latch. *Chill.* He tried to picture bringing Caroline home to meet his mother, to hang out on the corner with Murth and Sugar Butt, to eat smothered pork chops, sweet potatoes and macaroni and cheese at the small metal table his mother covered with a red checked cloth. He could picture everything down to the smallest detail--except Caroline. This made him curious. Was there a hole in her pictures when she did the same with him? Or did she even try?

"I'm just not ready," she said. "At least not for the parental visit. And not Bedford Heights. These people would skin you alive."

He tried not to flinch at her words, tried to grasp the lack of hearing in them. She might as well have said *string you up.*

"But look." Her hand was now on his hand, the one controlling the latch. "I know a place where we can meet."

Maybe she had her own sweet talk, and if that's what this was, then neither of them was ever going to get out of this ice cube. Sure, she'd meet him, at night, out of sight. At least then he'd see her in her street clothes, her street self, in some place that spoke of her. But his hand stayed put. Her offer wasn't enough to put *action-reaction* back into motion.

She stroked his hand slowly, as if to conjure words to her shivering lips. "A date," she said. "A *real* date. Pizza at the Medici. We'll hang out at Washington Park. I'll even show you the campus. Forget about Bedford Heights. You know it better than I do, all the fat cats and joy riders and everybody in between driving through. There isn't anything you could know about me here that you don't already know."

Curiosity satisfied. No pictures were running in her head of her mama, the kitchen table, her girlfriends in the hood. Not only was she missing in his pictures, he was definitely missing in hers. And so he couldn't entirely blame her for wanting to bring him to a place where she could picture him. Even if it meant he'd have no pictures of the place beforehand in his head.

So she still held the advantage.

"I hate pizza," he said.

Her laugh turned the *action-reaction* back on inside him. He pressed the door latch until it clicked open. "They have burgers and other stuff, too," she said, and squeezed his hand once, quickly, before hurrying off through the kitchen. Without the ketchup, he saw.

Chapter Fourteen: Service Bar

Rose and I ignored each other. I had no jokes to tell or gossip to share. Rose cared about here and now, while I was interested in a past she never spoke of, but that she nonetheless displayed: the rouge, the delicate blouses, the wrinkles on her face like strong nets that held up her defiant eyes. She seemed ancient to me, even older than my grandparents, but unlike them, told no stories about the past. But that August, as she reached across the service bar with two glasses of Chablis, she stared at me with a fierceness that announced to anyone within earshot they would soon hear exactly what was on her mind.

"Tight," she whispered in a dramatic voice. She placed the wine on my tray, slowly and deliberately, then leaned forward on her elbows. Her usual fan club had already scattered. For reasons I could not grasp, every man at the Stables flirted with Rose, with the exception of the bussers, who she barked at to haul ice and fetch syrup canisters for the soda gun. Her silver hair formed a thin net over her freckled scalp. She curled and sprayed it to gain volume, in an attempt to offset its tissue-paper thinness. Red circles marked the place where wrinkles buried her cheekbones. I could only think of that red as rouge, although no one called it that anymore. I pictured her dipping her finger into an ancient pot she'd hoarded all these years and smearing a spot on each cheek, just enough to spread out her red fingerprint. She wore bright lipstick that bled into the fine lines around her mouth and eye shadow that darkened the already-deep sockets around her pale blue eyes. Her skin was sallow, and along with her generous lips and flared nostrils, I gathered that she had once been, and still was, proud of her looks: pale skin, "good" hair, and light eyes elevating the earthy features she shared with her darker co-workers.

Despite her obvious aging, she insisted on wearing low-cut necklines wreathed in ruffles and sheer chiffon in pastel colors that brought out the blue in her eyes. Her delicate looks, however, contrasted sharply with her shipyard mouth, from which the most colorful curses and risqué jokes flowed. Lenny took his turn, like all the other men, to sidle up to the service bar's steel counter and ante up a few winks, slap his thighs, and lick his lips in exchange for some half-whispered complement and the filthiest jokes around, jokes that circulated the Stables for days after. At first, I didn't give his flirtations a thought. Rose was to be pitied; he was just doing his part to keep her ancient spirits up. Later, I changed my mind. Rose knew exactly what she was doing.

With no one else at the service bar to explain to me what she meant by "tight," I pretended I hadn't heard her. When confronted by incomprehensible behavior, my first instinct was to pretend I hadn't seen it-- just minding my own business--and get away as quickly as possible.

Then, as I reached for my tray, I started to believe I really *hadn't* heard anything. Rose was just tired, I reasoned, as she leaned forward the way she often did by the end of her shift, her wild eyes staring past me like caged things. Wild things in cages never looked at what was right before them. They always looked beyond.

The edge of my tray was quickly trapped in the vise-grip of her craggy fingers. Behind the bar, Rose had about three feet to move in any direction. She was very small, under five feet and slightly built, as if her body had adapted itself to the available space. Lacking room for even a bar stool or chair, Rose always stood. She complained about her feet during slow times, when Albert wandered over from the Tack Room to tell dirty jokes. Yet she showed up day after day; the few times she didn't appear, no subs were hired, leaving the Garden Room waitresses to trek over to Ernie the bartender at the Winner's Circle lounge. She was the only one who could fit that cramped and crowded space, and she knew it.

My second instinct was to agree with her, without revealing my lack of understanding, and again, make a quick getaway. "Right," I said solemnly. "It's tight in here." I gently tugged my tray away from her.

She tugged back, without spilling a drop of Chablis. "Tell me," she growled.

Instinct number three was to stall. "Can I drop these drinks first?" I smiled my most winning smile, as if we were the best of friends, and of course she'd understand.

"Now." She tapped the tray with one long, rose-lacquered nail.

My next instinct (it amazed me how quickly I could think on my feet) came surprisingly easily. "I don't quite remember," I said, shaking my head sadly. "You know how it is." I expected she would.

But instincts failed me when I realized she wasn't crazy, at least not in the ways I had assumed, when she said, "You like it, don't you?" Her red lips smacked as if every word was pudding.

My instincts exhausted, I now had to face the fact that no matter what I said, something could, and probably would, go wrong. As I followed her plunging pastel neckline to the rapid rise and fall of her chest, I realized how much she depended upon my story. I'd assumed that she worked because she was lonely, even compelled to work for some reason worthy of pity. Why else would she stand in that tiny, cramped space for hours at a time, for a few tips from the servers and maybe minimum wage, working a job no one else would do?   But whatever pity or even disdain I had felt suddenly dissolved. For once, I was interesting to her.

"Like what?" I said lamely, hoping for a way out.

She cocked her head and squinted her eyes, a grin spreading across her full red lips. My breath stopped for a second as I tried to anticipate what words she might utter.   Instead, she clutched my hand with hers, cold, smooth, and surprisingly soft for all the glasses she had to wash back there in the tiny bar sink, and chuckled, deep and throaty, like she already knew.

"You college gals got it bad," she said, patting my hand before releasing it and my tray. She kept chuckling and shaking her head as she picked up a bar towel and started to dry.

*

I can't decide what to wear on this date.   I open my dresser drawers, hoping inspiration will strike. Too hot for jeans, and shorts are too casual. I own exactly one sundress, one that I sewed myself back when I had time to sew: halter-style, with a long slit up each side. Not the sort of clothes you wear to the library.   That's what I've told my mother—I'm going to Regenstein to get ahead on fall readings. It's August; time to turn back to the books, I say, just wearily enough to sound convincing.

I pull on jeans and a tube top, slip into some Chinese flip flops with black velvet straps, and throw a western-style shirt over the tube top. Into my backpack, instead of spiral notebooks, pens, and index cards, I carefully place the folded halter dress.   I lay a pair of high-heeled, wood-soled sandals, the kind with one leather strap across the toes, next to the dress, careful to turn the soles in towards each other. Into a plastic baggie go the contents of my afternoon excursion to Walgreen's: Big Lash mascara, Yardley baby blue eye shadow, a stick of heather blush, and frosted pink lip gloss. The plastic baggie gets tucked between dress and sandals. I toss in a hair brush and my wallet, and I'm ready to go.

Mom looks up from "The Price is Right" as I reach for the door. "What time will you be home?"

I shrug. "Probably late."

"How late?"

We've had this conversation before. If I don't give her a set time, she'll say she'll worry. "That neighborhood" is her code for why she worries. But it's not just the neighborhood; she'd worry even if it was Bedford Heights. It's different for her if I'm with a man, but I can't tell her that it's a man I'm meeting and not my roommate from the dorm.

"After midnight." I can't bring myself to nail down the hour.

"Doesn't the library close?"

"They have a 24-hour room."

"Why do you want to study that long?" Her forehead wrinkles. In the background, Bob Barker announces the grand prizes for the final round.

"We'll probably go get pizza." I try to sound calm.

But she persists. "You just had dinner. I don't like the sound of this." She shakes her head. "Why don't you just study here?"

Big sigh. "I told you. It's reserve reading. I have to read it there." It helps that she never went to college.

"Well." She turns back to the television. "Do you have to work tomorrow?"

"Just dinner shift."

"Don't be too late." She turns back for one last, worried look. "Be careful. Lock your doors."

"I will."

Something tells me to meet him outside. I hug my arms to my chest; the lake breezes that cool Hyde Park skip Bedford Heights completely. I lean against the Medici's façade, then quickly straighten up as I meet the eyes of a guy in an Einstein t-shirt. He's startled by the long slit in my dress and the high heels that arch my feet. Before he can close his mouth, I rebalance on my stiff platform soles and glare at him. He ducks a head full of absentminded curls and lopes past, his backpack swaying more than his baggy-ass jeans.

I wonder how Lenny will make his entrance inside the Medici. I want to hear how he asks for a table, walk with him past students huddled over books or leaning across dim-lit tables, the smell of pizza and coffee and cigarettes overtaking us like a drug. As we choose which side of the booth to sit in, I want him to stare at me the way he does when we're alone. I want to show him the art posters and political graffiti, the cappuccino and the foreign languages being spoken all around.

Just as I start to head inside, he shows up. Shivering hard, I hope he'll drape his arms around me.

But instead of giving me a hug or even a kiss, he stops, grabs my left elbow, and jiggles it up and down. "Hey Care-o-lion," he drawls, grinning that I'm too cool smirk I recognize from the Star Dust. His eyes are already roaming the street. He's wearing a black, white, and gray silk screen shirt, unbuttoned below his collarbone, with two gold chains winking at a struggling street light. Tight trousers outline his ass and hips. Instead of khakis or jeans, Nikes or Adidas, he's in polyester and platform shoes.

"Hi." I'm still shivering, but now I don't want his arm around me. "Wanna go in?" I reach for the door.

He purrs under his breath as I brush past, but I want to turn around, go back to Regenstein and the narrow bathroom stall where I could barely hold my arms out to straighten the ties on my dress. I want to wipe all this crap off my face, stuff everything back into my backpack, then throw it in the trash. My feet hurt, my lips are sticky with gloss, and mascara is flaking into my contact lenses. The halter straps are cutting into my neck, and I can't loosen them without revealing my bare breasts.

As we wind our way through the Medici, it is painfully clear how much we stand out. Everyone else is dressed in jeans, painter's paints, hospital scrubs, and the occasional oxford shirt and pocket-protector. It's like we're extras on the wrong movie set, Annie Hall instead of Saturday Night Fever. Never mind that he's got the only afro in the place, unless you count the curly head of a Mediterranean-type. I fight the urge to turn around and instead keep moving towards a vacant booth in the corner, one of the few still empty.

Just as I'm about to slide in, I hear my name.

"Caroline." Kyle is sitting across the aisle. He's not alone, either; white-blonde hair cascades down the back of the chair facing him. "I'm not recognizing you for a moment," he continues.

"Dark in here, isn't it?" My jaw clenches and heat blooms across my face. I hear Lenny's breath grow shallow, but my eyes fix themselves on that long blonde hair swishing like a palomino's tail. He refused to come here when we were dating, claiming not to like "American" food, especially pizza, which I love.

Scanning the half-eaten pizza on his table, I calculate that I'll have to stare at him at least another fifteen minutes from my seat in the booth. Right now all I can think about is he's gone lighter, and I've gone darker.

Then Lenny reaches out his hand.

"Hey man," he says. "How you doing?"

Kyle accepts Lenny's hand, a bit cautiously, I think, and, while Lenny gives Kyle's a few hearty pumps, Kyle looks at me, distressed. In Kyle's world, certain protocols have to be followed, and one of those is being properly introduced. Grudgingly, I oblige.

"Kyle, meet Lenny. Lenny, Kyle."

Kyle nods at Lenny somberly then turns his attention back to the blonde waterfall. "Caroline, please may I introduce Marcia." Marcia swivels towards the aisle just enough to reveal a pink tube top covered by a crisp, tailored shirt with the cuffs folded back neatly to her elbows. Pressed Calvin Kleins and Dr. Scholl's sandals nudge Kyle's khakis and topsiders below the table.

"Hi." She's beaming. Her million dollar smile is worth at least a few thousand in orthodontist's bills.

If only Kyle was falling all over himself, eyes glued to her pale pink lips, I could at least forgive him for the half-eaten veggie deluxe pizza between them on the table. At least I'd know he was human, swept away by Marcia's blonde, blue-eyed demureness. Instead his eyes move up and down Lenny like an elevator, stopping at one floor, then jerking to the next with a mechanical jolt. Only the familiar tilt of his head against the back of his neck tells me what I need to know.

"Nice to meet you," I nod to Marcia. She beams at me, then Lenny, as if we are already dear friends. I shoot a glance to Lenny, wondering if her prim good looks are as potent to him as they apparently are to Kyle. Lenny beams back at both of them, secure in his self-sponsored spotlight.

"Would you like to join us?" Kyle asks. Despite the fact that their booth barely seats two, Marcia pats the edge of her seat invitingly. Kyle's choice is making much more sense now. I never pictured him chasing a trophy blonde; while he had always dismissed how his parents regarded my freckles and red hair, I knew he also felt guilty straying from their expectations. Yet I never understood the depths of his unhappiness over my "casual" style until confronted with Marcia's preppy perfection.

Lenny answers before I can. "Man, thanks, but you know how it is." He gives me the look I was hoping for earlier, not here, not now, not in front of Kyle's haughty face, Marcia's isn't that sweet? smile. He's made his claim.

Kyle straightens himself against the booth's unforgiving wood. "Yes. Well, then. Good to see you." His eyes are distant as he looks my way. "And to meet you." He is nothing if not proper.

I feel Kyle's long, straight nose follow me back to the booth.

The entire meal, everything seems a bit off, like a movie out of focus, or an off-beat drum. The pizza tastes like cardboard, and I wonder what it is about the long, rubbery strings of cheese that made me think he'd like it, too. Strange enough, he seems to enjoy the pizza, even the green olives, which he had once professed to hate.

The beer is warm and the pizza cold. The graffiti in the unisex bathroom is nothing but pompous platitudes and shallow wisecracks. The Toulouse Lautrec posters are pretentious, and our server, another baggy-assed guy, speaks in that nasally pseudo-intellectual whine. The worn wooden booths are way too hard, and I want a cigarette even though I don't smoke. The worst part of all is, Lenny is fine with it, so fine that he pays more attention to his surroundings than to me. He reads the menu twice, out loud, and asks the server to recite every salad dressing, every brand of beer, every sandwich condiment, every pizza topping, and every soft drink. He asks how espresso is made, and how that's different than a macchiato or a latte, and why anyone would order an Americano instead of just plain coffee? The server just eggs him on, one of those nerds who are into every little detail, a trivia collector of the worst kind, one who thrives on the kinds of things useful only for playing Jeopardy but even more so, thrives on talking about it. Or maybe he just thinks he'll get a better tip.

"Weird looking dude," Lenny says. "But he sure can get down."

My foot is tapping out a rhythm that Lenny doesn't hear. I'm anxious to go, but he's dug in. First he's guessing how much the server makes in tips. Then he's calculating how many tables one server can handle in a given hour, and then he's counting the seats or the number of steps from one side of the restaurant to another. He sounds old and boring, like my father, who has nothing to talk about except work. But unlike my father, who rarely speaks, Lenny won't stop talking.

"Do you like my outfit?" I finally say, exasperated at having to ask, three-fourths of the way through our pizza.

He leans over the soot-stained pizza pan and purrs, "I like it even better when we take it off." He grins and narrows his eyes.

I start drinking in earnest after that. I have no idea where to go after the Medici. The thought of locking ourselves in the bathroom here or sneaking one off deep in Regenstein's stacks strikes me as pathetic and desperate. But since I'm the one who set this up, I feel obliged to make it work.

When the baggy-assed server leaves the bill between us, I reach for it right away.

"What you doing?" Lenny says. He covers my hand with his.

I've never paid for a date before, and something in me is pushing me to take charge, settle things, show I'm in control. In spite, or maybe because of the reaction I expect, I jerk my hand out from under his and start checking the figures and calculating the tip.

"I invited you, so I pay. You pay next time." The minute I say it, I start to doubt a next time is going to happen. He's staring at me like he's never seen me before, an alien creature straight out of Close Encounters. Or maybe it's just the cool, matter-of-fact tone that has overtaken my voice, as if this was lunch with a co-worker and not a hot summer date, a first one, even if you don't count all the previous sex. Strictly business, that's what my tone says. I'm warmer with Stables customers than I am right now.

Maybe the best way is to split the bill, instead of one of owing the other. The smile spreading across his face, though, tells me it's too late. He's only too happy to pay me back later. He strokes my hand with the bill still in it. I start to panic. No place to go. Correction: No place I want to go. For all he cares, it could be under this table, or on the grass at Washington Park while dozens of people walk, jog, and bike past, or in a gas station. Just as long as we do it, he's satisfied. I haven't realized until now how much I want a place just ours, not sneaking around, hiding out, trespassing, not temporary, dirty, gross, weird. And I haven't realized until now that I have to find such a place, that I'd been counting on finding one and didn't even know it.

Heat follows his fingers up my left thigh, along the slit in my skirt. His eyes downcast, as if listening to something very soft or far away, he sways a little, back and forth, as if in a trance. His fingers glide seductively while he keeps his face serious, earnest, in imitation of all the other serious, earnest faces around us. Trivia guy comes by, takes the bill without a word.

"Keep the change," I tell him without looking, so he won't come back.

We take the Red Line north after wandering Washington Park. I take off my sandals to ease the ache in my arches. At this hour, nobody's riding, so we have only each other to stare at in the harsh bluish light. I collapse against Lenny's shoulder, suddenly tired, giving in to the train's uneven rocking. Devoid of any signs of life, this one car is too big for just us. We huddle together against our own reflections in the windows. Yet the faster we move, the harder it is to imagine ever getting off, rushing northbound for some purpose we don't exactly understand. It's as if we've always been on this train, harsh light and hard seats, no comfort except against each other's bodies, hypnotized by the shuddering motion and streetlights streaking past like comets.

Near downtown, the train slows and stops more often. Passengers get on, greeted by the metal whine of doors opening and closing, the forced breath of brakes, wheels grinding. We pass through the Loop slowly, in underground darkness that exaggerates every scrap of sound against tunneled walls.

After a few more stops, I've had enough of the underground, the vacant-eyed passengers, the endless criss-cross of orange, purple, brown, green, yellow, and red on the El maps above us. Some wordless, nameless impulse to keep moving overtakes me. And him, too: we grab for each other's hand as the train eases up, and when the doors slide open, we burst out into the sewer stink and ride its fetid wave up to street level.

Here the garbage smells and the sewers stink just as they did in Hyde Park, yet it's somehow easier to breathe. Or maybe I just need to breathe less, dazzled by so many lights carving soft hollows in the night. I know I've been here before; the smells are of steak and butter, fresh flowers and salt. Marine winds catch my dress and threaten to lift it to my waist. I head towards Michigan Avenue, feeling my drift, drawn by the roaming shadows of shoppers and tourists, high-rise sophisticates and shop clerks in sandals. My hand, still in Lenny's, holds fast as I move forward. No effort in this, as if the lights and movements of the crowded street compel me. I dissolve into its familiar grasp.

I hear Lenny's steps against mine, cautious, wary of sidewalk cracks. My own steps click lightly, oblivious to the potholes and the squared-off curbs, the sidewalk's rough textures and eruptions like shifts in tectonic plates. It is not hard for him to keep pace, hobbled as I am by my impossible wooden soles. The farther we walk, the more I feel the difference in our rhythms. Yet neither of us lets go of the other's hand, though plenty of obstructions have forced us to one side: an elderly couple shuffling ahead of us; a group of teens claiming the throughway for themselves; other couples, oncoming, themselves squeezed against each other by families and large groups of tourists oblivious to their presence.

At Michigan Avenue, the only direction for us is north; no point turning back towards where we started. Already my feet are complaining, but there's no way out of these shoes now. Lenny takes the turn easily, smoothly, as if we had planned it this way. Even in a crowd, he is tall, and in his platforms taller than most people we pass. I'm proud of his height; it makes people look up. Yet in this crowd, locked into his slow, cautious steps, he seems even taller, narrowed by the activity around him. Against my meanderings, he is clear, focused on each step. A stranger to this place, I realize. Or at least a stranger to the eyes that meet his and then, abruptly, look away.

I can't bear his hesitations, the tensions that freeze his spine and shorten his breath, even as his arms swing loose and his legs glide, however slowly. He cannot follow me into this meltdown, this fascination for bright storefronts, the tiny Water Tower castle dwarfed by high rises, the slender reach of locust trees against hordes of taxis, cars, and buses. I am unexpectedly lonely, after the empty train car and cavernous tunnels and zombie riders that fused us into each other's skin.

I squeeze his hand, grateful he has not let go, hoping for a glimpse of his face, to see what sort of portrait the lights, hum, throb, and bellow create. When he grins and winks, at first I think it's the same old I'm too cool bullshit. But when a passing headlight beams from his eyes, I see panic in being possessed by a place so completely.

As I gaze inside the John Hancock building lobby, steady lights and a brief line of tourists bring me to my own calculations—how fast the moving line, how much money left in my wallet, how much time left before the city drug wears off and we are alone again, naked, only with downtown eyes beaming out from each other's. I don't know why, but I've always trusted high places even though my fear of heights keeps me wary of ledges.

"C'mon." I tug towards the huge black X's stacked up on the tower's facade.

He stops in the middle of the sidewalk. The crowd splits around us like waves against a pier. Even with his towering height, I can still see his eyebrows climb up into his forehead, startled by the somber black behemoth I'm urging him to enter.

"Whoah." He hangs on to my hand. I squeeze tighter.

"I'm not your horse," I kid, knowing that what came out of his mouth comes from another, unscripted part of his brain.

His eyes don't leave the tower. His head tilts back, his baby fro brushing the back of his neck as his eyes travel up the tower's side, searching for the top, which of course, disappears. Still, his eyes squint and his forehead furrows, as if he can't believe what he's seeing, or he can't believe what he doesn't see.

"Baby, I don't know."

"You afraid?" I instantly regret saying this. His eyes cloud over as he sniffs the thick, damp air, smelling my fear. He nods, slowly.

"I get it. You never been before."

I shrug, sheepish. "Fear of heights."

"Mama took me. I was six."

"You like it?"

"I cry when we have to leave." He turns his head, looks away from the Miracle Mile towards darker shores up north.

For a moment, the flow of pedestrians eases and the street empties of traffic. The portrait that started moments earlier forms a cameo, the sudden, sweet absence of activity a tender song tracing the soft planes of his profile. Light kisses the tip of his nose, the bulge of his cornea, sparks the sweat that has gathered on his forehead. The thought of him, a small boy, bowed by tears, reluctant to leave the jeweled heights he'd just discovered, makes me reach for the soft hollow at the base of his neck and stroke its tender skin until the traffic light blinks green, pedestrians once again surge all around us, and motors whisper promises in our ears.

The big-shouldered city spreads out below us. Traffic along Lake Shore Drive flickers like fireflies while waves caress the deserted shore. The lake itself is empty and beautiful, and the beaches are empty and beautiful, too. Lake breezes are now heavy winds that whip my hair around, half-blinding me until I busy myself with braiding and rebraiding the loose ends. I study the locator maps so as not to feel the cold and to keep my eyes away from the edge of the observation deck. Lenny, however, is plastered against the guard rail, leaning as far forward as the safety fence will allow.

"Check out this airplane." Lenny pulls me against the fence that's supposed to keep us from falling. "See? We higher than it."

I force myself to look. A small plane is cruising towards Meigs Field. My eyes roam out across the lake, away from the Hancock, which, I suddenly realize, is swaying right under my feet.

"Shit. It's moving!"

He just stares at me.

"The floor."

He shakes his head and starts to shrug, but then mid-shrug he stops. A smile spreads across his face. "Oh man," he sighs. "Now I remember. The whole thing moves." He holds out his arms. "Way to be!" He kicks one foot back and makes a quick turn. "Super fly."

"You think pigeons come this high?" I ask, backing away from the fence. The real terror is being right up against the edge. Farther back, the views are more benign; it's easier to pretend I'm just watching a movie if I'm not actually looking down the side of the building.

"Uh-uh. Too much wind." He says this quickly, with finality.

"Unless they find someplace the wind can't touch." I'll say anything to keep the conversation going.

"First they got to get here." He stares at me, his lips pushed out, but their curled-up corners betray his amusement. "You think a lazy old pigeon going to fly in wind like this?"

"I don't know." At least now I don't have to stand near the edge. "I thought pigeons roosted on all kinds of buildings."

"Man, I can tell you no city girl."

"Oh yeah?"

"You probably think they cute."

I do, but now I'd rather die than admit it. "Not cute," I say. "But wild." My face flushes from the thrill. A thousand feet in the air and we're finally having our first real conversation.

Lenny doesn't hold back. He starts to pace a little, chopping at the air in front of him to make his point. "You think they so cute, you try living with them. No better than rats—they wild, too. Pigeon shit all over, on your car, the sidewalk, the steps to your front door. Feathers always floating around. Put they nests on the windowsill so you can't open the window. No sense at all. You spend half your time watching out for them cause they too dumb to look out for themselves," he says emphatically.

I raise my fists to my hips. "Now just who you calling dumb? Maybe I didn't grow up sidestepping pigeon shit, but I've seen them roost in some pretty high places."

"Not this high." He shakes his head solemnly. "No way they can beat this wind. No reason to, either. Plenty of places more easy to live."

The finality in his tone eggs me on. I swagger a little, let my eyebrows lift and my jaw drop. I sigh dramatically, careful to place myself on the inside wall of the walkway. *"Easier, is that what it's all about? Isn't it possible that some pigeon might buck the odds--"*

For a second his eyes cut at me, but he then recovers. *"Crazy chick."* Now he's laughing. He grabs me by the shoulders and shakes me, playing hard.

"--paving the way for other pigeons to follow?" I'm giggling the way I used to when my immigrant grandfather told stories about road apples and outhouses, and bags of shit he burned on front porches until someone from inside stomped the fire out. My whole body would go limp, and I'd fall to the floor and roll through the cramps the giggles grew in my gut. Instead of rolling on the ground, I lean against Lenny. He obliges by holding me up.

"Pigeons don't think. They do what all the other pigeons do," he persists.

"But some pigeon has to go first." I wipe my eyes with the back of my hand, and then wipe my hands on my skirt, which flaps against my bare thighs like a flag. *"Somebody's got to lead the way."*

"They just following instinct. Hey," he says, half-frowning. *"Now you got me started on this shit."*

"Do pigeons have revolutions?" The giggles start all over.

But this time he's on to me. *"All the time, baby. They always be revolting."* Now he's laughing so hard he can barely stand, either. Other people smile as they pass us. We're contagious.

"So, maybe they're not so dumb, then?" I reach around my backpack for a tissue.

He shakes his head. I'm a lost cause. *"You don't give up, do you?"*

I smile into the tissue and blow my nose. I'm as far from the guard rail as the deck will allow. I don't have to look down anymore. But I don't mind looking up. The stars drift overhead like floating lamps, almost close enough to touch. I lean back against the wall and sigh. I congratulate myself for this private victory: he never sees how scared I am to be this high off the ground.

We walk the observation deck arm in arm, weaving between other sightseers absorbed in the regal views. Around the west side, the wind calms. I stop to search the grid of lights below for anomalies: a parking lot, a baseball diamond, a smokestack, river, forest preserve. As long as I don't think about the swaying floor under my feet or look directly down the tower's sides, I can pretend to be a spectator to someone else's dream.

I press against Lenny's shoulder. *"Look at the moon."* I point to a fingernail floating upside down in the dark, its pale light streaming down over the suburbs.

"Hey, ain't that Comiskey? Shit, the White Sox playing tonight. Wow." *He puts his arm around me and pulls me to his side.* *"Imagine that. You can see a ball game all the way up here."*

Of course, I can't see the game, but the field is lit up, a miniature that fits easily behind my thumb. That's the charm of it—so much of every day disappears, leaving only a tiny fragment, and the stars, to tell its story.

"You going to have to drag me down. I ain't leaving."

In between gusts of wind comes a steady stillness. The noise and confusion only climb so high before its reach is exhausted. I wonder at exactly what floor the city's voice stops and the wind's takes over, how far down before the streetlights dull the stars and high rises blot out the moon, the lake, the shadowed horizons. With every burst of air, with every shimmy of the building's bones, I hold my breath, for a moment disbelieving that such a place is even possible.

"I guess we'll have to take over the penthouse, then. Or learn to fly," I say.

"Whatever it take."

But I'm not dreaming about how to reach the clouds, own the sky, or fly forever above the birds. I'm dreaming of a place whose walls whisper its secrets when we reveal our own to them, where the echo of our steps gives a rhythm to the floors that they give back over and over. A place where, when we call out, our voices circle back with a thousand variations. A place whose interiors we can surrender to without fear, carrying us close like children and rocking us until an extravagant babble bursts from our lips in the pause between you and I.

"You shivering," he says, and from behind me, he drapes his arms over my arms, hugging them tightly against my body. He rubs against me, swaying almost imperceptibly, like the building itself. Heat bursts from his crotch, and his penis lifts between my buttocks. I curl into his chest, strange pulsings traveling up my spine, to my throat, demanding release. But I keep my mouth closed to their incomprehensible urgings, suddenly self-conscious of the sight-seers all around. Yet this restless inner movement produces its own stillness: the curve of his collarbone as it presses between my shoulders, the infinite pause between one finger tip and another, the recognition that a tongue can never be totally still. What do we have to hope for except the contact our cells have conjured, that holds us up and yet also apart, and still, on some level, exchanges something of itself? As long as I am dreaming, wide-awake, caught in a rhythm right under my feet, answered by a fingernail moon, then I, too, don't ever want to leave.

*

Rose's chuckle tickled inside my throat. I didn't want to feed the gossip mill, thinking of how that would surely come back to haunt me, but neither did I want to totally deny having something to tell. After all, I was finally interesting to her. The tickle urged me to spill my guts in the kind of girlfriend talk that usually happened late at night, over mushroom and green olive double cheese pizza, in hopes that all would be forgotten in the morning, deep, dark secrets that everybody knew but acted like they hadn't heard.

My hand still felt the touch of Rose's amused and eager expression of sympathy as my mind sped through all the possibilities of what she might now be thinking about me. Could she really feel sorry for me, having it so *bad* yet unable to even say what "it" was? Did she even know what "it" was? What exactly *did* she know? And was it worth the risk of finding out?

And then my questions turned towards him, the unmentionable "it." What had Lenny told? Why else would Rose suddenly be asking me for my secrets? Did he now all of a sudden think he had bragging rights? And he was the one who had been so worried that someone here might find out.

Since denial seemed all but impossible now, I picked up where instinct had abandoned me and instead used a tactic that I had learned from my professors: I turned the question back on Rose.

"Why do you think I've got it bad?" I asked, trying not to sound as insulted as my voice seemed to want to. Beyond the disturbing realization that I, not she, was the object of pity, I really wanted to know what she saw. What was "bad" and how did she know? Or did she? Maybe she just assumed all "college gals" had something going on over the summer? Had she seen this before? Were we that predictable?

"Baby doll, you got to be blind not to see it." For once, her voice took on an almost kindly tone. More like sympathy than pity, really.

I was dying to ask her what she "saw." It occurred to me that perhaps she did know more than me, since I couldn't even say for myself what that "it" was. But something told me that was a question for which she had no answer, unless you counted the humming in her throat just then, or the sad-happy blues that suddenly broke through her lips: "I sweep the floor/ just to sit at your feet/ you're a dirty dog/ but I can't get enough to eat/ I'm chained to your love/ darling I'm all chained up by your love/ and there's no escaping this prison/ I'm a prisoner to love."

"Why are you here?" I was shaking so hard that I expected the Chablis to spill at any moment. "Why don't you just—How can you stand it?"

Rose shoved the bar towel aside. I'd heard her wisecrack and yell and shout and sweet talk. I'd watched her mix dozens of drinks without missing a beat, albeit to her slow and careful rhythms, and carry on flirtations like a teenager. I'd seen her handle the obstreperous Delores as she elbowed past whoever was in line ahead of her, slap her bar ticket down and demand her drinks be made first. Rose would barely glance at her, lips curling into a faint sneer, and, with heavy-lidded eyes, continue stirring a Manhattan or hanging an orange slice on the lip of a Tom Collins.

But none of it had been for me. And I had no clue how to ask her what it was she saw that made her think I had it "bad." How could I, when even I didn't know what "it" was?

"You the college gal." She snapped the bar towel off to one side, then folded it carefully, smoothing it over and over again like a satin pillow case. "You the one supposed to know." Detached was not a tone I was used to from her. Perhaps this was one expression she'd saved just for me.

"Sorry." She looked up as I said it. "This is a very frustrating place."

"Mm-hmm." She sounded as if she'd just tasted the best thing in the whole world. "Like I said, you got it bad. Now don't you have some drinks to drop?"

I used to think I wouldn't want her job in a million years, stuck behind the service bar for hours at a time, no relief except in the company of others whose feet hurt maybe worse, whose arms ached, who left every night with aches and pains that only more aches and pains could erase. Yet it was difficult to imagine the Stables without her. Not only because we Garden Room waitresses would have to walk so much farther for our drinks, but because just getting by--grinding through sore feet, stingy diners, and cranky cooks-- was not enough, and Rose was the one who reminded us.

Part IV

And all shall be well and
All manner of thing shall be well
When the tongues of flame are in-folded
Into the crowned knot of fire
And the fire and the rose are one.

---T.S. Eliot
The Four Quartets

Chapter Fifteen: Powder Room

Rumor had it that Mrs. Parkerhouse frequented the Powder Room, though she had declared it off limits to all staff except Viney. The only other ladies' toilet was next to the business office, at the very back of the Stables, where female staff had to squint into a crusty black mirror with only a bare bulb for light, since the Powder Room was for ladies only.

Mrs. Parkerhouse had very definite ideas about the Powder Room that she communicated to Viney through the signs she left behind: fancy cloth towels neatly folded in thirds and fanned out on the counter; toiletries and eau de cologne tucked in small wicker baskets; stark overhead lights replaced with dimmer decorative bulbs. The "Ladies" sign on its door didn't change, yet soon enough, everyone at the Stables knew to call it the Powder Room. Inside, it had expanded to include individual stalls with plantation shutters, a marble-topped vanity to replace the cracked basin sink, and wall-sized mirrors where low counters and plush stools invited serious primping.

Not even Billiard was allowed inside, so upkeep of the Powder Room fell solely to Viney. When Viney had first arrived at the Stables, the Ladies Room was just a toilet and sink tucked in a closet behind the maitre d' stand. At one point someone had nailed a sign marked "Toilet" to the door, but it had always been hard to find. Later on, two separate bathrooms had been added, so that ladies and gentlemen would not cross paths. "Toilet" changed to "Ladies" and "Gentlemen" painted right on the doors.

In this newest name change, only the "Ladies" had a Powder Room, underscoring Viney's sense that "ladies" were pampered, high-strung creatures desperate for camouflage. To encourage them to linger, Mrs. Parkerhouse had placed satin-backed powder puffs stamped with the Stables' horse-and-rider beside a box of pressed powder and a gilded tissue dispenser. Yet from behind those shuttered stalls, Viney knew that the ladies might still catch an uncamouflaged glimpse of each other primping before the ever-vigilant mirrors.

Shortly after the Powder Room's transformation, a low stool covered in needlepoint and a crystal dish shaped like a leaf had found a home within, next to a parchment "Tips" sign scrolled in gold ink. The stool stood far enough from the plate to be out of reach, yet close to a stack of fresh hand towels. That same day, Viney had heard from Mildred, who had heard from T.J., who had heard from Billiard that Mrs. Parkerhouse had a more "traditional" job in mind for Viney.

Mildred had added that T.J. had said that Billiard had told him that Mrs. Parkerhouse saw this new position as a "graceful" step towards retirement.

"She say that?" Viney asked.

"'Retirement?'" Mildred replied.

"No. 'Graceful.'"

Mildred nodded.

"I have my doubts before, but now I know. She think I'm a lady."

Viney had witnessed many Mrs. Parkerhouses come and go through the years, all puffed up with their own set of signs, only to wear themselves out against the Stables' stubborn sense of itself. In the early days, she had tried to warn them that those signs would be their ruin. In the end, she realized they weren't ignoring her words but simply couldn't hear them as such. Her words provided the necessary background to make their own voices heard.

Mrs. Parkerhouse, however, usually didn't tell anybody anything, except maybe Billiard. Everybody just *knew*. The air vibrated with "Mrs. Parkerhouse wants" and "Mrs. Parkerhouse says," and whether one person's view agreed with another's was not anyone's concern. Everybody was right, as long as they claimed Mrs. Parkerhouse had said so. This created a perpetual confusion, since sooner or later contradictions arose. One week the kitchen floor was waxed to an inch of its life, and the next week it was dulled by bleach. One day the bussers wore their collars down and buttoned; another day they stood them straight up with the top button open. One day ice poured from pitchers, and another day ice held itself at the pitcher's lip. Some days, the hurricane lamp flames stood still and straight, while other days they danced and flickered like demons. Everybody followed the signs through which Mrs. Parkerhouse made her wishes known.

Sometimes, when one story contradicted another, people argued about whose version was true and whose was just somebody trying to sound important. There were stories about Mrs. Parkerhouse's true nature, as determined by the signs those in dispute claimed to have seen; there were stories about her looks. In the latter stories, contradictions were more readily reconciled, given how one's looks were subject to change: thin to fat to thin again; red hair to blonde to silver to black to white; extravagantly frilly to mannishly severe to quietly demure. New staff learned quickly that nobody would let them get away with stories about first-hand sightings. And as for expressing any doubts about the truth of Mrs. Parkerhouse's existence, those ended as soon as they started.

"Who do you think hired you?" veteran staff would growl.

"Them," the new one would point to Joan or Mildred, Hal, Al, or Ernie, and sometimes, without thinking it through, to T.J. who, after all, wore the most impressive uniform.

"Hah," the old-timers would scoff. "Read your paycheck."

In fact, Billiard's, not Mrs. Parkerhouse's signature made its appearance on all checks, but by the time new workers received their first check, they knew better than to go looking for such proof. By then, they'd heard a dozen times over about something Mrs. Parkerhouse had seen them do and wanted them to do differently, things often nobody else could know about, like dipping their dirty fingers in the water pitcher or chopping onions lengthwise instead of cross wise, things sometimes even they didn't know they were doing. Sometimes new hires like Essie would just quit, when she was told her underpants touched the bathroom floor, and the bus boy with the light brown afro with the Greek name nobody could remember was told to stop practicing cartwheels after hours in the lounge. Some people couldn't live with the fact that their secrets were not their own.

Mrs. Parkerhouse's signs had met no real resistance until she named Viney Powder Room attendant and hired Mildred's cousin's niece, Sheila, to take over as housekeeper. Viney had promptly disappeared on Sheila's first day on the job and did not return until the young, eager-to-please woman with no work experience whatsoever quit in frustration. No one could tell her what she was supposed to do, Mrs. Parkerhouse's signs notwithstanding.

"Just as well," Mildred later had told Viney. "That poor child gone spooky. She done think she see ghosts."

"Well, maybe she do," Viney had replied.

Later that day Mildred told Viney that she had heard shouts coming from Billiard's office, along with door slamming and a flood of tears. Mildred was certain that the tears did not belong to Billiard.

"I declare, I never hear such a temper on any living thing. You think she seen the end of the world."

"I reckon she did," Viney said.

Mildred gave her a long look. "You scare me half to death disappearing like that. I don't suppose you going to tell me where you gone."

Viney shrugged. "I go where I be called."

"Sister, don't be playing with me. You telling me you hear The Call?"

Viney paused.

"If you mean Jesus, he ain't announced Himself as such," Viney said finally.

"Well, then who call you?" Mildred squinted.

Viney's stomach jumped as Mildred's breath pulsed hard against her face. She didn't blame Mildred for asking. To the day she died, Viney's own mama never knew what took her daughter away from Snowbird for good. Nor did Celia know why all of a sudden Viney left the two-flat on 26th Street and the ten children who'd grown attached to her. Both had prescribed being with her "people" as the best remedy for life's ills. Even her daddy had proclaimed "his people" as the reason he kept going down to the Low Country; moonshine had been just an excuse. But Viney's leaving had nothing to do with people, hers or anybody else's.

"Some things ain't got no name," Viney replied.

Mildred pulled a hankie from her pocket. "'Some trust in chariots and some in horses, but we trust in the name of the Lord our God,'" she recited. She wiped her eyes gingerly, as if they might shatter. "It's them things without names that trouble me."

Viney knew her friend could stand only certain truths unshuttered, and the memory of horses was not among them. For Viney to tell Mildred the simple truth, that it was the thoroughbreds who called her, would be like admitting she followed the Devil Himself.

During the Stables' racing days, Mildred never once visited the horse barn, never once pulled out an apple or sugar cube for a thoroughbred to rubber-lip. The few times some thoughtless person talked horses in her presence, a glaze would dull her eyes. Within that glaze, Viney saw scenes playing over and over: manes heaving in flame shadows, hoods masking horse and rider, hooves fleeing strange fruit spinning from high branches. Mildred had never spoken of these scenes; instead, Viney had grasped them in recollection of the silences between Celia's hushed words, King's rages against the Man, and verses her daddy used to sing on his trips up and down the mountain.

Over the years, Mildred had learned to live with these silences. Every few days she threw the Devil's bones into a pot big enough to stand in, seasoned them with hell-raising shouts, and boiled them bare to soup. The racket alone was almost enough to make Viney wish Jesus had ridden a fancy Roman horse instead of a humble donkey.

*

Before Viney comes North, she eats only from wooden bowls and plates, and wooden spoons. She picks up her meat to tear it loose from the bone; she seizes risen loaves and twists off her share. Mamaw has a bread knife, though, and she watches, cheeks propped on fists, whenever Mamaw saws off a slice with those tiny, even teeth to make sandwiches. At home, Mama splits cornbread with a sharpened stone and Daddy pushes his thumbs into the heart of a biscuit to lay it open for fixings. But Mamaw's steady, even slices allow for shallow ponds of jam to cover every inch. Even cold butter spreads, the slices are that smooth.

Now, every day at the Stables, remembering Mamaw's picture-perfect strokes, she takes her meals on bone china, her drinks in crystal goblets. The plates are rimmed in gold, the same stuff Daddy claimed was buried in the Blue Ridge, and the goblets sing a round, sweet note when she taps a fork on their rims. As for forks, she still cannot fathom why so much silver has wound up in something used for eating. Each fork, spoon, and knife must have at least ten silver dollar's worth of metal in them. Food tastes different when she spears a piece of Mildred's roast chicken or spoons up consommé from those bone plates. Not only tastes different—is different. It enters her without her ever laying a hand on it. She no longer knows the feel of her food except within the closed cavern of her mouth. The utensils, an extension of her hands, are powerful in their ability to do so much more, with more precise results.

She can still use her hands, as Mildred sometimes does, as T.J. is prone to do, and yet something stops her. Perhaps it is because she has a napkin that she has less desire to use it, to soil its brilliant red body.

Eventually she tires of the heavy silver and fragile plates. She longs for the taste of food from her hands. She licks them clean, she wipes them on her apron, or she sits outside in the Rose Garden and rubs her palms in the grass. She spends too much time washingdryingpressing those napkins to just use them up like everyone else, as if napkins are air to be breathed. One more napkin makes no difference, of course. But then each time she reaches for one more, the difference gets a little clearer. So she stops reaching, finding comfort in the wisdom of her hands.

At first Mildred scolds her. "Stop eating like a country gal. These new people coming in be proper city folk, not like them slummers. They expect they help to act civilized. Best watch yourself around the new bosses."

"You the only one see me eat," Viney replies.

Mildred stares, one eyebrow pointing at her forehead, the other diving to the bridge of her nose. "You know how many peoples dying to have a proper dish to eat from, let alone a clean napkin for wiping up they messes? I come too far to be wiping my mouth on my sleeve and drinking from my hands."

"It ain't the same."

"Child, I don't know how to tell you this, so I just say it straight. You are stuck on the old ways because them's all you know. You afraid of the finer things cause all your life you been told one way or another you ain't worth it. Well, I'm here to tell you you are worth it. Not many places let the hired help eat like paying folk. Maybe Barnswell done been too

cheap to buy us things separate from paying customers. But I think he want us to understand rich folks from the inside out, so we do better by them. He maybe not knowing it, but we done better by us, too."

Mildred has only said out loud what Viney has already heard whispered about country folk: backwards, ignorant, superstitious. Although Mildred herself is from the country, she's wasted no time in distancing herself from her Mississippi ways. Her one exception is food. She has no use for lobster, or for those huge steaks that she carves so expertly from carcasses in the cooler. *"Ain't got no taste,"* she'd complain.

"I ain't stuck," Viney says softly, as if walking across dynamite. Not even T.J. disagrees with Mildred head on. *"I like soft rugs and a warm stove when it be cold. I like light when the sun go down, and I surely do like doing my business in private, without wondering who be watching. But I don't need bone plates and a chest full of silver to know what rich folks is about."*

"I guess you told me," Mildred grumbles.

"They don't know what they missing. The best stuff all the things they don't want. I ain't about to tell them."

"Don't bother," Mildred snorts. *"Missing? What they be missing? Taking whatever gets shoved on you? Training your tongue to like somebody else's leftovers? Teaching your kids not to hope beyond what they got right now? Being grateful to work 14 hours a day just to make ends meet? At least now I got choices. Now I see what else there be to work for. Now I can dream past them old cotton picker dreams of a piece of land and a roof over my head. I done tasted what it be like to pick and choose your dreams, and I know that as real as you and me."*

"Some choice." Viney shrugged. *"Bone plates or no plates."*

"Give me bone any day."

It isn't for no reason that people don't take Mildred on. Once she gets a notion in her head, she hangs on like a bull dog and will not let go. That's why Viney can't tell her the whole truth. Mildred will only fuss and poke at her if she tells her why she can't abide those fancy things. No words can explain how the plates cry out each time she touches them, and the beautiful songs from the crystal soon turn into screams. Perhaps worst of all are the voices of the dead that speak through the silverware every time she takes a polishing cloth to their elaborate designs. Mildred would roll her eyes as if that is the craziest thing she's ever heard, but still keep one eye glued to Viney just in case she's telling the truth.

Mildred isn't about to give up what she never was supposed to have, what she didn't even know she couldn't have because she never knew it *was there. Maybe she hears the voices, too. Maybe, Viney thinks, she's learned not to listen.*

But since Mildred is her one true friend, Viney takes a chance. "Can't you hear them?" She has come so far and given up so much, including that easy quiet with Mama, and Mamaw's stories about the old days before the rest of the world stopped speaking. Viney would never have had to explain restless bones in her dishes or poison singing in her cups, or the dead weight of forks to either of them. Their land still spoke to them, and so did all things connected to that land, their ancestral home for so long that they remembered no other. Other places cried out with the shedding of their ancestor's blood, but not Snowbird. That was where they all came home to in the end.

To Viney's surprise, Mildred stops and listens, eyes roaming, up, down, back and forth across the kitchen. Then she slowly nods, still looking all around, and returns her gaze to Viney. Viney feels cold run up her gut and down her spine. She crosses her arms so as not to shiver while Mildred is staring so hard.

"I reckon there be a lot worse evil in this world than what be in them dishes," Mildred sighs. "No use dwelling on it."

From that point on Viney understands that Mildred inhabits a different sort of space, one built by choices fearless in design, determined by an armored "I" that will not be denied. In this room, Viney is background noise, like the buzzing of the Stables' swamp, mostly unnoticed by day, but at night almost loud enough to break somebody's heart. Almost, but not quite loud enough.

*

During her years at the Stables, Viney has heard all manner of buzzing, screeching, and scratching creatures steal their way inside the restaurant's sprawling mazes, guided only by their senses and traces of those gone before. Large and small, they burrowed, flapped, or gnawed themselves passage. Drawn by some unnamable attraction, they shifted their destinations away from the ditches, gardens, lawns, and lots of greater Bedford Heights to inside the Stables' painted brick walls.

For the most part, she welcomed them as wayward travelers who sometimes overstayed their welcome. Usually they left as soon as she cleaned out their roosts. But the stubborn few who stayed behind remained hidden beyond her reach. These she never tried to disturb, necessary exceptions to the Stables' rule of order.

In their determined ranks, Viney grasped the long journeys behind them. Like them, she had traveled great distances. Like them, she felt the push-pull greeting of the Stables, held close at one moment, slapped back at another, like a rude dance whose steps she had struggled to learn. Yet she had learned them well, without realizing how much they had changed her, until the dance suddenly shifted as wave after wave of new migrants stormed their way inside that summer, sending her scrambling to keep up with their arrivals.

By August, so many had squeezed inside the Stables that even the Powder Room was not without them, despite blue toilet water (one of Mrs. Parkerhouse's signs) and tightly closed taps at the sink. Hoards of miller moths circled the vanity lights until they fell to their deaths, exhausted or fatally burned. Every morning, dozens of pale wings lay scattered across the marble counter, their translucent bodies powdering desperate prints on the mirror. Sparrows, too, had found a haven there, building nests in the heating vents with shredded toilet paper and Kotex, and lining them with hair and lint.

Before long, the migrant masses grew so large that even ordinary shadows were pressed for space and began to shift and shiver in discontent until, restless, they broke away from the very things that cast them and wandered among all the rooms they had never known before. At night they joined other shadows in huge, restless hordes that roamed with no purpose other than to revel in their new found freedom, unsettling in seconds what took Viney hours to restore. Lacking any sense of their collective power, the shadows failed to notice the paintings that cocked their faces inquisitively at them, or the dust that leapt joyfully onto higher surfaces for a better view, or even kitchen drains that, in their excitement, burped up unspeakably foul odors. Nor did the shadows notice how rugs buckled and carpets rippled in an effort to follow the shadows that had abandoned them to their own stubborn substance.

Viney now often found herself an obstacle in the path of the shadows' euphoria. At least once a day she was forced to crouch under tables or hide behind seats whose shadows had not yet left them so as not to get caught up in their restlessness and thus neglect her duties. Each morning, she met with fewer interruptions as sunlight coaxed many to return to their places. Yet with more and more of them breaking free, even daylight left few places for Viney to steer clear.

She realized very quickly that the Stables would not long withstand the constant agitation that migrants and shadows alike had brought to bear. The horseshoe carpet, once a dazzling scarlet, soon faded to a reticent rouge. White tablecloths suffered so many stains and tears that Viney could no longer spread a spotless backdrop to each diner's meal. Bemused by this turmoil, tobacco smoke clung so fearfully to the walls, floors, and ceilings that the air itself glowed an asthmatic yellow. Lights struggled out of their fixtures, and their bulbs glowed too brightly, burning out before their time. Plaster cracks webbed the walls and chips of paint danced loose to settle on whatever would accept it. Door hinges that had never complained now issued loud protests, in solidarity with table and chair legs equally vocal in their discontent.

At the same time, Viney could not have anticipated how this restlessness would affect everyone else at the Stables. A constant hum hovered as customers started to pour in without end, a hum that grew louder as the cash flowed stronger. Fever glowed so fiercely in their eyes that Viney could not steer clear of the frenzy. Stray coins leapt from the floor into her hands, and overlooked dollar bills winged their way into her apron pocket. The familiar scents of currency, smells that before had been so common as to escape notice, now overpowered the air with sudden ubiquity, all because the signs left behind year after year were finally coming to fruition. Yet the very things those signs had once sought to preserve now proved obstacles to their ultimate end: to fill the Stables with vast oceans of wealth until the whole place was drowning in riches.

Viney mused how all her cleaningscrubbingshining had brought her to this even as she continued her buffingrubbingscraping, on hands and knees, just as she always had, noting the increasingly visible signs of wear. These were what Mrs. Parkerhouse's signs had foretold all along: the Stables would come to its preordained end, and Mrs. Parkerhouse would rise from its ashes in glory. And since everyone else took these signs as the Truth, nothing interrupted their ever-quickening pace towards resolution. Viney's own labors had helped to speed this process along. While she had never worked towards holding things together, neither had she worked to tear things apart. Whatever she cleaned, polished, or put back into place acknowledged an end, yet harbored no permanence. She attended to whatever responsibilities fell to her as she would an instrument tuned to pitches that could not ever be heard.

So separate were the worlds they occupied it had never occurred to Viney that one day she might see Mrs. Parkerhouse in the flesh. Later Viney realized that she should have known she was bound to run across the woman, since of all the rooms in the Stables, the Powder Room was theirs alone.

Viney was sitting in the far stall, resting on the stool that moments ago she had wiped clean of bird droppings. As she leaned over to gather a spider web full of dead flies from the baseboard, she heard the Powder Room door hinges complain. Although it was too early for customers, the hinges had spoken in those firm, insistent tones reserved for someone with the power to relieve them. But their complaints grew quiet as the door swung back to silence.

The stall's plantation shutters had not budged from the same half open, half shut position that they had been locked in for weeks, so the most Viney could see was a narrow slit cutting across her vision of wide, flat lapels, white woven cloth, and a garnet stick pin that sparkled like current jelly. As she stretched forward for a different view, new details appeared: iron gray waves; thick black rims; a forehead creased many times over.

She could have easily flipped back the door latch and stepped out before that woman who stood there clicking her tongue. Viney knew she could pass her, unseen, like a slight breeze against the skin, or a shadow in the corner of an eye, momentarily glimpsed, then quickly forgotten. Or Viney could stare so frankly that, in staring back, the woman would be so scared that she would question the truth of her own eyes. But at the moment it seemed the least harm would be to just let the woman alone.

Viney had resigned herself to waiting when, gazing at the floor, her breath sucked in. Just beyond the shutters on the black and white tile floor laid two dead moths. In the past, other managers had been all too eager to gas the whole restaurant upon such a discovery. But at those times, she always had had a chance to persuade the migrants to settle elsewhere before the holocaust hit. She, too, would disappear until the air had cleared, sometimes for days. But she knew that once Mrs. Parkerhouse found out, she would waste no time in saturating every nook and cranny of the Stables with an arsenal of poison clouds, leaving no time for Viney to warn the migrants to leave.

Fortunately, the Powder Room's inspection by those black rims abruptly ended, as the plantation shutters on the other stall squealed and its door groaned open, then slapped shut. A pair of white lace-up shoes with thick soles appeared below the mahogany wall separating the two stalls. Heavy, pale hose outlined two slim ankles, the kind that young women had before children and other responsibilities thickened them like tree trunks. A steady rain fell into the toilet, drowning out the woman's slow, heavy breaths and the creak of those lace-up shoes. Coffee piss competed with Glade Summer Bouquet air freshener, yet another one of Mrs. Parkerhouse's signs.

The latch dropped back silently as Viney eased her stall door open. She waited until she heard the toilet paper tear before she leaned over, straining against her own bulk, and snatched the soft, powdery bodies into her fist.

"Stop right there," commanded a voice from behind the shutters.

Viney let go of the stall door, which promptly slammed shut, its spring hinges too tight. Many latches inside the stalls had broken when the ladies had pulled too hard to get in, only to discover the sight of panty hose puddled around someone else's ankles.

Water whooshed and those white shoes squealed as the sound of cloth rubbing against cloth ticked in Viney's ears. In a moment, that voice behind the shutters would take on the fullness of a body, and Viney would finally see the whole of her, the one person everybody knew but nobody, except maybe Billiard, actually saw.

Viney rolled the moths between her thumb and forefinger, careful not to smash their wings as she started for the Powder Room door. It wasn't that she lacked curiosity, for, like everyone else, she had imagined her own picture of Mrs. Parkerhouse's face, drawing from the vast pool of Stables' speculations to form features in accord with the signs she left behind. Nor did Viney fear recognition, since it was a simple enough matter for her to be still, rag in hand, eyes cast down, the way all managers expected their staff to stand. Nor was it a matter of love or hate, for she had long ago accepted that Mrs. Parkerhouse and her kind just *was,* like floods and humidity and earthworms. She did not need the proof of her eyes to know the fact of Mrs. Parkerhouse's existence.

In fact, it was out of respect that Viney eased open the Powder Room's newly varnished door, giving the hinges a break from their complaints, and fell in with the marching shadows that marked the passage to the Tack Room. She didn't need further proof to affirm what she already knew to be true: Mrs. Parkerhouse was a ghost from a past that loved the Stables like a toothache.

She tucked the two moths, now twined in death, into her apron pocket. She figured all Mrs. Parkerhouse would remember would be a work-splotched hand wiping the black-and-white tile clear. Mrs. Parkerhouse's poison would wait for some other day when it didn't matter how deep it reached inside, when the walls themselves would take one long, last inhalation and, in their collapse, blow that killer's breath back upon itself.

Chapter Sixteen: Safe Room

Once Lenny told me about the Safe Room, going inside it became an obsession. Only two people had a key: Billiard and Mrs. Parkerhouse. Yet everybody else already seemed to know about it. Even Mary Beth and Sharon knew.

"Why didn't you tell me?" I complained when I overheard them mention it one day.

They shrugged and shook their heads. "No biggie," Sharon finally answered. She slid a glance towards Mary Beth. Mary Beth returned a long suffering eye roll. As the summer had progressed, so had their friendship. They even talked on the phone on their days off. But mine had stalled after the initial boost from the Star Dust baby shower.

More and more they'd taken to falling silent when I spoke, or ignoring me when I tried to join them. It wasn't out of sheer meanness; our rhythms were out of sync. In holding onto my secrets, I was awkward and overly careful. Either they were playing dumb, or they genuinely didn't know about Lenny, but no doubt they saw me as less than forthcoming. I never spoke to them without first weighing my words. When it came to conversation, I listened first and only later offered response. Unlike them, I did not launch a few words without forethought, just to see where they would go. I was ponderous; they were playful and mercurial. They relished jokes, wisecracks, stray bits of gossip. I couldn't keep up without risking my cover. So I stopped trying.

"Well," I said, careful to avoid a long explanation. "I just wondered."

They looked at each other, then me, their mouths pursed in tight little grins.

In exchange for saying no more, I left the conversation even more unsure about their silences. Did they or didn't they know about my rendezvous with Lenny?

By the end of August, Lenny and I had had sex in every conceivable place inside and around the Stables. Our discoveries had gone on for so long that I had expected we would soon run out of new places to do it, just as sooner or later I expected we would be exposed. Yet after so many times of escaping notice, I began to believe we would never be caught. Others had passed within inches of us sprawled together on the floor, had even stared us straight in the face, but still, somehow, they had not seen us. Some had even bumped into us, as if we were just another table leg or lettuce crate. I could not explain how, time and again, we evaded confrontation by some busboy, waitress, delivery man, maitre d', or even Mrs. Parkerhouse herself, who, of course, we never saw but, like everyone else, believed saw everything. For all we knew, she *had* seen us but wasn't saying.

The other possibility, one I had clung to for weeks, was that everybody had seen us; we were just the last to know they had. Lenny insisted no way, being so close to the grapevine through Mildred Aunty and Uncle T.J., who had a way of knowing what was happening even before it did. But even they had said nothing.

Each time I thought we'd discovered the last unsexified inch of the Stables, new ones presented themselves, as if the Stables was urging us on, steering us towards that next stolen spot, spaces within spaces of endless possibility. We couldn't stop even if we wanted to. Knowing that made surrender easier yet still exhausting, since I could not ignore what might happen if we were ever confronted. Until now, our actions could be considered by the powers that be as morally repugnant, unprofessional, disrespectful, or subject to some other stiff-phrased admonition. But none of these even approached being caught in the Safe Room without permission. Criminal. Attempted theft.

Money didn't matter. I knew nothing about safe cracking. But what I could steal was peace of mind. That was irresistible.

During one agonizingly slow dinner shift, having nothing better to do than avoid Billiard, I strolled past the business office, which closed most nights at six when Mrs. Parkerhouse left for the day. Billiard was sometimes gone by then, too, if he wasn't in the Tack Room or the Winner's Circle Lounge making small talk with patrons or in the kitchen annoying staff with curt reprimands. He'd bark at us college gals to get busy even without a single diner in our sections and with our prep work done for the day, then steal the chairs we sat on by the Garden Room doors while we waited for our tables to be seated.

The office windows were dark and the blinds drawn. I gave the door handle a little jiggle—unlocked. After checking to make sure no one was looking, I slipped inside, closing the door behind me. Unlike the sewer sweat of the dishwasher or the grill's greasy fog, the office was dry and slightly musty, like a library. The air was cool, even a bit chilly, and I shivered as I took in my surroundings as best I could without benefit of light. I picked my way around the cement floor, toeing a floor drain, brushing past first one desk, then another, rubbing up against the roughly smooth face of a cinderblock wall. Unlike other places where Lenny and I had had sex, the business office held little appeal, too cool, too dry, and above all way too orderly, although the avalanche of papers on top of one of the desks did give me pause. I inched my way to the Safe Room door and tried its knob.

Locked, of course. The disappointment hit me hard. Up until that point, everything had been so easy. Fate was on our side. But this obstacle seemed a bad omen. Could it be our luck had finally changed?

The next day, Lenny and I were killing time between lunch and dinner shifts when I told him about my discoveries. We were straddling the threshold to the back door, trying to survive the record-breaking heat while Lenny smoked. For days we'd been plotting when to get together in the Safe Room. He'd become as obsessed as I was. We'd assumed that just getting inside the business office would be a major hurdle. But when I told him I'd found the door unlocked, he threw down his smoke, grabbed my hand, and raced us outside, away from the broken lettuce crates, haloes of flies, and cigarette butts flattened like a welcome mat and around the corner to the west side where he had paced a nicotine-fueled path in the grass.

"You telling me that door unlocked?" he asked.

"That was yesterday."

"Then we gonna see about today." He fished a Camel Straight out of his breast pocket and struck a match under the hooves of the Stables' equine emblem.

"They leave at six," I said. He already knew that; I just wanted him to know I knew.

"Man. Freaking. They really leave that door unlocked?"

Now he had me curious.

"So what? The Safe Room stays locked." I couldn't get past the disappointment of an entry finally denied. Up until now I had trusted fate to be on our side. Fate, I concluded, was fickle. I had no more idea why it had been so generous for so long than why it had now started to withhold. None of it made sense.

Lenny chuckled and reached for a stray strand of my hair. "Baby, where you been? What you been doing all summer? Or do all you college gals walk around with your head in the clouds?"

I slapped his outreached hand and grabbed his cigarette. I took a drag, blew the smoke over his head, and thrust it back, butt end aimed at his nose. "It's not much of a place," I said finally. "I almost didn't tell you."

"Not much?" He shoved his hat back and let his head drop against his neck, staring at the sun overhead. "A room full of money and she say 'it's not much'?"

"I didn't see any money."

This time when he laughed, it came from his gut. He even started coughing; the laugh had caught him off guard. "She don't *see* the money," he proclaimed to the sky, waving, coughing. His hat slid off the back of his head.

My fists found my hips and rested there while my neck pulled away from my shoulders. "Well, I didn't," I answered, trying hard to sound belligerent when all I felt was hopeless. The Stables had finally denied us. *Us*! The spell was broken; we were no longer held in its magical grasp.

"Like you supposed to." He was still laughing at me. I stomped my foot in the dirt uncovered by his restlessness.

"That room is creepy. So sterile. Like a hospital."

"You ever stay in a hospital?"

"No."

"My cousin a nurse at Englewood. Hospital one of the filthiest places around."

I threw up my hands. "Ok, I'm a stupid college gal and you're so much smarter than me." I spat out *gal* like spoiled meat. I didn't mind being called "college" as much as I did "gal." I could forgive the old folks for that, but not Lenny. I suppose they thought "gal" sounded better than "girl." It put me in mind of middle-aged housewives who couldn't get away with being "girls" but who couldn't bring themselves to say "women." And then there was that pernicious southern "gal."

"At least we agree on something," he grinned, tugging at another of my stray hairs. I slapped his hand again. "But seriously, we got to check this out."

"What's to check out?"

He kissed me on the lips before sliding his cig between them. "That Safe Room the last place anybody find us."

Every time I was sure we'd found the Stables' "last, best place," another one presented itself. The more visible we thought we were to others, the less visible we turned out to be. So would the Safe Room have the opposite effect? Was our discovery more likely because the Safe Room was unseen by all but Billiard and Mrs. Parkerhouse?

I drew on that Camel Straight so hard it burned my finger tips then flicked it to the ground. My big toe ground it into other butts in various stages of decomposition as I sucked out bits of tobacco stuck between my teeth. A hot flush swept up and down my legs. My ass squeezed hard, and my thighs pressed together so tight they started to sweat.

"See you at six," I said.

Days went by, and we still hadn't made it to the Safe Room. Either one of us was off, or Billiard worked late, or our shifts were too busy to take a break. In the meantime, Safe Room fantasies consumed me. At first they trickled in but soon swelled to an unstoppable flood. First came visualizations: odors, textures, and shapes; shadows and light; the spaces between things and their playful echoes. Then more active fantasies: my waist leaning against the safe, both hands pressed flat on top, Lenny behind me, between my spread legs; on the top of the safe, spread open to eyes I could not see, only feel, Lenny's voice, odd, officious, chastising me with his probing touch.

Once they started, they refused to stop--no turn-off valve, no on-off switch, no dike or sandbags, no lock and key--demanding unconditional surrender. The more response they won, the more they wanted. Eventually I did respond, equally insistent, equally relentless, demanding ever more powerful performances. Even asleep, my dreams placed me inside the Safe Room, and I would wake up knowing I'd spent the night there, performing prurient poses with my partner in crime.

Until the Safe Room, the Stables' grip on my imagination would last only until I crossed Illinois Road. Each time I walked the gravel drive to go home, my thoughts emptied themselves into the swamp on one side or the drainage ditch on the other, releasing me from the gossip, rivalries, and petty intrigue that so powerfully bound the veterans to their jobs and to each other. That brief walk erased the day's events, like dreams lightly passing through my sleep.

On the other side of Illinois Road, every crack in the sidewalk, every spider web spun between branches, every rusty nail in the telephone poles held some memory for me. Here, the Stables retreated, an exotic but fleeting weft woven into the mundane warp of my imagination. On this side of a road forbidden me as a child to cross, the Stables held itself apart with regal reserve, its peaked roof, white-washed brick, and steady stream of cars an impeccable, albeit distant, vision.

That clean separation between one side of the road and the other, between the reality that was my life and the dream I had been living that summer, disappeared once the Safe Room took on a life of its own. Until then, my dreams had been generous, supportive, ever humble about their place. Now they erupted into fiery nightmares that turned every day life into a fleeting afterthought.

For the next couple of days, I fended off anxious looks from my mother across the breakfast table as I forced down wedges of dry toast with black coffee, the caffeine my insurance to make it through the next shift. My uniform, already too large, now swallowed me in earnest. In the bathroom mirror, I glimpsed eye sockets scooped clean of everything but shadows. A forgotten pack of Pall Malls from the Derby Room took up residence in my uniform pocket. Bent at one end like a child's drinking straw, they smoked well enough before joining the gestalt of abandoned butts plastered outside the Stables' kitchen door.

The week was nearly over when my mother ventured a comment. All summer I'd been ignoring her observations about how I ate, what I ate, what I should eat, and when I should eat it, to the point where, only two weeks before my return to Hyde Park, she had finally called a truce. Or perhaps she had conceded that I was a hopeless cause. Either way, she must have found my current behavior worrisome enough to reopen the subject.

"You look thin," she said as she spooned up a soft boiled egg.

I turned my head from the phlegmy ovum as it slithered onto toast and picked up a triangle of toast that my mother had set before me. As a child, I had preferred my bread cut corner to corner. She still remembered this whenever I came home. Until now, it had pleased me. But now the toast was just one more reminder that I could no longer sit at the kitchen table and let my childish tongue roam.

"Are you on a diet?" Knife and fork in hand, she carefully sawed the toast into brown rectangles drenched in yolk. Again, I averted my eyes.

"No!" If she hadn't before, she would now suspect a lie. I couldn't tell her how the egg steam, the scorched toast, the sharp wedge of morning light cutting across the kitchen table were almost too much to bear, their perfect impartiality painful reminders of my own turmoil.

She put down her knife and switched her fork to her right hand. In the dorms, the North Shore trust fund babies had wielded their cutlery "continental" style—fork in left hand, upside down, spearing each morsel after every cut. My roommate had teased me for cutting all my food at once, as if for a baby. Now I couldn't help but note the awkwardness of a style I had known not as a "style" but as simply the way to eat.

"You know you don't have to starve yourself," she said. She kept eating, perhaps expecting her example to rub off.

"I'm not hungry." In a normal frame of mind, I would have never admitted this to her. I slumped back in the soft vinyl chair and waited for the inevitable.

"Are you sick?" She peered into my shadow-sculpted eyes, her tone conveying not a question but a certainty.

In fact, I had no "reason" for not eating. I was hungry but nothing appealed to me. The only word that sprang to mind, the only "reason" I could conjure at this point, was that I felt unsafe.

Yet I couldn't tell her that. Her whole life as a mother had been to secure my safety in the world. Why else had she and my father sacrificed, dreamed, and struggled if not to ensure that most basic need? How could I not feel safe when they had dedicated their lives to that cause? Had I thrown away their gift? Had it been stolen from me? These were questions I was unprepared to answer.

"I'll eat later on break."

She sighed, laid down her fork, pressed a paper napkin to her lips as if to muffle her words, words she didn't necessarily believe but had resigned herself to. "I hope you're getting the proper nutrition…" She picked up the fork and resumed her diligent consumption of a proper breakfast. She was nothing if not persistent.

"It's enough," I said, brushing nonexistent crumbs from my hands onto my plate. That maybe was the biggest lie of all; nothing at this point felt like "enough."

Perhaps it was because her hair was showing wisps of gray, or that beneath her cheeks, on either side of her chin, little pouches of skin had begun to sag past the bone, or that her brown eyes had taken on an inscrutability that I could not account for, that I hadn't really noticed until now. Perhaps she, too, was feeling the uncertain press of time, but unlike me, had no room to change her responses to things unknown. She was already "safe" and thus could not afford to risk what she'd worked so hard to gain. Perhaps she already knew that she could not lure me back, nor proffer any threat or warning to make me change my course. But as I watched her from across the table, I knew I had to find my own "safe," even if she was never convinced of that. The only "safe" she knew was holding onto us, her family, in the home we shared. We were her "safe."

We stared out the window into the back yard, our empty plates before us. The keen light pressed my gaze back towards abandoned spider webs spun between the window panes, streaks on the dusty glass, sun rays split into infinitely fine strands of light, softening my eyes into a hazy brightness against which my mother's dark form was the boundary that defined it. I wanted her to believe that like her, I was looking outside of myself when, in truth, I was trying very hard to look in.

As sink water ran, rubber gloves squeaked, and clean dishes thumped into the dish rack, I sat motionless, gripped by these ordinary sounds that spoke in a language both intimate and remote. Even after my mother moved on to another set of chores elsewhere in the house, her sounds held me, reminding me of how much between us was still unknown.

Once the sun's angle shifted, I stood and stretched as if I had been asleep a long time. Later, as I prepared for my dinner shift, I thought how odd it was that until now I had believed, like a scientist or a saint, that all would be understood in due time. This time stepping into my clean uniform, still warm from the dryer powered by my mother's vigilance, was not a chore but instead a relief.

*

Taking a break next to the empty service bar, Lenny and I are relieved to discover we have the same night off next week. That never happens. We decide we must take advantage.

Neither of us wants to replay the awkwardness of Hyde Park. Bringing the other home isn't even a topic.

"What about the Dust?" he says.

"What about it?" There the talk would really fly. Plus, I'd have to borrow my parents' Plymouth and hope nothing bad happened to it parked on a city street. "You want everybody at the Stables to see us get it on?"

"What goes on in the Dust stays in the Dust. That's the rule."

"What about being alone?" My eyes dart across the empty service bar.

"I know all the good spots."

When I ask for directions, he frowns.

"How 'bout I pick you up? Say around eight?" he says.

I can't believe what I'm hearing. I want to scream and jump up and down. He wants to pick me up. He wants to make me squirm. He wants to show me off. He wants to blow my cover. He wants to test me. He wants to please me.

I try the practical approach. "Why drive all the way back to Bedford Heights to get me?"

"You going to drive all that way by yourself?"

"You sound like my mother," I spit back.

His open palms rise up, begging for mercy. "Whoa. I don't know what your mama has to do with this. All I'm saying is you ain't never drove that stretch yourself."

"You think driving straight down 75th Street is something I can't handle?" The anger takes me by surprise. I'm suddenly in the middle of a fight that I don't want but don't know how not to have.

"Baby, I just want you to be safe."

"Like hell you do."

This time, instead of begging for mercy, his hands ball into fists. "Hell, if I was your mama, I'd be worried about you driving alone through a strange place, too. Girl, you ain't got no sense."

My hand hits the service bar with a loud slap. Lenny jumps back a little. My voice strains to stay low as I reply, "Fuck you."

He sighs and runs his hand through his fro. "Look. My mama done worry about me driving here, too. OK? Ain't just a girl thing. You ain't got the experience yet to judge."

My chin drops to my chest and my shoulders sag. "I am so sick of being told what I don't know. How do you know what I know?" But the fight has left my voice.

"I get it. I should a seen it sooner. You still ain't told your parents about us."

He stares at me, eyes full of resentment. I stare back, trying to match his resentment with my own.

"Like you've told your mother about me?"

"Matter of fact, I have," he replies coolly.

"So I'm going to meet her?" I try not to smirk. I've got him cornered.

"Don't change the subject. We be talking about the Dust."

"My father would kill me if he knew I was dating you." My voice is flat and lifeless. I'd give anything to get out of this fight now, before I really get hurt.

Lenny must have read my mind because he starts to laugh. At first it's just a chuckle, but then it builds to a chortle and then into a guffaw. He has to lean against the service bar to keep his balance. *"And just what you think your daddy going to do to his little girl?"*

"You don't know him."

"Try me."

"He'll cut off my tuition."

"So you can keep working at the Stables?"

"He'll kick me out of the house."

"So you can come shack up with me? He ain't that dumb. Not if he sending you to that expensive college."

"I'm on scholarship," I bristle. *"Partial."*

"So what you scared of?" His eyes soften as he leans forward, stroking my cheek with one finger. *"Why you won't let me come pick you up?"*

I shake my head. *"I'm just not ready,"* I tell him. *"I don't feel— safe."*

The memory is strong but no words can explain how safe disappeared long before my summer at the Stables: Nine years old, I'm watching the news, something I never do. But this day, nuns have sent us home early, asking us all to pray for peace. My father comes in, stops taking off his coat to listen to the announcer's voice go back in time, to Selma and Atlanta, Montgomery and Memphis, and even up north to Chicago: *"Shot and killed yesterday on a motel balcony in Memphis."* A camera zooms in to a second story room, not unlike those where we've stayed on family vacations. *"Killer still at large."* The camera shifts to masses of people crowding the streets, weeping, shouting, shaking fists and folding hands in prayer. As I watch, the announcer's voice ticks off the names of cities where riots have begun. Chicago is on the list. Where in Chicago? Soon the camera's gaze provides an answer. It is only five miles from Bedford Heights to those fires on the West Side.

I turn to my father and away from all those desperate, angry faces pressing through the TV screen. My teacher had called the man a saint. *"He stood up for the downtrodden,"* she said. I search my father's face for his reaction to the news of a saint's assassination and a killer still at large.

"About time they shot the nigger," he says, and shrugs off his coat.

"Don't you worry." Lenny strokes my cheek with one, solitary finger. "I know a place we both be safe."

*

"You brought a flashlight?" I asked. It was actually one of those pen lights that my father often used. Whenever he had to fix something—a clock, the oven light, a blown fuse—he'd unclip it from his shirt pocket and shine its sharp light on the problem. "Where'd you get that?" I asked.

"Locked," he said, ignoring my question. "You right. Damn. Not much of one. But still locked."

"Let me see." I crouched level with the light. He was right—not much of a lock. This was the *Safe* Room?

I stood up, brushed my hands down my halter top, smoothing out nonexistent wrinkles thanks to my mother's ironing. We finally had the night off together and had snuck into the Stables separately on some flimsy pretense, agreeing to meet at the business office door after Billiard left for the night. "My sister's room has the same lock. I used to break in, no problem," I said.

"You a lock picker?" I knew without looking he was grinning.

"Was."

"You forget?" His hands kneaded my shoulders in big circles, like a coach prepping his star for a critical play. My head arced backwards against my neck. A sigh drifted from my lips. His fingers walked my spine, traced my hips, then cupped my ass.

"Forget?" My voice floated, an untethered balloon. "Ah. Yes. Forget." I was wrong about the business office. The dry, library climate was as potently seductive as any place in the Stables. I could already hear those loose papers plopping in soft piles to the floor as we shuffled each other on the scuffed wooden desk.

His tongue tested my ear with a burglar's touch, his hot house breath coaxing its bloom. "Nasty," he whispered. "Breaking into sissie's room."

Some garbled sound escaped my lips.

"Tell me," he continued, "How you do it? Nice and slow? Slow enough you get all tingly?" He took my right hand and slid it into the stiff denim skirt between my thighs. "What you do first? Jiggle the lock?"

As if pulled by a string, my head bobbed up and down.

"Stroke the knob?" Now both our hands between us squeezed tight against our thighs. "Turn it just a little bit? This way and that? Tell me," he insisted. "Tell me. What you do now?"

"Bobby pin." I was right there before my sister's door, bulbous tips pinching my fingers, metal arms locked flat against themselves, looped wide at the end, enough to admit a child's nimble finger and release a sturdy snap. "Bend it," I murmured, my back arching to Lenny's touch. "Bend it open."

"Open, baby, open."

My left hand brushed back against the bobby pins that held my hair in place.

"The keyhole," I said. I remembered its irregular shape, round and angular at the same time. "Wait a minute." Slowly, my back raised itself up. "Check it out." The bobby pin danced a figure eight in the air as I held it up. The Stables' magic was not through with us yet.

"I knew it. I knew it." He kissed the bobby pin along with my fingers. "Look out, Safe Room, we coming in." The pen light aimed itself back on the knob. I pried the bobby pin open and crouched for a better look.

Later I marveled at how easy it was, though it had been years since I'd picked my sister's lock. Bent straight, the pin's head found easy clearance. A couple of probes and then the familiar click. True, it was my hands that held the bobby pin, turned the knob. But they were simply responding to the lock's direction, the bobby pin the medium of our exchange. Once again, the Stables had found a way to open itself to us.

With the final click, my flushed face drained to chill. Even with Lenny behind me, urging me forward, spasms shook my arms, and my palms grew clammy. My teeth clenched and chattered furiously. His knees bent into mine, his belly pressed flat to my back, and his chest lifted my shoulders like wings. Unlike every other threshold we'd crossed, this next step forward felt inexplicably final. Perhaps it had felt that way before, but we had been so consumed by the intrigue that any sense of finality had been lost, neither of us believing that anything would ever puncture our delight in the Stables' ever-open doors.

Inside, the Safe Room's darkness was absolute. Even my hand, as it groped ahead, was impossible to see. Not a spooky darkness--no cobwebs or rot, no festering molds, no fetid decay. Beyond the officious scent of paper, smells were curiously absent here, an escape from the Stables' habitual fires.

Two steps forward drew a pull string across my face. In response to my tug on the string, a bare bulb cast its feeble light. Then the door clicked closed and Lenny's arms circled my waist as our eyes adjusted to this sudden sight.

From the outside, the Safe Room had looked barely wide enough for us to stand side by side, and not much longer than we were tall. Inside, however, revealed a more spacious room, its most remarkable feature its sparse furnishing. Like the business office, the cinderblock walls were painted white, the floor a spotless concrete slab. Aside from a lone dining chair and open boxes of coveted items such as creamers, steak knives, napkins, and monkey dishes, the only other item was, as expected, the safe. With a mottled gray texture like a small waves on a lake, the safe hunched over two wooden pallets that lifted its squat, square body level with our thighs.

"The King was in his counting house, counting out his money," I sang, turning to Lenny. He was busy dragging the chair over to the safe.

"No shit. And smelling it, and rubbing it all over his boney ass." He eased his own trousered ass carefully onto the red leather seat and leaned forward, studying the safe's impassive face.

"Know what comes next?" My denim skirt hiked up just enough to straddle his pants legs as I squatted, face to face, on his lap.

"Sing it, baby."

"Guess first." My hips rocked forward and back into his.

"King got him a Queen." His hands disappeared under my hair and lifted it over my head. "She be wearing her crown." His long, slender fingers stroked the curls as they relaxed back down my shoulders.

"And he his." My palms cupped the bottom of his soft, fine fleece. "What else?"

"Queen say leave the money alone and give me some sugar."

My laugh broke the whispers we'd confined ourselves to upon our entry into the Safe Room. "Close. Though I doubt the Queen would want him to leave the money alone."

"Ok, so King rub it over her big, juicy ass."

"No, before that." Both of us were laughing now. In that dim, sealed-tight space, our laughter had no place else to go, rebounding from one hard surface to another, proving the exception to the Safe Room's stolid rule, to house nothing save what could be stockpiled for safe keeping.

"I give."

"The Queen was in the parlor, eating bread and honey."

"Forsooth, baby. Let us fetch ye olde honey pot."

I didn't care if the safe was, in the end, impossible to crack. In fact, that was perhaps its ultimate appeal: to overtake its rule, if for just a short while, transforming the miser's grim accounting into the immeasurable delights of expending a treasured hoard.

Until now, it had always been just the two of us, apart from all else. Or so I'd thought. But when Lenny dragged that lone chair over, I realized then that we had never really been alone. All along we had been overtaken by desires that were not ours alone, silent shapers of our stolen passions. Unlike Billiard and Mrs. Parkerhouse's more obvious desires, that accounted for possessions either owned or held in trust, these other desires, instead of counting our parts, had formed themselves around us and, in turn, offered their forms to us, registering the rhythm of our cells, our molecular frequencies, the imprint of our being against and among their own, their mute yearnings finding voice through ours.

Our seat of transformation, the chair held us in its power, challenging our imaginations, speaking through us as we moved. Our bodies discovered shapes they did not know they knew, owing everything to fulfilling the chair's silent desires. I should have known that the "us" that had begun as two and, through the chair, had expanded to three, was bound to keep on multiplying. Yet even though my ears heard the key engage the Safe Room's lock, and my gut registered the knob's slow twist, my eyes did not expect any other eyes to join us. After all, the illusion of two alone had held sway over us for so long.

Perhaps Lenny, too, did not hear the lock's click, did not feel the cool kiss of air on his shoulders, so completely was he saddled by the chair's urgings to suspend all calculations. Instead, his head turned not towards the open door but to the hoarded stockpiles deep inside, either ignoring or simply accepting what his ears had sought to impress.

We responded not by stockpiling our mutual heat but instead throwing off what we still possessed, which in that moment could only be described as endless. We counted on our contagion to infect whoever stood at the door. With the chair spurring us on, we would burn without end, unaccountable and uncontainable, flame to eternal flame.

Yet somewhere in the heat, the ache, the salt, the slick we shared between us, my own calculations were still at work: how long we could last, how much it would take, weighed against the prospect of better future returns. But the eyes that appeared in the doorway reflected a different equation than the simple multiplication of "us." In a face pocked-marked and gray, its features frozen from long disuse shone a stony wisdom. Even as those familiar eyes began to multiply, we continued our race to throw off all that possessed us, that we possessed, until I felt certain there was no way to retrieve what we had relinquished, our holocaustic winds sweeping the Safe Room clean of all but what was held inside those fiery green eyes.

And when I smelled the scorched air that soon followed and breathed a smoke whose flames could not be seen, remembering how the horses I'd searched for all my life had always left a trail of fire, I knew through the housekeeper's fiercely loving eyes that there was no turning back. I'd come to the end of that run.

Chapter Seventeen: Business Office

T.J. figured all it would take was one, hard breath to topple the stack of papers leaning at Billiard's right. They didn't have far to fall, from Billiard's desk to the floor. Another stack stood ready to follow them, and beyond that, another.

Following T.J.'s eyes, Billiard chuckled, fingering his watch pocket. "I admit I don't have much patience for being a desk jockey. That's what Mrs. Parkerhouse is for. She runs the place while I run with the big boys."

Mrs. Parkerhouse's desk sat perpendicular to Billiard's, facing the business office's door and window. With the blinds often drawn, whoever sat there had little to rest their eyes on but those blank white folds. Not that T.J. had ever seen Mrs. Parkerhouse sitting there. The few times Billiard had invited him to the office to talk turkey, she was gone, the gunmetal green desk tidy, devoid of papers. T.J. figured she probably didn't mind staring at white blinds as long as those papers were on Billiard's desk and not hers.

Billiard's desk was a scuffed wooden monster that likely would take three pumped-up men to lift it. An ancient thing, it hadn't moved since the business office had been added to the back end of the Stables, back when the Stables was a members-only supper club. Memberships drove the paperwork up, although new members could be approved only on another's recommendation. Back in the 40s, GIs had been regulars, along with a whole new crowd of city folk for whom fine dining mattered less than brief but private reunions. In the 50s the private club craze had continued, prized for the privilege to pick and choose with whom you dined, elevating that privilege to a status symbol, not the legal problem it later became, a symbol that didn't hurt T.J.'s tips one bit. In fact, that was his real heyday, when patrons practically stuffed his pockets just to show off their newly minted wealth.

As usual, Billiard had called this meeting. With business growing through the roof , T.J. assumed the boss had new hires on his mind. Lenny had the job down now and was working as hard as two doormen, but cars still backed up on the driveway every Friday and Saturday night. The old guard, driving Olds 88s and Cadillacs, men in tailored suits and women in even-in-summer furs, had not disappeared, but their numbers were increasingly overshadowed by polyester pant suits, disco shirts with gold chains peeking through chest hair and, and slinky, skin-tight dresses with treacherously high heels. Among their ranks, they drove more Chevys than Lincolns, more Monte Carlos than Le Sabres. More of them chose to park across Central Avenue in the church lot, picking their way up the gravel drive, rather than tip a valet. T.J.'s tips were fine, especially now that the stable boys were black-faced again, and Lenny was hauling it in hand over fist. The extra business hadn't hurt them at all. They just had to work that much harder.

T.J. wasn't ready to utter the word, "retirement," yet more and more his thoughts drifted south to that front porch with a fishing pole propped up against the wall. Mildred, however, showed no signs of slowing down, on a mission to keep things going, the way she always had. Mildred had always had a mission. These kept her going.

As Billiard fumbled through his desk drawers, T.J. eased back into a worn leather armchair that creaked as he shifted. "Ah," Billiard said finally, holding up his prize. "I knew I had a couple left." He held out a black Cuban and bit the end off another. T.J. eyed the lint on his stogie and, while Billiard fumbled for matches, gave it a quick blow. Papers slanted precariously over the desk's edge as Billiard forced the stubborn drawer shut. Miraculously the papers did not fall.

With Billiard, cigars meant one of two things—celebration or bad news. And sometimes the celebration and bad news could even be one and the same. Two abandoned cigars that had sat unboxed for God knew how long tilted T.J.'s bet towards bad.

Billiard leaned forward, holding a lit match over all those loose papers. Following Billiard's lead, T.J. spit his cigar tip on the floor then stood up to meet the flame. Both thumped heavily back into their chairs, smoke catapulting from their lips towards the overhead lights that glared back with an icy clarity. A sharp twinge raced through T.J.'s left arm, but he ignored it.

"Just goes to show," Billiard cradled the cigar between two fingers. "Quality holds up no matter what crap comes its way." His second puff came much slower, as if the first had been just a test. "Nothing can mess up a good Cuban."

T.J. had smoked much better from the well-sealed confines of a humidor, but he kept that to himself. Billiard was talking on the fly, and T.J. wanted the man to get on with whatever it was that kept him so wrapped up lately that he rarely took time to greet T.J., let alone stop and empty his thoughts from under the Stables' canopy.

Even with the door closed, T.J. could smell rank odors drifting through the business office's cinderblock walls. Nothing could stop the kitchen's greasy wind from penetrating even the thickest walls. Greasy dust on the desk's edges testified to that. In fact, grease had lacquered every surface it could reach inside the office with whatever filth it carried. At home, T.J. was the last one to notice such things, but stuck inside this cave of a room, he couldn't help but pay attention. For all Mrs. Parkerhouse's influence, a woman's touch was sorely lacking in here.

"T.J., I'm not one to beat around the bush, so I'll get straight to the point. I'm about to make your life a hell of a lot easier." Billiard swiveled back and forth, his chair ticking like a bomb. T.J. suddenly recognized the chair from speakeasy days, part of Barnswell's private wine room. Once a tufted leather beauty with a quiet shine that spoke of comfort, it had fit unobtrusively into its surroundings like a well-crafted shoe. Now the same chair muttered its grievances as Billiard rode it like a toy.

"It's the future, you see," he said. Billiard was staring straight ahead, but not at T.J. Instead, Billiard's eyes shifted back and forth as if watching a silent movie on the blank wall before him.

"Business up, for sure. We got so many cars we almost out of room," T.J. offered by way of agreement. He would stick to the facts; the future would take care of itself.

"That's why I'm giving you a raise."

T.J. sank back into his chair as if struck in the chest. "Come again?" This was one bet that had escaped him.

Billiard smiled, a rare and hideously handsome thing. He leaned back, cigar scissoring between his fingers. "You heard right. A raise." His shoulders spread so wide that even that generous old chair couldn't contain them.

T.J.'s lips started to form themselves around words of praise, when from the corner of his eye he saw something moving on the cinderblock wall behind Billiard. Unlike the long, uninterrupted wall of Billiard's Future, this wall stood between the kitchen's stove and deep fryer, and the business office. From the far corner, the wall jutted out then cut back again to enclose a small room within the room. If Mildred's stories were right, that room was the Safe Room, home to the Stables' money. Its door was plain wood, solid enough, but unlikely to stand up to much pressure.

As Billiard kept talking, T.J. let his vision wander. That wall to the kitchen was moving for sure, softening like asphalt on scorching summer day. To calm himself, he told himself it was just a shadow, maybe a moth projected from that overbearing light. He rubbed his suddenly achy chest. Probably heartburn, he told himself.

Billiard's voice was relentlessly upbeat. "Forget about tips. I'm making you a salary man. Your parking days are over."

T.J. leaned forward to rest his elbows on Billiard's desk. He needed something solid right now. The kitchen wall kept dissolving until something like daylight, or fire, egged on the elusive shadows fluttering in the air. The two stacks that earlier had threatened to fall now cascaded to the floor. Hot grease stung his eyes; he couldn't see it, only smell it, but he knew that that was bringing on his tears. No cigar had ever done that, not even a bad one. Something was burning. Inside him, but outside, too. Something bigger than he ever remembered. Except now he remembered—the horse barn burning all those years ago. Why remember that now, he wondered?

"Over. Parking?"

"Right. No more valet-only parking. I'm filling in the swamp out front—high time, too. That thing's a breeding ground for mosquitoes. Now that Bedford Heights is incorporated, they want to spray DDT. Next thing you know they're going to fine me. So, good riddance."

T.J. eyes kept drifting along the dissolving wall as he continued to listen. The swamp stood between the Stables' parking lot, Illinois Road, and Central Avenue, marking a clear boundary between the Stables and the rest of Bedford Heights. Once-open land around the pasture had already been consumed by housing additions and a township clinic, but the swamp still held the Stables as a place apart. Over the years, T.J. had forecast many changes, but never once had he imagined the Stables without the swamp. He wasn't fond of mosquitoes any more than anybody else, but he had no quarrel with them. If anything, he found the frog drones and cricket saws soothing. Yet until now, he hadn't realized he had found them so; only the news that these would soon disappear now brought this truth to light.

"You'll stay at the door," Billiard continued. "We'll still offer valet service but only as an option. The whole thing's going to be paved, marked spaces and all. You'll take care of the door, offer valet to whoever wants it, and direct traffic to keep bottlenecks at a minimum. That's been our biggest problem, those weekend bottlenecks. People want to drive in and out right away. We can't afford to make them wait, especially if they can help themselves."

The air itself was burning now, lights waving their fiery bodies in shadows on the wall. He tried to unbutton his collar, but smoke from his cigar bit into his eyes as he struggled with the Grand New Uniform's still-tight holes. He tried to balance his cigar on the edge of Billiard's desk but found no room. Instead, he leaned over and laid it on the floor while Billiard stared at the wall before him. Finally able to loosen his collar, T.J. took a deep breath and promptly coughed. Even his lungs burned. Each breath produced another cough.

Doubled over from coughing, T.J. soon felt a hand pounding his back. His lungs were on fire from whatever had drifted into the airless room. Next thing he knew, a paper cone of water was thrust to his mouth. He grabbed it and swallowed it all in one gulp. The cone crumpled in his fist, he handed the wad to Billiard, who aimed it at Mrs. Parkerhouse's wastebasket. It landed on her spotless desk.

"You had me going there for a minute," Billiard said, returning to his chair.

T.J. just stared. What was it about this man that he missed what was going on right under his nose? Billiard's desk was practically dancing now, with papers sliding left and right to the floor, but he wasn't paying attention to anything but the blank wall on which he was writing the Future.

T.J. left his Cuban on the floor. Billiard's had somehow disappeared, although the room was now misted in smoke.

"We can't afford to lose you," Billiard said, leaning forward, elbows now finding room where the papers had once sat. "Mrs. Parkerhouse is right. You are an institution."

Papers kept falling like confetti, but both men watched them fall, as if in celebration of everything that was shifting before T.J.'s eyes. T.J.'s whole body convulsed in response to Billiard's words. T.J. *was* the Stables. There was no leaving it. His front porch dreams were just that, dreams. He'd become the place that he was supposed to leave someday, the launch pad to his dreams, but not the dream itself. If it was burning, he was burning. They would go down together.

"T.J.?" Billiard's voice reached his ears before shadows overtook him, and he passed out.

*

They may as well put up a tombstone, he thinks.

RIP
Thomas Jefferson Jackson
1914-1933
Beloved husband, father, and son
    Since the fire, his days have been like digging his own grave, hauling out charred beams and ashes. Even Barnswell puts on dungarees and pitches in to clean up the infernal mess left him. Nobody complains it isn't their job. It certainly isn't the filthiest job any of them have ever done. Maybe, though, the saddest. Their pride, their hope, their tickets to the Future have burned away to dust.
    Now as he loads two packed satchels into Barnswell's 1929 Studebaker, he hears Miguel's voice in his left ear: "I see the fire in your eyes, mi amigo. Los Dios are your fate. They are the ones who will carry you to your life. Easier to just give over to them than to fight, no?" He feels Miguel's wink like the closing and opening of forever. "Nobody can blame you when Los Dios take over. That is how it should be; you should beg for their mercy."
    Too late for that. He drops one satchel then the other into the cavernous trunk, then carefully arranges them to leave room for the rest of

Barnswell's belongings. Barnswell will take only what he can carry; the rest belongs to the Stables, and the Stables is no longer his. One car load, and he'll be gone.

T.J. is envious. How easy for him to leave the disaster behind. His friends from speakeasy days will pity him, stand him drinks at newly opened bars in the Palmer House and the Drake, light his Cubans and tell him it wasn't his fault, that some half-breed trainer lost control and set the horse barn on fire: " You think you know a person, but with hired help, you never can tell," they'll say, sucking tongues to teeth. They all know he was living on margins, like everybody did before the Crash, and he couldn't help it if the only hope he had of getting back in the black were three mares, two geldings, a stallion, and a colt. That and a gang of people who lived the high life whether they could afford to or not. No, it isn't his fault, just bad luck that the Stables went bust.

Barnswell wears his sad gentleman's face through it all. He does all the "right" things, including making sure the new owner keeps the core staff on. That is part of the deal, as Barnswell tells it. "Non-negotiable. He keeps the staff, or I walk." Not that Barnswell has any power to enforce that once he drives off for good.

Sure glad he asked us, T.J. thinks, more out of needing to vent than any real complaint; the simple fact is there are no other jobs, no place to go, not even to Angel Fair, who has passed on, leaving her men folk to fend for themselves. If only he could leave. Instead, he and the others who must stay are sold off with the rest of the place, lock, stock, and barrel. It is more than most owners would have done. For that, T.J. can't deny Barnswell is a gentleman. At least he doesn't put T.J., his wife, and their baby daughter in the street.

Once the trunk is full, the back seat is next, and finally the passenger side is crammed to the roof with boxes, bags, and a stray bit of riding gear. Thirteen years crammed into one car. Then finally the man himself, wearing a sport coat, slacks, and sunglasses, as if it's just another trip to the track. He is tight-lipped; T.J. suspects a quiver in that locked jaw. The Foster Grants hide Barnswell's eyes strategically. He waves in the rear view mirror to the little group standing in a horseshoe behind the car as he pulls forward, always forward, and does not look back. T.J. thinks it's shame. The man fell short of his promises to them, to everybody who invested in his Future. He doesn't tell them where he's going or how to stay in touch. He doesn't have to. He knows where they'll be, at least as long as the Depression lasts.

T.J. kicks the gravel, sending up a cloud of dust. Of course the new owner has Big Plans. He wants to lure city folks away from the see-and-be-seen places down town that cater to name dropping, gossip columns, and splashy photos in the society pages. The Stables is the place where the wearily famous and discreetly rich will escape all that tiresome hoopla, along with those rich enough to buy the memberships that will allow them to rub elbows with their personal gods and goddesses. Even post-Prohibition, being out in the sticks remains the Stables' great advantage.

But for T.J. and his family, the advantages, whatever they may have been, are no longer clear. The new owner is no sportsman; all business, he has set his sights on a reputation for exclusivity that no high-profile venue can ever hope to match. T.J.'s track days will no longer matter to the Stables. He'll still cultivate his patrons, privately, taking care to hide below the new boss's radar. But this means he'll see less of his own gang, the bellhops, doormen, club managers, and waiters who meet at Hawthorne and exchange notes, behind-the-scenes stories of visiting celebrities and dignitaries, and views on the next mayor's stand on vice.

Until now, T.J. has had the best of both worlds, city and country, black and white, south side and north side, because Barnswell had a passion for the race. T.J. doesn't doubt that Barnswell still has it. Nor does he doubt that Barnswell will hone in on whoever else shares that passion and round them up for his next adventure. But now that Barnswell is gone, and the thoroughbreds are no longer at the center of things, Bedford Heights seems a long way from anywhere.

Mildred, too, is restless. Their daughter is well out of the crawling stage, and Mildred has said dozens of time that she will soon outgrow confinement in the attic rooms by night and the grass outside the kitchen in the daytime. And then there is the question of schools, which isn't really a question, since everybody knows no Negro child sets foot in schools west of Cottage Grove Avenue. But just five miles east of the Stables, other black folks have started to settle, close enough for T.J. and Mildred to drive to work each day in their old Ford. Mildred's family will turn cartwheels at the news that their wayward daughter is returning to the flock, even though she never actually meant to leave. Her family had refused to visit, unwilling to drive out to some place that, for all they knew, harbored men in ambush, and where they would be left unaided, in the middle of nowhere, to suffer their wounds.

Mildred's elbows aim like arrows from her hips. Her eyes follow the Studebaker's dust plume up the drive and out to Illinois Road. She's already wearing the new uniform that's been provided her, the first sign that somebody other than staff would be frequenting the kitchen.

"Amen," she says, and squints at the speck that Barnswell has become.

T.J. turns to her, her forehead lifted into grooves that would, 45 years later, engrave a permanent expression of disbelief and surprise. "How you manage to make a blessing sound like a curse?"

"Sometimes not much difference between them." She lifts her nose and sniffs as if she has better things to do than stand around and talk about what is now creeping into the horizon of the Past. "I bless what been so it go peaceful, and I curse what been so it don't come back."

The others in the group of stay-behinds are starting to break up, headed for a little work, a little rest, one last breath before the Stables' mad race begins all over again.

*

"Hey man, what's up?" Lenny eyes darted past T.J. towards the driveway.

T.J. met Lenny's uplifted hand and squeezed it, one palm crossing the other. He tipped back the hat that shaded his eyes and grunted. He wasn't used to meeting Lenny on his own ground. No one in their right mind hung out on the west side of the Stables in the height of afternoon sun.

"This place never change," T.J. replied.

"Tell me about it."

"Another fire."

"Where the trucks?"

"They wouldn't a done no good."

Lenny searched T.J.'s eyes with blank curiosity, as if looking at a TV screen.

T.J. sighed heavily, as if the words he needed were too heavy on his tongue. "Aunty take care of it," he muttered. "Like always."

Lenny just stared back, either afraid to ask for a repeat or unsure how to respond to what he had just heard.

"You ok, man?" Lenny's voice was tender. "I hear you pass out again. Billiard call Aunty in to wake you up. She all worried now."

"Just the usual," T.J. said gruffly. He wanted Lenny to believe him but he was having trouble convincing himself.

T.J. tugged his hat's visor back down. No one else would want to fight the sun, or for that matter, the rain, without cover, or generally be so far removed from the Stables' inner workings so as not to smell the smoke when things got out of hand. But no doubt that's why Lenny had worn a path to the west side in the grass, littered it with cigarette butts, and traced a circle where it ended. So far as T.J. knew, Lenny couldn't taste the greasy air or feel its burn, or see lights flicker in panicked tongues. He couldn't hear his Aunty shouting at Opal not to throw water or the herd-like footsteps of everyone else that rumbled out the back door. He couldn't see the placid, almost bored faces of diners as these same images burst out into climate-controlled dining rooms and thundered past, knocking down a fork here, a napkin there, causing water to tremble in its goblets.

What Lenny could see was what was left of that achingly flat stretch of land once called a prairie, that little bit of Forever that ended where Illinois Road angled off to the southwest, and roof lines and tree tops took over. It was, after all, a good place to stand, in some ways better than the canopy cover T.J. had claimed for himself, where he watched traffic stop and go, filtered by cattails reaching out like hot brown pokers from the swamp. Lenny didn't have as much shelter as T.J. but neither was he bound to become an *institution*.

"I been here, what, five months now?" Lenny asked, staring out across the pasture. The stare told T.J. that Lenny wasn't looking for an answer. "You know what? I feel like I been here my whole life." Lenny's eyes sought out T.J.'s now, certainty bringing both light and firmness to his expression. He held T.J.'s eyes until T.J. shifted them away, towards the remains of Forever just over Lenny's shoulders. Suddenly that view looked trivial, even vaguely treacherous. Forever was something some people imposed on other people or things they wanted to control.

"I don't like that feeling," Lenny continued. "But that's what always happen. Before too long, I figure out the show. And it's almost always the same—somebody got power, a bunch of people don't, and then the pecking order that follow keep everybody on edge, wanting just a little bit more, sometime fighting each other to get it."

T.J's chin sank into his gold braided collar. A rush of recognition stung him, and familiar words crowded his tongue. But this time his mouth refused to open. He was done defending the *institution* he'd become.

Instead, T.J.'s thoughts circled around the stories he'd told Lenny over the years. His intention had been to help the boy learn to want the right things, things that had served T.J. and his family well, that would set Lenny on a path away from what the rest of the world bet on for boys like him: addiction, jail, an early death. T.J. had made work at the Stables sound exciting and himself important, putting a good face on what others might consider vice. T.J. had no doubt his time at the Stables was ten times more productive than that of others he'd left behind on the South Side, eaten up by all that was denied them.

"You sure know how to work this job, I give you that," T.J. said finally, a gruff respect kicking up gravel in his voice.

"Way before I take this job, I picture it, down to the littlest things, like how my wrists going to snap closing and opening doors for people, how I match my rhythm to theirs and get them to move just how I want. They can't help but reach for dollars instead of quarters when the time come. I have my lines down and my looks fly, down to the shine in my shoes and the crease in my pants. In my mind, I be the best."

T.J. felt another, familiar sting. This was where he was supposed to caution Lenny about humility, even take him down a notch, and return his gaze to T.J., the role model. But all T.J. could do was nod in recognition. He'd heard such words before; they were his own.

By now the sun was staring straight into T.J.'s eyes. But he barely felt it, sunk down deep inside the Grand New Uniform. Still, an urgency to respond to his own words, now formed by Lenny's mouth, gathered itself. He mustered all his strength to meet the cruel brightness that surrounded them.

"Being the best used to mean something," T.J. said.

Lenny's mouth dropped. "It still *do*," Lenny insisted.

"Not when they going to pave the parking lot and make your life work a *option*." T.J. hadn't expected to tell him this way. He'd planned on buying Lenny a beer at the Stardust and telling him in front of T.J's cronies, who'd shake their heads and speak their own stories of how, when it came to work, the story was always changing. That way Lenny wouldn't walk around with the notion that he was the first person to be betrayed by having his story changed. Their presence would prove they had lived to tell another story. They would welcome him into their School of Eyes Wide Open and tell him all he hadn't been ready to hear before.

"Man!" Lenny's hat sprang from his head and bounced on the worn-out ground. Before T.J. could blink the sun out of his eyes, Lenny was through the white board fence, legs pumping, like a shadow crossing the sun.

*

Sitting on the grave where he has buried his past, T.J. remembers the night his story changed for good. A real scorcher that August. Cars just keep coming and coming up the gravel drive. Gasping through the dust, passengers pile out, tell him the city is much worse. Even the half ton of lake ice that Barnswell brings in each week can't stand up to this kind of hot.

The band is in full swing, their drums a heartbeat sending shudders through the walls. Inside, it's even hotter, but after drinking shots of gin and dancing to distraction, the air will feel cool when the slummers finally stop. A few hangers-on at the door hope to catch a stray breeze, telling each other that anything is cooler than the city, where the pavement and brick buildings sit shoulder to shoulder, blocking lake breezes. Eventually the music persuades some to come in for the night while others stagger out in search of cool.

Tonight they pay T.J. just to listen to their sorrows. He gives in, without offering a word of his own. Later, when he empties his pockets, he finds more cash than he has any right to expect. What did he give except his ear to bend?

 Whoever has stayed late has either given over to the music or the booze. They are sweating so hard their shirts cling like they've been rained on. If only the rain would come.

 That night, the stable hands avoid the horse barn in search of distraction. They haul their bedrolls out between rows of corn and hope that beer is enough to kill the heat coiling around their bodies. It's that part of the night where early is long gone and late has just begun to knock when T.J. sees a shooting star graze the horse barn's roof and inwardly instructs his baby daughter, who he hasn't seen all day, to make a wish.

 The flames spread quickly, ruthlessly, before T.J. can call out for help. Stable hands stumble out of the corn stalks and run for the trough, soaking themselves first before grabbing anything that will hold water. One bursts from the tack shed with two feed buckets swinging. Another is wrestling the puny hose used to water the Rose Garden. Two others locate a wash tub and scoop water with beer cans, cupped hands, and old paint cans to fill it from the trough. T.J.'s mind registers a lost cause, but his legs hustle him up to the barn door, which is buried in smoke.

 Hideous screams shatter the air. It's all he can do to stop gagging. If only it were just wood and straw on fire. Instead burned hair and skin scorch his nose, eyes, every uncovered pore of his skin. Nothing real could be this hellish, he thinks.

 Hooves pound the barn walls, or maybe roof beams are crashing to the floor. He hunches low near the stone foundation, looking for an opening, some place a fire-crazed hoof may have broken through the wood. Miguel had warned him of the power of Los Dios: "If they don't want to stay inside, you better believe they gonna kick out! Anything you want from them, you have to ask first. Not begging—they don't like that. But if you ask with love and confidence, plant little pictures in their mind to show them what you want, then Los Dios find a way to you."

 Barnswell tries to douse the flames with two china tea cups full of water while Mildred flies out with an armload of bedding and flings it into the trough. T.J. hurries over, grabs a quilt, dripping, wraps it around his shoulders and head, then resumes his search. The wet quilt muffles the screams inside the horse barn. He throws it back off his head; he needs keen senses to find a way inside the horror.

 Smoke is so dark he can't see his own hand moving. Darkness has swallowed everything. As he creeps near the ground, his mind starts to wander, asking is he alive? He can't let those angry sounds inside the barn pound him to permanent slumber. The thoroughbreds' shrieks suddenly pierce the veil of sleep floating down around him.

Somewhere above him he feels light but doesn't see it. Cracking sounds explode on all sides. Soon he, too, will be sucked into the flames if he stays on this creeping course. As he reaches out to the barn's wall one last time, his hand falls forward and does not stop. He follows his hand into the putrid air then abruptly lands on a moist pile of muck. But the rest of his fall is broken by something more than muck.

He pushes himself up, feels shirt buttons digging into his palms. The buttons heave up and down. His fingers follow the buttons in search of an outline and ultimately an endpoint--an arm, leg, or head--to grab and drag outside.

The barn, however, has other ideas. Falling inside is one thing; pulling out is a different struggle. Fire coils into a tornado of hot wind that sucks him into its core. The thoroughbreds' screams whirl around him, some so close it's as if he is the one screaming, his jaw sore from the effort of staying open to breathe. The stench of scorched hair is equally strong, his own hair no doubt now part of the stench. He plunges his head into the muck, then yanks back, sucking sounds grabbing at his ears. Menacing roars pound at him, refusing the hope that he might yet rise to his feet. Instead, he slides backward across the shirt buttons, the metal suspender buckles catching on his soaked quilt. Gripping a waistband to steady himself, he pushes himself backwards down two interminably long legs to a pair of bootless feet.

Just as he tenses to pull those feet back out into the night, his own feet are yanked back, gripped around the ankles by some unseen force. He manages to hold on to the ankles in his grasp while he himself is dragged back out into dead calm air.

Away from the fire, clean air now attacks the smoke in his lungs. The coughs that struggle out give him an excuse not to look at what he has pulled from the fire, or to give his rescuer the look of gratitude he surely expects. It is all T.J. can do not to spit in his face.

He is anything but grateful, because inside the fire, he had heard his name; he had tried to answer. Los Dios—*their sweet voices had caressed the sounds that had first shaped him. He had wanted to tell Miguel he now understood completely. There was no going back to that life before* Los Dios *had opened up his walls. No going back to creeping along his foundations blindly like a beggar.*

Let them believe he has been saved, he thinks. Nothing anyone does can bring him back now.

For days after the fire, when T.J. is not hauling buckets of ash or sinking an ax into burned beams, Mildred weeps when she sees him. At first he tries to spare her his face, but then she cups his cheeks between her palms when he starts to turn away, with a tenderness even Mildred has never shown him before. Her tears pool slowly in red rims before they spill. She won't let him go until they do.

Her gratitude tears at his guts. She sings every hymn of thanksgiving that she knows, a considerable collection.

Just once she says it, straight to his face. "You saved my gal." But it's what she doesn't say that hurts. She has no tears for the thoroughbreds, now asleep in the dust. Only tears of joy: "Nor will we seek horses to ride; what we have made with our own hands we will never again call gods." The scripture verse hovered around her like the voices of cheerful murderers. Her relief was too much for him to bear.

Everyone tells him he is a hero. Of course, there is a villain, too, Mudrack's name now uttered in disgust. "Coward," they call him. But when the bones they do find are not only those of horses, their disgust turns into confused contempt.

Stories start to circulate. A lover's quarrel, one man left for dead, the other bound to be hunted for life. No secret Mudrack had his favorites among the stable hands. This time, the favor is fatal, but to which of the pair, no one can say, since both Mudrack and his favored one have both vanished without a trace.

T.J. can't accept being called a hero and yet doesn't know how not to be. He tries to deflect the title, instead expressing gratitude for the strong hands that pulled him and Viney out just before the roof caved in. Yet each time he says this, the looks he receives grow blanker and blanker. One night Mildred finally asks him as she heats water for his bath, "Why you keep turning peoples away? Can't you let them thank you proper?"

"I got somebody to thank myself."

Mildred looks at him quizzically.

"Nobody believe me when I say somebody done pull me out a there."

Mildred sets the kettle back on the kitchen stove and does not turn around. Finally, she says, "Who you think?"

"I don't know. Nobody around here take the credit."

"You know if credit there to be taken, somebody going to," Mildred replies, facing him again. "Maybe you just don't know your own strength."

"I do know it, and that's a fact," T.J. insists. He unbuttons his sooty workshirt and unbuckles his overalls while Mildred leans over to test the bath water. "And I know I did not pull myself and somebody else straight out of that barn. How else I get all scraped up? See the drag marks on my face?"

"Lot of things do that."

"*You want to keep me all puffed up in front of everybody, that's fine. I understand you want me looking good. But between us, we done always kept the truth. And the truth is, somebody drag me out of there. I got caught in a mess inside that barn and somebody come along and pull me out. And I'm grateful. That be all I going to say about it.*" He hands his clothes to Mildred and bends over to grab the side of the galvanized tub. Every night since the fire she has prepared a bath for him, so ash-covered and greasy from the clean up that neither of them could stand it if he went to bed unwashed. In the last couple of days he has grown fond of her extra attentions. It would be easy to carry off the lie that he had acted alone. Easy, but far from the truth. More than ever now he wants the truth.

But there is one thing he doesn't tell her because he doesn't know how. After no one comes forward to claim T.J.'s rescue, it comes to him. He knows that grip. He can picture the hands. And later, when the deputy fire chief of Cook County explains the burn pattern using one, cheap cigar, T.J. knows for sure. What he doesn't know is why, if Mudrack was an arsonist, he stuck around. The fire was going strong by the time T.J. fell through that wall. Of course, maybe that was part of the payoff, to see his evil in action. And some thrill to risk being caught on the scene. But a rescue from someone destroying his own life's work? Mudrack and T.J. weren't exactly friends, but they respected each other and never got in each other's way. Maybe Mudrack had regrets when he saw the extent of the harm to others, like T.J.? But what arsonist had regrets?

The barn door had been locked. They found the padlock and iron latch in the ashes. The stable hands typically used the hayloft ladder to climb in and out when Mudrack padlocked the barn at night, to keep the horses safe. Had he meant to lock Viney in? He must have known T.J. was not the only one he was pulling out. The weight was too much; he would have felt it in T.J.'s limbs as he dragged him backwards out of the smoke. Was she supposed to disappear in the fire? What would make an arsonist change his mind?

Or had it been an accident? They might never know, since the one skipped out that night and surely would never show his face again, while the other became part of the ruins.

Viney is the only one who might know. She walks around with a dull glaze in her eyes. Lacking eyebrows, she looks like a stone idol, ashy and unblinking. When Mildred takes her hand and feeds her milk soup and mush, and tells her she is her own girl, Viney sits, stone-like, her empty face signaling how the rest of her has fled. Mildred combs ash from Viney's scorched hair. What hair pulls free goes directly into the stove, in obeisance to Mildred's superstitions that evil spirits might find and harness it in the devil's service. She oils the raw skin on Viney's scalp and the remaining kinks of red hair that Viney no longer bothers to gather tight in a bun. But no matter what Mildred does to coax her, Viney says nothing when asked about the fire.

Mildred won't let the deputy fire chief interview Viney, nor will she permit Barnswell to ask questions. Instead, she tells them she will ask, in her own way, so as not to upset her friend, who, she says, is fragile to the point of breaking. For some reason the men listen to Mildred, but then, Mildred usually manages to make herself heard one way or another. Eventually they give up, or move on. The horse barn is gone. Business takes over, as it always does.

When the heat starts to ease and cool breezes return at night, making sleep bearable once more, T.J. comes across Viney in the attic hall late one night, wearing Mildred's spare night gown. He is on his way outside to relieve himself, preferring to turn his face to the stars rather than stare into a chamber pot.

"Doing ok, sister?" T.J. offers. Never has he spoken to Viney alone. Angel Fair had been proper about men and women mingling. While the Stables had, in so many other ways, turned that prohibition on its head, with Viney the old ways still seemed right. Yet now, in the intimacies of the wee hours, breaking those rules seems almost normal.

Viney's eyes grow round, as if startled by his voice. Her eyes stare past him, through him, as if he is a flicker of light or a shadow on the move. "Dead," she says, stony-faced.

On impulse, T.J. reaches for her hand. "Sister, you ain't dead. You standing right here with me."

"That nice," she answers. "Good spirits chase out the bad." Moonlight shining in on her face washes her skin gray. But her grip is firm and certain.

"I ain't dead!" T.J. blurts, a nervous laugh catching in his throat.

"Ain't so bad," she says. This time she looks at him straight on. "I can see in the dark now."

"What you see?" The words just fall out of his mouth.

"Love," she says and squeezes his hand.

Maybe it is because the full moon pours itself into everything like daylight that T.J. takes no false steps, suffers no stumbling on his way downstairs to stand before the Big Willow. Even in the dark, his path is clear and bright. He knows that grip. He can picture the hands. What else would keep an arsonist from fleeing the flames he sparked? Perhaps even Mudrack did not expect his favored one, the lone stable hand in the loft, to surrender to love's fire.

Outside, the stars call out a high-tuned melody and the earth, in low tones, calls back in kind. He can't recall ever being this awake before, unless he was asleep.

*

The sledgehammer was heavier than he expected. Every time he lifted it to take a swing, it was like someone was wringing his heart out.

The first blow took the head off the left one, leaving a chalky white gash across the shoulders. Before now, he hadn't ever stopped to consider what the stable boys were made of. All he knew was he wanted them gone. But the crumbly white powder that had scattered told him the insides were more vulnerable than he'd imagined.

He leaned the sledgehammer against the Stables' front door, catching a copper glimpse of himself with tool in hand. His reflection grinned back. All this time, he could have kicked those shit-eating grins right off. But he'd never even considered it. He was told those lawn jockeys were planted with Forever in mind, and he'd believed it without question.

With the second one he took greater aim at a more ambitious target. The red-jacket exploded from the lawn jockey's gut. It collapsed forward, but then slid backwards, his top half taking a quirky little bounce before it fell over on its side, those bug eyes now staring not up the drive, but instead at T.J. who stood over them, leaning on the sledgehammer's handle, one foot propped on its mallet.

If only he'd known sooner what he knew now. Strange thing was, he didn't feel bitter. He had too much that he wanted to do and no time to stop and brood on the past.

Oddly, he felt sorry for the lawn jockeys, now exposed to the elements. He took off his coat and draped the Grand New Uniform over the gutless one and balanced his hat over the one that lost his head. Then he breathed deeply, a weight finally lifted.

"Huh?" T.J. lifted his head, startled. Someone was shaking his shoulder.

"I declare, I know you sleep at the drop of a hat, but standing up, too? One of these days you going to fall over." Mildred was staring at him, her hand resting on his shoulder.

Sleeping like a horse. Of course he wouldn't say so to her.

"Dinner ready?" He rubbed his eyes as he spoke.

"You got to ask?" She smiled as she said it.

He'd been standing out back of the kitchen, finishing the last of Billiard's Cuban. Stale or not, it was still miles ahead of T.J.'s El Productos. Now fully awake, he followed Mildred inside to smells of calf's liver and onions. The dream followed him inside, spreading a warm lightness from his gut through his limbs, behind his head and between his eyes. It may have only been a dream, but the lightness told him otherwise, a dream so real he could feel the soft plaster of the lawn jockeys give way to ordinary force. It didn't matter that he knew that they were really cast in iron.

Mildred grabbed both plates with hot mitts full of burn holes and started towards the Derby Room. T.J. caught her elbow.

"Billiard go home?" he asked as she turned around, frowning.

"I reckon."

"Mrs. Parkerhouse?"

Mildred cocked her head. T.J. marveled that she didn't flinch at all, given how hot the plates, directly from the oven, must be with only those raggedy mitts to protect her. Another bit of Billiard's "frugality," as he liked to call it. Mildred called it just plain cheap. She was always vowing to bring in a pair herself, but she didn't want to let Billiard off that easy. Besides, after so many years of handling hot food, her hands were practically burn proof.

"I got some things to talk about, and I don't want no other ears listening in."

"Them two don't never come around this time of night."

"They ain't who worry me."

Mildred set the plates back on the counter. "If you be wanting to sit somewhere else, fine, but first just tell me what going on." Her eyebrows pressed together so hard they joined in a V over her nose.

T.J. motioned with his head towards the business office. "I'll tell you as soon as the door close behind us."

As they passed the narrow stairway that once led to their attic quarters, T.J. thought about how few rooms in the Stables had a door to close. Once upon a time, he and Mildred had had that upstairs, but then Barnswell had shared that floor with them; his privacy had depended upon theirs.

The door to the business office opened inward. T.J. stood against it, gripping the doorknob, his other arm stretched out, motioning Mildred in. Her eyes grew wide as she passed him. He directed her to Mrs. Parkerhouse's spotless desk, and as she set the plates down, he dragged over the worn-out chair he'd sat in that afternoon.

Mildred stood staring until he took her by the shoulders and steered her behind Mrs. Parkerhouse's desk. She eased down into the chair gingerly, as if afraid of triggering an alarm. Once seated, though, her cheeks softened and her jaw relaxed. The chair, covered in plush red, was like a throne, unlike any other seat in the restaurant, including Billiard's. Satisfied that Mildred would stay, T.J. closed the office door quietly, easing the latch back without a sound.

As T.J. sat, Mildred pulled two folded red napkins from her apron pocket and handed one to him. The other she spread across her lap, smoothing it over and over.

"So what you got to tell me with the door shut?" she asked, concentrating on the motions she was making in her lap.

"I got a raise."

Mildred's eyebrows lifted along with her head. "Good." The surprise in her voice betrayed the uncertainty behind it.

"And that got me to thinking." He took a bite of the liver. A little sweet, a little rich, and with the bacon, just enough salt to bring all the flavors together. He was glad she wasn't one of those women hounding their men about cholesterol and salt and God knows what other foods they were supposed to avoid. "You and me, we the ones holding this place up. But look at what we been holding up."

Mildred pointed her steak knife at him. "We done had a chance to leave, start our own place close to home. But we decide this place do better by us, even if it ain't ours."

"Point is, *is* ours."

"Yours and mine?" He nodded. She leaned forward, eyes roaming the desk's shiny, unmarked surface. She paused, studying a hint of herself reflected back in the metal. "Don't you mean we be *it*?"

"When Billiard tell me I'm going on salary, he say, 'T.J., you're an institution.' What other institution he mean?"

She nodded back. "News to me he think so. But that the truth. We make this place. Thing is, nobody ever put two cents behind us, til now." She slid a piece of liver between her lips and chewed thoughtfully. "Why now?"

"Mrs. Parkerhouse want what she call 'authentic.' That be us. The real deal. On top of that, I hear Billiard going to run for the new city council. He got a lot of wining and dining to do. This the classiest place in Bedford Heights by a long shot. Remind people of 'the good ole days.'"

Mildred sniffed. "'Good ole days' for who?" She stared past him to the closed door as if she could see right through it. "What about Viney? What they be saying about her?"

The wall behind Mrs. Parkerhouse's desk was just as blank as the others, but from behind Mildred's spine-straight body, all sorts of lights were now reaching out through the whiteness. He blinked once, twice, trying to satisfy himself that his eyes weren't playing tricks. When that didn't satisfy him, he just stopped blinking and let the lights in.

"What make you think they saying anything?" he replied.

"I always say this place a three-legged stool. You, me, and her the legs."

The silver fork fell to his plate. Mildred gave the sound one hard, quick look then returned her eyes to his. But his gaze had already drifted behind her, the wall's whiteness now shifting and turning in rhythms, ones that he could not help but surrender to, despite Mildred's insistence that he return his eyes to hers. In fact, what had captured him *was* her, but also what moved around her.

He couldn't look at her in just one way now; there were too many ways now to look. In one look, she was a rolling rise and fall of tangled flame; in another, she was the shadow the flames cast, unmoving in the midst of all that motion. Inside the solidity of her darkness, only her eyes stirred. Then suddenly, as in a dream, her eyes transformed into the eyes he'd glimpsed the night of the horse barn fire. He knew those eyes so well, and yet he hardly knew them at all, having depended upon Mildred for what he knew. Then, within those eyes, other eyes surfaced, their equine globes absorbing light in ways human eyes rarely did. Like blank spots in his memory, the memory of the horses' eyes brightened the other memories that were now coming through. No doubt those eyes had always been there, waiting to be remembered, but he had recalled only their absence. How long had he clung to them, thinking they were nothing?

Smoke bloomed in his eyes. His heart slammed against his chest. "Sister," he cried out. *He knows those ankles, the long, slim reach of their feet.* For years he couldn't see her. But he still knew she was there. "We got to get out of here." Charcoal rubbed up against his lips as he spoke.

"I can't leave her," Mildred was saying. Her voice stung his ears. "I can't just walk away from the fire."

Burning air drew tears onto his face. He didn't have to see the flames to know that they were there.

"Sister, we got to leave." The floor shook his thick-soled Florsheims, rattled the braid on his shoulders like bones. He could not be still and yet he could not move, caught between one place and another. Yet this was how it had always been for him, standing in places that were not places, instead openings to someplace else, doorways leading back and forth, from light to dark, quiet to noise, forgiveness to rage.

She is dead weight against his. And perhaps she is already dead. The danger is enough without trying to drag a dead body out of the flames.

As he pulls her body lengthens, her muscles softening in response. Perhaps she has not been dead so long that the give of her flesh has locked itself away. He pulls and it gives, then springs back. Pulls, gives, springs. Pull, gives, springs.

T.J.'s tongue was dead weight against his mouth. It struggled to shape itself around the sounds forming inside: "Who are these people seeing nothing but Forever?" Then he remembered a memory he didn't even know he had. Shit-kicking boots diving into the hole in the barn wall where T. J. and Viney had been dragged out. Mudrack. Too stunned by their rescue, he and Viney had turned their backs as he hurled himself into the flames.

Mildred's voice burned inside his chest. "I ain't going without her. She my *girl*."

Mildred, too, was coughing, as she did every morning when she first woke up. Her whole life she'd never touched tobacco, but she rose out of sleep hacking like an addict, her reward for holding up her leg of the stool.   Mrs. Parkerhouse's throne groaned as Mildred stood up, still coughing, and reached across their plates to grab his hand.

"As I live and breathe, my fire fighting days be done," she said. Her grip was warm and urgent. "But I ain't leaving her behind." Her fingers tightened around his; they trembled and stirred the dead weight of his hand.

"I ain't holding back," she concluded. Still, she clung to him.

Good, he thought. Goodgoodgood.

As long as she held him, nothing was still. The ground itself was in motion. As long as she held him.

"I ain't. Going. Back." Her words struggled between coughs.

No more holding up that stool. No more holding back.

Both her hands around his one. In his other hand, the weight of her wigged head, her soft cheeks.

"I'm going to tell her," she said.

His tongue, dead weight, lifted up on her words to speak. "She be coming with us," he said.

"Baby, I got to find her." His hand uncovered, again.

The floor shook below them and the walls dissolved to light.

"Right here," he said. "She be right here."

"I ain't holding back."

"Hold on." His full weight fell across Mrs. Parkerhouse's once-spotless desk to reach her.

She must have finally seen his eyes through the smoke, because she grabbed his hands and pulled him back up. "Holding on," she answered. She inched her way around the desk and stood right next to him, still holding his hands.

"Say it true," he said.

"I ain't gonna let go."

"Then we can go."

"Where my girl?" Mildred wailed.

But the smoke gathered so thick that his burning lungs pounded like hooves. No words came; all he knew was they had to get out before the smoke overcame them. His last thought before they scrambled through the office door was at that least they were together, finally, with nothing left for them to hold up. Instead, they were holding on to Now.

Chapter Eighteen: Swamp

No place else could be worse to Lenny as he stood inside the swamp: hot, buggy, creepy-crawly. He had never imagined it would be that way, waiting for her to walk home for the night. The buzz in his ears that had started as he'd stepped out the Stables' front door had only gotten louder as he had approached the swamp. Until that moment, he'd never noticed just how loud it was. Like jets circling Midway Airport or the constant jolts of traffic from Illinois Road and Central Avenue, the swamp's buzz had been background noise.

Now, as he stood inside the swamp, its buzz just about drove him crazy. And the smell. Like rotten feet. He could even taste the smell. He couldn't just close off his nose without also holding his breath to escape the stench, although he had tried holding his nose but had quickly grown tired of that. What he *had* imagined—the dry gasp of weeds as he pushed them aside, the shoe-sucking mud, the dive-bomber bugs—were bad enough. He just hadn't figured on the buzz and rotten feet. Nor had he pictured how deep in he'd have to go. The swamp weeds had thinned out in the heat, and until the sun set, he'd be easy to spot without at least six feet between him and the gravel drive. If he hunkered down, maybe only three feet, but no way was he going any closer to The Smell.

He told himself how much worse it would be if he was still wearing that uniform, those shoes, that hat. But now his uniform lay in a heap in the laundry room, smug in the certainty that one good wash and dry, maybe a hot iron, would erase all traces of him and how he hated it. Then again, if it hadn't been for that uniform, he never would have come here in the first place, waiting for her to walk her "sensible" shoes and uniform back home, as she did every night. Unlike him, she never changed clothes at work.

T.J. never changed clothes at the Stables, either, and kept after Lenny to stay in uniform for the ride home. "At least that way they know you got some business being here," he'd say. "Think about it. You want them hauling your ass to jail for a speeding ticket?"

But Lenny always brought a change of clothes, ready to party right after the last car drove off for the night, even if the party was straight home to Mama stretched out on the couch, asleep to the late show on WGN. The last thing he wanted was for her to fuss over his clothes. He never wanted her to waste her pride on that uniform. It wasn't that he lacked pride in himself, but he kept that pride separate from the monkey suit he had to wear. T.J. had taught him that much.

The buzzing rose and fell in layered waves around him. Inside that sound, his breathing shook the cattail stalks, packed so close together that the rise and fall of his chest rattled their dry husks. He tried not to lift his feet, which sank deeper and deeper into the muck as he struggled to stand still. Even worse than the smell was the sinking feeling, and the fear that he might not ever get out. Even though his mind knew he'd get out—after no rain for a month, the swamp had shrunk to little more than an oversized puddle—his feet told him otherwise. And even though the mosquitoes weren't so bad, he still found himself slapping at his neck, face, and arms, as sweat crept across his skin, intent on some mysterious destination. As far as the sweat was concerned, he was just another obstacle on its long trip to someplace else.

If only she hadn't put him off, he might have just let the whole thing go, might have told himself, Sooner or later she'll come around. Sooner or later she'd realize that everybody already knew about Them. Sooner or later, she'd take the next step and say out loud what the rest of them were already saying to themselves, that she and Lenny had something going. Or maybe not. All he knew now was that he had to see what lay past the line she had drawn. Before now, he didn't much care. In fact, he figured he knew. But now that she had drawn it and was keeping him from crossing, he had to know for sure.

I'm just not ready, was what she had said. *I don't feel safe.*

This was how she always answered now whenever he asked to pick her up. She never asked if she could pick him up, but he could forgive that as a girl thing. Not that she'd ever asked where he lived. She just didn't want him to come to her place. A clear line drawn.

She never said what would happen if he did come. She didn't have to; he could tell from the Bedford Heights cops' narrowed eyes, from stares at stop lights west of Pulaski Avenue, from T.J. pestering him to drive with the uniform on, what could happen. What she did say, over and over, was, "In the fall, it'll be different."

The sun was setting so fast now that he couldn't see his black leather platform shoes besieged by mud. She might come by in a few minutes, or maybe an hour. A slow night, he hadn't thought twice about leaving T.J. alone. He didn't even care if T.J. or anybody else spotted him, a crazy motherfucker hiding in the swamp. She was the one whose eyes he aimed to avoid.

He hadn't counted on the cattails not only hiding him from view but also hiding most of their view from him. The Stables' front door disappeared in a maze of cattail shadows. The Stables' roof was lost to him in an ever-dimming sky. Only the lantern lights at the main entrance glowed through it all. Beyond the Stables, only movement was visible: traffic stopping and starting, birds cutting back and forth to the cottonwoods along the ditch, jet streams dissolving in ever-thinning trails overhead. As he waited, he grew certain that he would not see her as she passed. But he grew equally certain that he would hear her. The buzz somehow heightened his hearing even as it heaved up other sounds: swamp creatures splashing, bird wings whistling through night air, tires mumbling in a steady drone. Maybe it was the rain-starved air that brought such clarity that even far-away sounds sounded near, as if he were inside them. When she did finally come, the gravel's rough voice would no doubt give her away. Who else would be walking that long drive but her?

At first, he had only wanted to know which of the nearby brick bungalows squatting shoulder to shoulder she called home. He knew she had to live close by; T.J. had noticed first thing that she never drove. And he knew she always walked down the drive, instead of cutting across the pasture, to enter the Stables' front door. Nobody else at the Stables walked to their job. Staff wouldn't dream of leaving their cars at home, even if they could. Anybody who resorted to buses was first ridiculed then offered a ride. Even patrons drove. Bedford Heights was a driving place. Only she walked, and always alone. Once when he asked, she said she had no car; her parents loaned her one of theirs when she needed one. She never asked him for a ride. "I like to walk," she insisted, after he asked her why she walked, the only person he'd ever met who was actually proud of walking.

Once, he'd almost asked her if he could follow her home. She'd never said not to, but the fact that she had found so many reasons to be alone had made her attitude clear. He wanted to see the house where she grew up, what greeted her after she left him, any hints of the life shut inside those brick boxes. He had thought she might agree if he promised to keep his distance and pretend he wasn't with her. She could act surprised if somebody spotted him. But she'd probably just roll her eyes and complain for the hundredth time about growing up in the midst of such "rabid narrow-mindedness."

Instead he decided to make it his own private game. She wouldn't have to *act* surprised if someone caught him—she *would* be. He would shadow her to her door, watch her go in and that would be that. No peeking in windows, crouching in bushes, eavesdropping—that was for wacked-out guys checking up on their chicks. She'd never know he knew.

Then when Sooner or Later finally came, when she did, finally, let him pick her up, he'd tell her, with a grin, that her secret was no secret. And they'd both have a good laugh, her for being needlessly worried about him crossing into the midst of such "rabid narrow-mindedness" and him for his fear of asking to cross.

After all, she kept insisting that she wanted to ease her parents into the idea of him. That, she claimed, would be easier once she was back in

Hyde Park: easier for her so she wouldn't have to face their daily disapproval, and easier for them to get used to the idea before they actually met him.

The longer he waited, the more agitated the buzz around him grew. Dim yellow lamps that marked the entrance to the Stables' driveway could not penetrate his place in the swamp. From where he stood, the cattails pointed to a sky he saw only in pieces, interrupted by the thick, dry growth that insisted that his eyes fix on it and not beyond. In return for its camouflage, it required his eyes to travel only so far before returning their gaze back to it. But that was a trade-off he was used to.

Footsteps scraped towards him from the entrance. Instead of focusing on their sound, he searched the air for a different sound, one that would contrast the steady pace of her steps, background riffs to sharpen his sense of what approached. He would wait in the arms of the cattails, their punky brown buds like furry cigars, their stems straight as sentinels, until the gravel grew silent, and the traffic on Illinois Road paused, and headlights were startled by her shadow as she slipped between bumpers to cross to the side forbidden him. Only then would he wrestle his boots out of the mud and run like a fool before he lost her.

The sirens kept coming even after he crossed: pump truck, hook and ladder, fire chief's wagon. Lights spun their strobe action so that the cattails looked like cornered criminals in a silent movie, their arms raised, guns still in hand, flickering like a bad dream. Outside of the daylight bolts of the fire trucks' spinning lights, he was thrust into a deeper darkness. Good thing, too—if she stopped and turned around, the fire truck's lights would seize her attention instead of him.

If she stopped. How many times had she, growing up just footsteps away, heard the sirens, seen the urgent parade, waited for the flames to die? Even after only a few months at the Stables, he, too, had come to expect the fire would always be contained. Think of what a lifetime of living just down the block would do.

*

Outside, a siren cries as Lenny palms Murth a stack of twenties. They are sitting at the counter of 40 Acres and a Mule. Sugar Butt is busy checking out the narrow bar for signs of action. The place smells like garbage, as it has all summer, a back alley room known only by word of mouth. Two taps—Pabst and Strohs—and bottles of Jim Beam, Seagrams, and Johnny Walker Red hunch behind the bar. One lone cop, who comes in once a night for free beer, looks anywhere except at the ADC checks passing hands or loan sharks leaning in for the kill, as he sits like a prince on his bar stool throne, half smiling, half frowning, while the men around him trade toasts that slash and dance, gaining applause as they go.

Big ole lion got his head way up his ass

When he blink his eyes he think he sitting on grass

Oblivious to all the signifying going on, Murth glowers back at Lenny in the dirty light. He jerks his head towards the cop three stools down.

Sugar Butt claps his hands as the toast ends and the rest of the room, except the cop, breaks out in laughter. "You hear them dudes go at it? Ought to have they own TV show. Picture that. Laugh-In for Homies. Flip Wilson doing the dozens. Hell, who need the tube when you got live jive."

"It's cool, man," Lenny says to Murth. "The Man ain't gonna mess up his gravy train just to bust your sorry ass."

Murth leans into Lenny's ear and hisses, "Nothing stopping him from jumping on this one."

Lenny leans back while Sugar Butt signals for two more boilermakers. "Well, I be getting off. I is cashing in," Lenny says, his voice low and steady.

Lenny has bet that Murth's anger at his bailing out of their deal will be blunted by passing him a wad of cash. Murth usually doesn't think in the long term; he won't dwell on losing Lenny as much as he will what it means right now to their business. Lenny isn't just paying out his end of their policy gig; he's paying off Murth so Lenny can go his own way. Two years ago, he started up with policy here at 40 Acres and a Mule, so this is where he will end it.

"Man." Sugar Butt lifts his chin to shotgun his whiskey, then tucks it to throw back the chaser. "We the three Musketeers. Can't get along with just two."

That is the problem; Lenny is tired of just getting along. For a long time he has thought it is because Murth always calls the shots. Murth makes the deals; he and Sugar Butt follow through with sales and pickups. It doesn't matter that more and more Lenny has had to bow out, his "straight" job eating up his nights. Often, Lenny has found himself too tired to go from an evening of parking cars to a night time of plays and pay outs. Still, Murth has kept him in the game. It doesn't make sense; Murth could have tapped plenty other dudes.

If only James were still around, Lenny wouldn't be stepping into this unknown so deep he might not ever get out again. The only ones who want to beat the system as bad as he does, who back him against whatever or whoever stands in their way, will be lost to him once he bails. But James— James was supposed to be the hero in everyone's success story. Instead he is in jail, a fallen hero that nobody likes to talk about except in stolen whispers.

James liked to read—he read all the time—and remembered every word of it. Had teachers eating out of his hand. They turned him into a scholarship boy; he headed to Northwestern for a dorm room and a rich Jewish roommate and a freshman year that he chronicled in letters to Lenny, who repeated his letters word for word to the blank walls in his bedroom. James kept urging Lenny to come see for himself, but Lenny found it hard enough to address his letters to Evanston let alone get on the trains and go there. What would he say to some roommate whose last name was the same as a local department store's? James, of course, had plenty to say.

James had a golden tongue, signifying to the most powerful folks that they could eat shit for supper yet make them laugh and grab his shoulders. He'd have that Goldblatt dude begging him to tell tales about how fucked up rich people were, introducing James to all his other friends, who James would tell with utter sincerity that they were all ass-licking slave masters in training, and they would listen and join in the insults, and invite him to insult them even more. James had facts and figures and clever turns of phrase to make him sound more educated (and he was) than all of them put together that awed them and made them realize they needed him on their side. But of course, James would keep the stream of truth flowing in their direction without ever crossing over.

And that may have been his downfall, not taking the side that the department store- (and hotel-, and grocery store-, and high rise- and other-) named boys stood on. Because after a glorious year of highs and lows, of breakthroughs and hitting bottom and everything in between, James found himself in jail, accused of killing a white woman all the way out in Lake Forest. His name-brand friends, shocked, insisted he was innocent. But they offered no alibi, and no money for defense, and eventually, not even their support. They (those on their side of the truth) simply didn't have friends in prison.

Lenny went to see him once. If James had read all the time before, now he read nonstop, except, of course, to talk to Lenny through a window, on a phone. Even then he had books stacked by his side: Stokeley, Malcolm, Gandhi, the Tibetan Book of the Dead, LeRoi Jones, the Upanishads, the Koran, along with volumes on state law. The smile was gone. Death row had a way of straightening lips into a flat line, no ups or downs, no curves. When Lenny kept telling James he couldn't believe he had been convicted, was going to die for a crime he didn't commit, James didn't hold himself out as a warning, or a sign, or anything that was supposed to make Lenny hunker down inside himself. Instead, James had simply told him, "Get right with yourself."

And you weren't? Lenny wanted to say back. What difference would it make for James to be right with himself only to be shot full of poison? And how was reading a bunch of books going to do that, anyway?

"Man, it don't matter. They get you in the end no matter what," *Lenny replied.*

"That's the problem. You're focused on THEM. Get focused on you. On US. Stop listening to other people's lies. Find your own truth."

James kept writing him even after Lenny stopped writing back and stopped visiting Stateville. Lenny kept the letters in a drawer but never read them. It was too much to take in. The games they'd played, the jokes they'd told, the violations they'd risked when they were growing up had turned too real for him. He had then turned to Murth and Sugar Butt for comic relief.

"Find yourself another Musketeer. I is outta this shit." *Lenny stands up, brushes his pants off, both hands at once. The cop turns his porky pink face and locks eyes with Lenny, sensing a fight.*

"Dude, you killing me," *Sugar Butt shakes his head.* "What about 'together forever'? What about our blood? Man, who gonna watch your back?"

Murth stands up slowly, facing Lenny. The cop still stares, bored, yet hopeful. "You be fucking it up for all of us. I don't take this shit lying down."

Somebody starts another toast, and the cop turns away to listen:

Way, way down in the jungle deep
The badass lion stepped on the signifying monkey's feet.
The monkey said, "Motherfucka, can't you see?
You're standing on my god damn feet!"
The lion said, "I ain't heard a word you said."
Said, "If you say three more I'll be steppin on yo muthafuckin

head!"

Now, the monkey lived in the jungle in an old oak tree
Bullshittin' a line every day of the week.
Everyday before the sun go down,
That lion would kick his ass all through the jungle town.
But the monkey got wise and started using his wit,
Start telling "I'm gonna put a stop to this old ass kickin shit."

Nothing Murth has said or done so far surprises Lenny. Murth is nothing if not predictable. That may have been part of his appeal, so totally opposite of James, who continued to surprise him day after day, year after year, until he, too, got caught and became part of the prediction: after so many years of evading it, he got his ass hauled into jail. "A cliché" is how James would have put it, had it not been so painfully true. Now the only question is whether Murth is going to come out swinging right now, in front of the cop, or take Lenny outside to beat the shit out of him.

Murth's eyes flicker with the rage he always carries in his pumped-up arms, legs, and torso and turn directly on Lenny like a murderous spotlight. Murth's hesitation has nothing to do with calculating the cop's reaction; the cop is there to be entertained, not to keep the peace. Instead, Murth musters all his strength, nostrils pumping, mouth shut, chest rising and falling smoothly, as if preparing for an Olympic match. Murth's muscles will dictate what he will do, and right now they are deep in communication over how and where they will release into a fight.

Lenny has seen Murth even more agitated than this, but never directed at him. Anticipating Murth's reaction, Lenny has had some time to think about what he should do. Physically, it's not even a question; Murth is far stronger and will fight to win, not just put Lenny in his place. Once challenged, Murth will not relent. So Lenny's choices are either running or taking whatever Murth delivers. If he runs, he will have to keep running, since Murth never forgets a betrayal. If he takes what Murth dishes out, then he might be able to walk away with some bruises, cuts, even a break or two, but with all debts settled.

Lenny has expected he will hold firm and face Murth's rage, but now that Murth is right there, pumping himself up, Lenny has doubts, goes back to his calculations. Murth never crosses beyond what he already knows, so if Lenny runs away, leaves the hood for good, Murth won't track him down. Lenny just has to find new ground.

The calculations have shifted Lenny's eyes away from Murth's, long enough for Murth to finish transferring his rage from his eyes to his fists, long enough for Sugar Butt to let loose a stream of trash, "Oh, shit, mutherfucker, you fucking, hoe sucking, dirty down dog," but not long enough for Lenny to know if it is him or Murth that Sugar Butt is signifying.

One jab is all is takes and Lenny is out, cold. And when he wakes up, he is out in the stinking alley, pushed up against the trash cans. Alone.

*

The headlights coming at him on Illinois Road were Murth's eyes all over again. He walked fast but did not run across the road: nothing like a black man on the run to raise suspicions.

He could see her, on the sidewalk, a shadow moving between streetlights. The worst thing he could do was act like he was hiding. Somebody sitting on their porch or standing on its steps for a smoke would instantly assume trouble. But as he scanned the rows of two-story brick houses, he realized few had porches. On a hot summer night, the doors were closed and air conditioner compressors were huffing. If the curtains weren't shut, they revealed the blue light of TV screens. Chances were nobody was looking.

Including her. Amazing: all she had to do was cross the road, and she was back in a world where the Stables and everyone inside it was just a dream. He kept his steps light and soundless, giving her no reason to turn around.

When she turned the corner, she stopped under the streetlight and shook out the braid in her hair. The red curls sprang to life between her fingers. His legs kept going even though hers had stopped. Trees beckoned him to hug their dark trunks, and bushes whispered promises of camouflage, but his feet kept rocking, heel to toe, inside-outside, against the cement, knowing she would not stay there long, shaking out her hair in that hazy orange light, light so different than the white glare he was used to in the city. These lights' reaches went farther but were softer, illuminating instead of punishing.

To him, this world, with its forgiving light, its clean streets, its self-sufficient homes, was the Dream imparted to him growing up. And, as it happened, this was where she lived.

He thought she might still spot him now that she was perpendicular to him-- a corner-of-the-eye grasp, some echo of his step, some faint reminder of his scent across the empty air. But her eyes never veered from the path straight ahead. All of a sudden, she disappeared behind a tall, cone-shaped evergreen. He cut the corner to keep up; he couldn't risk losing her.

Approaching the corner house on the block, she slowed down. The porch lights from the other houses lit her hips that shifted beneath the black uniform dress, those round, muscular haunches heaving up like an eruption and stretching down in release. Every night, every heat, those hips rising and falling to a silent rhythm, arching over grass, through lights, across asphalt, into brick, moving through every last thing in their path. Somehow they kept moving, unaware or just not caring, holding secret what it was that sustained them.

And then it wasn't just her hips but everything around them in motion, liquid against her liquid, waves rising and falling, her movements dancing in circles with theirs. Not *she* but *them*. She was part of them.

"That's the problem. You're focused on THEM. Get focused on you. On US."

But James was in prison. And she was free.

"Caroline." He whispered loud enough for her to hear but not so loud as to wake the blue faces from their TV dreams.

Now she was all hips, hair, and hooves, colliding in a three-way dance. This was a world in which wood and glass and brick and steel were simply smoke, and light the movement through them. Her world. He had no doubt that the house she would enter had doors that required no effort at opening, yielding to her intent. He even pictured her racing through the walls, although the sealed-tight houses that surrounded hers suggested she would move more with caution than abandon.

"Caroline!" This time his voice echoed back to him. She stopped, two feet shy of the corner house's front steps. Unlike the other houses, it was wide rather than deep, split into two levels, two-story on the left, one-story on the right. Unlike the other houses, it boasted a grassy yard that reached all the way to the corner, and two towering trees flanking either side. Unlike the other houses, the curtained picture window was close to the ground, leaving little room between him and whatever lay behind it.

Her feet stopped but her hair still moved, swirling, springing, and rearing.

She turned towards him, drawing him into the sweep of her movements, just as he remembered from their nights together. Then he, too, was swirling, liquid, as he reached out for her hand.

"What?" she blurted, startled. She blinked hard, as if staring out from deep water. "Oh God," she sighed. "It's you. What are you doing here?" She was whispering now, her back to the door. He stood beside her on the top and final step that led inside her world.

"Get focused on you. On US."

US was the two of them moving as smoke, penetrating all obstacles in their path. But in this, her world, *US* masked their light, pretending that they could not move as they really could, so as not to shatter the blue light dreams around them.

She grabbed him by the arm and led him away from the door, to a gate with a chain-link fence, and through it into the shadow of one of the guardian trees.

"Oh my god," she said once they were hidden behind the huge old trunk, out of view of her parents' windows. "Ohmygod ohmygod ohmygod."

Her voice rose and fell along with her curls. Going up, it was sweet; coming down it was rough. She tugged on his shirt sleeve as she spoke.

"Lenny, are you crazy? What are you doing, following me here?"

He waited until she stopped tugging and he could find her eyes. For the first time, he heard some part of himself that wasn't anybody else— not James, his mother, Murth, Sugar Butt, his teachers, his disappeared father, T.J., other chicks, not even himself, but some new voice giving directions: *No bullshit.*

"Caroline." He said her name a third time. This time she took a step back. He didn't say it with the usual play on her lying or being a lion.

This time it was just straight on, no jive, her name as her name. A shiver traced his body from limb to limb; she shook her head as if hearing him for the first time.

"What?" She stared as if that would bring words to his lips. When he still didn't answer, her eyes softened. She reached out again, only this time instead of tugging, she smoothed her hand up and down his sleeve.

"Baby, do you miss me that much?" she leaned over, whispering in his ear.

What was it about her breath? That sour milk smell from little babies, a churchy smell because that's where he'd held them, Sunday gatherings in the church basement over plates of fried chicken and slaw. This cousin or that neighbor or Mildred Aunty herself shoving the babies in his face, saying, Ain't he sweet? later on asking him to hold Sweet while they fixed themselves a plate. The never-sure-if-he-liked-it smell of what everyone else insisted was Sweet.

Back then, he knew better than to answer that question and risk a slap upside the head for being impolite. Now he wondered why he hadn't smelled her baby breath before, or if he had, why it hadn't at least given him pause.

"This ain't about missing you. This about you shutting me out," he replied. Her predictable eye roll followed. "You know how they are—"

He interrupted with, "Yeah, I know." All of a sudden, it wasn't him staring at her; his eyes were now Murth's, and they cut her mercilessly. It wasn't a game anymore. He'd left the uniform behind, left policy and his partners, had left the church basement, and just moments ago had left the swamp to cross the boundary she had set because that was the only thing left that mattered. With so much behind him now, he had to keep going.

Tears flooded her eyes. "No you don't," she hissed back. "Don't you see what can happen? I need time to work this out."

"And just what you working out? Tell me, 'cause I sure can't tell."

"I can't believe you followed me. What do you want?"

The swamp ooze, he discovered, was still sucking at his shoes. His ears buzzed with its insect songs, and all he saw as he looked around him were splinters of struggling light. He was sinking so fast that when he opened his mouth to speak, the muck was so thick his jaw would not move. And, he discovered, nor would his arms, and now, not even his head. He'd entered the swamp willingly, confident that this was where he would find her. He was still unafraid; even its smell was something of a relief after her sour baby's breath, clear hatred being preferable to the uncertainties of Sweet. He hated that swamp. But more importantly, he loved that he hated it. At least that much was clear.

"I want to see where you live."

"Shit." One of the second-floor windows lit up. She pressed her hand against his chest, moving him backwards behind the tree. She held it there, both of their chests heaving, until the light went out again. Her hand on his heart. The light out and her hand still there, moving through him, through the brick and wood and glass of his chest to touch his pulse directly, nothing between them. *US.*

Slowly, her hand dropping, gliding down his shirt buttons, skating off his belt buckle, then rising to repeat the hold on her own heart. "Scared the crap out of me," she whispered.

The shape of her outline softened. Her breath became quiet. Her hand drifted back down to her side. "Well, here it is. Here's where I live." The other hand swept up and out abruptly, then dropped hard. "Not much to it, but you wanted to see it, so here you go."

In the dark, it seemed smaller than he'd imagined, and he hadn't imagined it as anything all that big. True, it stood out among the bungalows he'd passed, two-story rectangles that sat shoulder to shoulder with only narrow gangways between. Her house had a yard and no other houses on two sides. And yet, somehow, it was smaller than he'd expected. Like the other houses, it, too, had that sealed-tight look about it, air conditioners hanging their behinds out some windows, the others shut up, blinded or with curtains. But mostly it seemed small because it was so set apart. The corner yard, with its trees, bushes, and grass, swallowed it up.

Being in the swamp made a lot of things clear, turning sour newborn breath into the kind of Sweet people weep over and spend their lives always wanting more. But as long as she stood outside of where he stood, as long as she refused to join him inside the worst stink, the endless sink, the maddening hum, then whatever had lead them here, that could not bear to part with them even after he'd crossed into her world, had no sweetness or light, just a sealed-tight certainty that was the opposite of free.

Staying outside with her left him with nothing but sour milk breath with no chance of Sweet.

"You going to invite me in?" he asked.

She barely waited for him to finish. "Not tonight."

"When?"

She threw up her arms, turned, started pacing circles in the well-tended grass. "Why are you pushing this? It's not about them." She jerked her chin towards the dark house. "It's about us."

He shook his head.

She stopped circling, stood full face before him. Two jagged V's etched between her brows. "I want to be with you."

For a moment, the swamp returned him to *US* under the sheltering old tree, some tone or vibration, a clear note or two in the vast buzz of night. At least now she'd said it. She wanted to be with him.

"When?"

She stomped her foot, shook back her hair. For a moment, he believed her, believed that *US* was not just what Sweet brought them but *was* them.

"Why isn't now enough?" she replied. "For now?"

What had he been thinking before, about her being free? And all his fears of James' words, as if those might lead him into the same prison where his oldest, smartest, truest friend dwelled, what were those fears, anyway, but a similar, foot-stomping, head-shaking frustration about having to think beyond *THEM*, to forget about what *THEY* said about the way things were, too scared to realize that an *US* was already here, now, and that they could move through anything as if it were smoke, that they were smoke, as long as they were *US*.

"It is. But you're not here."

US had him fully in their sight now, and he intended to stay there, as they raided yards, ignored fences, nuzzled those sealed-tight houses open just a little more. Like so many times before, he was ready to run, only this time, he knew he was ready, and his running would be for a purpose. *US* would take him through every sealed-tight house, into every blue light dream, so that even the slightest bit of forgotten dust would be its intimate. Nothing was forbidden; everything belonged to *US*. Everything was *US*.

In her eyes he saw many eyes unfolding from their mossy depths, filling their green spaces until the water they held spilled onto her eyelashes and onto her cheeks. He took a deep breath, feeling the release. All that water that lay inside her, stagnant and still, had now found its flow.

She wiped her eyes, brushed the back of her hand across her nose. "Come inside." She took his hand. "They're asleep now." She nodded up to the second floor window, now dark. "We'll go in the basement. I'll turn on the TV like I always do when I come home. They never come downstairs once they've gone to bed."

Thing is, he was telling her without telling her, *I been in the basement and now I am out. I am out, and I'm not going back.* That much was true. She was still in the basement and wanted him there, too. It didn't matter how long. She was in the basement. She wanted him there with her.

If he was Superman or Super Fly, the way he used to imagine, he'd go in there and snatch her up in his arms and fly them both to a far away place. *Rescue, man. She want rescued.* And not too long ago, that's what he would have tried to do. But that was before sirens and smoke, tornados and hail, hoofbeats and manes swirling everything into *US*. In *US* there was no rescue, only a long dance towards something more than itself.

Her tears kept flowing, dripping off her chin. She held onto his hand as she brushed them clear, wetting his skin in the process. "I wasn't expecting this," she said. "I didn't know we mattered this much."

Neither did I. But instead of saying what he thought, he said, "They gonna pave the swamp and let people park themselves."

She nodded, dry-eyed, and squeezed his hand. "Those assholes," she said. "They don't know what they're missing." She sighed. "Not much reason for you to hang around."

Now he was the one with the tears. "No use trying to go back there. You right. No place for me there. So I got to keep moving. I can't wait around."

He took her other hand and squeezed it as hard as he could, as if by squeezing it he might still find a way to stay, go inside, make love to her two stories below her parents' dreams and hope that was enough to set her free. But that would only make the basement more like a place she didn't want to leave.

She nodded, a clearness edging into her eyes that he hadn't seen before. Instead of moss, a fine-tuned light. Her jaw set. A little laugh escaped her lips.

"I'm not used to this," she said. "You're really serious."

"I ain't fucking around." As soon as he said it, he realized how he had been doing just that. When had he been serious about anything?

"So what do you want? What should I do?"

At least she said it. Nothing in his memories of her told him that she wanted to know what he wanted, beyond fucking around. But still, she said it. She wanted to be *US*. And who knew? Maybe she would. Maybe he would. She was right; it was all so brand-fucking-new.

"I want you."

"You got me." She didn't waste a breath answering.

"Come with me." He held out his hand.

She frowned. "Where?" Still, she took his hand. "Where are we going?"

All this time, waiting and fucking, laughing and hiding, screwing up and screwing off, he thought he had answers. But how could he have answers when he never had any questions? He never questioned whether they were *US* because he never thought to ask. And now that they were, he realized he never considered they needed some place to be just that.

He grabbed her other hand and squeezed both, hard. "You tell me." He stared straight on; she held his gaze. Squeezed back. She fucking squeezed back.

"We'll find a place." She sighed. "Give me a chance to look around. OK?"

"You mean it?"

She nodded. Her brow still furrowed, but she was smiling. And still holding onto his hands. Now he was the one who had to let go.

He took off running, flanked by rolling hips and muscular necks, rising and falling like his own breath, through fences, past roses, into walls, beyond roads. Somewhere, his oldest, smartest friend, James, was waiting, letters in hand, to show him the truth on the other side of all these things, of which he now knew he could never get enough.

Chapter Nineteen: Broom Closet

It did not start off as a closet, and it never held brooms. Behind the big wooden desk in the lobby, where the inner walls backed up on each other, the broom closet was simply dead space. Sometime during speakeasy days it had acquired a door. The maitre d's used to sit inside on a three-legged stool and grab a smoke during election year raids staged by the cops. The door didn't look like a door, just another panel in the mahogany walls. The handle was inside, and the panel opened inward. The lock worked from the inside, too, invisible from without.

Only Viney had a key. Not that it mattered. No one noticed it was a door, not even Mrs. Parkerhouse, who noticed everything.

The broom closet was the one place in the Stables that Viney did not clean, a place between places, frozen in time. Sawdust still fringed the floor where nails had entered two-by-fours that had not lost their raw, piney smell. The air held a stillness of things untouched. Not even dust found passage inside. Only Viney knew a way inside, and she was careful to leave no trace of herself. Here, with nothing to clean and no one to answer to, she felt the stillness that much more.

One owner among the parade of them had once stood an usher's broom and dust pan inside that dead space. When the evening rush died down and the maitre d's had nothing better to do than review the next day's reservations, the owner enjoined them to tidy up. This way, the owner assumed that the maitre d's thoughts would stick to cleanliness, not skimming the cash drawer. As a result, Viney's morning visits to the lobby would reveal a spotless carpet, dust-free mantle, and end tables without ashes or trash. This should have lightened her work, but the opposite occurred.

Mr. Owner (that was what she had called him; he had never actually introduced himself) had had a vivid imagination for dirt. He saw filth otherwise invisible to the human eye, including Viney's. "Look at this mess," he'd say, running his finger along the top of a picture frame. Try as she could, she saw nothing captured in the whorls of his fingertips except his own skin. No matter that she had already dusted, swept, washed, and wiped everything he touched. He always found something. Repetition was something the staff learned to live with, unless they wore out first. Fortunately, O (what Mildred called him) wore himself out before too long, carted off for a "nervous condition."

Mildred called it justice.

The broom and dustpan disappeared along with O. After that, no one ever used the broom closet again.

The ghost horses had never come there. After the horse barn fire, they had at first stayed in the pasture, grazing all day and night. They sought no shelter from the rain, wind, or sun, and ate grass out of habit, not hunger, which they had lost along with their bodies. With no nights in the barn, no handlers and grooms, no apples and sugar cubes, no oats in a feedbag, they no longer seemed to notice, or care about humans.

What they had seemed to miss was the racing.

Sometimes she'd catch a couple of them in full gallop across the pasture, running headlong for the fence. At the last minute, they'd swerve, their training still strong enough to override their instincts to run straight on, without thought of collision.

Shortly after the horse barn fire, yet another fire changed their direction.

It had been one of those sunsets that bled flames across the sky. She had seen few others like it: the sun a brilliant ball balancing on the earth's rim, shadows stretching across the turf, their long, ghostly fingers gathering stray remnants of daylight. The sun was so low it seemed she could walk straight inside it. Upcountry sunsets had been nothing like this. There, the sun had disappeared in great swaths of color well before its light withdrew. Shadows lasted long, familiar as friends. Heat did not blaze up in one last, defiant breath but instead lingered longingly, until darkness tucked it into the valleys below.

The thoroughbreds had been grazing in the pasture, as they had since the big fire, with Queen's Shadow inching the herd towards longer grass along the fence posts. From the west, the sun hurled its last heat against a darkened east. The stallion spotted the sun's flames first and so began to bolt. Soon his panicked cries were joined by the geldings, two mares, and then, finally, Queen's Shadow and Baby. Until now, they had had no reason to run away. Everything familiar and expected was right where they stood. Only this strange and startling fire could return them to that night inside flaming walls that had seared their skin, melted their bones, and emblazoned the pulse of their nerves. Reduced to dust, what had survived was their passion to run. And so they had, straight out of their bodies and into the lives of ghosts.

If only she could tell them what she already knew about being dead.

But only fire could do that.

As they fled the failing sun, the horses had raced in circles. Mentally, she had urged them towards her on the other side of the fence, where she stood next to the Stables. The stallion had run straight for the fence and this time did not stop. He did not follow his training to take the curves and mind the rail and fly at full speed only after a rider had spurred him. This time the stallion flew straight through the fence and kept going until he'd left the sunset long behind within the Stables' walls.

She knew then it was just a matter of time, and fire, before they found her once again.

In their own time and in their own season, the thoroughbreds had continued to race through the Stables, spurred on by fires both inside and out, and until this summer, had left no traces of their presence. Yet not once had they passed through the broom closet.

This was where she would finally wait.

No other room was so cleanly quiet, so perfectly preserved that just standing there, eyes closed, spine straight, brought back all of what had come before. In those moments when she grew weary of keeping one foot in daylight and the other in shadow, all she had to do was enter that stillness, and it would take her back to where she could listen to everything, giving it its proper due. As Mamaw had once taught her, "Iffen you get quiet enough, you can hear the earth a turnin."

Viney had never questioned whether she could hear the earth turn, nor had she questioned why she should want to. Some things could not be explained; Mamaw's life had been a picture of respect for the secrets that surrounded her. "Learning is secret," she had liked to say. When Viney used to press her, she would raise one taut finger to her lips and let her eyes soften. When Viney followed suit, her questions disappeared. Instead, she became her questions.

And now, in the years since the thoroughbreds learned how to run through walls, she had become that stillness inside the broom closet that, given time enough, and fires enough, would show them how to stop running and be with her once more.

*

Each time a fire breaks out in the kitchen, she hears their hooves clattering across the floors, smells their damp coats, watches the panicked patterns they trace in the air as they thunder past, eyes rolled back to white. But now, with a baby resting in one arm, she stays still, does not try to follow, or calm, or otherwise convince the horses that she, too, lives as a ghost. Holding the infant halts all her efforts to divert them from the nightmare they still race to escape.

Had her baby not been stillborn, it would have never been so perfect. In its undisturbed sleep, yet another ghost has joined her in her vigil for the horses. She is blue-black like King, same oval head, and long, tapered fingers whose touch turns every day into brand new. Having never opened her eyes, her gaze lingers in the ghost world. Her lashes feather the slight arc of her lids. She has flown into Viney's arms, sole companion in a world where the horses she has depended upon no longer stop for her.

The infant's mouth is open, frozen in surprise or hunger. Her hair is a fine, red fuzz, setting flame to her well-formed head. She slipped out of the womb easily, without a cry, as if she knew she was better off silent. Viney hadn't planned it that way. She hadn't tried to hide her extra weight; it just happened that her man's clothes made her belly disappear, and in uniform, the starched apron flattened out the curves. When the baby's head finally pushed to daylight, nobody had to tell Viney it was too soon. Some people count the weeks and months; she felt the baby's weight as if plumbing a melon for ripeness, appraising the tautness of her belly for its give. The ripening had gone unfinished. The baby slipped out easily, quickly, the pains little more than a charley horse. The channel was clear, and she fit it perfectly. But only because the ripening fell short. She came out a hard, tight bud closed off to light.

She could not have been more beautiful.

As long as something is left to burn, Viney knows there will be fire. Her child has been born of fire and now carries on its spark. At any moment she may break into flame. Viney holds her close to her chest, closeting her brilliance. Eventually Viney realizes what she has to do.

At first Mildred refuses to leave her friend behind while the Stables, no longer a speakeasy, is being remodeled for its new life as a private supper club. "Where you going to sleep? What you going to eat? I ain't going to stand idly by and let you live low like a critter."

Viney says nothing. She holds the baby closer, tucked inside her man's shirt, against her left breast. For all anyone knows, she is holding her heart. The bloody towels have joined the ash pit. Her red-soaked skirts have fed the furnace. All that remains is the creature herself, curled up tight against Viney's skin, as perfect as perfect can be. Even Mildred has not fathomed what Viney holds so near.

Mildred turns to T.J. "You just going to stand there? She got to listen to reason."

"Sister, it ain't safe, you being alone here. All these men coming in and out, they bound to take advantage of you first chance they get."

"How you know they ain't already?" Viney says.

T.J. tugs his hat rim down, shifts from one foot to another. He turns and slams the Model T's trunk closed.

"The Devil's talk." Mildred crosses herself. "I'm a get you a place close by ours. We can drive in mornings and go home at night, us three." She turns to T.J. "Her and her country ways. She ain't never lived

right and now she got a chance, she can't picture anything past what she already know."

"You can take the gal out of the country, but you can't take the country out of the gal," T.J. mutters.

T.J. waits for Mildred to pull her legs inside the auto then eases the passenger door closed. "As long as we got wheels, we can go wherever we want," she says.

Viney waves as they drive off down the gravel drive, still holding her heart. The cottonwoods lining the ditch wave back, their leaves blushing yellow in the cool, late summer wind.

It is a comfort to live low, like Upcountry days when she might eat nothing but scotch broom and jewel weed, and drink water from her fingers straight out of the stream. At what used to be the horse barn's trough, she takes water from the hand pump. Rose hips in the Rose Garden are plump and plentiful; she fills her pockets before the backhoe rips out the bushes and buries them in a heap. At night, she lies on blankets from the tack shed spread across the broom closet's floor. Harnesses and bridles, brushes, bits, and blinders now decorate the walls of the newly named Tack Room. The tack shed itself will soon be destroyed, victim to a new owner who prefers memories to the life that such memories recall.

Inside the broom closet, she listens to the nearby furnace shudder and bang as the coal within releases its oily flame. For the first time since she left her mama's country, she is her sole companion.

Except for the infant whom Viney has named Jewel. Her fellow ghost. Her spirit daughter. The last reminder of King, who fled and never looked back. If there is such a thing as perfect, Jewel is that. She exists in an attitude of quiet, frozen into the shape in which she entered the world: lips open wide in hunger and trust, eyes fixed on the stars inside, hands clutching air, head dropped back to sky. Her body fits in Viney's hand, from wrist to finger tips. Unlike every other living thing, Jewel does not change. Even her skin is always the same smooth surface, no matter the heat or cold, damp or dry. Nothing disturbs her; even a corpse, in its dance towards dust, cannot approach her stillness.

Viney gives Jewel everything she has, regardless of the hammers and saws, the digging and pounding, as the Stables endures its reconstruction. Men in overalls groan and sweat while fancy men point and squint, their coins and keys jangling inside fine pockets as they finger the watch chains that tether them. Viney, too, wants more time. But unlike those who care only for the future, she searches for a peaceful place where both she and Jewel can dwell.

Until Jewel she wanted nothing. The horses had always brought her everything before she ever thought to ask. But Jewel has changed that.

Now Viney wants a place where Jewel belongs, the dark, still bud that never fades, the heart open beyond open, beyond death, beyond the fires that shaped it.

*

From inside the broom closet's dark stillness she heard the *cleaningscrubbingbuffing,* the *scrapingsweepingbending.*

Mamaw. Mama. Even Celia came to help.

Mama, the strongest, lifted the chairs, pushed the sweeper, scrubbed the stains. Mamaw's keen eyes spotted the candle wax on the wall, the loose bulb, the hole where the mice had gnawed through. Celia was quick, doing twice as much in half the time, having learned from raising ten children to make the most of what she had.

Even before the horse barn fire, Mamaw's listening had already been at work on Viney. Yet it had always given her time to adapt; the listening was clever that way. She hadn't noticed how much it had changed her. Now that it insisted on her total attention, she locked herself into the one room where she could surrender and listen without pause. Now she did not stop for anything, not for sleep, nor pee, nor food, nor breath. Mamaw's listening poured through her, lighting the walls, the ground, the deadly still air.

Inside the stillness, she was not she. It was useless to think that way. At the same time such thoughts flew in and out of her like knives, or wings, slicing open skin, or wind, yielding until another came hurtling along. Thoughts strung themselves together, pictures of a life lived as she had dreamed it. Yet she was not dreaming it; there was no she.

She had no need to move from where she was; everything was already in place. She had no reason to be still; everything was in motion and there was no difference between her and it. There was no her, no it. There were no shadows, only horses racing back and forth, without pause. The Stables itself was racing, and the horses stood still, the whole place moving forward with abandon, into horses that with just as much abandon stayed in place.

The stillness dreamed the shadows as if the shadows were dreaming it, as if stillness could not happen without shadows to contain them. Soon the shadows disappeared, while the stillness kept moving.

No shadows remained, only horses racing, intent on the race, on the stillness they were becoming.

*

Every night before she collapses into dreams, she stokes the coals inside the furnace's belly. She could easily let the fire die down, wait until morning before loading more fuel. She could let herself grow cold except for Jewel, who shines with each pulsing ember, each trembling flame. To let the fire die is to give up on Jewel. Without fire, Jewel grows weak, and her brilliance dims. Her skin grows dull with each fading coal. Viney will not gamble that Jewel, like the fire, can be revived. As much as she believes in Jewel's perfection, Viney cannot bring herself to test its truth. She cannot risk the one being in her life that loves her without question.

She does not let Jewel out of her embrace, always carrying her close to her heart. Sometimes she cups Jewel in her hand, while other times she cradles Jewel inside her man's shirt, snuggled against one suspender and the waistband of trousers riding high on her waist. She believes it is impossible for them to separate, even if she wanted to. They are one and the same.

But in one, fleeting moment, the spark that has brought them together suddenly cleaves them apart, and after that, nothing is the same. Nighttime, in the pasture, she is alone with the thoroughbreds who, for the moment, are not fleeing. Instead, they stand in the grass, away from the bare, scorched earth newly crowned with chickweed that used to hold the horse barn. Their heads are lowered as if grazing, though as they bite and tear and chew, each sturdy blade stays upright and alert. Their ghost bodies cannot touch it.

Viney stands outside the freshly whitewashed fence when Baby first approaches. She stretches out her right hand and finds it cannot reach him. Then, with her left hand, she reaches for Jewel, curled inside her flannel shirt, and balances her atop a fence post, still sticky with new paint. She then extends both hands to Baby, who continues to move her way. She can see him, feel him, hear the ghost breath blow through his nostrils.

At first she thinks the burning comes from Baby, as if he still carries the coals of that fire inside him. But as Baby turns and flees, the burning grows more intense. Light shoots from the corner of her eye. She twists to face the fence post sparking and smoking. Jewel, as always, is perfectly still.

Viney snatches Jewel from the smoldering post and tucks her back inside her shirt. Later, Viney's fingers explore the raw, raised skin Jewel has left behind on Viney's hands while Jewel sleeps on, her eyelashes flying her into far-away lands. Like the thoroughbreds, she is unreachable. For the first time, Viney understands how far away Jewel really is, how much she must long to return to that fire which had borne her, of which Viney herself was made, and to which she must ultimately go.

*

In the stillness, she was running. She smelled the smoke, felt the flames rake her flanks, searched the darkness for signs of the herd as hooves clattered from room to room. To run was to escape, but there was no escape, only more running. Running was necessary; running was joy: a race for survival, the first expressions of play. Even when plagued by some predatory desire, running still clung to those deeper instincts that eventually circled back to their source. To run was the most intimate connection. It was intimacy itself; it was the voice of all that did not otherwise speak.

*

The raked coals inside the furnace speak, their glow hot and throbbing. She pauses, beads forming on her forehead and cheeks, bathed in wavering light. Tucked inside her man's shirt, Jewel grows slick with Viney's sweat. Heat presses into her eyes, forcing tears that blur the cavernous light before her. She squints, then shuts her eyes, blinking back the tears. The heat claims them greedily, sucking them dry.

She knows she cannot stand in front of the furnace too long before her skin cries out, and her flannel shirt scorches the tender skin it is meant to protect. Jewel, of course, does not move, except to mimic Viney's labored breath. She feels Jewel slide up and down against her breasts, over her heart. Jewel's skin is perfectly smooth. As she slides, Viney feels the texture of her own skin. Compared to Jewel, the surface of her skin is coarse, full of friction, and oddly stubborn. The burn creeps up on Viney, slow but steady. Jewel herself is not the source of heat; instead she is the medium through which the flames travel.

To join with Jewel, she can no longer hold her. Nor can she put her down. King's laugh cuts a jagged bolt across her sky. He knew what was to come. He knew she could not help but open her arms to greet it.

His laugh hangs in the air as she unbuttons her shirt. Jewel's skin is cool but the furnace's heat is unbearable. As Viney lifts Jewel, her perfect sleep stays undisturbed. Still, Viney waits. How can she release her, this cherished curve, this rhythmic weight, the last note in her daddy's whistle as he drove his pride-ful Morgans back down to his Low Country home?

In the end, it is the fire itself that moves her, loosening her fingers with its insistent heat. Jewel slips, falls headlong into the glow, her back curled into itself as her body traces a perfect arc through the shimmering light. In an instant, a flame rises up: no spark, no sound, no foretelling of its arrival, only its luminous body reaching out from an invisible source.

*

She did not have to see the flame-twisted walls to know that Mildred was no longer fleeing the horrors held inside her dreams. She did not have to smell T.J.'s El Producto to know he had run out of Cubans as well as regrets, for having had fine smokes and for having no more. She did not have to hear the yells to know that the cooks in the kitchen were scrambling for an exit. She did not have to hear the cubes shifting inside the ice machine to know that the bus boys had abandoned their pitchers, nor did she need to hear candles hiss inside hurricane lamps to know that every last diner still expected to be served. She did not have to smell soft skin blossoms to know that the lovers had already crept towards some other, darkly hot place to swell all over again. She did not have to feel hooves pounding her chest to know that the thoroughbreds were still running.

She did not have to hear the sirens' shout to know that the horses did not hear them, too frantic saving the lives they had already lost. So this time, when fire reached out for her from deep inside the stillness, she greeted it as she greeted her own face in the dawn.

She was on fire. She was fire.

Now the horses could not help but see her.

She sang out their seven names. Not the names they'd been bred to but those she'd held secret, whispering them daily into each hairy ear. The names had barely left her lips before the thoroughbreds arrived, rolling red-streaked eyes, sweat carving fast currents through soot-crusted skin. As their scorched manes filled the air with smoke, she doubled over, retching, holding her dress to her face to escape their overpowering stench. Their charred and tattered flesh stunned her. She flinched at fierce yellow teeth that clattered like dull blades, while piercing cries poured out between bleeding, blistered lips. As they jammed and jostled, their furious chests heaving, threatening to crush her, she curled tight into herself, as if to disappear. Nothing had prepared her for this devastating return.

Too scared to move, too scared not to, she resumed her singing, desperate for distraction. This time came a melody that King's band had played late at night, when nobody seemed to mind, too drunk on gin or sex, too tired to care if they ever saw dawn, too busy counting the night's gains, the kind of song that Barnswell normally forbade, fearful that patrons would be fatally bitten by its sorrow. But they had always come back for more. They could not speak their own sorrows nearly as well.

At first, she could not bring herself to lift her head. Nothing she could give them would ever be enough. Still, the song insisted; she needed an open throat to sing. She raised her head and opened her mouth, letting the sound flow through.

Seven heads lifted and lowered. Queen's Shadow pushed forward, as black and restless as ever. Baby hugged her side, barely visible against her darkness, his white star brightening his forehead. The two geldings stretched their necks, fear overtaking their usual cool. The other two mares kicked and bit at each other, hungry for attention. And the stallion, instead of plotting his moves on the mares, stood with haunches pointed towards the others, his neck twisted, ready to flee yet watching for signs from the herd. For all their awfulness, they were strangely familiar.

They had answered her call, but in the end, she could not surrender to the ruins that they had become. The song died on her lips. The horses did not move. The silence was unbearable.

*

In the silence of Jewel's departure she remembers Mamaw's instruction. Some learning is best kept secret, Mamaw says. Not everybody can countenance the truth of their own lies. Sooner or later we all come to a place that can't be crossed. The only mercy is that sometimes the killing stops, and folks get a chance to find a different way.

The Old Ones say it's the stories that cross back and forth, their homing instincts as sharp as any bird's. They say the stories have always existed, there for anyone who looks. But their learning is secret; other stories cover them up, to confuse those who would destroy them. Still, the stories are always there. They sprout up, sometimes in answer to somebody's call, sometimes for no reason, sometimes to remind the People that they exist. The stories live in-between the words that hold them, with no beginning and no end, opening up places for the People to be. They don't do much, but when they do, it happens in the night. They undo everything that the daylight demands, beheading cornstalks, scattering anthills onto graves, twisting roses into nipples that refuse to be sucked. And for those that seek the stories, that is how they learn to be, if they are wise enough to listen.

*

The habit of listening was strong, stronger than silence, stronger than the smoke that filled her then returned to its invisible source. Her nose filled again with the smell of charred skin. Her eyes blurred, and her chest heaved as smoke closed the spaces between the thoroughbreds and her. Sweat soaked her dress and dripped down her legs. She followed the smoke as it entered her: *ahahahah.* With each breath in, a little more smoke lingered inside. With each breath out, a little more of her mingled with the smoke outside: *eeheeheeheeh.* Soon she was breathing nothing but smoke, her tongue heavy with its taste. Her eyes clouded, and her skin sealed shut. Her limbs sagged from the weight of all that smoke while her hands struggled to grasp something, anything, to hold herself up.

Just when she thought the smoke had finally taken her, she cried out. Startled by a sharp pain in her hand, she instinctively thrust her fingers inside her mouth. Blood. Baby.

Unlike the others, he looked to her for more. He sawed at her fingers as if they would release the milk he still expected. She let him suck; her blood did not dissuade him. He kept sucking, pulling harder with each suck, determined not to release her until he'd had his fill. He might never have his fill; the thoroughbreds might never find another place to be. She started to weep, but did not withdraw her hand. The urge to exchange the tender flesh he'd awakened with her own, love-crazed teeth twisted her around. Her mouth hovered a breath away from his. Her teeth told her to break through, go beyond the skin's seal to the pulsing flow below, while her tongue anticipated its long-awaited taste that was at once what held her and what she herself held. What else could either of them do except consume the other until nothing was left but charred bits of bone and hair burnt to its invisible roots, the remains of the fire that was their beginning and their end?

She did not return Baby's passionate bite. Her blood had already entered his, just as his had entered hers, just as her blood had entered whatever and whomever in her life that she had ever touched. She had entered the world and it had entered her, and it had only been because the horses had no longer stopped for her that she had forgotten those crossings back and forth, back and forth, each time erasing all that had come before. Now they were back, and they were waiting; they were listening. She was listening, as she knew now that she always had been, holding them inside that listening, just as they were holding her. There was no place to go; there was nothing to do. Only ashes remained. Ashes the only things she, Baby Divine, now bent down low to love.

Author's Biographical Note

Mary Ann Cain lives near the bend in one of the three rivers of Fort Wayne, Indiana, where she teaches prose writing, rhetoric, and Women's Studies at Indiana University Purdue University Fort Wayne. She also teaches creative writing for the Three Rivers Jenbe Ensemble, a West African drumming and dance group for young people and is a jenbe player herself. India has claimed her as well; she meditates in the tradition of Paramahansa Yogananda and traveled to India where she interviewed devotees of the legendary Anandamai Ma, spiritual advisor to Indira Gandhi, to learn about Indian women's spiritual practices.

Her fiction, memoirs, and blurred genre work have appeared in numerous literary journals, including *The North American Review, The Denver Quarterly, The Sun: A Magazine of Ideas, Thirteenth Moon, Many Mountains Moving*, and *Hawai'i Pacific Review*, among numerous others. She is the recipient of an Indiana Arts Commission Individual Artist grant, two residencies at the Mary Hambidge Center for Arts, and one at Hill House Writers' Retreat. Her book on writing workshops, *Revisioning Writers' Talk: Gender and Culture in Acts of Composing*, was published by SUNY Press in 1995. Forthcoming from Heinemann Boynton Cook is *Breathing Space: Composing Public Places for Writing and Teaching*, with co-authors Michelle Comstock and Lil Brannon. She and her husband, poet George Kalamaras, share a 1929 Tudor-style house with their beagle, Bootsie.

Down From Moonshine was one of eleven finalists in the Carolina Wren Press national contest, from which it had to be withdrawn since it was already in press at *13th Moon*.